W E B   O F   S I N #3

PROMISES

Book #3 of the WEB OF SIN trilogy

Aleatha Romig

New York Times, Wall Street Journal, and USA Today
bestselling author of the Consequences and Infidelity series

COPYRIGHT AND LICENSE INFORMATION

PROMISES

Book 3 of the WEB OF SIN trilogy
Copyright @ 2018 Romig Works, LLC
Published by Romig Works, LLC
2018 Edition
ISBN: 978-1-947189-32-4
Cover art: Kellie Dennis at Book Cover by Design
(www.bookcoverbydesign.co.uk)
Editing: Lisa Aurello
Formatting: Romig Works, LLC

2018 Edition License

PROMISES – WEB OF SIN BOOK 3

The twisted and intriguing storytelling that you loved in Consequences and Infidelity continues with the epic conclusion of the all-new alpha anti-hero in the dark romance series Web of Sin, by New York Times bestselling author Aleatha Romig.

Have you been Aleatha'd?

Learn the truth behind the secrets and lies.

Surrounded by secrets and lies, can promises be believed?

Promises is book three—the epic conclusion—of the widely-acclaimed Web of Sin trilogy.

WEB OF SIN BOOK 3

Promises

"The woods are lovely, dark and deep. But I have promises to keep, and miles to go before I sleep." - Robert Frost

PROLOGUE

Araneae

The end of Lies, book #2 of the Web of Sin trilogy

When we finally arrived at her door, he said, "I'm staying right here. Get her and bring her back. We'll go back to the office and forget this happened."

"You don't mean that."

"Please, Araneae, talk to her. If she intends to stay employed by Sinful Threads, she'll come back with you. If not, it's her choice."

"My company," I said with less zeal than before.

He didn't answer.

Taking a deep breath, I knocked on her door. When she opened it, her eyes were red and swollen, and her face and neck were covered in red blotches. "Winnie..." I wrapped her in my arms as we stepped inside. As the door closed, I asked, "Winnie, what is it?"

"Ms. McCrie?"

I gasped as I stood straight again, taking in the man who had appeared from the bathroom. I knew him immediately.

Knew was the wrong word.

I recognized him, his blond hair, and his boyish features. "Mark?" I questioned.

Hanging from his belt was a badge.

I took a step back, my shoulders colliding with the wall. "What is this?"

The man placed his finger over his lips. "I know you're being watched. I know there's a man outside who won't hesitate to enter. I need you to listen to me."

"I-I thought you were in trouble..." Winnie cried, her words surrounded by quick inhales of breath. "I-I thought..."

"What did you do?"

"Ms. McCrie," Mark said, speaking quietly as he came closer, "I'm certain you were told elsewise. May I formally introduce myself? My name is neither Mark nor Andrew. I'm Wesley Hunter, a field agent with the FBI. For the last two and a half years I have been infiltrating the world of Chicago's underground."

My lips came together as my head shook. "That-that has nothing to do with me."

"You didn't correct me on the use of your birth name."

"My name is Kennedy Hawkins." I fumbled with my purse. "I-I have my ID."

Mark, I mean, Wesley, lifted his hand. "If you want to play that game, it's your choice. You have a long history, Ms. Hawkins, Ms. Marsh. Or is it, Ms. McCrie? While infiltrating the world that *has nothing to do with you,* the FBI became aware of your connection—or should I say your father's? Because of that, there is concern for your safety. For most of your life you have been a sought-after individual. For that reason, once you were discovered, I tried to stop you from becoming involved. Wichita? Perhaps you recall? As you know, that didn't work."

My head was shaking. "This doesn't make any sense."

"Kenni," Winnie said, "I'm sorry. They came to me, told me you were in danger. Your behavior...I thought I was helping."

"Why?" I asked, this time louder. "Why not come to me?"

"I thought with the odd behavior," she said. "I thought...the FBI said...you were in danger...that you were being forced...and then today you said...I left the office to inform Agent Hunter that the FBI was wrong." Her head shook. "I'm sorry."

"Agent Hunter," I said, finding my voice yet purposely keeping it low so as not to alarm Patrick. "Am I under arrest? If not, I'm going to leave this room. I appreciate your concern; however, I guarantee that I'm safe."

He reached for a folder lying next to the TV and flipped it open, revealing Sterling Sparrow's picture. "Ma'am, this man is dangerous."

"He's in real estate."

"You're believed to have information that could be detrimental to him and his future. We have it on good authority that his plan is to get that information by any means possible. Are you in possession of the information?"

What could I say?

"I don't have anything like that."

"The FBI is willing to offer you, Ms. Douglas, and the

cofounder of your company, Louisa Toney, witness protection in exchange for the information in question. Certainly, you want to save your friend's soon-to-be-born child?"

Oh my God. This was the same way Sterling convinced me in the first place—blackmail.

I shook my head. "I don't have any information."

"You have been marked by Sterling Sparrow."

He had no idea.

"We've tried for years to find something that would finally stick to Sterling Sparrow. We believe you have it."

I shook my head. "I'm leaving." I took a step toward the door.

"Upon further research," Agent Hunter said, "into Sinful Threads, it has come to the notice of the FBI that there are some unusual real estate deals regarding your properties that are connected to Sparrow Enterprises."

"Yes, that company deals in real estate," I said, standing taller. "My company needs properties."

"The deals you received are significantly below market and below that offered to other customers. That leads us to question the complexity of your agreements."

I shook my head. "Those agreements go back years. I only recently became acquainted with Mr. Sparrow."

"If you're not willing to share the information that you have with the FBI, possibly incriminating evidence against your new acquaintance, we are prepared to offer you an alternative. This is a onetime offer. Once it's made your decision must be imminent."

"I don't need an alternative offer. I don't have any information, and I've done nothing wrong."

Wesley crossed his arms over his chest. "It's very easy. All you need to do is take my place, infiltrating and ultimately testifying against Mr. Sparrow."

"What?"

"The evidence regarding real estate combined with some questionable bookkeeping and inventory irregularities at your Chicago warehouse implicate Sinful Threads as a possible means for illegal activities. We have the records."

"No, that's impossible. Louisa and I go through every line. Besides, it couldn't be him. He's in real estate," I said it again as if repeating it would nullify his other dealings. "And I just met him."

"Lying is what men like him do."

My phone buzzed and *STERLING* came onto the screen.

My mind was a battlefield as my lungs forgot to breathe, and my gaze went back and forth between Sterling's name and the FBI agent across the room.

Who should I believe? Who was telling me the truth, and who was telling me lies?

STERLING

*M*y gaze narrowed to meet my assistant Stephanie's as I entered Sparrow Enterprise's private office suite. There was no way she wasn't aware of my ire regarding the interruption of my morning plans; however, just in case, my scowl pointed her direction should have been a clear indication of my current disposition. As our eyes met, her furrowed brow, wide eyes, and tilt of her head led me to widen my inspection of the room. My stance grew taller, my neck straightening, and chest inflating with a deep breath as the blue-eyed gaze I'd known my entire life burned my direction.

Standing in all her regality, dressed and styled to perfection, wasn't the woman I'd prepared to meet but the one who the last time I'd seen her, I'd told her to leave my home, the one who gave me life.

"Sterling," Genevieve Sparrow said, my name rolling off

her tongue coated with enough sweetness that was I diabetic, I'd need an immediate insulin injection.

Turning away from her greeting, I stepped closer to Stephanie. "Judge Landers?"

"Sir, I took her to conference room four. She was visibly..." Her gaze went to my mother and back to me. "...agitated."

My mother's skinny hand landed on my arm. "I need to speak to you alone."

My nostrils flared as I inhaled, her sweet perfume taking over my senses. Everything in me wanted to tell her to make an appointment, to come back another day, or leave and try a phone call.

Stephanie continued, "Mrs. Sparrow accompanied Judge Landers."

Turning on my heels, I stared down at my mother. "In my office."

Together we stepped down the hallway. As we passed conference room four, through the slender window beside the door—though the blinds were pulled, they weren't completely closed—I caught a glimpse of Annabelle Landers, pacing near the table, wringing her hands.

With a momentary smile, my mind went to Araneae and how she did the same thing when she was thinking or concerned.

Once we were within my office, I shut the door and gave my mother a one-word question. "Why?"

Her lips pursed as her chin rose. "Things are out of hand. There has been some discussion...amongst those of us who remember what happened."

"The old guard. Tell me, Mother, what have you old

biddies decided? That is, as long as you're aware that it's only my opinion that counts."

Genevieve shook her head. "We are older than you, you're correct. *Old* however, is a state of mind, and none of us are that. Sterling, power may give you many things. It doesn't, however, give you wisdom. That, son, comes with age and experience. I told you the last time I saw you that what you've done will irreparably damage our lives—all of our lives. I warned you. I've been warning you since you were a child, imploring you to allow the dead to stay that way."

Sitting behind my desk, I brought my phone out of my pocket and placed it before me, hopeful to find a message from Araneae or Patrick. There wasn't one. Under normal circumstances—normal being a subjective word—multi-tasking wasn't a problem. With both of the current figurative fires involving Araneae, I was having trouble focusing on my mother.

With a huff, she sat at one of the chairs across from my desk, perching on the edge, her slender legs daintily crossed at the ankle, her knees pinched tightly together, and her handbag clutched in her lap. It was as if all of my life she'd been a walking, talking example of ladies' etiquette. The part that never aligned with that facade was her ability, all the while appearing serene and genteel, to debase or chastise, her words venomous as her smile remained intact.

"There are times," she went on, "when we ladies have needed to step in, to forget for a moment our differences, and concentrate on the future of our world. I implore you to listen to me."

"You have three minutes."

"May I remind you that I'm your mother?"

"That seems like a waste of your first ten seconds, but by all means, mother, spend your time however you choose."

Sucking in a breath she squared her shoulders. "The tensions were incredibly high around the time Annabelle gave birth." She swallowed. "Daniel McCrie was wrong to leverage stolen information. He put Annabelle, their child, and himself in danger.

"While Annabelle and I went different paths, we've known each other for nearly...well, ever. We went to the same schools. Our parents ran in the same circles."

My mother came from old money, steeped in the history of Chicago. Originally her ancestors came from Ireland, some of the early arrivals. Their specialty was farming. It wasn't until the next generation that their horizons were broadened by the construction of the Illinois and Michigan canal, allowing the shipping of goods from the Great Lakes to the Mississippi River and down to the Gulf of Mexico. That was in the mid-1800s. Not long after, her great—a few greats—grandmother married a man willing to risk the family fortune on the idea of expanding shipping beyond the waterways onto rails. Twenty years later, refrigerated train cars improved the transportation of meats and produce. Chicago became a main railroad hub. Those railroads opened the way to transport lumber, and then came steel. Demand required factories and warehouses. Employment opportunities abounded. The city grew. Her great—how many times—grandfather's investment paid off, propelling the family into the upper echelon of Chicago's elite. Money begot money.

Her family's wealth gave Allister what he needed to make Sparrow Enterprises into a well-known name, a competitor on the world market. His family's influence supported his other endeavors.

Though I didn't know Annabelle's family history as well, I was aware that her family also dated back to the beginnings of Chicago and included generations of lawyers, bankers, and investors. These were the people who worked beside the entrepreneurs. Together they forged the city where we now live.

"Your time is running out," I said.

"It was incredibly difficult for Annabelle to see that girl with you." My mother's voice lowered. "This is not to be repeated; however, she admitted herself for rest."

I nodded. "I'm aware."

"How would you know that?"

"If it happens in this city..." Or should I have said originates? "...I know."

She shook her head as I looked down at my watch, silently reminding her that her time was about out.

"When Annabelle came home from the spa, she called me," my mother said.

Spa.

Hmm.

Otherwise known as the psych ward at an out-of-state hospital.

"I'm well aware of the stories your father told you," Genevieve continued, "about a future for you and that...that *girl*. He convinced you that she was Annabelle and Daniel's daughter. Old wives' tales and fables." Her chin rose higher. "It's time for you to come clean and tell Annabelle the truth, that you have no proof of the girl's paternity. That the identity you've given her is simply based upon a story created by a man who's now gone. Your father planted fiction in your head and you tended it, letting it take root. Give poor Annabelle closure. Closure that she can only find by confirming that the baby she held and buried was her child and that part of her life is over."

I took a deep breath and shook my head, recalling Pauline McFadden's words to Araneae: *The real Araneae McCrie would never betray her family like that. Your fabrication will never work. I don't know who you are or why you've allowed this man to convince you otherwise, but Araneae McCrie died. Some second-rate imposter who stole a bracelet won't get away with threatening our family.*

"I can't and won't do that," I said. "I doubt very seriously that my father told a fable. As you may remember, he was never the bedtime-story-type of man. Out of curiosity, was Pauline McFadden around for this cackling-hen session?"

"Yes. She was as well as Ruth Hillman. We all remember."

Ruth was Wendell Hillman's wife. She'd also been at the club the night Araneae was poisoned.

"Essentially, you're telling me that you, my mother, Genevieve Sparrow, sat down with three McFaddens."

"Martha Carlson was also there. Technically, Annabelle isn't a McFadden." She shrugged. "Nor is Martha." Martha Carlson was the wife of my father's consigliere, Rudy Carlson, one of the men in the room the first time I saw Araneae's photo. "Not by blood."

Taking another look at my phone, I stood. "You came here today to ask me to tell Annabelle that Araneae is a fake, an imposter." Though it was a question, I delivered it much more as a confirmation.

My mother looked up, her gaze never leaving mine. "Sterling, I'm asking you to do what's right, to save the world where we all live. Rubio is poised for his presidential bid. You have the power here in Chicago. You can be instrumental in burying old hatchets and finally do what your father never could do—coexist. The possibilities are endless if we work together instead of against one another. As president, Rubio could do much for Chicago. There is nothing good that will come from...her."

Leaning forward, I splayed my fingers over the top of my desk moving my weight to my arms. "*Her* has a name. Her name is Araneae McCrie. I can tell you that in the weeks since she's come into my life—where I brought her—when it comes to that woman, not a girl, everything has been good."

My mother stood. "Tell me, Sterling, do you have proof? Do you have more than war room stories made up by vengeful men?"

"Your time is up. Do you plan to join me for my discussion with Judge Landers?"

Her head shook ever so slightly as her lips pursed. "No. Annabelle asked for my help to talk to you, to see you. Whatever the two of you discuss is none of my business. My only concern is you."

"Hardly, Mother. Your concern is maintaining the life you've perfected, the one that's shiny on the outside and filthy on the inside. That secret information that Daniel McCrie supposedly tried to leverage unsuccessfully, how did you feel about that?"

"I-I don't know for sure what it was. Your father never told me those kinds of things. I didn't even know that Daniel came to him for help until years later."

"Wait, what do you know about that? Daniel came to my father for what kind of help?"

With the hand not holding her purse, she slapped the side

of her thigh. "Leave it all buried. I told Allister the same thing when he had that tiny coffin exhumed."

I thought back through our extensive research. "There's no public record of that. There would be something listed with the coroner's office or medical examiner."

"Oh, Sterling, it wasn't here in Chicago, not even in Illinois. At first, Annabelle and Daniel didn't tell many people where they buried her. Of course, Rubio and Pauline were at the small funeral."

I knew where Araneae's body had supposedly been buried; however, I waited to hear if my mother would divulge the truth or more of her lies. "There would still be a record."

"Even if you looked in the right place...you remember your father. He didn't go to the authorities. What excuse would he have to request an exhumation? Instead, he ordered it himself, having his men dig her up and put the casket back."

"When?"

My mother's complexion paled as she began to pace a trek to the large windows and back. "If I tell you this, will you please tell Annabelle the truth?"

"I will tell her the truth."

"It was years later. You were too young to remember when the infant died, when it all began, but this—the exhumation was over a decade later..." She shook her head. "...no, even more recent than that. I believe you were home from the army and at Michigan. I don't know for sure when it was...time goes fast and it's hard to keep up."

She stood at the window, looking at the city and lake yet appearing to see neither. Her mind was back to a time before I was in power, a time that I had no way of remembering.

"It took years," she said wistfully, "but finally McCrie had gotten himself to a place where he was working again with Rubio and occasionally Allister, convincing those around him of his loyalty. With Rubio's help, Annabelle had been appointed as a federal judge. Rubio was spending more time in Washington than in Chicago. Things were looking up for everyone.

"One night, your father was upset, more agitated than normal. Usually he didn't say much in front of me, but we all knew something was happening whether it was said or not. That one night he'd been drinking. After Rudy left the house, Allister was livid, and I was the one who happened to be present. Your father ranted about being played by Daniel. He said that he'd demanded Rudy confirm that the buried infant wasn't..." She let out a long breath. "Later, Allister told me that his men exhumed the body. He had doctors who did the testing. They confirmed the remains were of Annabelle and Daniel's child." She pleaded, "You see, there's no public record. It wasn't carried out by a governmental agency. Tell her the truth."

Sighing, I shook my head. "My father lied to you, Mother."

Her blue eyes turned my way. "No, because after, it was when..." She turned back to the window. "Something had gone south again with McCrie. Just like around the time of her birth, both families were again at odds."

I leaned back against my desk, watching my mother's reflection in the glass window, the way her lips tensed and brow furrowed.

"It was when McCrie..." She bit her painted lip and shook her head. "...I know what was declared publicly, but it was a hit. I always wondered if it had to do with the information about the infant." Her head shook. "But your father swore it wasn't from the Sparrows. He even met with Rubio to confirm that it wasn't Sparrows.

"Don't you understand? If he hadn't, there would have been a war like Chicago had never seen. But it didn't make sense. If it wasn't from the Sparrows, it implied that Rubio had authorized the gruesome death of his own brother-in-law. It was a dangerous time. Finally, the conclusion was made that the hit was a family from Philly or New York capitalizing on our infighting.

"Like we just did, we ladies came together and made a plea for peace before it was too late."

I stood and walked closer. "Does Annabelle know what you just told me? Does she know that my father authorized the exhumation of a body, one she believed to be her child?"

My mother shook her head. "No. The exhumation wasn't confirmed. The church where that girl is buried is in a small town in the middle of nowhere Wisconsin. A few months later, Annabelle was contacted by someone telling her that they believed there might have been tampering—they blamed it on kids' pranks. The church told her that the ground had been dug. They didn't know if the casket had been reached or not. You see, it happened in the dead of winter. It wasn't reported to Annabelle until after the snow melted, nearly three months after Daniel's death. Annabelle didn't pursue it."

"So you're saying, she never got that information."

"Heavens, no. DNA results are hardly the conversation topic for social events. Pauline, Martha, Ruth, and I were the ones to know the truth."

My phone buzzed. On the screen: *PATRICK*.

I swiped the screen.

. . .

"SHE'S STILL INSIDE. I DON'T HEAR ANYTHING."

What the fuck?

I texted back:

"I TOLD YOU NOT TO LET HER OUT OF YOUR SIGHT."

"Sterling," my mother asked, "is everything all right?"

My gaze narrowed. "No, everything is not all right. We're done. Allister lied to you. Araneae is who I say she is. I have the proof."

Next, I sent Araneae a text.

"YOU HAVE FIVE SECONDS TO GET TO PATRICK OR YOUR ASS IS MINE."

Fucking follow one damn direction. Once.

Araneae wasn't the only one who would hear about this.

Why the hell would Patrick let her out of his sight?

ARANEAE

*S*TERLING was on my screen, indicating a text message. I looked back up to Agent Hunter and then to Winnie.

"Winnie, we need to leave." I laid my hand on her shoulder. "Please come with me."

"I-I...do you still want me?"

"We need to discuss it privately."

"Ms. Hawkins," Agent Hunter said, "this offer expires when you step across this threshold."

I stood taller. "It can expire immediately. I have no information. I'll admit—off the record—that I was told about an old wives' tale stating that I did have something, but you must understand, I was an infant. How would an infant obtain and retain information from before her birth?"

"Were you told what that information involved?"

"I wasn't given specifics."

He reached for the folder that had Sterling's picture. "I can show you specifics."

I lifted my hand. "I'm leaving."

"It might not be as easy to dismiss my offer or willingly walk back into the clutches of Sterling Sparrow if you took a minute to see the victims. We're not discussing a victimless crime here. These were and are children."

Are... it made my stomach turn, yet Sterling had promised that he was no longer involved.

Why should he pay for what his father did?

My mind went to Jana and Missy, the sister of Sterling's friend. I doubted Jana was the only victim he'd helped. There were so many people loyal to him. Could there be others whom he'd saved?

I shook my head. "The Sterling Sparrow I know is in real estate. I refuse to let you poison my mind otherwise." I took a breath. "Your infiltration of this supposed underworld, Agent Hunter? Were you or were you not posing as Andrew Walsh?"

"I can't discuss—"

"You brought it up. Who was it that you worked for in this infiltration?"

"I've always worked for the Federal Bureau of Investigation."

I shook my head. "You know that isn't what I meant."

"Ms. Hawkins."

"Are you insinuating you worked for Mr. Sparrow," I asked, "the real estate mogul? If that wasn't the case, then why would I need to be saved by you in Wichita?"

"No, ma'am, I wasn't working for a real estate mogul. Why try to save you? Your identity had been made public. It was meant to be a preventative measure, to help you before things got out of control."

"I'm having trouble following. If you hadn't been working for Mr. Sparrow, why are you pursuing him? Wouldn't or shouldn't you have enough evidence to bring down whomever it was who ultimately ran whatever outfit you worked for?"

"As I said, I can't discuss—"

I tilted my head. "In Wichita, did you mean to *save* me or *enlist* my help as you've offered today?"

"You don't understand," Agent Hunter said.

"No, I don't. How much time did you say you were undercover?" I answered my own question. "Two and a half years? And still you don't have what you need. Perhaps what you seek doesn't exist."

"Without particulars," he said, "let me simply say that power operates inside a vacuum. It works the same with crime, government, and any other institutions where power rules supreme. If one powerful entity is taken out, removed from the situation—or city—then the remaining powerful force, by the elimination of the counterforce, gains ultimate power."

My chin rose. "You're saying that you want everyone gone?"

"In a perfect world."

One of my cheeks rose. "Good luck on that perfect world, Agent Hunter. I suppose optimism is a positive attitude."

"Heartbreaking really. Too often we see what is right..." He lifted his hand and closed his fingers around his outstretched palm. "...in front of us. It's right there, within reach, and yet even when it's presented on a silver platter, it isn't seized. Optimism would believe that when a good person, such as yourself, is given the chance to do what is right—save children and lessen this city of crime—that you would willingly oblige."

"I believe we're done," I said.

Winnie stood as I started toward the door. As I passed, Agent Hunter reached for my upper arm.

Fire burned from my gaze as I stared from his grasp to his eyes. "Let go of me."

"You didn't ask for any of this," he said, his grip still secured. "You shouldn't have to carry the weight of what was thrust upon you as an infant. Life isn't fair. We're giving you the safest option with the bonus of helping others, not only strangers but your closest friends."

"I suggest you let go of me..." I tugged my arm away. "...and never consider touching me again. If I scream, I promise you'll regret it."

Though his grip was gone, his blue eyes begged for me to listen. "Don't tell him."

"Why? Why wouldn't I tell him that I was ambushed, that Winnie was lied to? Why wouldn't I be honest with him?"

"Because he hasn't been honest with you."

You don't know that. He's been brutally honest. He's told me more than anyone. He'd even told me about the exploitation and trafficking. His father may have been involved, but Sterling wasn't.

I couldn't and didn't say any of that, yet my heart did.

Sterling had trusted me with not only my secrets but his. I had no plans on breaking that trust. I turned toward the door again. "Winnie, we're going."

Agent Hunter shook his head as he moved in front of me, his volume lowering. "Listen, I want to help you. If you tell him about this, your one avenue of escape is gone. Winifred has my number."

"You said that your offer expired."

"I won't leave you without an option."

"I don't need an option," I replied.

"You might soon. It would be a shame to not have one," Agent Hunter said as he stepped into the bathroom, closing the door.

Taking a deep breath, I pulled the door to the hallway inward. Patrick materialized, his hand at his side, beneath his suit coat. It didn't take a genius to know what he was packing under there.

"We're ready to go," I said, looking him in the eye.

"Ma'am," he said, his gaze searching what he could see of the hotel room.

It wasn't until we were back in the car and my phone buzzed that I recalled I had a message from Sterling.

Two text messages. The most recent was from Patrick.

I read his first.

"NOT IN FRONT OF WINNIE. TELL ME WHO ELSE WAS IN THAT ROOM."

I allowed my eyes to close in an extra-long blink before my gaze met his in the rearview mirror. As we stared, I searched for my answer to his question.

What should I do? Should I trust a man I barely knew who claimed he could help me or the man I'd become very accustomed to who had already shed more light on my life than anyone else?

Instead of answering, I looked down, opening Sterling's text message.

"YOU HAVE FIVE SECONDS TO GET TO PATRICK OR YOUR ASS IS MINE."

Warmth filled my cheeks until the sentiment changed to betrayal. I looked up. "You told him I went in there alone?"

Patrick's wide shoulders moved with his exhale as we emerged from the depths of the parking garage into Chicago late-morning traffic. "You were gone longer than I expected."

"It's my fault," Winnie volunteered, her eyes still glassy though her speech was clearer. "I thought she wouldn't want me back at Sinful Threads. Kennedy was trying to convince me."

I took a deep breath, wondering what to do and say to Winnie. What had Agent Hunter told her? I peered at the woman at my side and reached over to her hand. Giving it a squeeze, I smiled reassuringly. "You asked me if I wanted you to stay at Sinful Threads. My question to you is do you want to?"

"You and Louisa have..." Her head shook. "Being your assistant has been the best job—no, career move—of my life. Each day you've allowed the responsibilities to grow. Working for you has given me opportunities I never could have imagined, and watching the success...I am sorry for what happened."

My eyes went to the rearview mirror as I inhaled. "We can

talk more about that at the office. Are you telling me that you'd like to continue?"

She bobbed her head. "Very much."

How was I going to tell Louisa what happened?

What about the insinuation that Sinful Threads was involved with illegal activities?

That couldn't be true. I knew who I needed to trust.

I pulled my phone from my purse and sent a text.

"WE NEED TO TALK."

STERLING

"*S*terling, please..."

It was the last thing I heard my mother say as I stepped from my office, leaving her alone, and made my way to conference room four. My mind spun in a hundred different directions. As I reached for the handle, my phone in my pocket buzzed with *PATRICK* on the screen.

"I HAVE THEM BOTH. WE'RE HEADED TO SINFUL THREADS."

Thank God.

My fingers itched to text Araneae, to warn her what was coming the next time we were alone. Clenching my jaw, my cyclone of thoughts whirled with theories and concerns of what Winnie and Araneae discussed while they'd been alone in that hotel room.

"Do not leave Patrick's sight," was what I'd told her more than once.

Was it too fucking hard for her to just once follow my instructions?

And then my gaze moved to the window. Judge Landers must have seen me outside the doorway. Her steps had stilled, and her eyes were opened wide as she waited for me to enter.

It wasn't that I saw her often. I didn't. Nevertheless, since the night at the club she'd lost weight. Her pale skin seemed to hang from her bones, making her appear frail, not the picture of a distinguished federal judge.

"This is for Araneae," I told myself as I placed my phone back in my pocket and opened the door.

"Judge Landers," I said, taking charge of this conversation, "this is highly unusual. It's customary to contact my assistant to arrange a meeting, not my mother."

Her head nodded as her noticeably shaky hands reached for the back of one of the padded chairs surrounding the table. "Mr. Sparrow, I apologize for the irregular approach. The truth is that I was afraid you wouldn't agree to see me if I took the normal channels."

"Tell me why I should see you now."

"Because..." She took a deep breath as her fingers gripped tighter to the upholstery, and moisture gleamed in her eyes. Swallowing, she lifted her chin. "...I need answers and I believe you are the only one who can help me."

Her approach was contrary to both Pauline McFadden's and my mother's, having me both curious and intrigued. Inhaling, I answered, "Judge, I don't have much time." I gestured to the chair. "Please have a seat and you may ask what you want. I can't guarantee I'm able or willing to answer."

"Thank you, Mr. Sparrow." She pulled back the chair and sat, not at the edge as my mother would do, but settled on the seat, placing her hands on the table, like the judge she was. "I appreciate your candor."

Joining her at the table, I sat and asked, "What do you believe I can answer that you don't know?"

Her eyes—the exact color as Araneae's—blinked as she appeared to collect her thoughts. "I've been wrestling with this since the night at the club. While I have a million questions, the one that I keep returning to is how is it possible?"

"You aren't going to ask me if she's really her?"

"I-I...I would like confirmation; however, I believe that when I saw her in the bathroom of the club—when our eyes met—I knew. In my heart, I knew."

I nodded.

"Please understand this from my perspective," she said.

"I'm not sure that's possible."

Her head tilted as a sad smile floated across her lips. "I didn't give her up. It was a choice I struggled with at the time. It was an option presented to me, to protect her. I considered it, yet I couldn't. I was selfish. Instead, I vowed to protect her. The sad truth was that even if she would have been safer with other people, I couldn't do it, despite the things Daniel had done. When the time came—when she was born—the decision was taken from me.

"I wanted her more than I wanted life. As a matter of fact, when she died—when I thought she died—I contemplated going with her. I couldn't harm myself, but I didn't eat. I slept for days, for weeks. I was so grief-stricken that I was even beyond inconsolable." She looked down at her hands on the table, one wringing the other. "When you entered the club, there were whispers. Rubio was furious. Her name was being repeated in all directions. My mind knew it couldn't be true." A lone tear trickled from her soft brown eye. "I'd held her in my arms, her lifeless body. I cradled her and told her all the things I could—that I loved her, I always would. That she was now my angel."

She inhaled and wiped the renegade tear away. "Well, being there at the club, her sitting at the bar...I couldn't take it. I went to the bathroom to gather my thoughts, telling myself that you were a Sparrow. You couldn't be trusted and this was a ruse."

I sat taller.

"I'm sorry, Mr. Sparrow. It was what I thought. I'm being honest. And then as I was washing my hands, she came out of a stall." A new smile floated across her lips, bringing a gleam to her eyes. "I always imagined my daughter would look like me, my hair and eyes. The infant that I held had dark hair, and I never saw her eyes.

"When our gazes met in that mirror, it was as if I were seeing my own reflection in a twisted time machine. I-I became momentarily paralyzed. All of my dreams and all of my visions for the child I carried were suddenly alive, wrapped up in the astonishing young woman at my side.

"I knew, in my heart. And then I had the confirmation when I saw her bracelet. It was supposed to have been buried with her."

"Bracelet?" I couldn't remember which bracelet Araneae had worn that night. There were too many other things on my mind. And then I recalled mentioning it outside of the elevator before we'd entered. "Why did you want that old charm bracelet buried with her?"

Judge Landers shook her head. "I know your time is limited. It's a long, boring story. My point is that even without more proof, I believe you. I don't understand and I may never, but I believe." Another tear rolled down her cheek. "Maybe it's wishful thinking. If it is, it's the most I've had in...twenty-six years.

"Mr. Sparrow, I don't know if you have more proof or not, but I pray to all things holy that you're not lying, trying to get to Rubio with a charade. I want better than that for both my daughter and for me."

"Judge Landers, I have DNA proof. I'm certain it doesn't make sense, but I wanted her to be Araneae McCrie—"

She gasped.

"What?"

"The way you pronounce her name."

"Yes? It was the way I was told."

Judge Landers shook her head. "*Uh-rain-ā* was how Daniel wanted it pronounced. I wanted it pronounced *Uh-ron-e-eye*, just like the spider." She waved her hand. "Never mind, please go on."

Interesting.

"I also wanted her to be who I was told she was. I didn't want to be disappointed nor did I want to bring someone into this world, *this world*," I repeated, believing she'd understand my meaning, "who didn't belong."

"But how?"

"Hair. Yours and hers."

"Mine? How?"

I shook my head. "The particulars aren't important. What is important is that you and Araneae share mitochondrial DNA. We didn't have access to your husband's DNA, but from what I was told, only women can pass along their mitochondrial DNA to their children."

Her fingers came to her lips as she gasped again. "What does she know about me?"

"Nothing until you said something at the club."

"I-I was in shock."

For the first time ever with this quest, I felt a twinge of guilt for the way this played out, not for making the statement that Araneae was mine, but for Annabelle.

How could we have known that she had also been lied to?

"I would like to," she said, her soft brown eyes pleading, "do a better job of introducing myself."

"Your sister-in-law met with her this morning. I'm afraid she didn't pave the way to a family reunion."

Judge Landers sat taller. "Mr. Sparrow, I have never had problems with you. With your father, yes. Is she...is my daughter happy?"

"That's my goal."

She nodded. "I implore you to let her know that I've dreamt of reuniting with her one day—away from this earth. As time passed and I've made necessary decisions, I feared that those decisions would never allow that reunion to happen. Surely my innocent daughter ended up in a better place than I one day would. And now you have provided a means for that reunion to occur. Please let her know that I'm sincere."

"She was upset by Mrs. McFadden."

Annabelle's chin rose as she inhaled and exhaled. "Pauline

has a way with people. She doesn't believe that she's really Araneae. Pauline said that her real name is Kennedy Hawkins. Is that true?"

"*Real* is a subjective term. Araneae McCrie was declared deceased. Her legal name is Kennedy Hawkins, and when it comes to Ms. Hawkins, I'm certain you've done your research."

A smile broke out across her face. "I have. Silk fashions. Isn't that...something?"

My phone vibrated in my pocket, yet I remained focused on Judge Landers. Nodding, I added, "Your daughter *is* something. I'll talk to her, but meeting with you is her decision and hers alone. My only stipulation is that neither Pauline nor Rubio McFadden or his men are allowed anywhere near her."

"Surely you don't believe the old wives' tale."

"Which one would that be, Judge Landers?" I asked.

"That my daughter somehow possesses evidence that Daniel hid."

"You don't?"

"I don't," she confirmed with a shake of her head. "I was there with my husband. I refused to learn the details. In my position with the courts, I couldn't. I believe that whatever Daniel knew died the night he took his own life."

That had been the official story—not the accurate one but the one that helped people sleep at night.

"Then again," she went on, "I never believed my daughter was alive."

I debated telling her that Araneae didn't have the information. Annabelle may be upset with Pauline, but when it came to Rubio, I couldn't be certain that she could be trusted. "Nevertheless, Araneae will not be put in harm's way again. That includes Rubio, Pauline, and any of McFadden's men."

Judge Landers began to stand. "Mr. Sparrow, I won't keep you any longer." She reached into her purse and handed me a card. "Here are my private numbers. I thank you for your time."

Joining her in standing, I nodded. "I want you to know that I didn't find her to hurt you." I wasn't sure what compelled me to tell her that, but I did.

"No, I believe you found her to hurt Rubio, and I don't care. You found her." She reached out toward me and stopped, placing both hands on her purse. "Somehow, because of you, life and hope have been allowed to bloom in a place where I never thought that would be possible. I choose to believe that you're sincere in wanting her happy. It's all I've ever wanted. No matter the reason you found her, thank you."

ARANEAE

*J*ana met us with wide eyes upon our return. "Is everything okay?"

If only there was a simple answer to that question. Instead, I deferred. "Did anything happen while we were away?"

"No, mostly quiet."

"Please hold all calls—*all*," I emphasized, knowing there was one man who could be persistent.

"Ms. Hawkins?" Patrick asked as I headed toward my office.

I turned his way. "Winnie and I need to continue our conversation from the hotel room. We were on a time limit."

Though disagreement rippled off of Patrick in waves and I knew he wanted an answer to the question he'd texted me, he didn't return my statement with a rebuttal but simply a nod.

Once Winnie and I were inside my private office with the

door shut, I gestured toward the table—the one still cluttered with sketches for Mrs. McFadden. "I don't have anything stronger, not here. Would you like a cup of coffee or water?" I asked.

Shaking her head, she sat. "I am sorry."

After silencing my phone, putting it into my purse, and securing it in the drawer of my desk, I made my way to the bookcase where the coffee decanter was located. Pouring myself a cup of the hours-old yet still-warm java, I added cream and stirred. Watching the swirls, I collected my thoughts. After a deep sigh, I went on, "You do keep saying that you're sorry. Do you have anything in the safe within your hotel room?"

Her blue eyes looked up. "What?"

"You obviously can't stay in that hotel room another night. I'd bet it's bugged."

"Kenni, who are you? What the hell is happening? The person I know—knew—wouldn't even think that way. What Agent Hunter said about Mr. Sparrow being dangerous, he convinced me that it was true. He made me believe I was helping you by getting you in touch with the FBI, like you were being forced to do something...unwillingly."

Taking a deep breath, I carried my coffee to the table and sat. "Sterling is in real estate."

"You have mentioned that many times. It seems that maybe there's a middle ground between the monster Agent Hunter described and this man who swept you off your feet. Or maybe it's hard for you to see with all the dollar signs swirling around."

Dollar signs?

I looked up. "Explain."

"You said you're living with him."

I nodded.

"You have your own personal bodyguard. You're wearing expensive clothes. I can assume the trip to Canada was his idea. And you look..." She waved her hands my direction. "...I don't know—different. You've always been the most confident one of us, the one willing to take chances. Now it's as if you seem...regal." She shook her head again. "I don't mean like you think you're better but that you actually are. There's an air. It's not...damn, I'm not saying this right."

"Of us," I said.

"What?"

"You said *of us*—I was the confident one of *us*."

"Yes."

"I suppose if I'm being honest," I said, "I feel betrayed and disappointed. Why would you choose to discuss Sinful Threads and me with someone else, not Louisa but a stranger? If there is an us, shouldn't we first bring our concerns to one another?"

Winnie leaned back. "As you know, Louisa is busy with both work and preparations for the baby. And the concerns about you weren't only mine; we'd all shared our unease. Louisa and I talked about your odd change in behavior. You went days with hardly a text or email.

"He, Agent Hunter, isn't a stranger, not now. He came to me in Boulder. At first, he wasn't upfront with me about who he was, saying he was an insurance adjuster and asking questions about your apartment."

Oh my God. The blond insurance adjuster the lady from my apartment spoke about.

"Go on," I said. "You happened to start talking about my behavior to an insurance adjuster?"

"He brought you and your apartment up, and then he asked me out, Kenni. I hadn't been on a date in..." She sighed. "...not a date with someone I thought was attractive. I've got a thing for nerds—he was a numbers guy. And bonus, if they're handsome..." Winnie leaned forward with her hands on the table. "Wesley was all those things and easy to talk to. I agreed to drinks. We started talking. Now I feel like a total idiot. He didn't ask me out because of me but because of you."

Wesley.

"When did he come clean about who he was?"

"On our second date."

I closed my eyes and inhaled.

"By then," she said, "I'd talked about my job at Sinful Threads. I'd even talked about how we were expanding our offices to Chicago and that you'd offered me the ability to commute. I was very excited. I talk when I'm excited." She looked at my cup. "Do you mind if I get coffee?"

As I shook my head, she stood and continued talking. "He told me that he liked me, and that was why he came clean. He said he couldn't lie to me anymore, even if it was for his job."

"Did you give him specifics about me or Sinful Threads?"

"No, I promise. At least I don't think so. He knew. Once he told me who he was—what he was—he told me about the inventory numbers in Chicago not meshing. Everything he said was something we'd all discussed. He mentioned that you'd been seen publicly with Sterling Sparrow and he feared that somehow Sparrow would influence you to allow him to use Sinful Threads for a front."

She sat back down with her cup of coffee. "I only knew about the real estate. I'd never heard of anything else about him. Are those other things true?" she asked.

My palm slapped the tabletop. "Is it true that I'd allow anyone to do anything to hurt or jeopardize Sinful Threads? Is that what you're asking me?"

Winnie's expression fell, curiosity morphing into sadness. "I hadn't thought of it like that." She looked up from her coffee with more tears in her eyes. "I know you wouldn't do anything to hurt Sinful Threads. It's just that there seemed to be circumstantial evidence that backed up everything he said."

"Are you...dating Agent Hunter?"

"No," she answered too quickly. "I agreed to talk to you while I was here and feel out the situation. I didn't want to believe what he was proposing was true. And then this morning I called him to let him know he was wrong, that whatever the FBI thought, they too were wrong. You weren't doing anything against your will. You were...you are...in love with Sterling Sparrow.

"Wesley told me to meet him in my hotel room. When I got there, he was already in it." She stood and spun. "That freaks me the hell out. He was in my locked room. I mean, who does that kind of thing?"

I could think of a list of candidates at this particular moment; however, I stayed silent, hedging on the idea that her question was rhetorical.

"Wesley said," she went on, "that I needed to give him a chance to speak to you."

"Now that you did all that, what do you really think? What do you, Winifred Douglas, believe?" I asked.

"I think I let you down, that you should tell Louisa, and I should be fired."

I closed my eyes and inhaled before opening them again. "What do you think about what Agent Hunter told you?"

"I think he's wrong. I don't know about the numbers. We should have Jason look into that. You know, a fresh pair of eyes? If someone is using Sinful Threads for something illegal, we need to be open with the FBI. If it's happening, my money is on Franco Francesca. If he is doing something, he should go down, not the company." She shrugged. "Maybe wishful thinking. I don't want to believe that it's you or a man you care about."

"I guarantee it isn't me or Sterling. Think about it, Winnie, when Sterling can't be with me, he has Patrick beside me twenty-four seven. He knows how much Sinful Threads means to me. The real estate deals Agent Hunter mentioned are accurate. Sinful Threads has received better-than-market deals. That's not illegal. And there are no strings attached."

"None?"

"Not regarding business." My cheeks warmed as I pushed away the thoughts of strings or scarves and our four-poster bed. "I think I do need to tell Louisa but not until after Kennedy is born. She doesn't need the stress. As for firing you..." I thought about talking to Sterling and Patrick and then remembered what I'd been saying: Sinful Threads was my company, mine and Louisa's. "...I don't want to do that. However, what I do need from you is a promise that you and Wesley Hunter are done."

Winnie nodded.

"The other things you heard such as about my name..." I let the sentence go incomplete.

"I-I don't have any idea what he was saying. I still don't. He never mentioned any of that before."

"If I asked you to forget about it for a while, could you?"

"Is it true? Are you three people?"

"No," I said, unsure how to accurately explain without too much detail. "I'm one person who has had three identities, all by the age of sixteen. I never lied to you or Louisa. By the time I moved to Boulder and she and I met, I had become Kennedy Hawkins." When Winnie didn't answer, I said, "I was adopted as an infant. The only parents I remember weren't Phillip and Debbie Hawkins. Those people never existed. When my adoptive mother sent me to Boulder, she told me to become Kennedy, for my safety."

Winnie's eyes were wide as saucers.

I shook my head. "For that reason, for your safety as well as mine, it's better if we keep it at that. If my true adoptive parents are still alive, I don't want to risk their safety. I recently had confirmation of my birth name. That's part of the reason for Patrick. My birth father did something, and there could be people who want to do me harm." *Perhaps my own uncle.* I couldn't say that either. I took a sip of coffee. "Can you leave it at that and trust me that I'm not doing anything illegal?"

"Yes. If you can forgive me."

"I can. I understand now that I should have shared more with you and Louisa earlier. I truly was too swept off my feet to even imagine how it looked from the outside. Now," I said, "tell me how you feel Jana is doing."

"Well. She's a fast learner. I wanted to show her how to access inventory at all of our various locations and cross-reference that with pending and filled orders, and then how to keep that in line with production. With the new dresses, the production team is working overtime. Dresses take longer to create and produce than a scarf or bangle."

I smiled, hearing Winnie discussing Sinful Threads, confirming that I was making the correct decision by keeping her as part of our team. "I want you to show Jana all of that today. I think you should go back to Boulder tomorrow. And tonight, Patrick or Jana will book you another room, probably in a different hotel. They can also have someone move your things and check you out of the Hilton."

"But...I was going to be here until Friday, show Jana other things and look further into my friend."

I shook my head. "My friend said if your friend wants to be off the radar, there's not much that can be done. Besides, Louisa could go into labor at any moment. I know Cindy and Paul are at the office, but I'd feel better if you were there."

"You don't want me gone—completely—from Sinful Threads...after what I did?" Winnie asked.

"No, but I need to know you're secure. As you said, Agent Hunter entered your room without your permission. He was there for God knows how long. It isn't safe."

Winnie nodded. "I do have things in the safe."

"Give the combination to Patrick."

Before she could respond, the door from the front office opened.

"Jana..." I began to say, turning, when the energy shifted, causing my heart to beat faster. Meeting my gaze was the dark stare of the man I decided I loved. His expression wasn't one of adoration and was only momentarily directed at me. His granite features were fixed on Winnie.

How much did he know?

"This is..." I turned to Winnie as she paled before my eyes. "...Winifred Douglas." I turned back to Sterling. "And this is Sterling Sparrow."

STERLING

*P*atrick had informed me of his concern—that there had been someone else in the hotel room with Winnie. He hadn't yet had the opportunity to confirm it with Araneae, but that didn't matter. We had our ways.

We had Reid.

Seventy-two minutes before Winnie returned to her hotel, Andrew Walsh entered her room, using a master key. Prior to the meeting, Reid hadn't looked back in time, only forward. Our facial recognition system confirmed him as Andrew Walsh, the one of McFadden's outfit, the one from Wichita. The difference between the man at the airport and now was that currently there was a badge hanging from his belt that hadn't been there before. Closer inspection of the badge through the security footage confirmed that it was FBI. With that new bit of information came a new search by Reid.

. . .

A few minutes ago on the telephone~

"Sparrow, I'm sorry. I didn't look backward," Reid said through the phone.

I tried to rein in my anger. Araneae was safe and back with Patrick. That was the ultimate goal. Now I needed to know what happened in that room.

Why did Winnie have an FBI agent in her room?

"Find out who the fuck he really is."

If anything had happened to Araneae, I would need a new set of trusted right-hand men. They'd both fucked up. Reid hadn't researched the security footage well enough, and Patrick had allowed her to go in the room alone.

Hanging up with Reid, I called Patrick. "What the fuck part of don't let her out of your sight was difficult to understand?"

"Sparrow, she can be...convincing. It was a one-room hotel room. I never would have done it if I couldn't be right outside. I was. I would have kicked the damn door in if necessary."

I knew too well how convincing Araneae could be.

"It was a direct order to both of you." I reminded him.

"You also told me, in front of her, to listen to her. She likes to remind me of that."

Rage and hysteria must be closely related. While I was on the verge of taking out my wrath on my trusted friend, listening to him speak about how convincing, how conniving Araneae could be, made me smile—hell, I almost laughed.

Almost.

"Where is she now?" I asked.

"She and Winnie went in her office and closed the door. I told Araneae I wanted to speak to her and she...well, she went in her office with Winnie to complete the conversation from the hotel. She said they'd been on a time limit there. Now she wanted to talk."

My head shook as I listened, imagining Araneae's pert lips and straight-as-a-stick neck with her shoulders squared. When she was determined, it radiated from her every pore.

"So you haven't confirmed with her the presence of the FBI agent?"

"No."

"I'm on my way to Sinful Threads. Earlier, Araneae said she wanted to take that getaway. I'm all for that. After this FBI business and dealing with Pauline McFadden, my mother, and Judge Landers—"

"Your mother?" Patrick asked. "How did she get in the mix?"

"I'll fill you and Reid in together. Basically, the old guard of Chicago busybodies convened. They tried to convince Annabelle that Araneae is an imposter. Annabelle wasn't sure that I'd meet with her if she called for an appointment, so she asked my mother for help. Before I spoke to the judge, Genevieve ran interference, asking me to tell Annabelle the same story the old biddies had concocted."

"Did you?"

I looked up at the front seat at Garrett. "Like I said, I'll fill you both in. I'd prefer to only tell a story about my mother once. Don't let Araneae or Winifred leave the office. I'm on my way."

I shot a quick text off to Stephanie, telling her I'd meet with the contractors on one of our projects this afternoon at the job site and to send me anything else via email. I planned to be out of town for the rest of the week. There was a yacht waiting at the Columbia Yacht Club still tethered to a dock, one that should be floating in the blue waters of Lake Michigan.

The damn car was not moving. The downtown traffic was at a fucking standstill. I watched the pedestrians as they hurried by. I could get to Sinful Threads faster if I walked.

My mind went to Andrew Walsh or whoever he was. In Wichita, he'd told Araneae his name was Mark. I sent that in a text to Reid, to see if it would help.

My phone vibrated. *REID* was on the screen.

"WESLEY HUNTER, AGE 27, FIELD AGENT FBI, CHICAGO FIELD OFFICE."

The only word coming to my mind was fuck.

Apparently, it was on repeat, working for each situation.

Hunter wasn't even the same age as his alias. What did this mean? What had Hunter learned in McFadden's outfit? What did he learn about the Sparrow outfit? Why was he with Winnie, and more importantly, what did he say to Araneae?

The car finally sped up, increasing to a breakneck speed of over ten miles per hour. When we stopped again, I spoke to Garrett, "Fuck it. I can see the damn building. I'm walking. Park in the garage—if you ever can get there—and I'll let you know when I'm ready to leave."

"Will you need me or Patrick?" he asked.

"You. I have a meeting this afternoon."

"Yes, sir. I'll be waiting."

The heat of the summer washed over me as I opened the backdoor and stepped onto the street. Dodging barely moving cars, I made my way to the sidewalk. With long strides my loafers clipped along the concrete, crossing the bridge over the canal, until I reached the building on South Wacker. An elevator ride later and I entered Sinful Threads.

Nodding to Jana, I made my way to Patrick and closed the conference room door. "Tell me they're both still here."

"They are."

"Did you get Reid's message?"

"About Hunter?"

"What the fuck do you think this means?" I asked, taking a seat.

"We need to learn what happened in that hotel room."

I wasn't planning on chastising Patrick again over his mistake. Instead, I let my glare do the talking. Finally, I asked, "How long have they been in there?"

He looked down at his watch. "Twenty to twenty-five minutes."

Taking a deep breath, I stood. "This is done. Book Winifred a flight. She's headed back to Boulder this afternoon or tonight. Whatever you can get."

Patrick had the good sense to simply nod as he looked down and began hitting the keys of his laptop. "There's a four this afternoon and a 7:20 later tonight, both direct flights to Boulder."

"I'd prefer the four o'clock, but we should let her finish the day with Jana and take the 7:20 flight. Do you believe Jana can continue with Winifred and keep her cool?"

"She can," Patrick said. "She and I spoke after we came back. I told her to be careful about any discussion not centered on Sinful Threads. She's solid, Sparrow. She'd take a bullet before she disappointed you."

Nodding, I stood and opened the door to the center office.

"Mr. Sparrow," Jana said.

"Jana, I hear things are working well with you at Sinful Threads."

"I'm trying, sir." A smile spread over her face.

If I cared, I'd notice that it was more genuine than her usual smile on the plane. Maybe I did care because my cheeks rose too. "Thank you for your dedication."

"Thank you for your faith in me."

"This job was due to Patrick with the final decision being Araneae's. Sinful Threads is all hers—well, and Ms. Toney's." I tilted my chin toward Araneae's office. "I'm going in."

Jana stood. "Sir, she asked not to be disturbed."

Did Jana think she could stop me?

"Did she?" I asked, my eyes widening.

"Well...um...she said to hold all of her calls—*all.*"

I nodded. "Then continue to do that, Jana. No calls."

"But..."

I didn't stay to hear whatever she planned to say. Reaching for the handle to Araneae's office, I opened the door and surveyed what was inside. Considering all that had occurred, seeing Araneae and Winnie chatting over coffee was not what I expected.

Araneae turned my way while at the same time, Winnie turned ghostly white.

"This is," Araneae said with a smile, "Winifred Douglas. And this is Sterling Sparrow."

I stepped closer to Araneae. "Kennedy." The name felt foreign on my tongue.

Not only was it incorrect, but in my opinion, the name didn't fit her. Araneae sounded strong and resilient like a spider. There was nothing wrong with the name Kennedy; it just didn't describe the stunning, amazing woman before me, the one who was mine.

"Sterling," she said, standing.

"Ms. Douglas, I've heard a lot about you," I said, deciding I'd keep the FBI talk to Araneae.

"As have I—heard about you," Winnie said, rising to her feet and extending her hand.

After shaking hands, she retook her seat.

I looked to Araneae—her smile, poise, and confidence.

When I'd entered this office, I'd planned to walk in and tell Winnie she had to leave today. I wanted her gone because of the FBI and because of her association with Leslie Milton. Now, however, standing here, I knew that wasn't the right move. If Winnie was leaving, it needed to be Araneae's choice. This wasn't the time to make my usual unilateral decision. "Your text," I said, referring to the one saying that we needed to talk.

"Yes," Araneae said to me. Turning to Winnie, she continued, "If you could excuse Mr. Sparrow and me. Find Patrick and give him the information on your hotel room and safe. He'll arrange to get all of your things. He can also book you another room for tonight and find you a flight for tomorrow."

Winnie nodded.

I cleared my throat, causing both women to look my direction. "I believe he may have found a flight for tonight."

Araneae straightened her neck as her eyes narrowed my direction. And then instead of arguing, she turned back to Winnie. "Find out the times. If one is late enough, you can work with Jana and not bother with another hotel room."

Winnie nodded. "I am sorry."

"So am I," Araneae said, reaching out and hugging Winnie's shoulders. "We'll get through this. Louisa needs you back in Boulder."

"Thank you, Kenni," Winnie said as she hurried toward the door.

There were a million subjects ready for me to address, and yet when the door shut, my first instinct was to reach for Araneae's hips, splay my fingers over her ass, and pull her against me. As her tits crashed against my chest, my mouth found hers, tasting coffee and sweetness. Nipping and tugging, I persisted until her lips parted and our tongues moved in sync. As her hands moved up my chest to my shoulders, her office filled with the soft sounds of her moans and whimpers.

When we pulled away, I stared down into her velvety chocolate eyes and my grin turned menacing. "I'll be the secretary as long as I am the one fucking you." I shook my head. "And after your stunt today, your ass—"

Her lips turned upward as she silenced me with her finger. "We need to talk first."

I reached for her hand as we sat at the corner of the table, our fingers intertwined. "I think we need to institute a new rule."

"Oh, you do?"

"Yes, no talking until the fucking is done."

Her slender shoulder shrugged, highlighting her long, sensual neck. "Now, there's a rule I could probably live with."

"I spoke to..." we said in unison. It was the conclusion of the sentence that was different.

"...your mother," I said.

While simultaneously, Araneae said, "...an FBI agent."

We both took a deep breath.

"You were right," I finally said. "We do need to talk."

"You're not upset?" she asked.

"That you went in that room alone? I'm livid. That you're telling me the truth of what happened?" My head shook. "I told you before. Never be afraid to tell me the truth. We'll deal with whatever comes our way together. Only fear my reaction to lies and half-truths because..." I ran my finger along her cheek. "...those are the same thing."

She nodded. "I hope you mean that because I have a lot to say." Her head tilted to the side. "And I want to know about my...Annabelle."

"There's something more important that I need to say first."

"What?" she asked.

"It's about something you said earlier today."

"Damn, Sterling, a lot has been said."

Lifting her hand that was in mine, I brushed my lips over her knuckles and took a deep breath. This needed to be said before anything else.

ARANEAE

"*B*efore we parted ways," Sterling said, "you told me something. With everything that has been happening, what you said was in the back of my thoughts. Seeing you here..." Sterling's gaze scanned me from the top of my head to the toes of my shoes. With each inch, his stare sent sparks over my flesh until fire smoldered in his darkened orbs and my skin was ablaze. "...has brought your declaration back."

Goose bumps prickled beneath the burn as I recalled telling him I loved him. "Sterling, I—"

It was his turn to silence me with a finger to my lips as he leaned closer and the spicy scent of his cologne filled my senses.

"No, Araneae, I brought you into a shitstorm." His head shook. "The fucking thing is swirling around us, and yet when I'm with you, holding your hand, looking at how strikingly beautiful you are, regal and strong in the middle of this mess,

I'm awed." His free hand caressed my cheek. "You amaze me, continually. Whether you're dealing with assholes the likes of Pauline or facing whatever in the hell happened with Winnie in that hotel room..." He took a deep breath. "...if I were half the man that people think I am, I would do everything in my power to give you back the life I stole from you. I'd put a hundred men and women in Boulder to keep you safe and let you get out of this shadow world. I would let you live your life as Kennedy Hawkins."

Wait, what? Let me out of this?

My head shook yet he continued.

"I can't do any of those things." His chiseled jaw clenched. "That's not true. I could, but I won't. I will never let you go. You're mine. Today you told me that you love me."

My lips turned upward as I nodded.

"It should go without saying..." He took a deep breath. "...that I'm a coldhearted man capable of horrible things."

His finger was now gone. "No, Sterling, that's not what I see."

"I'm glad. I don't want you to see that. When I'm with you, even I can forget that part of me. Araneae, I've known you were mine since I was thirteen years old. I've never doubted it."

He cupped both of my cheeks and peered into my eyes as the silence around us grew. With each second, my heart beat faster as I anxiously waited for what he was about to say. As the clock ticked, I feared that maybe my sentiment wouldn't be reciprocated.

Finally, he spoke. "Like I've said before, I knew you were mine. I watched you. As you grew older..." His free hand brushed the side of my breast. "...and you became so fucking sexy, I knew I'd have you. I'd make you mine. None of that came as a surprise."

"Sterling?"

"Araneae, even with all of that, I never expected to love you. I never expected to love anyone—ever." His lips brushed over mine. "The story you told Louisa and Winnie, the one about me sweeping you off your feet?"

With my face still within his grasp, I nodded.

"Sunshine, you had it wrong. From that first meeting at the Sinful Threads distribution center, you've had me completely swept off my feet. I should have told you that night when I had your sexy body pinned against the wall that I loved you, but if I had, you probably wouldn't have believed me. I hope you believe me now. Araneae McCrie, I love you."

We both leaned forward until our lips united. As our kiss deepened, warmth flooded my circulation like a warm spring to a frozen stream, each second thawing the winter's ice.

Sterling may see himself as unlovable; however, what he didn't understand—nor maybe had I—was that without realizing it, I'd felt the same way about myself. If I were lovable, I wouldn't have been abandoned twice by the age of sixteen. Every other relationship since then, except with Louisa and her family, I'd ended, perhaps because I feared that if I didn't, then once again I'd be left behind or made to leave.

Sterling's possessiveness, his declaration of proprietorship pissed me off and reassured me at the same time. I was his, which meant he was mine. The shitstorm—as he called it— could continue to blow as long as we were together.

When our kiss ended, I smiled, staring into his dark gaze. "I meant it. I love you too, and I believe you. I believe every- thing you've told me. I know you're not perfect; neither am I.

What matters to me is that when we're together, we're honest with each other—no lies or secrets. When we are, we make one another better."

"I don't fucking deserve you."

"You're stuck with me," I said with a grin. "Will you tell me how it went with my mother?"

Sterling nodded. "I will. First, what happened with Winnie?"

After asking Jana to order us lunch, we sat at the table and talked.

I was completely honest, telling Sterling how Agent Wesley Hunter had approached Winnie in Boulder, at first pretending to be an insurance adjuster. And then how he'd asked her out.

"There are eyes on your friends in Boulder. I'm pissed that they didn't see this," Sterling said, now standing and pacing as I told him the story.

"They had no reason to suspect federal agents. Are those eyes...Why?" I wanted confirmation.

Stopping in front of me, Sterling reached for my shoulders and encouraged me to stand. "You asked me to keep them safe. Everyone associated with you could be considered a liability. Do you see that now? That's what Hunter is doing, capitalizing on your friends."

Swallowing, I nodded. "He said they would offer witness protection to not only Winnie, but Jason, Louisa, and the baby. He accused you of using Sinful Threads for illegal dealings, threatening my company. It reminded me of when you threatened the same people and thing to get me to Chicago."

"Sunshine, I told you I do bad things. That doesn't mean

I'd let anything happen to anyone you love or a company you conceived."

"Then first and foremost," I said, "keep yourself safe because you're one of those people." It was then I recalled something else. "It seemed like Hunter has information on McFadden from when he infiltrated the McFadden outfit. He said he couldn't discuss it, but he laid out the pieces. If you hadn't told me...I wouldn't have understood. Hunter isn't satisfied with only bringing down McFadden. He wants both of you and wants me to help him get evidence that will stick. He said something about power working in a vacuum."

Sterling chuckled. "He's a fucking idiot."

"Why?"

"He's not an idiot for saying power works in a vacuum. He's right. He's an idiot if he thinks removing the McFadden *and* the Sparrow outfit will solve the crime problem in Chicago. Think of..." He contemplated. "...nature."

"Okay."

"A long time ago, the Great Lakes were surrounded with forests. The ecosystem was balanced. And then with time, the predators, the large ones, were killed by man or pushed north." His smile grew. "Remember what Rita told you about hiking in Ontario?"

"Bears," I said with a shiver.

"Right. It's a balance thing. Bears don't kill to kill. They kill to survive, to eat. When the ecosystem is in balance, the smaller creatures are monitored and their population is kept in check. Today, hell, probably literally today, if you drive the country roads of Illinois or Wisconsin, you'll find multiple deer lying on the side of the road, dead from an automobile. The population of deer is so high they starve in the winter. Their natural predators are gone. Even the smaller predators, foxes and wolves, are being pushed away or killed."

"Why does that make Hunter an idiot?"

"Because he thinks that if he takes out the top powers, Chicago will be crime free. He's got it completely backward. If McFadden and Sparrow were both gone, every two-bit petty thief, drug dealer, numbers runner, and pimp would be vying for that top position. Right now, we keep those lowlifes in line. Without us, this city would implode."

It made me think of *Lion King*, of what happened when Scar allowed the hyenas to rule the land. I nodded. "It's your job to keep Chicago looking good to the outside."

Sterling smiled. "You've been listening."

"I have. I think that's why I didn't believe him when he said you'd been lying to me."

"He said that?"

"Yes. And if you hadn't shared my secrets and yours with me, I suppose I could have believed him." I reached for Sterling's large hand and held it in the palm of one of mine. Running my fingernail over his outstretched palm, I traced the lines until I looked up at his incredibly handsome face. "I'm not sure what kind of person it makes me, but I'd rather never know the things that keep you awake at night. What I do know, Sterling Sparrow, is that these hands can be loving, sensual, and protective. They've brought me more adoration and pleasure than I ever imagined having."

"They can also redden your ass, and after that stunt at the hotel, that's on their agenda for tonight."

I tilted my head and looked at him with veiled eyes. "You see, if Patrick had come in that room, I would never have learned what I did about Agent Hunter and the FBI's plans. So really it was a good move."

A knock on the door refocused our attention.

As we both turned, Sterling whispered, "Nice try. Your ass is mine."

With a new layer of goose bumps, I called to the door, "Who is it?"

"Jana. I have your lunch."

"Come on in."

Once we were alone again, Sterling asked, "Hunter wants you to report to him about me?"

I nodded.

"He actually offered you that option?"

"Yes. I told him to go fuck himself."

Sterling's lips curved upward. "While I don't think those were your exact words with the agent, they were when you said that to me."

I grinned. "Maybe I've learned my lesson with that." I tilted my head. "I'd much rather have you fuck me."

He shook his head. "That makes two of us."

Looking at the grilled chicken salad before me, I asked, "If you tell me about my mother, will I lose my appetite?"

"I've told you that Reid, Patrick, and I've done research."

I nodded as I took a bite.

"I was also honest that there were some things we had to hypothesize. Today, I learned something I honestly never assumed."

"What?"

"Annabelle Landers didn't give you to the Marshes."

I set my fork down. "What?"

His head shook. "No. She...damn, this isn't easy to say."

"Tell me, Sterling. You promised." He had promised to be with me when I learned the good or the bad.

"She wanted you very much. She still does. She was nothing like Pauline had been. Her demeanor was..." He seemed to weigh the best words. "...respectful and hesitant. She told me that after she gave birth, she was handed a deceased baby, one with dark hair. She held it, thinking it was you."

Oh my God.

Tears stung the back of my eyes. "How is that possible?"

He grinned. "That was the same question she had. How was it possible that the dead infant she held and buried is now alive?"

My stomach twisted as the little bit of salad churned. "Maybe...maybe you're wrong. Maybe I'm not Araneae." Panic bubbled in my stomach. "Oh God. What if you are wrong?"

"You saw her—Annabelle," he said. "What do you think?"

"I-I don't know what to think. Our coloring is similar."

"Her first question was *how*, not *if* you are who I say you are. She said that when your eyes met in the bathroom mirror of the club, she knew. In her heart, she knew."

I stood and walked to my desk and back, wringing my hands as I recalled that night. "She scared me. The way she was looking at me." I remembered her grabbing my wrist. "She asked me about the bracelet."

Sterling nodded again. "You two even have some of the same mannerisms."

"Have you? Did you?" I asked, unsure if I could open my heart to another mother.

"Have I proof of your lineage?"

"I mean, you seemed very confident, but she's saying she saw me die."

"She said she saw you dead. That's not the same thing, but I didn't think of it at the time." He gestured toward the salad. "Sit down and eat."

I took a tentative step toward the table but didn't sit.

"I do," Sterling said. "Mitochondrial DNA. It's only passed from a mother to her children."

The tears that had only threatened now flooded my eyes. "She didn't give me to Josey? Then how did I get there?"

Sterling reached out and held my hand, pulling me closer until I fell into his lap. "Sunshine, we're going to find out."

I nodded as more tears flowed and my breaths grew ragged. "She wanted me?"

His arms surrounded me, hugging me closer to his solid chest. "She would like to reintroduce herself."

"W-what did you tell her?"

"I told her that the decision was all yours."

My temples throbbed as I leaned against him, his heart beating in my ear as I cried. It was so much. A month ago, I would never have imagined the opportunity to meet my birth mother or defend my boyfriend to my friends or an FBI agent.

Who could imagine those things?

The meeting with Pauline McFadden had been my worst nightmare—more rejection. I'd expected the same thing from Annabelle. Now that she'd responded differently, I was too confused to make a decision.

"Shh," Sterling soothed. "I have her number. You can call—"

I shook my head. "Not today. It's too much."

"I understand." His chest inflated and deflated with a deep breath. "In *this* world, for Judge Landers to go to my mother and ask for her help and then for her to come to my office...it took a lot of fortitude."

"Your mother?"

"Don't ask."

"She doesn't like me."

"She doesn't like the possibility that you could ruin her perfect crystal world."

"I don't have any information."

Sterling reached for my chin and with the pad of his thumb wiped the tears from my cheeks, one and then the other. "This isn't about my mother. It's about yours. If you won't call Judge Landers, I will. After her show of bravery today, she deserves it."

I nodded again, sensing Sterling's newfound respect for the woman who gave me life. "Okay. Tell her that I'm considering it."

He kissed my forehead. "I will. I need to get to a meeting." He looked down at my uneaten salad. "After you eat, go home..." He inhaled and rephrased, "Will you consider having Patrick take you home after you eat? We have a yacht waiting, one with an empty deck where tomorrow I plan to have you naked in the sun."

I smiled.

He'd said will.

My cheeks rose. "Mr. Sparrow, whoever said old dogs can't learn new tricks never met you."

His finger came to my nose. "I'm not old."

No, he wasn't.

"But you are learning new tricks."

He helped me to my feet as he too stood. "I have some more tricks in mind to teach you after we complete our discussion of your disobedience today."

My eyebrows rose. "Discussion, that sounds reasonable."

He winked as he headed toward the door. "Sunshine, enjoy sitting for the rest of the day."

That shouldn't make my insides twist, but it did.

REBECCA/JOSEY

Twenty-six years ago ~

"*W*hat did you say?" I asked, staring at my husband of five years. He'd awakened me when he arrived home early in the morning, apprehensive and nervous to tell me his news.

As I worked to still the shaking of my hands, I realized his anxiety was contagious.

"Becky, I don't know how to say it...other than to say it. He made me an offer. I'm not sure there's an option B."

I stood, walking warily away from the kitchen table where I'd been sitting, and moved to the stove. Lifting the teakettle, I gave it a shake, confirming its lack of contents. As I moved, Neal continued staring my direction, waiting for an answer. I didn't have an answer. I was having difficulty comprehending his statement.

Did a statement even need an answer?

My husband's head was down in defeat as he leaned

against the counter, his arms crossed over his chest. Adding water to the teakettle, I placed it back on the stove. Twisting the knob, I waited for the pilot light to ignite the burner. First a hiss and then with a burst of blue flame it came to life. I adjusted the heat.

"Are you going to say anything?" Neal asked.

"Would you like a cup of tea?"

"Becky."

Sitting back down on the hard wooden chair, I shook my head. "I-I don't know what to say." I looked up at him as he eyed me from under his furrowed brow. "May I ask what happened or how it happened?"

"You know that I can't answer that."

"Is this because of your brother?"

Neal formed his lips in a straight line as he shrugged his shoulder. "Isn't everything?"

"Why us?"

Neal shrugged. "He knows he can trust me—us. I owe him. He knows that I'll never get out from under the debt. If we do this, we'll be free."

"Free? How are we free if he's still watching us?" Neal didn't answer. With my frustration growing, I asked, "Whose baby is it?"

"We're not supposed to know."

"How are we getting it? Does he expect us to kidnap this kid?"

"No, he's got it all arranged. It's our chance for a family."

My stomach twisted with equal parts terror and anticipation as my emotions began to build. "Damn it. This isn't fair. You know I've been trying to get pregnant for years."

Neal came forward, kneeling near my chair and placing his

hand on my robe-covered knee. "I know that, Becks. Of course, I know. I've been the one to watch helplessly while you cry every time your period starts. This is our answer. Think of this as a gift."

My neck straightened. "Allister Sparrow isn't God. Babies come from God, not a man like him."

Neal's lips attempted a smile. "Aren't you the one who says God works in mysterious ways?"

"What if Mr. Sparrow changes his mind? What if we agree to all the terms that he's laid out, and then one day he comes and snatches the baby away?"

"No. We won't let him."

My stomach twisted more. "Who's going to stop him?"

"It's a chance at a whole new life for us," Neal said again. "Think of it. You, me, a kid...he said it's a little girl." My husband stood and lifted my hands. "The pressure we've been under and the debt, it'll be gone—vanished with this one assignment." He gestured around our simple nine-hundred-square-foot flat. "This offer comes with a whole new identity —for both of us. I'm going to be able to do what I've always wanted. Have a legitimate job. He offered Boeing." My husband's face grew brighter. "And you'll be able to do what you wanted, be a mom. Think about it. We'll have a house in a decent neighborhood with a yard and other kids living nearby. We'll raise her like she's our own."

"There's a catch," I said. "There's always a catch with Mr. Sparrow."

Neal and I should know. From the time Neal was young, his mother's drug problem was supported by turning tricks. Her pimp was in Sparrow's outfit. Obviously, my husband didn't have the best childhood. That didn't mean his mother didn't try her best with Neal. Her options were limited. To hear him tell the story, she did what she could to help him avoid her path, including bragging about his various abilities to her pimp.

Though I didn't know the details, according to Neal, some kids had it worse. In order to avoid darker options, as soon as Neal had been old enough, he'd gone to work for his mom's pimp and became part of Sparrow's outfit.

He started running drugs and sometimes numbers. His responsibilities increased until the day his mother injected more than her fragile body could handle. Out of the blue, his grandparents reemerged, vowing that now that she was gone, they'd get him out.

Moving him to Indiana, they paid for his college where he studied data analytics. Neal took what he'd learned running numbers and counting cash and turned it into a valuable education.

There was a kid a few years younger than Neal, who he'd helped through the years. Though they weren't blood relatives, they called themselves brothers. Joey's mom had the same profession as Neal's mother. Her fight with drugs ended earlier.

Neal did all he could to help Joey while they were young, working to keep him in the lighter side of their dark world. Neal hadn't told me the particulars, but according to my husband, running drugs, selling to kids, or helping with the backroom gambling was the better option. Others were much worse. The problem was that as Joey grew older, he did more than work the gambling. He lived it, losing money as soon as he earned it, and finally, skimming.

When Neal and I met at Purdue University, I had no idea

of his past. We married our senior year. It was upon graduation that he learned the hard truth. He could move beyond
doing grunt work for Allister Sparrow, but leaving the outfit
was impossible.

Neal's affiliation preceded him, making employment away
from Chicago impossible. The only way to be hired in or
around Chicago was to go through Sparrow. The way Sparrow
saw it was that Neal had gotten his start in the Sparrow outfit.
Neal was given the choice of jobs as long as they benefited
Sparrow Enterprises.

My husband's dream had been aerospace not real estate.

When we returned to Chicago after college and marriage,
Sparrow had Neal working both sides of the legal fence. The
job Allister offered Neal at Sparrow Enterprises was simply a
legal hook to keep him in the illegal Sparrow outfit forever.

"I don't know if there's a catch," Neal said. "Mr. Sparrow
means business with this. The baby is due soon. We have to
become new people, even physically. He has some people who
can do some of that stuff. I don't know what it includes, nose
jobs and cheek bones..."

I scrunched my lips. "Surgery? Why?"

"He wants us hiding in plain sight."

"We could move away from Chicago."

"Becks, he has this all worked out to the second."

The teakettle on the stove began to whistle, like the shrill
alarm of Allister Sparrow's timer. Our time was up, and we
needed to make a decision.

Standing again, I removed the kettle from the burner,
turned off the flame, and opened the flimsy cupboard above,
removing two mugs. My steps stalled as the window above the
sink caught my attention. Beyond the dingy glass panes was

the world in which we lived, roof tops with chimneys and brick walls. The sky was gray, filled with early March snow-laced clouds. I reached for the counter as the dishes in the sink rattled, and the 6:15 train sped by on the nearby tracks.

"What if we say no?"

"I can't be sure. Look what happened to Joey."

The year after we graduated college, Joey's body—or what was left of it—was found floating in a fifty-five-gallon drum of acid behind an abandoned warehouse in South Chicago. Since that time, Neal's been held responsible for the money Joey skimmed. With the accumulating interest—points—it's been a debt that he could never repay.

"If we say yes?" I asked.

"I call him tonight. They'll come and get us." He gestured around the room. "We leave this all behind. Mr. Sparrow said that we could be having surgery tonight or tomorrow. Next will be our identities: new names, a house, a job—a life out of this dreary apartment." He turned me by my shoulders toward him. "The life you deserve."

"What about my job now and yours? What about friends and my family?" It wasn't like we had much. Neal had no family and all I had was a sister who lived in Evansville, Indiana, with her husband and two kids.

"We have to disappear—vanish into thin air. Just imagine a baby girl in your arms. We will be a family."

I took a deep breath. "If we say no, what happens to her—the baby?"

Neal shrugged. "I can't say. Honestly, I don't know."

My mind filled with the horrors of the Sparrows. What would that man do to a baby? I couldn't even think about it. I turned to Neal. "Then yes."

"I love you, Rebecca Curry. I'm saying that now because all I know is that tomorrow your name will have changed."

It was too much to process. "Do you know what my name will be?"

"I'm not supposed to, but I saw it on his desk. You will be Josey Marsh."

"You?"

"Byron Marsh."

ARANEAE

Though my head was still pounding midafternoon when Patrick and I arrived back at the apartment, my demeanor changed the moment I heard activity in the kitchen. It was a little after three and for once I'd made it home before Lorna finished cooking.

With her earbuds securely in place, she didn't hear us come into the kitchen as she spread ingredients over the counter. Placing my satchel on the floor, I moved closer.

"Oh! Araneae, you scared me to death. What are you doing home?" She looked up as Patrick came in behind me. "And I see you brought Patrick."

"Technically, he brought me because as you know, I can't make the damn elevator work." I looked up at Patrick. "Or drive...or... I'm certain if I keep going, there's a number of other things I'm no longer allowed to do."

Patrick grinned. "Money's on you, but don't forget, I'll deny it."

"Thanks."

"You've had a long day. Are you all right? Do you need anything before I go downstairs?" he asked.

I shook my head. "Not from you. I think I do from Lorna."

Her big green eyes peered my way. "From me? What?"

"Let me give you the night off from cooking. I'd like to do it."

"Are you sure? Patrick just said your day was long. You could go upstairs and take a bath or something."

"Have you ever had a day where you're tired of thinking about it?" I asked. "A day when you want something else on your mind?"

"Oh, girl, have I."

I motioned toward all the items on the counter. "I think you have the perfect solution."

"I can help you," she offered.

I kicked off my heels and walked in my stockings across the marble floor. "Nope. Thank you, though. I have no idea what I'll make, but I want to make it." I laid my hand on Lorna's shoulder. "Why don't you go soak in a nice tub? I have bath salts upstairs you're welcome to use."

She giggled. "Who do you think does the shopping? I have a generous supply downstairs."

"Good. I'm glad to hear that."

Lorna looked from the counter to me. "Are you sure?"

I waved my hand toward the direction of the private elevator. "Positive."

She reached out and covered my hand with hers. "You seem...surer about being here."

My cheeks rose. "Remember when you told me that love wasn't something that can be controlled?"

"Yes..."

"I know I haven't been here or even with Sterling for that long. Yet it seems like we've always been together. It's hard to explain."

"And..."

I snickered, enjoying how easy it was to talk to Lorna. I'd told Louisa and Winnie that I loved Sterling. It seemed that if Lorna was my new friend, I shouldn't leave her out. "And I'm falling in love with him."

"Falling...?"

"Hell no. I've fallen, head over heels. He can be absolutely exasperating." It felt cathartic to be talking to someone who knew him. "He's overprotective and overbearing." Smiling, I remembered the addition of *will* to his request for me to go home. "And he's trying to do better. I think my biggest barrier is trust."

Lorna nodded. "Do you trust him?"

I did, but I wanted her answer. "You've known him longer. Is he trustworthy?"

Her lower lip disappeared behind her front teeth. "You said the other morning that all three men share a brain." She scoffed again. "They share more than that. To one another they're harshly honest. I'm not sure there's anything they won't tell one another." Pink filled her cheeks. "Okay, I thought of one thing. Those men all respect women too much to share our intimate secrets. When it comes to anything else, their honesty knows no bounds."

"Why do I feel there's a *but* coming?"

"It's more of a clarification. I believe everything Reid tells me—and everything Patrick and Sparrow tell me too. I also know that there are things they do, see, or know that they don't tell me. I believe it will be the same with you." She shrugged. "Some could see it as lying by omission. I hope you don't. I hope you choose to see it as I do—protection."

I exhaled. "I've heard that word a lot since this all started."

"Araneae, they believe it to their core."

I recalled what Sterling had said about telling him the truth. "Wouldn't omission be considered a half-truth?"

"Sparrow has told you where the three of them became friends, right?"

"Basic training and then they were stationed together with someone named Mason."

Lorna sucked in a breath. "He told you about Mason?"

"Not a lot, why?"

She shook her head. "Not my story to tell."

That was the same thing Sterling had said about Jana. "I feel like there's more."

"Honey, if he has told you that much this fast, he trusts you. That should mean something."

I nodded. It did mean something.

"So," Lorna said, "back to the army. He told you that they did two tours together."

She hadn't really asked a question, but I nodded.

"Is it a half-truth if he hasn't shared what they did, what they saw, what they experienced? Do you need all of that for it to be the truth?"

I thought about it. "No, I don't. If he ever needs to share, I would listen, but it would be so outside of my realm of knowledge."

"Exactly. Back to your question, do I think he's trustworthy? I think that I can believe one hundred percent of what Sparrow, Patrick, or Reid says. I also know in my heart that I'm only told maybe sixty percent of what they know."

"And you're all right with that?" I asked.

"I am. Life is too short to spend time worried about things I don't want to know. If it's important to me, Reid will tell me. Otherwise, I'd rather spend my time with my man doing other things."

That made me grin.

She lightly slapped my arm. "I was talking chess. Where did your mind go?"

"Definitely chess." I shrugged. "Maybe checkers?"

Lorna and I both laughed.

"Last chance for help with dinner," she said.

"Nope, I've got this." I looked toward the pantry. "Any chance that there's a box of macaroni and cheese in there?"

Her eyes widened. "Tell me you're joking or I'm not leaving."

"I'm joking."

"Have fun. By the way," she said. "I dust in Sparrow's office. I've noticed his chessboard and none of the pieces have moved."

My cheeks warmed as I felt the sparkle in my eyes. "Hmm."

With salads in the refrigerator, homemade vegetable lasagna in the oven, and a fresh loaf of French bread ready to bake, I slipped upstairs to finally change out of my work clothes. I couldn't believe I'd just chopped and mixed and created a meal dressed in the same expensive dress I'd worn to the office.

My mind had been too consumed with the meal to think about my clothes.

As I contemplated something comfortable, my gaze went to the part of the closet with dresses too fancy for work, more for dinner parties or celebrations. Running the luxurious materials through my fingers, I momentarily thought of Sinful Threads and Winnie. Shaking my head, I refused to dwell.

I'd called Louisa and told her that Winnie was on her way home, she'd worked out well, and we could discuss the arrangement further after the baby was born. And then I'd sent Winnie a text asking if her trip back to Boulder was set. She replied saying it was.

I knew I could call Patrick and learn the particulars, yet right now, I was exhausted with dealing with other people. I was ready for an evening that included only one other person.

After a quick shower, I redid my makeup, and instead of styling my hair up, I brushed it out. From being up in a twist all day, the long tresses flowed down my back in blonde waves.

With fresh thigh-high stockings as my only undergarment, I shimmied into the red dress I'd first seen on Sterling's airplane—yes, it had been dry cleaned. After a quick jaunt to the jewelry drawer in the closet, I added the diamond earrings and long platinum necklace. The only other accessory from that first night was the pair of Saint Laurent red patent-leather sandals.

With the bread and oil/seasoning mixture on the table instead of the breakfast bar, our two place settings ready, including wine glasses, and the lasagna cooling on the stove, I waited for the sound of footsteps.

It was nearly seven when rather than footsteps, the distinctive sound of the elevator's pocket door alerted me to Sterling's arrival. Lighting the candles on the table in the dimmed kitchen, I waited as the sun settled lower over the skyline, filling the sky with hues of red and purple.

STERLING

With my mind vying between the meeting with the contractors and my follow-up call with Judge Landers, the last thing I expected was the elevator to stop on two. When it did, I let out a long breath and made my way to the sensor that would open to our command center.

"Should I even ask?" I said as I was met by Patrick. "Where's Reid?"

"This won't take long. I just saw it."

"What?"

He tilted his head toward the computer screen. "Reid has certain traffic cams set for surveillance."

I looked up. "That's Judge Lander's house."

"Yeah, and Rubio McFadden is in there with her."

I shook my head. "Fuck, I wanted to believe her." I'd filled in both Reid and Patrick on my morning conversations.

"I'm not certain that you can't."

"Is there any way to listen in?" I asked.

"No, she's excessively careful."

"Excessively?"

Patrick laughed. "Yeah, it's as if she's lived in this fucking world her whole life and knows that most common technology is vulnerable."

"Any ideas what's happening in there?"

"From the look on his face, he's not there for a booty call."

"Send Sparrows over there. Tell them to stay in the shadows." I ran my hand through my hair. "This is fucking ridiculous, but if she's going to end up meaning something to Araneae, McFadden's not going to do anything to her on my watch. I'm sure he heard from Pauline about the meeting at Sinful Threads. If he knows Annabelle came to Sparrow Enterprises, he may be unhappy." There wasn't anything I wouldn't put past that asshole.

"Will do," Patrick said. "What's the line?"

I took a deep breath. "You'll know it when he crosses it."

Patrick nodded. "Go upstairs."

My lips curled upward. "That's where I was headed."

"By the way, Winnie has boarded her flight. It's taking off in twenty minutes."

I exhaled. "I-I don't know how I feel about her. If she weren't so closely connected to Araneae, she'd be eliminated."

Patrick stood taller.

"Tell me what you're thinking."

"I don't fucking know," he said. "In my observation, she's as bullheaded as Lorna and Araneae. I think Hunter played her. He capitalized on us."

"On us?"

"He saw a weakness, the fact that Araneae—sorry,

Kennedy—hadn't been communicating. He used it. I can't blame Winnie for that. It's the same damn thing you did to Araneae, capitalizing on her friends. From what I've seen, Winnie lives and breathes her job at Sinful Threads. She's close to Louisa and Kennedy. I have to think that she didn't set out to hurt Kennedy. She thought she was helping."

"You believe that?" I asked.

"Boss, I try to think about how others see the world. If I don't, I can't fathom their decisions. You, me, and Reid, we see everyone as a potential threat. Even Lorna is weary with good cause. People like Winnie and Araneae see the world differently." A smile came to his face. "Today Araneae told me she was glad I was scary." He scoffed. "I asked her if she thought I was and she said not to her. It's a trust in others that you and I can't even imagine."

I shook my head. I did have that kind of trust, in two people. I wanted it in three, but could I? Had she proven it today with how she reacted to that agent?

"Keep an eye on Winifred," I said. "Maybe you and Araneae are right and she was simply trying to help. I'm not convinced."

He nodded. "That's why Sparrows stay on top. We require proof."

"If she has any more contact with Hunter, I want to know about it."

"Sure thing, boss."

As the elevator doors closed, I did a mental rundown of the day.

A fucking FBI agent had offered Araneae the chance to be an informant. Though she'd been honest and told me about it —as well as refused him—I couldn't help but worry about her thoughts. She'd even said he insinuated I'd use Sinful Threads to further illegal activities. I wouldn't. If it mattered to her, it mattered to me.

What did something like that do to her—mentally?

Did it plant doubt in her mind about me?

Did she wonder if he was right?

I wanted to believe she didn't, that she meant what she said about the way she felt.

A stupid smile floated across my face.

She said she loved me.

Fuck, I should have said it then or sooner. The truth was that I was as shocked as anyone. Who knew that Sterling Sparrow was capable of love?

The scrumptious aroma of something in the air met me as the elevator doors opened to the penthouse, reminding me that I'd left most of my lunch in Araneae's office. Though I'd considered first going upstairs, a faint flicker of light drew me toward the kitchen.

A moth to a flame?

No, I was a bird, a Sparrow.

And yet as I turned the final corner, I was once again floored by the sight before me—the sight that washed away my earlier concerns and caused my heart to beat faster.

I'd never admit it to anyone except her, but a spider—no, *one* spider—could bring this damn bird to his knees.

Araneae was fucking gorgeous, standing near the table in that damn red dress, her golden hair flowing down her back, her tits heaving as she wordlessly watched me with a bright red smile. I scanned downward. The neckline of the dress showed half globes of her perfect breasts. And then around her waist was an apron—a fucking 1950's apron—and lower still her shapely legs were covered in silk and her feet were in those sky-high heels.

Holy fuck.

The array of dirty thoughts going through my head right now were all a result of how incredibly sexy she looked. This woman who ran Sinful Threads like a Fortune 500 CEO, who told off Pauline McFadden as well as an FBI agent, was doing all kinds of things to me dressed as a demure, sexy housewife. My cock was growing by the second.

As I stalked toward her, I fought back the smile that itched to come to my lips, doing my best to be the predator and not the prey because that was what she did to me. I had said over and over that she belonged to me. It was fair to mention that it worked both ways. I was absolutely captive under this beautiful, strong, and intelligent woman's spell.

Araneae's pert painted lips opened with a gasp as my hand splayed over her lower back, pulling her sexy curves toward me, not stopping until my growing erection probed against her stomach and her tits smashed against my chest.

This woman in my arms was all that I wanted in this damn world.

Her light-chocolate eyes sparkled with the candles' reflection as she stared up at me.

"You're fucking stunning." It was an understatement if ever I'd said one.

Her cheeks rose. "You're kind of handsome yourself."

In one fell swoop I lifted her ass to the end of the breakfast bar, and tugging her legs apart, I wedged myself closer.

"Whoa, Sterling. I have dinner waiting," she said with a playful laugh to her voice.

I lifted an eyebrow. "And I intend to eat." I inched the

hem of her dress higher, exposing the tops of the sexy-as-fuck stockings. Tilting my head, I asked in my deepest tone, "Tell me what I'll find under here."

Her red painted lip, the same color as the dress, disappeared for a moment before her tongue darted out and licked. "S-Sterling..."

I walked my fingers higher. "That's not an answer, sunshine."

With a sweep of my hand, I cleared the counter behind her, the contents moving back as I splayed my fingers over the exposed skin between her breasts and pushed her until her back was flat against the cool granite counter, her blonde hair spilling around her in a halo framing her gorgeous face as her eyes were opened wide.

"Don't move, I want you just like this, and I need my hands for something else."

"Oh...Sterling..."

I never gave my name much thought. It was what it was, a name—one written on letterhead and on the top of tall buildings. However, each time it came in a breathy whisper from her lips, it was like fucking Viagra.

A jolt of life to my dick.

I lifted each of her feet, until the tall heels were on the counter and I had the optimal view of the answer to my question, her perfect pink uncovered pussy.

My lips curled. "Good girl."

Pulling her hips toward me, the tall heels slid on the hard surface.

She was fucking perfect as her breaths and whimpers filled the kitchen. It was as my tongue found her folds that she cried out, her shapely legs wrapping around my shoulders.

"Oh, Sterling..."

Her hands flailed as she reached for anything to give her leverage.

Fuck no.

This was my show. She may have set it up, but damn, I couldn't resist taking it over.

My licks became nips, small bites to her inner thighs, as I held her in place. Her hips bucked as I let my fingers join the assault. Winding her tighter and tighter, I worked her to the edge and eased her back, again and again, until I needed a release as much as Araneae.

Pulling back, our eyes met. "What happens to good girls?"

Her breasts heaved as she sat forward or her elbows. "Don't be an asshole, Sterling."

My grin returned as I offered her my hand and helped her to the floor. Turning her toward the bar, I again pushed her upper body toward the counter, her back bent, tits flattened, and her legs stretched as she moved to her toes in those sexy red shoes.

She peered back at me over her shoulder. "What are you going to do?"

I lifted the skirt of the dress just as I'd done on the plane and ran my hand over her shapely ass, dipping my fingers in her wetness and then again rubbing my palm over her warming skin.

I leaned over her, my lips near her ear as I whispered menacingly, "Your choice, sunshine. You shouldn't have gone in that room alone."

"I-I..."

Standing straight, I shook off my suit jacket, unbuckled my belt, and undid my fly, letting my hardened cock spring free. Damn, I was in agony. Blue balls and a weeping dick had to be the worst punishment ever, yet I had a point to prove.

Her lip again disappeared behind her teeth. "I-I want to come."

"Then what does that mean?"

She laid her cheek against the granite as her arms came to a rest on either side of her head. "Fucking punish me, as long as I get to come."

Damn, I'd say it again. Araneae was the ideal woman.

Unfastening each of my cuff links, I let her wait and contemplate the decision she'd made. Her feet shifted in anticipation as I rolled up my sleeves, yet she remained in place. All at once, the kitchen filled with the sound of her shriek mixed with the slap of my palm contacting her ass. I leaned back to admire the perfect representation of my hand, her skin raising and reddening as my palm tingled. Another to the other side and another. As her ass grew redder, my desire for pleasure overruled the need to enforce my rules.

Pulling her hips toward me and gripping my hardened cock, I found my way home.

"Sterling!"

"You're so damn wet." *And tight*. Her pussy was strangling me and it was amazing.

Araneae hummed as she pushed back, taking me completely.

Easing in and out, I leaned over her again. Planting a kiss to her neck, I teased, "You're fucking soaked. I think you may have liked that punishment too much."

She craned her neck backward as a smile blossomed across her face from her lips to her sparkling velvet eyes. "If I never admit that, you'll keep doing it."

Fucking perfect woman—made for me.

With each thrust, Araneae pushed back, her body convulsing and pulsating around me. Reaching forward I found her clit. The kitchen filled with her moans as we wound one another higher. The sounds weren't only from her; we were both making noises, primal and savage. The need to not only find pleasure, but please the other one overwhelmed me as a fog of our connection grew stronger, swirling in a cyclone around us.

It wasn't until we both found our release that I stilled, our bodies still connected, and laid my upper body over hers. With my heart beating too fast, I teased a bit of her long hair away from her beautiful face. "I love you."

"I love you, too. And I like saying it."

I kissed her lips. "I like showing it."

She wiggled beneath me. "I like that, too."

As we finally broke our union, I went to the sink and dampened a paper towel. Bringing it back, I tended to Araneae. Once I was done, I looked around the kitchen and asked, "What did Lorna make us?"

After standing and smoothing the skirt of her dress back into place, Araneae's hands landed on my shoulders and she looked me in the eye. "Nothing."

What?

"But I can smell—"

"I made it. I came home early and convinced Lorna to let me cook. And now, after your little welcome home, I'm famished."

"Little?"

She laughed. "Hardly."

I lowered my forehead to hers. "I doubt whatever it is will

be as good as what I just ate..." I let the smile spread over my face as Araneae's cheeks turned pink. "...but I can't wait to try it. Is it ready?"

Leaning back, she lifted herself to her tiptoes and kissed my cheek. With veiled eyes, she then said the words I'd never thought I'd hear from her.

"Yes, Mr. Sparrow."

ARANEAE

Sterling's strong arms came to the railing as the warmth of his body radiated behind me, heating my sundress-covered back. Sighing against my neck, his prickly chin nuzzled against my shoulder while the aroma of sunscreen mixed with cologne replaced the fresh scent of water. Before us was the never-ending blue of Lake Michigan, the surface sparkling like diamonds in the sun as the yacht cruised through the waves, taking us back south to Chicago.

I leaned back against his solid chest, taking in the beauty as the wind blew my hair and the light fabric of the sundress covering my bikini.

"You're quiet. What are you thinking?" he asked, his words tickling my neck.

Instead of answering, I shrugged.

"I'll tell you what I'm thinking," he offered.

Spinning within the cage of his arms, I wrapped mine around his bare, toned torso. Looking up, I replaced my view of the blue waters with the darkest brown eyes. "What are you thinking?"

"That next time we have a yacht, it has fewer crew members."

My sun-kissed cheeks rose as my head shook. "I'm very disappointed in my tan lines. I was promised there'd be none."

Leaning away, he reached behind my neck to where my bikini top was tied and tugged at the knot. "Me too."

I didn't protest as the knot came loose, knowing that Sterling wouldn't expose me if others were around. That was the whole reason our nakedness had not included the multiple decks of this giant yacht; instead, it was limited to our private cabin, more specifically the master suite. My smile turned sultry as under the sundress, the top of my bikini fell, now only secured around by a string behind my back.

"Make that no crew," he said.

"I like that. Can it be a sailboat?"

"If you want a sailboat, we'll have a sailboat."

"Do you know how to sail?"

He ran his finger over my cheek. "Have you found anything I can't do?"

"Not yet. I'll keep trying." I looked up at his chiseled features as he stared beyond me to the water. "That sailboat..." I said, "...something small for just the two of us."

This yacht was bigger than I imagined, like everything with Sterling Sparrow—his plane, his cabin, his apartment, and now a chartered yacht. At nearly a hundred feet in length, the main level of the cabin was larger than my apartment in Boulder—two of my apartments. At times it was easy to forget that we'd cruised from Chicago to Mackinac. While the captain said it could be done quicker, Sterling chose to let us enjoy the solitude that comes with each other and a staff of twelve.

Yes, twelve.

Sterling's expression darkened. "You know it can't be only us."

I nodded. Even on this boat, we had members of his security—part of those twelve—people watching our backs, making sure that we were protected. "I hate that we get a vacation, but others have to work."

"It's the way the world works."

"Do you ever get tired of the constant surveillance?" I asked, not for a friend.

"I don't think about it, other than to know it's there, and then there are places where they're less obtrusive."

"Like home."

He nodded. "I love hearing you call it that." He lifted my chin. "Have you enjoyed yourself and our getaway?"

"Have I enjoyed five uninterrupted days of sun and sex?"

"Have you?" he asked, his grin growing as his dark eyes gleamed.

I lifted my arms to his broad shoulders. "Yes, Mr. Sparrow."

"You know that every time you say that, I get hard?"

"I think the answer to that would be the same." *Yes, Mr. Sparrow.* I turned back toward the water. "And Mackinac Island." I laid my hand over his on the rail. "It was fun to be regular people."

"Sunshine, there was security."

"Don't tell me that. Let me think that for one day we were free."

His chest rumbled with laughter. "Let's just say that your change in our plans wasn't as enjoyable for some."

Smiling, I shook my head and thought back to the day. I hadn't even suspected that we were being watched. I'd thought it was the only time we'd been alone, alone in a crowd. The yacht had stopped just beyond the unique island where we were met by a smaller vessel that after cruising around the island, docked at a private marina.

Three days earlier-

Mackinac Island was like stepping back in time. With no cars or motorized vehicles—other than fire engines—it was truly a memorable experience. The only choices for transportation were horses or bicycles. I'd heard of this island, but seeing it was unexpected and exciting.

With my hand in Sterling's, we walked the sidewalks around the historic town, stopped in shops, and ate amazing fudge. We toured Fort Mackinac. In a horse-drawn carriage we rode up a hill to the massive front porch of the Grand Hotel where a table was waiting inside for our dinner. The green-striped chairs and elegantly dressed waitstaff were like nothing I'd ever seen—classic, not the glitz and glamour of Chicago or New York.

After dinner, as we were headed back to the marina, I tugged on Sterling's hand. "Are we on a schedule?" I asked.

"No, next on the agenda is getting you back to the cabin of the yacht and making love to you under the lights of Mackinac Bridge."

It did something to me when Sterling used the words *make love*—a warm, fuzzy feeling that buzzed through my circulation, tingling my skin and twisting my core. It wasn't the same adrenaline rush as when he said he wanted to *fuck*. That was intense, an electric charge to my lady parts, such as the highest setting on the vibrator Sterling had described prior to our first date, the one that so far we'd only played with in the privacy of our bedroom.

Both descriptors brought a smile to my face. That was who Sterling Sparrow was—a man who could make me want whichever side of sex he offered and apparently a decadent toy or two.

For the record, the vibrating butt plug was still a solid no.

Warmth filled my cheeks as I contemplated his plans: the gentle sway of the yacht, the lights of the famous suspension bridge out the window, and Sterling monopolizing my every thought as he brought pleasure to my body. "I like the sound of that," I said.

He stopped walking and looked down at me. "I'm hearing some hesitation."

"Not about your plan. It's that...I don't know if you'll want to do what I want to do first."

"Sunshine, you'll never know if you don't ask."

I leaned my head toward a bicycle rental shop.

Sterling's eyes grew wide. "Bikes? You want to ride bikes?"

"One bike," I corrected, dropping his hand and pointing at a bicycle with two seats, one behind the other. When I looked back to him, I saw the wheels turning in his head. "You can say no."

His chest inflated as he took a deep breath. "I'm just a

little worried you won't keep up your end of the bargain and I'll end up pedaling us both—"

"All the way around the island," I interrupted with a smile. "I heard that family next to us in the restaurant talking about it."

A young man from the shop came out. "Can I help you folks?"

Not waiting for Sterling, I asked, "How long does it take to ride all the way around the island on a bike for two?"

The young man shrugged and scanned Sterling. "It's 8.2 miles. With him pedaling, he can probably do it in under an hour, but if you stop, it takes longer."

Well, that seemed like an obvious caveat.

I turned to Sterling and tilted my head, silently making my plea.

With a sigh, he reached for his wallet. "How much for the tandem?"

Yes, that was what the bicycle-built-for-two was called—a tandem.

For the next two hours we rode around the island on the paved M-185—the only state highway in the country that bans cars. While the island was beautiful, my view of Sterling was sometimes hard to resist. We weren't as close as we'd been on the ATV, yet with his broad shoulders and ass right in front of me, more than once my thoughts slipped to the next item on our agenda.

As we biked, we were sometimes alone while other times we were surrounded by people—couples and families. We did as the young man had said and stopped to see some of the sights we otherwise would have missed, including bluffs over-looking the water and natural formations like Arch Rock. As the ride progressed, I was very thankful for the enlarged seat, and I did pedal but not quite as much as Sterling.

Back to present–

"So because of me, some poor bodyguard had to ride a bike."

Sterling scoffed. "Two actually. I told Patrick about it, and he said he was glad to still be in Chicago."

I shook my head. "I liked not knowing that they were there." I turned back to him, my back against the rail. "You asked what I was thinking earlier. I have a strange feeling. I think I'm afraid to go back to Chicago."

Lifting my chin again, Sterling brought my gaze to his. "No."

"No?"

"That is something I can control and do. You're safe. You're as safe there as you are here." His lips quirked. "As you were on that bike ride."

I exhaled. "That's not what I mean. I know you and Patrick..." I peered over his shoulder. "...and any of these other people will keep me safe. It's just...I don't know. Maybe afraid wasn't the right word. I'm trying to decide why I feel...anxious. I think it's because I need to talk to my...mother. I've been thinking about it the entire trip and well, it's time to face it. Face her."

"I'll be with you, if you want."

I nibbled my own lip as I thought about it. I didn't know if that was the right answer; then again, if I learned something, Sterling had promised to be with me. Avoiding an answer, I asked, "Should I go to her or should she come to me?" My eyes widened. "Maybe we should meet at a neutral point. A cafe or something?"

Sterling's head shook. "No neutral place." His finger caressed my cheek. "I want to trust her, for you. However, under no circumstances do I trust McFadden. Wherever you meet, I need to know it's secure."

I turned back around, facing the railing. "How long until we're back to Chicago?"

"Right now, we're moving at approximately twenty knots."

"Is that supposed to mean something?" I pointed out to the water. "If I could see land, where are we?"

"Since you can't see land, we're in Lake Michigan. We have been the whole time, except when we were in the Straits of Mackinac."

"You're being an asshole."

He pointed to where I'd pointed. "Wisconsin is over there. If we went to the other side, it would be Michigan."

I shook my head. "Seriously, Sterling, the sun is moving that way. I know west. I also know geography. Give me a city."

He spun me back to face him. "I have, Araneae. Chicago is yours."

A smile came to my lips. "You're lucky you're handsome."

"Approximately, south of Milwaukee to the west," he said, "and south of Holland or Grand Rapids to the east."

"Thank you."

"In nautical miles we're seventy-five away from Chicago."

"And at twenty knots, we should be back to the yacht club in..." I left the sentence unfinished.

His broad shoulders shrugged. "Three hours."

I reached up on my tiptoes and kissed his cheek. "Well, I'm going into the cabin to retie my swimsuit."

Sterling's gaze darkened as he slowly shook his head. "No, sunshine. When I get you in the cabin, I'm going to untie the rest of those cute little knots until I have your sexy curves and every inch of your tantalizing body at my disposal."

With my heart beating faster, I eyed the man before me up and down, taking time to visualize what was under his swim trunks. "I believe my deal was that I'd agree only if you were dressed accordingly."

He reached for my hand, tugging me toward the cabin door.

As he was opening the door, a gentleman dressed all in white named Willis came around the deck. He'd been very attentive the entire cruise. "Mr. Sterling."

Something resembling a growl came from Sterling's throat, bringing a smile to my face.

"Willis, I mentioned that we're not to be disturbed."

"Sir, I understand. It's that—"

Sterling lifted his hand in a way that would stop most people.

Nodding, Willis backed away. "Sir, I thought that you'd want to know that Mr. Murray is on the secure network. He said it's important."

ARANEAE

*O*ur five days of bliss washed away with Sterling's news, no even before. From the second he returned from talking to Reid, I knew something was wrong.

"I told the captain to go as fast as possible," Sterling said, standing, still wearing his swim trunks in our suite on the yacht.

I paced back and forth, wringing my hands as I tried to comprehend his words. They were playing on repeat in my head yet I couldn't grasp that they were true. This couldn't be happening.

Sterling continued to speak, "We'll be back in Chicago in close to an hour." His tone was reassuring, though by his expression, the tenor was solely for my benefit—as if anything could reassure me. "I could have a helicopter sent out to us, but by the time it gets here and back, it wouldn't make that much of a difference."

My knees gave out as I sank to the edge of the large bed,

and my mind filled with memories. "W-where could she be?" I looked up at Sterling. "You told me she was safe."

"She was. Reid and Patrick are trying to find out what happened. They've sent others there or have them on their way. I told you there were eyes on people you care about. There were. I don't have all the information. Louisa and her husband were last accounted for around eight o'clock last night, Boulder time.

"Reid said this morning that Winnie was awakened to a deliveryman. Inside the package was a note telling her not to contact the police—*any* law enforcement. The note said they knew she'd been in contact with the FBI. It also said that Louisa wouldn't be harmed if Winnie followed the directions and to wait for further instructions."

Who besides us knew about the FBI?

My head was shaking as my stomach twisted in revolt. Tears stung the back of my eyes. "What about Jason? What about the baby?"

"Araneae, I didn't talk to Reid that long. After he told me, I wanted to get back to you." He let out a long breath. "From what I understand, immediately after Winnie received the package, she tried calling Louisa and Jason. Then she thought to call Patrick."

"I didn't realize he'd given her his number."

"He told her to contact him if Agent Hunter called again."

I nodded.

"Patrick told her to stay put," Sterling said. "She didn't. She went to Louisa's house. It was empty."

"Empty? Like all their things?"

"No, empty meaning there were no people. The note didn't mention Jason, only Louisa."

"I could try to call him."

"So far, all calls to either of the Toneys have gone to voicemail."

My stomach roiled as my body quaked, trembling uncontrollably from my fingers to my toes. I held my own hand, trying to make the shaking stop, yet it was as though the temperature in the cabin had plummeted to twenty below. "God, she's pregnant. Someone took her? Who would do this?" I found the strength to stand as the acceleration of the yacht propelled me forward, causing me to lose my footing and fall into Sterling's arms. Immediately, I backed away with my head shaking. "Will they hurt her? Is this about me? Is this about you? Sinful Threads?" I took another step back. "This doesn't..." I shook my head. "No...tell me this wasn't you."

Sterling staggered backward as if my words had physically struck him. His dark eyes sent bolts of lightning my direction as his chiseled jaw tightened. "Do you believe after everything that I would harm your best friend or have her harmed?"

I wasn't certain what I thought.

"I-I don't know." Tears were now trickling from my eyes. "You threatened them."

Sterling's hand ran through his hair. "Fuck, Araneae, I care about who you care about. It wasn't a threat as much as me capitalizing on your weakness. I told you that. I wouldn't—" Like a caged lion he turned a small circle as the cords in his neck tightened.

"Sterling, you're the one who keeps telling me you do bad things," I said. "Whoever kidnapped my pregnant best friend is doing a bad thing."

He nodded. "Yes. That's why we'll get her back."

I started thinking about what he'd told me. "Wait. Winnie woke up to the first message?"

Sterling nodded again.

"I-it's evening. There's only an hour difference in time. Why are we just now finding out?"

"Patrick's already in Boulder. Reid waited to contact us until they knew more."

"Do they," I asked expectantly, "know more?"

"More than this morning. It's why he contacted us. Whoever has Louisa sent a new message: they want to talk to you—Kennedy Hawkins."

"Me?" I stared up at the granite features as my pulse increased, my blood flowing too fast, making the room waver. "Okay. If that will help her, I'll do it."

"Fuck no."

I took a step toward him. "Sterling, this isn't a time for you to be overprotective."

"The hell it isn't. It's exactly the time for me to be overprotective. Someone kidnapped Louisa. Jason is missing. Patrick is with Winnie who wants to call the police. He's convinced her not to do that yet. Shelly, the person who was supposed to be watching everyone, is searching for Louisa."

I shook my head. "I remember that name—Shelly. She drove me. She's the one who helped Jeanne Powell." I reached out, laying my hand on Sterling's arm, remembering the cats and Jeanne's new place to live. "I'm sorry. I know this wasn't you, but it has to have something to do with me if they want to talk to me." I shook my head. "Isn't the fact that they asked for Kennedy and not Araneae a clue? I'll do whatever they want."

"It's a clue or a smoke screen. When we get home, we'll know more."

"What about Lucy and Calvin, Louisa's parents, and Lindsey, her sister?"

"We'll ask. Reid didn't mention them."

My head fell forward on my neck as more tears came. "I've been such an awful friend. She's due to have a baby soon, and I'm sailing all over Lake Michigan. I should have been at Sinful Threads. I should have been in Boulder. I don't understand..." My words came between gulps of air as memories of Louisa and I played on a loop, from our time in high school, to college, to Sinful Threads. The last time I'd seen her was weeks ago when I left Boulder. Memories came of her wedding, her talking about naming her baby Kennedy, and times with her family. "...if Reid and Patrick have known, they should have alerted us. We could already be back in Chicago."

Sterling's arms came around me, holding me close to his bare chest and surrounding me. This time, I didn't back away. I lingered, enjoying the way his protective cage around me made me feel.

"I can only assume that Reid and Patrick thought they could handle it." His words reverberated through me—not only hearing them but feeling them. "I extend a lot of leeway when it comes to Reid and Patrick, more than with anyone else. I trust them to make the right decisions. I believe they thought delaying telling us was right."

I tilted my chin upward and stared at his handsome features, his strained neck, tightly clenched jaw, and furrowed brow. "Sterling, there's more that you're not telling me."

He nodded his chin above my head. "They were also making sure we're safe—you were safe."

I exhaled. "Right now, all that matters are Louisa, Jason, and baby Kennedy. I'll do whatever Louisa needs. I'll tell them to take me and let her go."

His embrace tightened. "They are not all who matters. You're first on that list. There's always a concern that when something outrageous happens—like this—it's a diversion to let down our guard. And as for changing places, the answer is hell no. I won't allow you to do that. We'll get this figured out. If it's money they want, paying it goes without saying."

"I can't ask you to—"

"You didn't."

Laying my head against his chest, the rhythm of his heart and scent of his skin eased a bit of the tension as our yacht sped south.

I looked back up as Sterling continued his embrace. "I-I— this has to have something to do with me."

"We don't have answers yet."

My brow scrunched. "I'm surprised that you'd be willing to make a deal. I guess I thought you, Reid, and Patrick were more the guns-blazing type."

He took my hand and led me to the bed where we both sat. Exhaling, he said, "Reid believes this is a statement to get your attention."

I let out a long breath. "Fuck, send me a text. Don't kidnap my best friend."

The pad of his thumb gently ran over the top of my hand. "We'll confirm that she's safe, and then we'll find out what they want."

"Do you think this is my uncle?"

"You know I do."

JOSEY

Twenty-six years ago ~

The infant's cries came through the baby monitor, waking me as the clock on the bedside stand read 2:40. The darkness beyond the windows confirmed it was the middle of the night, or perhaps more accurately, the early morning.

At two weeks of age, Renee was waking every four to five hours, and although I was exhausted, the baby in the nursery next to our bedroom had already stolen my heart. Rolling out of bed, I left Byron—using our new names was the hardest part of this assignment—sleeping in our bed and made my way to the nursery.

Our new home was everything we'd been promised and more. With three bedrooms and two and a half baths, set in a quiet cul-de-sac in a picture-perfect neighborhood, it was a dream. Living in Mount Prospect, Illinois—a northwest suburb of Chicago, a suburb with the motto "Where friendliness is a way of life"—was nothing like our flat in South Chicago.

While it was still March and cold, there were neighbors out and about, walking dogs and shoveling sidewalks. Many even came to our door to welcome us to the neighborhood.

My cheeks were still bruised from the cosmetic surgery, as were my eyes. Thankfully, it was now more manageable and easier to conceal. My hair had been changed from brown to a darker black and cut into a popular style, longer in the front and shorter in the back. I missed my long hair, but admittedly with a newborn, this style was easier to manage.

The last two and a half weeks had been a whirlwind. Renee was born earlier than expected, in a small hospital in rural Wisconsin. I tried not to think too much about what happened, how they convinced the woman her child was deceased, or even where they came up with an infant's body for her to hold.

As I reached down into the crib, the gold bracelet on my wrist reflected the illumination of the nightlight in the corner. I couldn't explain what drew me to wear the bracelet. Maybe it was a tribute to the woman, a way for me to feel connected to her and her to Renee. She wanted it buried with her daughter. It only seemed right to keep it close to her daughter.

"There, there, my sweet Renee. Mommy has you," I cooed, lifting her tiny body to my chest and supporting her small head. My fingers gently ran over her soft halo of blonde fuzz, so light it was almost invisible. "You're so strong." She arched her back and lifted her own head before allowing it to fall back to me.

In seconds she relaxed, no longer fussing as I hummed a lullaby I faintly recalled. Laying her upon the changing table,

I continued talking, telling her what I didn't want to forget, what I knew I couldn't say when she was older.

"Renee, your real name is Araneae. We're calling you Renee for short. I don't know exactly why we were given you —other than you are a gift—but we believe it was to protect you. One day, you'll be stronger and so smart. You won't need us, but before that day, sweet girl, I'm here and so is your daddy. Always know you were loved." I fought the urge to cry, thinking of the woman who would never hold her. I couldn't change that, but I could let Renee know she was always wanted and always loved.

Byron had been able to piece together a hypothesis—his theory.

It was no secret that something big had gone down with an attorney in Chicago who did work for Allister Sparrow and Rubio McFadden. It was all over the news. The FBI raided his office and house. His name, Daniel McCrie, had scrolled along the bottom of the TV screen.

And then, we saw the obituary:

The McCries, Daniel McCrie and wife, the Honorable Judge Annabelle Landers, regret to announce the unfortunate loss of their daughter, Araneae McCrie. The infant passed away less than an hour after birth. The family has decided that there will be no public services. Condolences may be made in the form of donations in their daughter's name to the University of Chicago School of Law.

It was the name, the same name the woman in the hospital said she'd named her daughter. It wasn't common, such as

Mary or Susan. A name like those wouldn't be identifiable. The name, Araneae, had been what the woman in the hospital had said. There was no way we could chalk it up to coincidence. The baby in our care belonged to an attorney and a judge living in Chicago.

Why Allister Sparrow had gone to the effort to keep this baby hidden in plain sight still escaped us. All we knew was that we'd been pulled into this web. The gift of keeping the little girl safe and raising her had been bestowed upon us.

Renee's little legs kicked gleefully as I worked to tuck them back into the tiny pink sleeper. Her soft brown eyes stared upward as I snapped each small snap, keeping her warm on this chilly spring morning. Lifting her up, I snuggled her against my chest and made our way to the kitchen.

As I turned the corner, Neal—no, Byron—was already there. "What are you doing? You have to start work soon. You need your sleep." He'd been given a delay, time for his surgeries to heal.

A smile came to his lips. "I'm warming a bottle."

"You are?"

He came closer and placed a gentle kiss on Renee's head and then one to my lips. "We're a team. We're going to do this and save her from whatever her parents did."

A lump formed in my throat. "Do you think we can?"

"This real job, the one at Boeing, comes with real money." He looked around. "The house is paid off. Right now, our only obligation to Sparrow is keeping him updated on Renee. If he can make us into new people, one day, we can do the same."

I laid Renee back in the crook of my arm. "Did you hear that, sweet girl? It's going to be all right."

The microwave dinged and Byron opened the door, lifting

the bottle and gently squeezing the bag of formula inside. "Feels about right."

I started to sit in the recliner in the living room when I stopped. "Do you want to feed her?" I asked.

Byron's eyes opened wide.

"You won't break her, I promise."

His Adam's apple bobbed as he took the seat and extended his hands. As he settled her into the crook of his arm and brought the bottle to her ready lips, my chest ached, knowing we'd finally been given what we'd always wanted— knowing that our gift was at the expense of others.

STERLING

"We need confirmation that Louisa is safe," I said into my phone as Garrett drove Araneae and me toward the apartment away from the yacht club.

Looking to my left, seeing the fear in Araneae's eyes since I told her what was happening had me ready to jump out of my own fucking skin. I reached over and covered her hand with mine, reining in my anger and trying to offer her what she needed. Her chocolate eyes turned my way, glassy from crying.

It will be all right, I mouthed.

"Since the messages have been coming via a messenger—real people and not technology—we don't yet have a way to respond," Patrick said through my phone. "Reid has traced each package, but the sender information is varied and leads to dead ends."

"Where are they coming from?"

"Denver."

I sighed. "That's a good sign that they haven't moved her far."

Araneae's eyes widened as she looked my way.

"What?" I asked her.

"Oh God, Sterling, they can't move her far. What if she goes into labor?"

"That's why we're working on this," I answered, and then speaking back into the phone, I asked Patrick, "Is Winnie with you?"

"Yes." His voice lowered in volume. "I'm afraid if I leave her alone, she'll do something to make this worse."

"I want to talk to her," Araneae said.

"Put her on the phone. Araneae wants to talk to her." There was a hesitation in his response. "Patrick, she knows what's happening. She only wants to be sure at least one of her friends is all right."

"You're the boss."

I handed the phone to Araneae. As I did, the car we were in lurched forward, sending all three of us forward only to be snapped back by our seatbelts. "What the fuck?"

The echo of screeching tires came through the protective glass of our windows.

Garrett's complexion paled. "Sorry, sir. That car."

My head moved from side to side as a black SUV raced down a perpendicular street with smoke coming from the tires. The traffic light before us was green and traffic behind us was a chorus of horns.

"He didn't stop at the light, just barreled on through," Garrett said.

"Fuck," I said, "did you see the license plate?"

"No," he responded, moving us forward. "I'll give Reid the cross streets, and see if he can pick it up on traffic cams."

"I'll text him right away." I looked to Araneae still talking on my phone.

Hell, in Chicago it wasn't unusual for drivers to speed, avoiding stopping at traffic lights when the conditions allowed —when traffic wasn't at a standstill. Then again, with everything happening, I had a hard time accepting that what had just occurred was a coincidence.

"...nothing, just something with traffic," Araneae was saying, her knuckles blanched as she held on to my phone. "...please let Patrick stay with you. We need to know you're safe."

Talking to Winnie seemed to calm Araneae, giving her a sense of control that we both needed. After she said goodbye, promising to see Winnie soon, she handed me back my phone. "I told her we'd be there tonight."

I nodded, knowing she wouldn't be happy with the plan Patrick, Reid, and I had concocted. "We're going home first. I need to see Reid. Then the plane will be ready."

"I'd rather go now. I want to be with Winnie and if whoever this is wants to talk to me, I need to be there as soon as possible."

"Reid first, not negotiable."

She let out a long breath and turned toward the window.

If this was McFadden's doing, I was certain his people would be watching the airlines as well as my private plane. "If this is who we think, we're probably being watched right now. The only truly safe place is in the apartment."

She turned my way. "No glass towers. This is my best friend. I'm going to Boulder."

I reached out to her cheek. "Sunshine, the plane is being fueled. If you wanted to go rogue, which you can't, commercial airlines wouldn't get you there as fast as the Sparrow plane even with the stop at home."

She sighed. "I'm...I can't even think. What kind of sick person kidnaps a pregnant woman and where is Jason? Oh, if anything..." Tears again flowed down her cheeks.

Her sadness was the match to the raging fire within me, the one I was doing my best to keep contained. Expressing my anger and concern that Louisa had now been unaccounted for for nearly twenty-four hours wouldn't help Araneae. We had only recently gotten confirmation of a white van backing into the Toneys' driveway at nearly eleven last night. Reid had found the footage from a neighbor's video doorbell, one that activated with movement. The snippet of recording was only a few seconds long. There's no recording of anyone getting out of or into the van. The next recording shows the van leaving fifteen minutes later. Reid explained that the doorbells are set for sensitivity. From the distance of across the street, only the movement of the van activated it. Not the movement of people.

If this was tied to McFadden, I would find great pleasure in exposing his connection, after we made sure Louisa and Jason were safe.

I typed out a text to Reid, telling him about our near miss with the SUV, telling him the cross streets, and asking him to find and run the plates.

"How long before we can leave?" Araneae asked.

"I'm not sure. It depends on the information Reid has found. Why?"

She looked down at the dress she was wearing, the same one that covered the bikini I was never able to untie.

"I was going to do it on the plane, but if I have time, I think I'll take a shower and pack some things for Boulder. I need to call Jana and tell her that I won't be in the office on Monday."

"We don't know any of that yet."

"Sterling, it's Saturday night."

"A lot can happen in twenty-four hours." That was what worried me.

My phone buzzed with *PATRICK* on the screen.

"SHE'S ON HER WAY. I THINK THIS WILL WORK. LIKE I SAID BEFORE, THE LIKENESS IS UNCANNY."

I texted back:

"KEEP HER UNDER WRAPS UNTIL I GET THERE. GUARANTEE THERE WILL BE EYES. WE'LL ARRANGE FOR IT TO LOOK AS IF SHE'S WITH ME."

PATRICK:

"LET ME KNOW OF YOUR ARRIVAL TIME. MARI-ANNE HAS THE PLANE READY. AND JANA HAS AGREED TO BOARD WITH YOU."

I texted back:

"WHERE IS SHE?"

PATRICK:

"CONFERENCE ROOM ON ONE."

This had to work.

I looked over at Araneae as she watched out the window, concern lining her forehead. I would take this all away if I could. One thing was certain. I sure as hell wasn't letting her walk into a trap. While I'd only seen pictures of the woman Patrick had hired to be Araneae's decoy on the airplane the night the 737 crash-landed in Iowa, I could agree that she strongly resembled Araneae, or more accurately, Kennedy Hawkins.

On top of her resemblance, she worked for Sparrow. She understood the danger and could handle herself in a way I'd never allow Araneae to try.

I texted back:

"ONCE WE GET ARANEAE TO THE APARTMENT, I'LL GET JANA AND WE'LL BE TAKING OFF."

Garrett brought the car to a stop in our garage in front of the elevator. I didn't wait for him to open the door before I was out and Araneae was close behind.

"Take our bags to one after we go up to the penthouse."

Araneae's eyes widened, though she didn't say a word as I reached for her hand and tugged her toward the elevator. Placing my hand on the sensor, we waited in silence. I half expected another comment about her ability to call the elevator. When it didn't come, I let go of her hand and wrapped my arm around her, pulling her body close to mine.

"It will be all right. You have to trust me that we're doing what's best."

Her soft brown eyes peered toward me. "I do. I'm scared."

The elevator opened. Once we stepped in and turned around, I nodded to Garrett.

When the doors closed, she asked, "How long until I'll have my bags?"

"Not long."

"You're serious about not letting others into the penthouse. Don't you trust him?"

"Sunshine, I don't trust many people. He's proven himself trustworthy enough to drive me, and now, you. No one enters the penthouse, not even with bags. Floor one is accessible to trusted employees. He'll take the bags there and Reid or Lorna will bring them up."

Her head shook. "This is like some spy movie."

"No, it's real life. And with real life, I don't take unnecessary chances." I reached for her chin and brought her gaze to mine. "Remember that. It's for your own good."

"Sterling, I want to help my friend."

I kissed her lips as the elevator came to a stop on P. "I know."

ARANEAE

"Shouldn't you go to Reid?" I asked as Sterling accompanied me up the stairs toward our bedroom. "I'm going to change clothes too."

I looked down. Though he'd put on a t-shirt and slipped his feet in canvas loafers, he was still wearing his bathing trunks. I shook my head. "I guess it goes to show my mind isn't here. I almost forgot we were on the yacht enjoying the sun a few hours ago."

His lips brushed my hair. "It's understandable. Believe me, we're working on this."

"I just want to get to Winnie and hug Louisa."

"You will."

I wish I shared his confidence. Though I didn't, I kept reminding myself that Sterling was better versed in these kinds of situations. It was another case of being outside my understanding. Then again, wasn't kidnapping outside most people's understanding?

Once we were inside the bedroom with the door shut, I thought about our bags, but I didn't ask again. Lorna had our bathroom so well stocked that there was truly nothing in that bag that I needed to get ready to travel to Boulder. "I'm going to take a quick shower. I can be ready to go as soon as you let me know."

Sterling came from the closet, his bathing trunks gone and a pair of jeans in their place. The black t-shirt from before had been exchanged for a fresh gray one with a V-neck that fit well over his toned torso and bulging biceps. His dark hair was mussed and he still hadn't shaved, leaving his chin and cheeks with a dark shadow. In the middle of—as he'd called it—the shit-storm that was now my life, seeing him so casual gave me strength.

My sundress was gone, leaving me standing in our room in only the bikini from before. When our eyes met, he stalked toward me, his bare feet gripping the floor as his powerful strides met me near the entrance to the bathroom.

With one arm snaked around my waist, he pulled me close. The clean scent of his clothes combined with the mixture of lake water, cologne, and sunscreen.

"Sterling."

"I love you," he said, his dark eyes staring down at me.

I leaned into his chest. "I know. I love you too. I just don't want this new life to hurt my friends."

He lifted my chin. "I want you to know, we're doing every-thing we can."

I sighed. "I believe you."

He leaned back as his gaze scanned me, warming my skin as it moved from my toes to my eyes, lingering at sensual places in between. "Once this is over, I'm untying those sexy knots."

I nodded. "Deal." I took a step back. "Now go to Reid so we can leave."

Cupping my cheeks, his lips crashed with mine, lifting me to my tiptoes with his possessive pull. When we settled back to earth, he pulled away, yet his eyes remained fixed to mine. "I brought you here. I'll make this right."

I nodded as he turned away toward the doorway.

Why did it feel like he was saying goodbye?

I pushed the thought away, recognizing that I was simply emotional over what could be happening to Louisa.

Sterling disappeared behind the closing bedroom door as I stepped into the bathroom. Untying the knot behind my head and back, I removed the bikini top and shimmied out of the bottoms. As I pulled the tie from my ponytail, my hair fell over my shoulders. In the few days out on Lake Michigan, my skin had tanned and hair had lightened.

Was I becoming a different person as Winnie had said?

Refusing to dwell on it, I turned on the shower's hot water. Stepping inside, I stood under the spray. As the water cascaded over me, more tears formed, wracking my body like a sledgehammer as sobs erupted like mushroom clouds within my chest and throat, each one blooming bigger and bigger as the reality of what was happening overwhelmed me.

Too many questions.

Where was she?

Where was Jason?

Was she safe?

Was he?

Was she scared?

How was baby Kennedy?

My knees bent as I fell to the bench and water continued to pour over me.

"I'm so sorry, Louisa. I'm so sorry." I spoke aloud, my shoulders shaking as I admitted what I knew, what Sterling had tried to shield from me. "Lou, this is my fault. I brought you into this life, not to protect you—because look what's happening. I did it selfishly because of my curiosity. I know you can't understand, but Sterling offered me more than a new life. He offered me *my* life, the one I'd been born to live. I never meant for that to hurt you."

I sniffed and sat taller. "Stop it, Araneae. You're stronger than this."

The emotion wasn't helping Louisa. It wasn't, but I would.

I stood again, determined that I'd meet with whoever this person was.

Winnie had said I seemed different. Maybe that was Sterling's doing, but not entirely. Being with him, having him love me and my loving him in return, had given me a new strength. I lifted my face to the spray. I wasn't afraid to do what the kidnappers asked because I knew Sterling, Patrick, and Reid would keep me safe. I knew that in my heart and soul.

I didn't care what Agent Hunter said. Sterling had been honest with me and I with him. We would do whatever was necessary to save Louisa and Jason...and baby Kennedy.

No. No more emotion.

After quickly washing and rinsing my hair and using a soft cloth covered in bodywash to clean away the sunscreen, I turned off the water with a new sense of determination. Wrapping a plush towel around myself and running another over my wet hair, from a distance, I heard the ring of my cell phone.

Securing the towel over my breasts, I hurried to the bedroom suite. There on the bed was the bag I'd been carrying from the yacht. Reaching inside, I pulled out my cell phone.

STERLING was on the screen.

"Are you ready?" I asked as soon as I hit the green icon. "I'll be downstairs in five minutes." I'd worry about everything else on the plane. All I needed to do was throw on clothes and some shoes.

"Shelly found Jason." His voice was stone cold. In my mind's eye I saw his granite features and dark expression, hearing them drip from the simple statement.

My stomach dropped as I began to pace, my head growing faint as my circulation sped up. "Oh, please tell me he's all right."

"He will be. She found him in time."

I gripped the phone tighter as my steps stilled. "What does that mean?"

"Araneae, he was unconscious and dehydrated..." Sterling took a deep breath. "...and a little bruised. He'd been locked in a shipping container on the property of your design facility."

My pulse accelerated as I collapsed onto the edge of one of the overstuffed chairs near the big windows. The sight of Chicago's lights coming to life wasn't even registering. "Is he in the hospital?"

"We can't risk that. He's still unconscious, but Patrick said his vitals are improving."

"Improving?!" My voice shrieked. "Jason needs medical

help. He needs to wake up to tell us what happened and where Louisa is."

"Listen to me. We're going to get him medical attention, but until we find Louisa, we can't risk the police."

I nodded, trying to keep myself calm. "All right. I want to see him."

"You will."

"Has Shelly searched all of Sinful Threads' properties for Louisa?" In my mind I thought of all the different places: the design center, the offices, and the storage facility.

"She has. She has help. They're searching. Currently, it's a needle in a haystack as we wait for another message."

I shook my head. "Has Reid found the couriers?"

"Legit companies. Legit employees. A different one each time. Patrick had a few men question them. They've been employed for years. Reid confirmed it. He's trying to get a read on the customers in security footage. We also have people watching all the possible couriers. It appears the customers are two different men, both with their face obstructed from the camera. Of course, they paid cash."

I shook my head. "He'll get something. You and Lorna keep telling me how great he is."

"He is."

"Okay. I'll meet you downstairs in five minutes," I said, standing, seeing my own reflection now in the large window and thinking that despite the sun of the last week, I was nearly as pale as the white towel wrapped around me.

"That won't be necessary," Sterling said.

"What?"

"We're about to take off."

"I-I don't understand what you're saying."

"Araneae, you're safe at home."

"What the hell, Sterling?" My hands began to shake. "You can't go without me. The people want to talk to *me*." My sentences were coming faster and faster. "Don't you dare do this."

"I'll call you with any more news. Don't call Winnie. There's a good chance her phone is tapped. No emails either. Reid's already gone through the emails sent to you or Louisa. It's better to stay offline so you don't pop up on his searches."

Now, my entire body was shaking—trembling—as tears returned. "You asshole. You can't leave me here and order me to stay quiet. These are my friends."

"I can. I just did."

My queasiness from before warmed to a boiling rage rolling through me.

"Damn it, Sterling! You promised to be with me."

"I also promised to take care of this and keep you safe. This is the best way. I'll call you, Araneae. Don't even think of leaving the apartment. You're in the safest place right now."

Oh my God. My mind was a cyclone of thoughts, most of them erratic and disconnected.

"I can't leave. You have me locked in a fucking glass tower." Before he could respond, I went on, "How?" My free hand hit my towel-covered thigh as I paced between the sofa and bed. "How can you do this without me if they want me?"

"We have a plan. I love you."

The phone went dead.

"Oh no you don't." I hit the green icon to call him back. As soon as it connected, his voicemail answered.

With shaking hands, I hammered out a text.

STERLING

*E*xhaling, I looked down at the screen of my phone. One missed call and one text message. *ARANEAE* on the screen.

"DO NOT DO THIS! YOU CAN'T HOLD ME CAPTIVE IN A DAMN GLASS TOWER. LOUISA IS MY BEST FRIEND. COME BACK AND GET ME OR I SWEAR TO GOD, I WILL FIND A WAY OUT OF HERE. THERE'S ALWAYS THE FUCKING FRONT DOOR."

I sent a reply.

"I SUGGEST YOU STAY AWAY FROM THAT FRONT DOOR. IT WON'T WORK ANYWAY. IT'S MONITORED. IF

*YOU TRY, YOU'LL REGRET IT. LET US TAKE CARE OF
THIS. IT'S WHAT WE DO. YOU STAY SAFE."*

Exhaling, I looked up as the door to the plane closed. Marianne was in the cockpit and Keaton was on board. Though it
was no longer her job, so was Jana.

"Mr. Sparrow," she said, "may I get you something?"

She'd removed the blonde wig the minute we boarded the
plane; however, she was still wearing the clothes Reid had
provided. Though she was not quite Araneae's size, he'd
managed to get her a nice dress and designer shoes much like
what was stocked in Araneae's closet. While in the car with
Garrett and me, Jana did her best to mimic Araneae, her body
language and mannerisms. From working together for the last
weeks, she'd done a good job picking up on a few. Jana only
resembled Araneae from afar, but hopefully, it would be suffi-
cient if we were being watched.

"Jana," I said, "have a seat. I appreciate your helping us out
at a moment's notice. Patrick will arrange for a flight back to
Chicago, and you'll be back to your husband and son by
morning. If the boy sleeps in, he'll hardly know you
were gone."

A smile crept over her lips. "Thank you. You know I'd do
anything you or Patrick asked. I've spoken with Mrs. Toney
over the phone." She hesitated. "I don't know what's happening, but if my pretending to be Ms. Hawkins for a few
minutes helps, I'm glad to do it."

I nodded. "Thank you, Jana."

She looked down at the clothes. "I'll return these to
Patrick next week."

"What? No. They're your size. Consider the clothes a bonus on top of what you'll be paid."

"I couldn't. They're too nice."

I tilted my head toward the area to the rear of where I sat. "If you'll excuse me."

"Of course," she said, beginning to step away.

"Jana?"

She turned back my way. "Yes?"

"Remember, you're a guest on this plane for this trip. Relax. I just need you to disembark with me when we land. And then you'll learn from Patrick when you can go home."

Her smile returned. "Thank you."

As she turned toward the partition, I pushed the button at the round table, raised the computer screen, and finding the keypad, I brought it to life. Once I was alone, I began looking into all of the findings from Sparrow. No one was taking this lightly. Reid had a team on it as well as Patrick.

I sent Reid a message.

"MONITOR THE FRONT ELEVATOR. NO ONE GOES UP OR DOWN. TOTAL LOCKDOWN WHILE WE'RE DEALING WITH THIS SHIT. WE NEED TO KNOW THAT EVERYONE IS SAFE."

REID appeared on the screen.

"BACK ELEVATOR? LORNA?"

. . .

My decision wouldn't be popular, but popularity wasn't my goal. I replied.

"THE APARTMENT IS FULLY STOCKED. I'D RATHER NOT TAKE A CHANCE. DOUBLE-CHECK EVERYONE ON ONE TOO. YOU KNOW THIS BETTER THAN I DO, BUT THE WAY TO US IS THROUGH THOSE WOMEN. I WANT THEM BOTH SAFE."

Besides, I believed Araneae would take her time in the apartment better if she had company. That didn't negate the chewing out she'd give me when I returned. I'd take it. I'd take her calling me every name in the fucking book as long as she was safe.

Message from *REID*:

"I'LL PASS ON THE MESSAGE. HOPEFULLY THIS IS SETTLED SOON."

I scrolled my secure messages until I found the picture of Bridget Anderson. She was twenty-seven years old—a year older than Araneae and from California—yet their likeness was uncanny. This could work.

Message to Patrick:

"GET BRIDGET UP TO SPEED. IF SHE NEEDS TO TALK

TO SOMEONE, SHE NEEDS TO HAVE SOME KNOWLEDGE."

PATRICK replied.

"AS WE SPEAK...WINNIE IS HELPING."

I leaned back in the chair, finally realizing that we were off the ground. The sky beyond the windows was darkening, yet we'd be heading west, chasing the sunset. Exhaling, my jaw clenched at Patrick's message. This was one of the times I had to trust Patrick's instincts. He'd been right about Jana. I had to believe he was right about Winnie too. Bridget needed to be well-versed on Sinful Threads and Kennedy Hawkins. She also needed to know that she wasn't limited to one name. She was also Araneae McCrie. McFadden's people would certainly know that. In a nutshell, Bridget had to convince whoever questioned her that she was Kennedy/Araneae.

And then there was Jason. If he'd wake, hopefully he'd be able to shed more light on what happened.

What about the baby?

I recalled that nearly a week ago she'd texted Araneae about being dilated. I knew less about childbirth than nearly anything else in the world. I could talk real estate holdings, architecture, investments, money laundering, and gambling—even human trafficking. Yet with something as natural as childbirth, I knew nothing.

What I did know was that if anything happened to Louisa

or the baby, Araneae would blame herself. I refused to let that happen.

Fuck, my mind was all over the place.

Twenty-four hours was significant in abductions. What we had to keep in mind was that this wasn't a stereotypical abduction. It may fit the pattern. Women were kidnapped more than men. Over sixty percent of adult female kidnappings result in sexual assault or extortion. I was too aware of those statistics as well as those involving children. Things were different with Louisa.

Reid, Patrick, and I all agreed, this wasn't random. It was to get Araneae's attention. That bit of knowledge gave us hope. If Bridget could get them to play into our hand, we'd hopefully learn more.

With only two messages, we didn't have much to go on.

A message bar popped up on the side of my screen with the name *PATRICK.*

"JASON IS IMPROVING."

I sighed.

"Mr. Sparrow," Keaton said, entering the area of the plane where I was working.

"Keaton."

"May I get you anything? Something to eat or drink?"

"Water."

Nodding, he turned away.

I should be hungry. Araneae and I last ate a midday meal on the yacht.

Fuck. That seemed like days ago.

The memory made me want to message her and tell her to eat; however, I'd have to trust that she'd do that on her own. Opening a line of communication right now was no doubt a bad plan. I would listen to her tirade after I had Louisa safe.

As time passed, I decided that working on anything for Sparrow Enterprises was a waste of my time. Thankfully, I'd kept up on everything while on our getaway. Now, my mind couldn't concentrate on contracts, architectural perspectives, or even job bids. All I could think about was Louisa. I'd never met her, yet I'd seen enough pictures that I felt as though I had.

She mattered to Araneae, so she mattered to me.

I ran my hand through my hair.

How the fuck had we screwed up?

It was simple. We'd underestimated McFadden. We'd protected Araneae to a fault. He knew he couldn't get to her, so he went for someone more vulnerable. Patrick had Shelly watching four people in Boulder plus other Sinful Threads employees. There was an array of people watching Araneae besides the constant presence of Patrick or myself. We'd allowed the coverage to be too scarce on Araneae's friends.

With our destination approaching, I went back to the bedroom and showered. After a quick shave I dressed less casually—trousers and a button-up without a tie. The attire fit for the way the two Araneae imposters were dressed. I went back to the computer and continued to monitor the situation.

Two and a half hours after wheels up, the wheels of the Sparrow plane set down, taxiing on a runway in Boulder.

Being after ten at night in Boulder, the sky was dark, but there would be lights on the tarmac.

We'd be visible.

As the plane rolled to a stop, Jana returned to where I'd been sitting. She once again wore the blonde wig as well as a long, light jacket over her dress. Its collars pointed over her cheeks obstructed part of her face.

I looked her up and down. "Again, thank you, Jana."

She nodded.

"May I rest my hand on your back as we leave the plane? It would look more natural."

She swallowed and lifted her chin. "Thank you for asking first."

I'd spent too much time with men and women who'd endured horrendous hardships I could only imagine. With time came knowledge. I'd helped countless individuals find education, jobs, and careers. What I couldn't give them was peace of mind. That was up to each one individually. They had to choose that. I simply did what I could to pave the path.

Throughout all the years Jana had worked for me, I'd never nor would I—under normal circumstances—touch her. She had to know that she had her own personal space.

"May I?" I asked again as the door popped, the seal breaking as the stairs began to descend.

"Yes," she replied.

I looked down at my phone. "There's a car waiting. Keep your face down and once we're in and out of the car, your part is done."

She nodded as we moved to the door, her face down, watching the tall heels walk down the stairs with my hand guiding her.

ARANEAE

Through the fog of my desolation came a knock at the bedroom door. It was there, rapping in the distance, yet I didn't want to hear. With my phone secured between my hands, waiting, praying, and hoping for a call or a text message, I was too angry to answer the taps that continued.

No, angry wasn't the right word.

Angry didn't even come close to describing my feelings—my swell of emotions.

Livid.

Enraged.

Incensed.

My list continued as I ignored the knocking.

Hurt.

Disappointed.

Beyond consolation.

"Araneae," Lorna's voice came from the other side of the door, adding to the knocking.

I'd cried a bucket of tears, worrying about what was happening in Boulder, and while it seemed that none should be left, more came as I finally stood, my head pounding and my body drained.

Throughout the last hours I'd tried to think of ways to escape.

How fucking sick was it that my best friend had been taken and I was the one who needed to escape?

I wanted to throw something through one of the giant windows, but even if it would break—which I doubted it would—I'd be staring down at Chicago from ninety-seven stories in the air. I'd need a damn parachute for me to make it to the ground.

I'd contemplated the elevators. I didn't need to test the one at the front door—the one Genevieve Sparrow had used —to know it wouldn't work. Sterling had told me that in a text message. His words about leaving the apartment from weeks ago came back to me. *"Cannot. As in...are incapable of, not only forbidden but physically unable. Is that spelled out enough for you? Obviously, following rules voluntarily is not your strong suit. The choice for you to go against my will regarding leaving the apart-ment has been taken away from you."*

Trapped.

The weight of that reality was unbearable.

If I felt this way, how was Louisa feeling?

"Araneae, please. I know you're in there."

Walking from the chaise where I'd been sitting by the window, I dredged myself across the massive bedroom—my prison—toward the bedroom doors. The burden of my capture made moving toward Lorna's voice difficult, like the process of walking through knee-deep water in a lake with a mucky bottom. Each step was harder than the last, pulling me down.

With my last bit of energy—while knowing that I was a walking, talking, blubbering mess—I yanked open one of the doors while keeping my chin down. I'd made it to her; that didn't mean I wanted to look at her. She was one of them, one of the people I'd trusted who now had me held prisoner.

I didn't care how fucking beautiful Sterling's apartment was.

A gilded cage was still a cage.

Avoiding Lorna's eyes, I kept my gaze pointed downward, concentrating on her colorful tennis shoes. They were bright pink with purple. Even the swirl of colors couldn't ease my stupor.

"I thought..." She began before exhaling. "...how are you?"

"I-I'm..." I wasn't sure what I was.

Abandoned.

Demeaned.

A fucking child grounded to this apartment while her friend was in danger.

A person who had opened her life to possibilities only to have it ripped away at the agonizing price of everything: my best friend, my company, and my freedom.

My head shook.

How had I been so stupid?

The reason that I couldn't look up and face Lorna's green-eyed stare was because I didn't need to tell Lorna any of those things. She knew. She knew what I was. She knew and she'd helped. The strong, determined CEO of Sinful Threads was reduced to rubble, and she knew.

It hurt in a way that words couldn't describe.

Standing there looking at me, Lorna was a witness to my misery.

That was what she was.

It was bad enough for me to experience the wreckage of what was my life—I didn't want a witness. I shook my head again as I started to close the door.

"It isn't just you," she said, bringing my attention up to her pretty face as she reached out, blocking the closing of the door.

In that second, there was a flicker of something different. "What's not just me?"

Lorna tilted her head. "May I come in...I-I won't if you don't want me to. I've just never been on lockdown with someone before. You never know how long it will last and the men are all inaccessible. It's...so many emotions."

"Lockdown?"

She nodded.

I took a step back, allowing her entry to my cell. As she crossed the threshold, I noticed that other than that Lorna had on shoes and I only had socks, we were dressed similarly —yoga pants and t-shirts. Apparently, there was no need for formal attire during a lockdown. "You've gone through this before?"

She continued walking until she came to the small table and pulled out a chair. Sitting, she looked up at me. "I know this is all new to you, but I warned you." She shrugged. "I'm not sure you remember, but I mentioned it the first morning in the kitchen. I said that they would disappear for days on end. Sometimes it coincides with things we're aware of, like this..." She gestured about. "Other times, they're just gone."

I sat across the table from her. In the window behind her was my reflection. My emotions were broadcast over my face, written in tear tracks, swollen eyes, and splotches. "I can't believe he did it. He didn't even have the balls to tell me. He left me. I thought I was going. This is my best friend who's in trouble."

Lorna's head shook. "Did he tell you that you were going?"

"Yes..." I thought about it. "I think. He insinuated." My palm slapped the table with less force than I would have hours earlier. "Fuck, I don't know. I thought I was. Maybe it was just me. He kept saying things like that they were taking care of it. He said he had to talk to Reid, and the plane was about ready. He said he loved me." With my elbows on the table, I lowered my head to my hands. "I don't feel loved. I feel abandoned. I feel..."

"Like a child being locked in her room," Lorna said, completing my sentence.

I looked up to her emerald stare. "Yes." My lower lip began to tremble as salty tears burned my sore eyes. "I-I can't do this."

She reached over to take my hand.

Tentatively, I relinquished it to her, but quickly took it back. "I-I also don't know if I can trust you." My filter was gone. "I think he sent you to me, like you're here to smooth this over for him. Sterling doesn't deserve for you to do that. He screwed up. My friend's life and her baby are at stake."

She nodded. "I guess it may look like that, but that's not why I'm here. My intentions were what I said—I'm glad you're here."

I exhaled, wanting to believe her.

"Five days."

"What?" I asked.

"Five days was the longest. I had no communication with any of them. This place was as secure as it is now. We're always well-stocked on food. Shit, if I'd made a dinner for the three of them, I could live on it, three meals a day for five days. But the isolation and uncertainty were unbearable. I've seen some things no one should see, but the unknown is the worst."

I nodded, currently feeling the fear and total isolation she was describing. "Sterling said he'd call, but he hasn't."

"Reid and I had a serious knock-down, drag-out when they got home that first time. He was oblivious, not seeing my point of view. It was all about safety and protection."

My stomach turned. "Do you know how sick I am of hearing those words?"

A small smile skirted across her lips. "I have an idea." Lorna went on with her story. "Well, I told him that I loved him, and if he loved me at all, he'd never put me through that again. I needed communication." She took a deep breath and leaned back. "That was right after we were married. This life was new to me. I swear, I thought I was a caged animal. I spent five days afraid he was dead or Patrick or Sparrow or all of them. I worried that if that were true, I'd never get out."

"But you have the handprint thing, right?"

"Yes, but they can change it, making it so no one but them can get up and down. I mean, what if something happened to them and I'd been trapped?"

"So now?"

She shook her head. "No, I can't make it work either.

Lockdown means that these two floors and our apartment level are the only accessible floors. No garage and no bat cave."

"Bat cave?" I asked.

"It's where Reid spends most of his time. When he's gone from here, I know things are bad. He usually runs things from within while Sparrow and Patrick take to the streets."

"Where is he now?"

"I really don't know. I'm telling myself he's on two—the bat cave." She pulled her phone from a pocket on the side of her pants and laid it on the table. "He promised me a call or text message. That's what we do now. Even if he's on two, if the world is in emergency or lockdown, I may not see him for days."

I sighed. "Lorna, I don't know how you do it."

"I'd tell you that you get used to it. I could say that these otherwise considerate men are overprotective assholes and you get used to it, but honestly, it isn't that easy."

Overprotective assholes.

That made the tips of my lips move upward until they fell again. "My friend is...missing."

"I didn't know for sure. Reid only told me it had to do with Boulder. I know that's where you're from."

I swallowed the tears forming. "Her name is Louisa. We've been friends since high school..." For the next hour or more I rambled on, telling Lorna everything about Louisa—high school, college, and Sinful Threads. I talked about her family, her parents and sister. I told her about Jason and how they'd met. I even included how since Sterling came barreling into my life, I had been an awful friend. And how that now, I believe it's because of me that she'd been taken.

After I was done, Lorna got up and came to my chair. "I'd like to hug you."

I nodded, standing as I let my new friend give me support for my dear one.

"Hey," she said after taking a step back, "I looked up your company after I learned what you did. Damn, you guys are good."

"Thank you. It's been our baby, both of ours."

We were still standing.

"Goodness, it's nearly one in the morning," Lorna said, "but would you like to go to the kitchen and get something?"

I narrowed my gaze. "That sounds like Sterling."

She lifted her hands. "No, it's me. I've been pissed since Reid informed me of the lockdown. I'd love a glass of wine. Maybe some cheese and fruit."

I was tired, but the crying and worrying had me too wound up to sleep.

"Do you have a kitchen besides the one downstairs?" I asked.

Her eyes widened. "I do. Would you like to visit?"

"And get out of these two floors, hell yes."

"I'm not sure if—" She stopped and squared her shoulders. "Fuck them. Let's go."

It wasn't much of a rebellion, but I'd take it. "Let me grab my phone. I'm hoping for a call."

STERLING

A few hours earlier~

*N*ews came as soon as Jana and I entered the secured car. We weren't taking any chances. Like most of our vehicles in Chicago, the one we were riding in had reinforced metal and bulletproof windows. The driver was a man I recognized from our Chicago outfit, and I knew that Patrick had arranged for his temporary relocation—as well as for others from our outfit.

Patrick had also contacted an outfit—a cartel—in Denver. It would cost us, but they were helping with the rescue. The deal was something about allowing a percentage of their heroin to be sold on the streets of Chicago.

Quid pro quo.

That was how this world worked. Patrick negotiated the deal, and I'd authorized it.

"A new package just arrived," Patrick said through the

phone. "There's a cell phone in it. Kennedy is supposed to call the programmed number."

"Shit. Bridget looks like her; does she sound like her?" I asked.

"I sure as hell hope so."

"Isn't she with you?"

"She is," he said, "and to me she doesn't, but I know Araneae. To someone else, maybe."

Fuck.

"What about the courier?"

"He was legit, but the customer..." His voice trailed away as if he were distracted.

"What?" I asked, my ire growing.

"Carlos's men followed him to an old trailer in the middle of nowhere up in the mountains."

Carlos was the Denver cartel leader who was now welcome to sell drugs in my city. Not drugs—heroin—one drug. I'd have some upset gangs and dealers, but it didn't matter. My city, my streets. They deal with me or they don't sell. At least if they'd found the location where they were hiding Louisa, the deal with Carlos was paying off on our end.

"What are the logistics?" I asked. "What are the chances that's where they have Louisa?"

"Logistics are awful. It's high enough in the mountains that the trees are few. There's no good way to surprise them other than to rush it. Chances that she's there, I think, are good. Reid has been searching for aerial views. He's tapped into some real-time satellites and according to what he's seeing, there's only one access road. Carlos has drones that are able to see if the road is guarded, so they'll go in prepared. His drones also sense temperature. Soon we'll know how many people are in the trailer."

"Fuck. Drones? Won't they hear them?"

"He says," Patrick went on, "that they're used all the time to watch for DEA and ICE. Says they're so common out in the mountains and desert areas around here that people are as used to them buzzing around as fucking mosquitoes. His words, not mine."

"The call can't be made until we're there. Remember, Araneae..." I looked at Jana sitting to my side. "...is with me."

"We know. So do they. The note said that as soon as she arrives, she needs to call."

"You're being watched." I hated having an emotional attachment to this mission. It was a liability, and McFadden was capitalizing on it. I looked at maps on my phone. "We should be there in less than twenty minutes. No news to the women until we know for sure, until we have Louisa safe and sound."

"I'll pass that along to Reid. At this moment, he's too busy comparing images and watching to say a word."

"I don't want to disappoint Araneae," I said. "Fuck, we need to do this tonight."

"See you in twenty."

I turned to Jana. "Winnie's place is being watched. I'm going to need you to walk in the house with me."

She nodded and let out a long breath.

"You're going to be safe," I said.

"I believe you."

I spent the rest of the drive looking at images Reid sent as well as corresponding with both him and Patrick. Though the resolution on the satellite images weren't great, it was interesting to see how close to the ground a satellite in space could focus. Those images were nothing compared to the drones. The FAA regulations limited the drone's altitude to no higher than four hundred feet. Higher than that and they would interfere with national airspace and potentially set off alarms. We didn't need to let that happen. The problem was that the tree line or timberline in the Rocky Mountains varied from 11,000 to 12,000 feet.

The trailer in question was in a sparsely populated, secluded area outside the national park.

PATRICK came on my screen.

"REID JUST CONFIRMED THREE PEOPLE IN THE TRAILER. ONE IS THE WEASELLY GUY THEY FOLLOWED FROM THE COURIER."

I texted back.

"WHAT CONFIRMATION DO WE HAVE ON MCFADDEN'S LOCATION?"

PATRICK replied:

"LAST SEEN IN WASHINGTON DC FRIDAY NIGHT AT A DINNER WITH HIS WIFE."

. . .

I doubted that Rubio would be here in Boulder. It wasn't his modus operandi to get his hands dirty. That didn't mean he hadn't ordered it. My skin itched with determination, the need for retaliation. However, I didn't want to have it done in front of Louisa. She didn't need to see that any more than Araneae did.

I sent another question.

"ARE WE SET TO RUSH THE TRAILER?"

PATRICK:

"YES."

The car came to a stop in front of a simple house in South Boulder. From our earlier research we knew that Winifred Douglas's house was a rental. She'd lived in it since before she became employed by Sinful Threads. The financials were all solid. South Boulder, where she lived, was south and east of Boulder while the trailer in question was west, up into the mountains.

Hurrying with my hand again on Jana's back, we practically ran into the house. As we did, she kept her face down, her cheeks covered with the coat's collar and her long blonde wig secured in a ponytail similar to one Araneae would wear.

The door opened immediately to Patrick, and we hurried inside, the door shutting behind us as we entered the house full of people. This had become Patrick's command center, yet from the outside it didn't appear as so. The cars for all of these people had been hidden so as to not alert the kidnappers. Quickly, Patrick made introductions. Most of the people were from Chicago, Patrick confident in their loyalty. Only one man present was one of Carlos's cartel.

"Where is Winnie?" I asked.

"She's in her bedroom with Jason."

I looked down at my wrist. "It is nearly eleven. Are you sure they're secure?"

"Yeah, Jason woke." Patrick tilted his head to a woman sitting on the couch who he'd introduced as a physician. "Dr. Moore has been watching him."

The woman nodded.

"He doesn't remember a thing of what happened," Patrick continued. "She had to give him something to calm him down. Now he's groggy and keeps asking for Louisa."

I shook my head. "I want to get them both back in their home with a twenty-four-seven bodyguard and let them think this was a bad dream."

If only the flashy things in the old movie *Men in Black* existed. It would make our job a lot easier.

Patrick nodded and handed me the last package. "Here's what arrived."

"Mr. Sparrow."

I looked up to the unfamiliar voice. She'd not been present during introductions. Her eyes were a darker brown and there was something different about her lips, but I had to agree: this woman's similarities to Araneae were astounding. "Bridget, I presume."

"Yes, sir. It's nice to meet you. I'm sorry about the circumstances."

"If you pull this off, you will be well compensated."

She inhaled sharply. "I've spent hours with Winnie and Patrick, trying to know the answer to any proposed question."

"Where were you born?" I asked.

"I was told Chicago, but recently I learned it was Wisconsin."

I nodded. "Your name?"

"I was born Araneae McCrie, raised Renee Marsh, and at the age of sixteen became Kennedy Hawkins."

"Family?" I continued asking basic questions.

After she answered with knowledge of the Marshes and limited knowledge of the McCries, she mentioned the fictitious Hawkinses, killed in a car accident.

"Louisa?"

"My best friend since high school. Pregnant with her first child." As she answered, her voice cracked with emotion.

"Your voice is too deep," I said. "Try again."

"My best friend—"

I lifted my hand. "Much better. Remember that."

"Yes, sir," she said, her tone closer to Araneae's.

"Eventually, they're going to want to meet with you in person. Go along with whatever they say. We need to know their plan. Even if we get Louisa tonight, we need to understand what they're after."

She nodded.

"Very good." I turned back to Patrick. "I agree, during the call is the time to do it. We'll have eyes and ears in the trailer if they allow Louisa to speak."

She was our wild card. If they allowed her to speak, would

she play along with Bridget pretending to be Kennedy? It was why we'd decided to rush the trailer sooner rather than later.

"Are Carlos's men set?" I asked.

"We are," Mandy, the man from the cartel, said. He was shorter than most of my men, but in no way did it diminish his aura of power. This wasn't Carlos, the head of the cartel, but he was a trusted associate.

Patrick nodded, his eyes on the tablet in his hand as well as a laptop open on the table. He'd been on the ground here for nearly a day. I had faith in his command of the operation.

"His men are set," Patrick said, "and our men are waiting to take her after Carlos's get her out. His men know this area better."

My heart was beating incredibly fast, though on the exterior I appeared as calm as Patrick. "Let them know—"

"Mr. Sparrow?"

I turned to see Winnie standing in a narrow hallway, eyeing her living room and kitchen that were filled with people. Her complexion paled as she came closer.

"I wanted to tell you that I'm sorry about what happened in Chicago. If any of this with Louisa is my fault—"

"Ms. Douglas, when we make it through tonight all is forgotten."

Swallowing, she nodded. "I want to forget it all." Her glassy eyes moved from me to behind me.

Looking the other way, I saw Jana, still wearing the blonde wig, standing quietly while leaning against the wall. I tilted my head from Jana to Winnie. Jana nodded as she moved through the room and made her way to Winnie.

"How about a cup of tea?" Jana asked, wrapping her arm around Winnie.

"If we can get in the kitchen," she replied.

I turned to Patrick and Bridget. "Let's do this." I spoke directly to Bridget. "Remember, try to speak to Louisa. If you do, we'll have confirmation that she's there and alive." I hated saying those words—of admitting doubt. That was why this wasn't Araneae in front of me but a professional.

JOSEY

Twenty-three years ago ~

I leaned against the kitchen counter as Byron shrugged his shoulder in response to my question. I was beginning to get used to his blond hair and the shape of his nose. The old Neal had been hit in the nose when he was younger, making it wider and less defined. The plastic surgeons had straightened as well as thinned it. Remarkably, it gave him a completely different look. What would never change were his green, almost golden, eyes. I don't know what I would have said if they'd talked about changing our eye color.

Probably nothing.

It wasn't like we had a voice in what was done.

They'd even put veneers on our teeth, giving our mouths a different shape.

Three years ago when it all happened, we both lost days, maybe a week. Much of the surgery, oral and facial, was done while we were under anesthesia. We literally woke as new people.

Sometimes it was easy to forget, to fall into the routine our lives had become. It was as if we had awakened into a fairy tale in suburban America, the nearly perfect family. We didn't have the 2.5 children, only one, our Renee. Yet last year we'd added a gray kitten to our family. Renee named him Kitty. It wasn't the most masculine name for our tomcat, so we added a mister to the front. Mr. Kitty came to his name as readily as the three of us had adapted to our new names. Most importantly, Renee adored him. And even though he was a big cat, he tolerated her affection to a fault.

Yes, I could slip into the security brought on by our new names and lives.

And then something would happen, something seemingly innocuous that would set my heart to racing and bring a cold layer of perspiration to my skin. Today it was a man who came to our door, saying that he was doing a survey for the next census.

At first, I was fine, no alarms sounded, until Renee came running up behind me and peered up at him from the safety of behind my legs. Though the screen door was between us, my pulse sped up as the man smiled, a smile that twisted my stomach into knots. He lowered himself to his haunches and spoke directly to Renee.

"What's your name, beautiful?"

She looked up at me with her chocolate eyes as I shook my head no.

"Come on, sweetheart," he said. "You can talk to me. Your mommy was talking to me."

I ran my hand over her soft, silky hair. I'd pulled what

little bit she had back into two pigtails, reminding me of the youngest child on a show I watched as a kid. We teasingly called her Cindy when her hair was like that, me for the daughter on the *Brady Bunch* and Byron because he thought it made her look like Cindy Lou Who from Dr. Seuss, some of her favorite books for us to read.

I tucked her behind me. "We're teaching her not to speak to strangers," I said, my neck straightening as I stared down at the man still staring at our daughter.

Finally, when she wouldn't answer, he stood back up to his height. "She sure is pretty, ma'am."

"Thank you. I believe we're done with your survey."

He looked down at his clipboard. "Just the three of you living here?"

"And Mr. Kitty," Renee said in her sweet three-year-old voice.

He bent back down. "You have a kitty?"

Renee nodded. "That's his name."

"Kitty is your cat's name?"

She nodded again, once more moving to behind my legs.

He stood tall again. "I believe, Mrs. Marsh, that does it for now."

I started to take a step and close the solid door when he paused. "You all stay safe."

My stomach twisted, knots on top of knots, as my hands shook as I fumbled with the solid door and lock. Trying not to alarm Renee, I casually walked about the house. Door by door, I moved until I'd confirmed each outside door was secure.

"Mommy, Mr. Kitty is out there," Renee said, pointing to the backyard. "Memeba, you let him outside?"

I peered beyond the taut white curtain obstructing the windows on our back door. Sure enough, sprawled out on the back deck, lying in the sun, was Mr. Kitty. I told myself he'd be all right. The backyard was fenced, a six-foot-tall wooden fence, and the gates were always closed and locked.

"Go get him," she said, her eyes pleading. "I don't wants him outside with that man."

I looked again at the deck. Mr. Kitty hadn't moved. Steeling my neck and shoulders, I unlocked and opened the door. Mr. Kitty's head turned my way as my gaze scanned the yard beyond the deck to Renee's swing set and sandbox. "Come on in, Mr. Kitty," I said, talking to him while watching. As I reached down to lift him, I saw it out of the corner of my eye. The side gate was open wide.

Carrying Mr. Kitty and shooing Renee back into the house, I again locked the door.

"Why did you say you didn't want him with that man?" I asked, wondering what she'd seen.

"'Cause he was a stranger."

That didn't answer my question though I hesitated to push, to alarm her in any way.

Now, I was here with Byron, wanting him to share in my alarm, as Renee was in the living room singing and dancing to one of her Disney sing-along videotapes.

He shrugged again. "I don't know, Josey. I might have left it open after mowing the yard."

"You never leave it open. What if Mr. Kitty had gotten out?"

"I don't have an answer." He reached for my shoulders and kissed my forehead. "I understand why you worry, but there's nothing to worry about."

I lowered my voice. "Do you know that? Have you talked to Mr. Sparrow?"

"No, Neal Curry is dead to the outfit. I can't just call him. You know we have very specific instructions on sending information on Renee. I can't just show up at Sparrow Enterprises. Remember, I also walked out on my job there. I'd be shot if I approached the house."

"What if that man was Sparrow's?"

"Then he saw what he was supposed to see. Renee is still here. So are we. We're doing as we were told."

"I don't like it. Maybe we could get away sooner rather than later?" I asked.

"We need to save money. I'm doing that, but it takes time."

"What if Mr. Sparrow knows about the money? What if that man was a warning?" I stood straighter. "He told us to stay safe. Who does that?"

"Maybe a kind gentleman who wants people to stay safe."

"I saw McCrie on the news the other day. He's back to working for McFadden."

Byron shook his head. "Baby, that life is over for us. Don't fixate on it."

"I still don't understand why if McCrie works for McFadden, if his sister is married to Rubio, why McCrie would arrange for Allister Sparrow to watch over his daughter."

Byron opened the refrigerator and took out a beer. "When's dinner?"

I closed my eyes. "Think about it."

"I have," he said through a clenched jaw. "I've spent three years thinking about it."

"And what have you decided?"

"Maybe he didn't ask for Sparrow's help."

I shook my head. "I don't know what you mean."

"The paper said that..." He dropped his voice to a whisper. "...they announced the death of their child. Maybe neither McCrie nor his wife know she's alive." He shrugged. "I mean, I don't know."

"McCrie was at the hospital. I think he knew."

"You went to the hospital? Why haven't you ever told me?" His hand went to his hair. "Oh my God, Josey, what if Sparrow would have found out."

"He's the one who sent me." I shrugged. "One of his people. I was supposed to get Renee. I couldn't imagine giving up a child. I had to talk to the mother." Tears came to my eyes. "She didn't know. I wanted to tell her the truth so badly, to ease some of her pain. But what could I say? Your daughter isn't dead, but I have to take her." I peeked around the corner to the living room, confirming that Renee's interest was on the television and not on us. I lifted my right arm. "She gave me this bracelet, telling me to please have it buried with her baby girl, Araneae."

"Araneae? Is that why you wanted her name to be Renee?"

I nodded. "I hoped the one request could be granted by Sparrow's people, the ones with the documents."

"I thought that was some old bracelet, one you said you didn't want to leave behind."

"I didn't lie to you, Byron. It is."

He lifted my wrist and looked at the charms dangling from the gold links. "What are you going to do with this?"

"I don't know," I said truthfully. "I imagine one day giving it to Renee, telling her it was from her birth mother and that she loved her too, like we do, so much that she knew that giving her to us was best, safest."

Byron shook his head. "You can't tell her any of that. She can't know how we got her."

"She knows she didn't grow in my belly. When she asked about Patricia, next door, and why her tummy was getting bigger, I told her that babies grow in their mommies' bellies. She made the natural assumption. I told her that even though she didn't grow inside me, we loved her very much and she was our gift."

"She's three years old."

"And she accepted it. No more questions."

He took a deep breath. "Next time, talk to me first before you tell her anything that could come back to hurt her."

"That's what I'm trying to avoid, hurting her. I'm being as honest as I can. She's smart. She asks questions. She watches and sees. That's why I'm afraid she saw that man in our yard."

"You don't know that," Byron said.

I didn't reply.

"I'll get new locks for the gates."

"Thank you."

STERLING

*T*he note in the package with the cell phone had directions for Kennedy to call as soon as she arrived from Chicago. If we were right and the house was being watched, our time was nearly up. The entire house silenced, holding a collective breath, as Bridget put the phone on speaker and pushed the call button.

I nodded to Patrick and Mandy, telling them to send in Carlos's men. Patrick had set this operation in motion, but now that I was here, I was in charge. Both men nodded as they sent their appropriate messages. The only instructions to the cartel men had been to rescue Louisa. If possible, I wanted the chance to question the kidnappers, but not as badly as I wanted Louisa safe. If the cartel got their kicks taking McFadden's men out, they could go for it. Reid could trace all their electronics to confirm their connection to McFadden. If it wasn't him, we were back to square one.

"Ms. Hawkins?" a deep voice through the phone's speaker asked, "Kennedy Hawkins?"

Familiar chills of anticipation ran down my spine. This life wasn't for the faint of heart. It took the right men and women to stare death in the face and walk away unscathed. To willingly face it time after time was either insanity or incredible fortitude. All of us gathered here were standing on the edge of a cliff, the spot where adrenaline kicks up the pulse and fingers blanch as they clench into fists. It was the fight-or-flight instinct that in people like us was defective.

There was no flight, only fight.

No backing away. No receding into hiding places.

It was kill or be killed.

Though I could say that people like Reid, Patrick, and I, as well as others in my outfit, acquired that psychological response in the army or in other branches of the military, it wouldn't be completely accurate. With the three of us, I believed we honed it in the army, in the desert, and in decimated towns. However, to truly stand tall and unwavering and stare down the grim reaper time after time, that defective instinct had to be wired into your DNA. Only men and women with ice-cold hearts could do it and come back for more. We were a unique breed, a brotherhood when we worked together, mortal enemies when we didn't.

For most in this small house, we qualified, and today we were brothers and sisters working for one cause.

Perhaps that DNA was another thing I should thank my father for.

Maybe I would, when we met in hell.

For others, this life—this business—was unbelievable, unfathomable.

I couldn't worry about Winnie or the doctor and how they would deal with the aftermath. Patrick had found the doctor through the cartel. She'd be well paid and if she talked, she'd die. It was the simple truth she understood well. If she didn't comprehend that, she wouldn't work for them.

As for Winnie—and hopefully Louisa if she survived—their rose-colored glasses would never fit again. It was the hard truth.

My eyes went to Patrick, wondering if he thought the voice on the phone sounded familiar. There was no distinct accent or unique characteristic. As I ran his question— "Ms. Hawkins? Kennedy Hawkins?"—through the databases of my mind, his voice sounded like every man while at the same time no man whom I knew.

Thankfully, Reid was doing the same thing as I but not mentally—technologically. He was running the voice on the phone, via a connection on Patrick's laptop, through thousands of voice patterns, looking for a match.

"Yes, this is she," Bridget replied to his question.

I pointed upward. Her tone needed to be higher.

Bridget cleared her throat—which I hoped sounded like nerves and not what it was.

"May I please speak to Louisa?" Bridget asked, her voice quivered appropriately with a sprinkling of fear.

"In a minute," he replied hastily. "First, I'm going to tell you exactly what you need to do to see your friend again, and I mean not in a morgue."

I nodded, encouraging Bridget to get to Louisa.

Her eyes were wide on me as she listened and spoke. "I want to be sure she's all right. Please let me—"

"Answer my question. Who's your mother?"

My stomach tightened. That wasn't a simple answer.

"My birth mother or the woman who raised me?"

"Kennedy Hawkins's mother."

"On my Kennedy birth certificate, it says Debbie Hawkins."

I exhaled.

"Now please—" Bridget continued.

"My client," he interrupted, "wants the information—the evidence—your birth father hid."

She must have answered the question the way he wanted.

Wait? Client?

"I don't have any information. That's an old wives' tale," she said immediately as I said a silent thank-you to Patrick for his thorough work with briefing Bridget.

"He thinks you do," the man said. "He thinks that you have the key. Stop lying and get me the evidence. Once you do, you're going to call me on this phone and arrange a transfer. Those CDs for Ms. Toney."

CDs?

"I need to hear—"

He continued to talk. "We have eyes. We know Sparrow is your fucking shadow; he won't let you out of his or Kelly's sight. Otherwise, it would be you here instead of your friend. Can you live with yourself if you let her take this fall?"

"Please."

Damn, my hands fisted tighter, itching to strike. I wanted to climb through the fucking phone and take out this guy. At the moment, I didn't care if it was in front of Louisa or not if I got to just watch him bleed out for the way he was talking to Araneae—even if it wasn't her.

"Better hurry..." He chuckled. "...and get Sparrow to help

you because this lady here is about to have a kid—like any minute. We aren't set up for no babies. Hate to have to kill two people because you can't follow directions."

I sucked in a breath and looked to Patrick. I fucking wanted to hear commotion on the other end of this line.

Where were Carlos's men?

"Please," Bridget pleaded again, doing a great impression of Araneae, "let me speak to her. I need to know...She's my best friend...May I-I see her?"

It was risky for her to initiate a visual call, but keeping him on the line and confirming Louisa's safety were the priorities.

"Once you get the evidence," he said, "you—not your bodyguard or Sparrow—will bring it to me. I suppose you know not to contact the police or feds. If I so much as hear a rumor that you've talked to the feds again..." His words trailed away before coming back louder, "What the fuck?"

The line went silent, but not before a woman's distant scream and the crackling and popping of gunfire erupted on the other end. It sounded like someone had set off a packet of firecrackers.

I sucked in a breath.

Bridget's hand shook as she looked down at the screen that indicated the call had ended. "Was that? We didn't get to talk to Louisa," she said, tears coming to her eyes. "I don't even know her." She looked up at me. "I'm sorry, Mr. Sparrow."

Winnie and Jana were staring at Bridget, their eyes also moist with emotion as they held on to each other's hands for comfort.

My mind spun, wanting answers, worried about Louisa,

and imagining the unimaginable task of telling Araneae news that would break her heart.

"The man on the line said he was going to let her talk," Patrick said, breaking the dooming silence. "That means she's there. It also means that as of a few seconds ago, she was able to talk and that..." He turned to Mandy. "...your men are at the right place."

"I want answers," I declared to the room. "We're being watched. This house needs to be secured."

Under the cover of night, three of our outfit's men slipped out the back door and into the shadows. South Boulder wasn't ready for a gun battle in a quiet neighborhood, but if we were approached, it would get one.

The clock ticked. Yet time fucking stood still as the walls of Winnie's house figuratively closed in around us.

ARANEAE

$\mathcal{I}$t felt good to leave our apartment, if only to the floor below. The elevator opened to an open area, a communal sitting room with sofas and chairs, reminding me of a lobby of a hotel.

"Do you use this area much?"

"No," Lorna said. "Just another place to clean."

"I'm sorry. I should do more upstairs. It isn't fair to you."

She waved her hand. "Don't mind me. I'm upset about the lockdown too. Hopefully it will be resolved and your friend will be safe. I'm fine with what I do. I don't have an amazing silk fashions design house to run."

My mind went to Sinful Threads and then to Louisa, Jason, and baby Kennedy. "The last time I talked to Sterling, he said her husband was found and should be fine." I looked down at my phone. "I can't believe I haven't heard another word from him."

"Have you called or texted?"

"A million times right after he left. Now, I'm as mad as I am curious. I hope he, Patrick, or Reid will tell me what they can, when they can."

She led me to the door on the right. "Come on in. Welcome to Reid's and my home."

It made me smile, thinking that we all lived together, yet Lorna was able to consider this space theirs. "Do you mind my being here? I don't want to intrude."

"No," she said with a grin. "I like it. As you can imagine, this life doesn't allow for many—okay, *any*—visitors. Having you here makes me feel like..." She shrugged. "...like I'm having a friend over for wine."

"And cheese," I said. "You mentioned cheese."

As she opened the door, I stepped behind her and looked around at their home. "Oh goodness. I love it. It's so different from upstairs and yet so spacious and you."

"Me?"

Eclectic, a bit hipster chic, and at the same time homey.

I stood at the doorway, taking in the large living room that connected to the dining area of her kitchen. The wall to the right and the far wall were made of all glass, the same tall windows as upstairs. The living room was sleek with colorful paintings, many like the ones in Sterling's office. The gray sofas and chairs were littered with accent pillows and throws in varying colors matching the paintings.

I took a step toward one of the paintings on the wall. The signature was from Jean-Michel Basquiat. "Sterling has one of these in his office."

She nodded. "I liked his, so Reid surprised me with this one. I can't believe we own something that is similar to what they hang in museums. He's good at picking up on what I like and don't like."

"Like chess?"

Her smile broadened. "Hmm."

"I guess it's easier to think about that than being left alone for five days," I said wistfully, hoping and praying it wouldn't be five days. Five hours had been unbearable enough.

Lorna turned on lights, and hitting another button, she brought their fireplace roaring to life. "I know it's summer, but when I'm upset a fire with wine makes me feel better."

I watched the flames for a moment, trying to comprehend that it was now Sunday morning and only twenty-four hours ago, Sterling and I were on a yacht on Lake Michigan, and now, Lorna and I were in some strange reality where something called lockdowns not only existed but removed us from the real world.

I pulled myself away from the flames and trailed after her to the kitchen. "I like the fire. It's a good idea." When I turned from the dining area, I stopped and took in Lorna's kitchen. While not as large as the one upstairs, it held all the same fancy appliances and hard-surface counters. One difference was the backsplash. It was colorful tile that brought sparks of red, yellow, and orange to the walls. When she hit another switch, LED lights made the tile glow, as if like the fireplace, they were made of real fire. Hanging from cords over the island were more lights. These were shaped like flames with bulbs within them that gently flickered.

"You like fire," I said.

"I like warmth. I hate being cold."

"Do you cook in here too?"

"Sometimes. It depends. One day I'll only cook here and

take the food upstairs. Another day, the opposite." She shrugged. "Depends on my mood and it changes things up." Turning, she opened a wine refrigerator built into the cabinet and asked me what I'd like.

"Moscato, white if you have it."

Lorna grinned. "Like I said, I do the shopping. I keep us well stocked."

I looked at the size of the wine refrigerator. "If this is going to last for five days, we may run short."

"Oh, there's plenty upstairs, too."

After I helped Lorna slice some different cheeses and took the plate to the living room, I grabbed the bottle of moscato and a stemmed glass and went back to one of the sofas. As I sat down, I again took my phone from my pocket and laid it on the table.

On the screen I saw the icon indicating I'd missed a call.

STERLING on the screen.

"Oh my God. How did I miss it?"

"What?" Lorna asked, coming from the kitchen with her own bottle of wine and a glass.

My hands shook as I lifted the phone. It was after two in the morning now, and I wasn't sure I could listen to a message. I didn't know if I could handle the news. What if it was bad?

Sterling had promised me that he'd be with me when I learned good or bad. He'd made that promise about my family, but damn, Louisa qualified as family. For years, the Nelsons had been all I knew.

"What?" Lorna asked again.

I pointed at the phone on the table. "I-I missed a call from Sterling."

"How? You've had your phone with you the whole time." When I only looked wide-eyed at her and back to the phone, she went on, "Did he leave a message? Are you going to listen to it?"

I tried to swallow. "I'm so scared. I wish he were here." I looked up at Lorna as she sat beside me. "Don't get me wrong. I'm pissed as hell at him. I want to scream at him, call him every name I can conjure up, cuss like a sailor, and beat my fists against his fucking chest."

Lorna nodded. "And then you want him to wrap you in his arms and tell you it's all right. Your friend, her husband, and their baby are all safe and healthy. You want him to tell you that he, Patrick, and Reid are all home and safe. You want him to tell you that life will go on."

Tears were again raining down my cheeks. "Yes. I want all of that."

"Hey, while you're making demands, don't forget about your hand on the sensor. I have ten dollars riding on that."

The throbbing in my temples resumed. "I need to listen to his message."

I lifted the phone as if it were a snake capable of injecting venom, and I swiped the screen.

"How long ago did he call?" she asked.

"Just five minutes ago. I don't understand how I missed it." I checked the ringer. "It doesn't make sense. The ringer is on and it should have vibrated."

"It's 2:22 here," Lorna said, opening the wine bottles. "Boulder is only one hour behind, right?"

I nodded as my heart beat wildly like a drum vibrating in my chest, the pulsations reverberating to my hands and making them shaky. Taking aim, I touched the voicemail icon and lifted the phone to my ear.

Sterling's deep voice came through the phone. "I hope you're asleep. We'll be on our way home in another hour. I know I promised to be with you when I gave you news."

More tears formed at the sound of his voice.

"I know you're upset with me, but our plan worked."

Worked? What does that mean?

"I think that just this once, I can break my promise. I think you need to know sooner rather than later. And if you wake and see this message, I don't want you to worry any longer. Louisa and Jason are safe. She's on her way to the Lutheran Medical Center outside of Denver, by ambulance. Not because it's an emergency. That hospital is where they have the top NICU department on-site. She's not in labor. This is strictly for prevention. I'll tell you more in the morning. Not only are they safe, but we're also arranging around-the-clock individual surveillance until this thing is settled."

What needs to be settled?

"I need to go. We have a few things to wrap up.

"Sunshine, you can hate me, but I needed to concentrate on Louisa and know you were safe. You can hate me, but it won't stop me from loving you."

The voicemail ended.

My cheeks were covered in tears and my nose was running. I was as far as one could be from the picture of regality Sterling had told me to be at the club what seemed like a million years ago. Laying my phone in my lap, I turned to Lorna. "She's safe. They did it."

She leaned forward and gave me another hug. "Praise be."

I nodded. "I'm still mad at him."

"I don't blame you."

"But I guess I understand."

Lorna poured moscato in my glass and then something red in her own. After handing mine to me, she lifted hers and said, "To Louisa."

Our glasses clinked before we each took a sip.

"Do you think it would still be all right for me to do all the things I said?"

"The yelling, hitting, cursing...? That stuff?" Lorna asked.

I nodded, taking another longer sip.

"I would, after you wrap your arms around him and tell him how grateful you are that Louisa and the baby are safe."

I shrugged. "It seems like the wrong order."

Lorna winked. "It will keep him on his toes."

ARANEAE

At a little after three in the morning, Lorna rode up the elevator with me to the first floor of Sterling's and my apartment. When the doors opened, she smiled. "It will be better in the morning."

"Now that I know Louisa is safe, I want to do that," I said, pointing at the sensor.

"Ten dollars on you."

The elevator doors shut, leaving me alone in the vastness of the penthouse. My stocking feet slid on the marble floor as I made my way to the stairs. With my hand on the banister I stopped and turned toward the archways to the sitting and the living rooms. With the only illumination the moon's glow coming from the windows, the apartment took on a silver hue.

Although nothing about the penthouse had changed since going down to Lorna and Reid's apartment, it felt different—in a good way.

I still couldn't make the elevator work, but I knew I was safe. I knew Louisa and Jason were safe. As wrong as the world and my life might be, it was right.

I was home.

Walking up the stairs toward our bedroom, I smiled, recalling Reid and Lorna's conversation. It occurred minutes after I'd listened to Sterling's message. Not only had Reid given Lorna the same information, he let her know that lockdown should be over after Patrick and Sterling returned. The part that made me smile was when he also mentioned that he knew I was in their apartment. Lorna just laughed. When she hung up, she repeated what he'd said and reminded me again that when it came to those three, I should accept that they will always know our whereabouts.

It seemed overwhelming, overbearing, and even overkill, yet knowing that I wasn't alone, that Reid was the same way with Lorna, somehow gave me the willingness to accept it for what it was. Sterling said over and over that the world he'd brought me into—the one I'd been born into—was dangerous. As long as he and Patrick and Reid were able to save Louisa, my momentary internment in the gilded cage seemed less upsetting.

Our bedroom was quiet as I switched on a few lights turning the giant windows into mirrors. Like the apartment as a whole, the bedroom no longer felt like a prison cell. It was where I wanted to be until Sterling returned and I learned more about Louisa and Jason.

In Sterling's message, he'd said I could hate him but he'd keep loving me. That sentiment played on repeat in my head as I readied for bed, washing my face and brushing my teeth. As I pulled a long satin nightgown over my head and it slid down my body, I decided that I could do both. I had. I'd been upset—irate. I'd hated him in that moment and the moments that followed. That didn't mean that I'd stopped loving him.

I'd heard once that love and hate were the flip sides of the same coin, so closely related that you couldn't experience one without the other.

Climbing into our big bed, I settled with a sense of contentment that a few hours earlier I never imagined having. Pulling Sterling's pillow to my chest, I inhaled his lingering scent, the combination of clean bodywash and his cologne. The realization that my coin had flipped came as his aroma comforted me. Before I could give it more thought, sleep quickly took over.

I woke to the rhythm of Sterling's breathing, his warm, hard body wrapped around mine, my back to his front, secure in his embrace. I hadn't heard him enter the room or the bed. Blinking, I focused on the bedroom filled with sunlight, having no idea what time of day it was or how long I'd slept. The sky beyond the large windows was blue with large fluffy white clouds in the distance. As I started to move, his embrace tightened, pulling me closer.

"I'm not letting you go." The gravelliness of sleep infiltrated his deep tenor as his warm breath skirted over my hair.

I remembered all the things I wanted to say, the way I wanted to fight back for what he'd done, yet for some reason, none of that came out. Instead, I marveled that he was here, still sleeping with me when I woke. As I settled against him, my emotions came out in salty tears.

Sterling rolled me toward him, my front to his, as he gently wiped a tear from my cheek. "She's safe. No more crying."

I nodded, letting my forehead fall against his chest, yet the tears continued. My voice was muffled as I swallowed the tears. "Thank you for what you did for her."

"Patrick and Reid should get most of the credit."

I peered upward to his gaze. "I want to go to her, to see her and Winnie. I can't imagine what they went through."

"Winnie saw it from the outside. She understands what happened and the importance of keeping quiet. Jason doesn't recall a thing. Louisa knows that she was taken, but she never saw her captor. She has no idea why it happened. We convinced them to keep the police out of it. After we got Louisa to Winnie's house we called the ambulance and had her taken to the Lutheran Medical Center just outside of Denver to be checked out. She told the EMTs that she wasn't feeling well. They're going to keep her for observation. If all is fine today, she'll probably go home."

"Sterling, I want to see her—in person."

He nodded. "I know. You will."

"Is she safe?"

"I'll be completely honest with you. This isn't over. That's why we have Sparrows watching everyone. Before, it was one watching Jason, Louisa, and her parents." He shook his head. "Now they all have one, including Lindsey in Boston."

"Do they know?" I asked.

"Louisa and Jason do. She asked that the ones watching her parents and sister stay low. She was afraid it would upset her mother. Lindsey's isn't new. He's been there for a while."

I nodded. "Will it end?"

"I believe it will. You have to trust me, trust us."

Finally, I lifted my chin, searching for the reassurance of

his dark stare. I did trust him, yet I too needed to be honest. "What you did hurt me."

He nodded, pulling me close. "What we do isn't something I want you to see, to know."

"But this wasn't a random situation. This was my best friend."

"Which, if it hadn't gone well, would have made it worse." He caressed my cheek. "I won't stand by and allow the sunshine in your eyes to fade. Always know that whatever I do is for your safety."

Before I could respond, he placed his finger over my lips and continued, "I'm certain you're tired of hearing that, but I won't stop saying it. Araneae, you are mine. Keeping you safe, protecting you...it will always be my first priority, always."

"I'm not a child. I need to be informed and consulted. I'm not saying that I won't be mad. I probably will." My fist came to his shoulder though my punch was nothing like I'd envisioned—a tap against the bulk of his hard muscle. "Don't do that again. If I need to be on lockdown ever again, be man enough to tell me to my face. I don't want to go through the emotions I had last night ever again. I thought I was going with you."

Lifting my chin with his thumb, he watched my eyes. In his brown orbs I saw a million emotions battling for supremacy, for the right to be said and the right to be heard. I'd come to know that Sterling Sparrow would only voice the one that won.

Finally, he replied, "I don't make promises that I can't keep. Last night, I broke one, and I won't make another that may need to be broken."

I leaned away. "So you're saying that you won't promise not to leave me here against my will?"

"Araneae, tell me. Are you here against your will? In *our* apartment? In *our* bed? In *my* arms? Are you here unwillingly?"

I sighed. "No."

"I can't make the promise you want to hear because things happen that are beyond my control. I will promise that if it's possible for me to tell you in person, I will." His head shook. "You're right about yesterday. I should have told you; however, I never said you were coming. You assumed that."

"And you let me."

"I did because I didn't want to fight with you. I needed to learn what Patrick and Reid knew. Louisa had already been gone for too long. I had to jump into the situation with both feet. I can do many things, but with you it's different."

"How?" I asked.

"You've made me want what I've never before wanted. I never gave a shit about what people thought..." His shoulder shrugged. "...with the exception of the people in this apartment. That being said, I make decisions based on what is best for Sparrow and for Sparrow Enterprises. I learn the facts and move from there. It's not about emotion. Emotion is a weakness in my world that I can't afford. Emotion changes things and blurs the goal. Cold hard facts, gut intuitions—that's what fosters success. Once my decisions are made, they're carried out. I don't wallow in the consequences. I move on.

"With you, I fucking care what you think. I don't want you to see the side of me that went into action last night. I want you to see a man who loves you and for you to look at me like you are now." His finger again moved over my cheek. "I want those fucking gorgeous, light-chocolate eyes of yours to see a man who will do anything in the world for you, not to see what that means."

"I see that man. Last night..." I searched for the right words. "...what you did...I can understand it, but I was beyond angry. I don't like feeling out of control or like a child who's been punished. I love you. That didn't stop even when I was hating you. One day, when this is settled, I need you to promise you will allow me more control."

"There will always be dangers."

"Yes, that's why I need to have some control."

"When this is over," he said. "I promise."

I sighed, melting against him, my softness against his hardness. We were opposites in so many ways, yet we fit together perfectly as our hearts beat as one.

ARANEAE

*S*terling's large hands splayed across my lower back, moving downward over my behind as he pulled me closer. My nipples grew tight beneath the satin of my nightgown, and his growing erection probed against my tummy.

A soft moan escaped my lips as he bunched my nightgown, his fingers trailing over my skin, pulling the material higher until I wiggled, allowing him to bring it over my head and leaving me bare.

Sterling sat taller, taking me in, inch by inch. I lifted my hands above my head as the desire in his dark eyes seared my exposed skin. His gaze moved from my face downward. Time passed painfully slowly as my flesh pebbled with goose bumps from the heat of his stare. By the time he brought his eyes back to mine, my breaths were shallow and my core wet.

That was what Sterling Sparrow could do, without a word or a touch. He made me want what only he'd ever given me, taking what he claimed and giving much more. My body was primed and yet we'd only begun. Tipping his face toward my neck, he sent a shiver through my nerves and up my spine.

"You're so fucking beautiful," he said, his words warm puffs of breath on my scorched skin as he nuzzled his prickly chin against my collarbone. Running my fingers over his shoulders, my back arched as his kisses moved lower, taking one nipple into his mouth, pulling it taut, while caressing the other with his talented fingers.

In his hands I was a prized instrument and he was the musician. Together we created a beautiful melody that rang through our bedroom with his words of adoration and my sounds of ecstasy.

By the time his fingers found my core I wanted more. "Please..."

That wasn't how it was to be.

As simply the instrument, I was at his disposal. It was the musician who orchestrated the tune. I was his to play, and like that prized instrument in the hands of a talented musician, he did, tuning me, winding me tighter and higher until I was his to arrange. Sterling moved me to my knees. With my weight forward on our pillows and my ass in the air, he spread my legs, dipping his fingers as I squirmed under his touch.

"I love your sexy ass."

Taunting an opponent I could never beat, I wiggled it back and forth.

"This is mine," he said, with a light slap to my butt cheek. "And this," he said, again dipping his fingers inside me. "Say it."

I lifted my head as my breasts swung and my voice came in ragged breaths. "Yes, Sterling. It's yours."

Another rub over my ass as he continued the torture.

"What's mine?" he asked, leaning over me with one hand on my stomach keeping me in position.

"Me, I'm yours."

Again, his fingers strummed my core as I added more notes to our song.

"This pussy," he corrected.

I nodded.

"Say it."

Oh God. I wanted him inside me.

"Yes, my pussy is yours."

My entire body tensed as he took my essence, moving his finger to a place I'd never been touched. "Sterling."

"Relax, sunshine. Close your eyes and feel. Don't think."

"I-I..." I did as he said, my eyes fluttering closed as I concentrated on his movements.

Around and around he tantalized until my entire body was feeling his actions. Not only where he was touching, but everywhere, as if my tight ring of muscles was hardwired to nerves all throughout my entire being. My breaths stuttered as hairs on my arms and the back of my neck stood to attention, tiny lightning rods ready for the strike.

"This is mine too," he declared.

As I fought back the anxiety his proclamation created, the bed moved. I turned toward him, feeling the loss of his presence behind me. "What?"

He opened the drawer of his bedside stand, where he kept the vibrator we'd tried. My eyes opened wide and heartbeat accelerated as he removed a different case. He didn't need to tell me what it was because as soon as he removed it from the satin interior I knew.

"Sterling...I'm not..."

"Trust me."

Nodding, I lowered my forehead back to the pillows, nervous about what he was going to do, yet trusting him to do it. Again the bed shifted as something cool drizzled over my behind. Using one finger he resumed the circling.

"Relax, Araneae. You were almost there. I told you that you are mine, all of you. This is part of you."

I let out a breath as I concentrated on his movements. Slower and slower he circled, the gel warming under his touch until I gasped as he breached the ring of muscles. "So fucking tight. I can't wait for my cock to feel this."

"I-I..." Words weren't forming.

"Not today, sunshine. We'll start with a butt plug. You need to stretch before you can handle me, and I want this to feel as good for you as it does for me."

Sterling's words reassured me as once again the muscle was breached. This time I knew it wasn't his finger, but the toy I'd seen him remove from the case.

"How are you doing?" he asked.

"I-I don't know."

He pushed it slowly, bit by bit, in bearable increments.

"I-it feels...different."

"It's all the way in," he said. "Can you hold it there?"

My core clenched at the odd sensation beside it. "I-I think so."

I let out a loud shrill as the plug within me began to vibrate. "Oh, fuck, Sterling..."

He didn't answer as he leaned over me, kissing my neck and shoulder blades. His lips moved down my back, creating a trail down my spine as the toy continued to move. With tiny explosions throughout my nervous system I was losing all sense of what was happening.

As Sterling's cock joined the party, I pushed back, wanting him to fill me.

So full.

My lungs fought for breath as he stilled, letting me adjust to his size as the toy continued to vibrate.

"Oh God. This is..." I couldn't find words adequate to describe the sensation.

"Holy shit," he said, holding onto my hips. "Fuck, Araneae. It's vibrating my cock."

Thrust by thrust we fell into our own rhythm. My skin dampened as perspiration coated it, yet my mind was centered on what he and the toy were doing, lifting me higher beyond the ninety-seventh floor up to the clouds. His grasp of my hips tightened as he slammed into me over and over. All at once, my core clamped down and fireworks detonated behind my closed eyes. Complete annihilation. Like no other orgasm before it, my world disappeared as my insides convulsed and I screamed out his name.

Rendered useless, my body collapsed.

Lifting me and rolling me to my back, Sterling kissed my lips before continuing and bringing my body slowly back to life. The toy was still in place, yet it was the man making love to me that had my full attention. Peering up at his handsome face, I marveled at his intensity. The muscles of his jaw clenched as his biceps bulged under the strain. My hands roamed over his broad shoulders and chest, following the indentations of his definition as once again my core tightened.

I couldn't believe I could have another orgasm, not after the last one—and not so soon.

And then as the room filled with his guttural roar, the cords of his neck strained, and his hips stilled, my back arched as a fresh wave washed through me. Not as intense as the one before, yet this one lingered as Sterling's cock throbbed and my body held him tight.

A smile filled both of our faces as our unity broke and he stopped the vibration and eased out the plug. Taking it to the bathroom, he returned with a wet cloth and took care of me. Once he was done, I wrapped my arms around his neck and pulled him back to the bed. "That was..." My smile grew.

"Better than I imagined," he said.

"What? You've never done that?"

His grin grew as his dark gaze sparkled my direction. "No. I made it up for our date." He shrugged. "But once the idea was set, I couldn't get it out of my mind."

There was something about being the first one to experience that with him that filled my chest with warmth and pride. Still, I wanted to be clear. "I'm never wearing that out of this room. So put that idea out of your head."

"The other vibrator?"

He was talking about the one with the remote control. I shrugged. "No promises."

"That's better than a flat no."

My nose scrunched. "And I don't know about the other thing. You're kind of big."

His finger caressed my cheek again. "Sunshine, we have forever. There's no rush."

"Are you going to tell me more about last night?" I asked.

Sterling nodded. "Yes. Let's get cleaned up and lunch first. I'm hungry."

"Lunch?" I looked at the clock. "Oh, jeez. It's nearly noon."

He offered me his hand to stand from the bed. "That's why I said lunch."

STERLING

J was struck by the reality that all five of us were back in the kitchen eating sandwiches and salads as if the entire world hadn't been ready to implode the night before. Araneae and Lorna were saying something and smiling. Reid told me that Lorna had taken Araneae to their apartment last night. And while I wasn't sure how I felt about it, I liked that she hadn't been alone. I recalled the first time we'd left Lorna on lockdown. She was a tough lady, yet we hadn't considered her fear. To us, she was safe. Since then, Reid's done his best to keep her connected when things go south.

The two ladies were saying something about chess. I'd need to ask Araneae if she played.

The thought brought a dark shadow to my lighter thoughts. Would it seem odd to buy a new board for our bedroom if she wanted to play even though I had the set in my office? Would I need to tell her why I couldn't move those pieces on the board in my office? It had been an ongoing game with Mason, and since he's been gone, the pieces haven't moved. For nearly six years they've sat exactly as they were. Lorna's feather duster was the only thing that touched them.

I'd worry about that after this deal with McFadden was settled.

After Carlos's men shot up the trailer, confirmed the men inside weren't part of their cartel, and delivered Louisa to the Sparrows, two Sparrows went back to the trailer for cleanup. Leaving dead or nearly dead bodies lying around was never good. In Chicago they could easily be moved to a believable location, adding to the veil of deception that worked to create Chicago dwellers' false sense of security.

Boulder was different.

When our men arrived, the man who'd spoken on the phone was dead, a gunshot wound to his temple, his phone destroyed, and a gun in his lifeless hand. The cartel was good. They'd left him wounded and ready for questioning. Maybe they weren't that good because, somehow, he'd found a gun and taken his own life. It was a sure sign that he'd rather die by his own hand than go through our questioning or McFadden's punishment for losing Louisa.

The young kid who was the one going to the couriers wasn't as resourceful. According to his ID, his name was Ricky. Ricky had been shot in both knees, so moving was impossible. Yet he was alive. There's something about the thought of lying in the wilderness, your body a smorgasbord for rats and other vermin, that helped you do what you could to survive and get out.

Too bad for him, he thought that would happen with his cooperation.

It didn't take too much persuasion by the Sparrows to get Ricky to sing. He didn't know the name of the client, only his instructions through his partner. The kid had helped nab the Toneys, shooting them both up with a tranquilizer after placing a rag with chloroform over their sleeping mouths.

That was part of the reason we insisted on transporting Louisa to the hospital. While Dr. Moore assessed that she and the baby would be fine, both with strong heartbeats, I wasn't willing to take any chances that the drugs caused harm.

The tranquilizer was why Jason had no memory of the abduction. The temperature in the storage unit caused his dehydration. It truly seemed he was as lucky as Louisa. If he'd been left in that container longer, his body would have shut down.

Ricky said they snuck into the Toneys' house near eleven at night to drug them. The van arrived a little later—the one Reid saw on the neighbor's video doorbell. The client instructed them to ditch the husband, saying he was only interested in the woman.

Ricky wasn't even sure of his partner's name. The man had only hired him for this job, but he recalled hearing someone on the phone call him Sly.

While the kid would no longer be alive to experience the vermin invasion, that didn't change the fact that as we ate lunch, Ricky was now feed for Colorado's wildlife. It would more than likely begin with bigger prey: cougars, black bears, or wildcats. As a species, the felines were more carnivore than the bears, but meat was meat. Eventually, the smaller vermin and insects would finish the process.

It was no different than what would have happened to him if the job had gone the way Sly planned. The only reason to hire a nobody in another town was to set them up for the fall and silence them before they had a chance to rat you out. Ricky's future was set the minute he agreed to work with Sly.

As a rule of thumb, don't accept a criminal endeavor for promised cash from a stranger. It was a good rule to follow.

With the kid's phone and Sly's—though it was destroyed—Reid was certain he could confirm the connection to McFadden. He'd already gotten a hit on the man's voice on the phone call: Sylvester Hicks, a McFadden capo.

That meant that the client Sly mentioned was McFadden, and he wouldn't let this drop until Araneae produced the evidence.

"I spoke with Louisa," Araneae said to Lorna. "She's confused but healthy. I felt bad not telling her that it happened because of me. She doesn't know why she would be kidnapped and is eternally grateful that you..." She looked around the table at Patrick, Reid, and I. "...were able to jump in and help." She turned to me. "I told her that I was coming down soon."

I took a deep breath, not responding, and by the expression on her face, if we were alone she'd be pushing the matter. It wasn't that I disagreed. It was that first we needed to bring this old wives' tale to an end.

"I think it's time for a one-on-one with McFadden," I said, trustful of everyone listening.

Araneae's eyes opened wide. "Not if it's dangerous, you're not."

"Sunshine, it's like gasoline and matches, but we can't go on grasping at straws. Last night we learned that he believes you have the evidence from your father. You know you don't. I know you don't." I motioned around the table. "We all know that. The subject even came up with your mother. She said she doesn't believe it exists. That leaves McFadden. I need to find out why he's so hell-bent on this."

Lorna shrugged. "I'd bet it has something to do with his candidacy for president."

We all looked her direction.

"What? I'm more than a pretty face," she said. "I listen. I also have news apps I follow. There's speculation he's announcing soon."

Reid shook his head. "You're definitely a beautiful face, but, babe, it's the end of August. Midterms are coming in November. No one announces this early. It would be over two years ahead of the election."

"I'm just telling you what people are saying," she said. "I may not get out much, but I stay informed. The senator wants to get out in front of the pack. There won't be an incumbent in the next race. His campaign manager leaked that it's McFadden's time."

Reid, Patrick, and I stared at one another as wheels turned in all of our heads.

"It would make sense," Patrick finally said, "that he wants confirmation the evidence exists or doesn't exist before the announcement."

I ran my hand through my still-damp hair—from our shower earlier—and turned to Araneae. Her long yellow hair was also damp and braided over one shoulder. With very little makeup and the remains of the sun's tan from the yacht, she was absolutely radiant.

We had to get this figured out before McFadden pulled another power play. I looked to Patrick and Reid. "After we finish eating, we'll go downstairs and brainstorm. I think Lorna's onto something."

Araneae turned my way. "We also need to talk about my upcoming one-on-one."

I shook my head. "You lost me."

"With my..." She let out a breath. "...mother."

I looked to Patrick. "We need a secure location. Either my office or hers."

"Hello," Araneae said. "You two are doing it again. Don't make my decisions for me." When no one responded, she added, "Maybe I could invite her here?"

My jaw clenched. There were too many damn fires happening.

"No," Araneae said, turning to Lorna, "I can't because I can't operate the damn elevator."

Lorna turned my way. "If you don't give her access to the elevator soon, she's going to stab you in your sleep."

Araneae laughed, covering her lips. "I almost spit out my salad."

Reaching under the table, I squeezed her knee. "I think I'm safe."

"How about to access A?" Lorna pushed.

"Lorna," Reid said in a tone I recognized, "not your battle."

"Like hell. I have money riding on this."

"What?" I asked.

"Nothing," everyone said in chorus.

"Not to the garage until this is settled with McFadden," I said, looking directly to Araneae. "You will stay with one of us at all times when you leave this apartment." I turned to

Lorna. "A is your floor—all of yours. I'll leave that up to you, but all three of you have to agree."

Lorna turned to Araneae. "You have a yes from me." Both women turned to Reid.

"Look at you two ganging up," Reid teased. "I don't have a fucking choice in this, do I?"

Lorna shook her head.

"Fine by me," he said.

We all turned to Patrick as his hands went in the air. "Oh hell no."

"No?" Lorna and Araneae questioned together.

"Oh hell no, I'm not standing in the way," Patrick clarified. "I have to spend most of the day with Ms. Hawkins. Having her mad at me is scary."

Araneae smiled, tipping her head with all the sweetness she could muster. "You're the scary one."

Patrick grinned. "I don't think you've met the woman who thought I tricked her into going to the distribution center. She's one tough cookie."

"Then it's settled," Araneae said. "My glass tower just grew a bit."

"That is all until—"

"I know," Araneae said, interrupting me. Her soft brown eyes pointed my way, "until this is over." She waved her hands toward the doorway. "Then go, you three, figure it out. I want it over."

"See," Patrick said as we all stood, "scary and bossy."

"That's right. Remember who's in charge," Araneae called as we headed toward the elevator.

JOSEY

Twenty-one years ago ~

*a*s we pulled up to the elementary school, I forced myself to remain calm. We'd known this time would come, yet that didn't make it easier. As Byron turned my way with a weary smile, the car came to a stop in a parking spot. The one-story building loomed before us. To the average parent it was probably beautiful, a recently constructed school with all the amenities including a rubber-covered ground for the playground, a small backstop and field for kickball games, and a soccer field with child-sized goals on each end.

The thing was that I wasn't concerned about a skinned knee on a playground or if Renee would enjoy recess. My stomach knotted as I took in the open space around the school and the chain-link fences. My gaze darted to the surrounding streets.

"Are you ready to show me your new school?" Byron asked, looking at Renee in the rearview mirror.

"Yes!" Renee replied, bouncing in the back seat.

Byron reached over and took my hand. "She's going to be okay."

"It's so open here. What if they're watching her?" I asked in a low voice.

Undoing her seat belt, Renee scooted toward the back door. "Come on. I want to see my class again. Oh, and my teacher, Daddy, she's real pretty. Her name is Miss Macdonald..." She looked at me. "Right, Mom?"

I grinned. We'd been working on learning her teacher's name since the day we came to meet her. That was a week ago. Miss Macdonald was young with dark hair and an infectious smile. She'd greeted each child by bending down, talking directly to them, and calling them by name. She'd taken each child's picture and promised to know all the names by tonight.

School started tomorrow.

"She's excited," my husband said. "Let her be excited."

I inhaled and exhaled, trying to live in the moment, and for once, not let Sparrow's shadow haunt what should be an enjoyable milestone in Renee's life.

With Renee holding my hand on one side and Byron's on the other, we walked into the school surrounded by other parents and children.

"Do you remember the direction to your classroom?" Byron asked.

I was busy looking at the entry. It was large and nicely decorated with glass doors that led to the outside and a web of hallways.

"This way," Renee said excitedly as she pulled us along.

Byron peered at me over her head. *Be excited for her*, he mouthed.

"I wonder if they lock the school during the day," I asked quietly.

"Look around at all of these students," he replied. "They know what they're doing here. This is one of the newest schools in the area."

Renee continued to tug until we came to her classroom door. On the wall beside the door was a colorful bulletin board covered in construction paper to look like a giant apple tree.

"Look!" she said. "It's me."

Sure enough it was.

On the tree hung cutouts of apples, and on each apple was a child's picture with their name spelled out beneath.

"It says Renee Marsh," she said, pointing to the name. "That's me."

"Yes, sweetheart," Byron replied, "it is you. Now where is this Miss McDonald?"

"No, Daddy. It's Macdonald like the song, not the restaurant."

I smiled. It was how we'd practiced, singing *Old Macdonald had a farm*.

"You're right," he said with a laugh as she tugged us through the door.

"Oh," she sighed as her brown eyes grew wide and she took in the classroom.

In the last week, Miss Macdonald had turned the relatively plain room into a kindergartener's delight. There were tiny desks all in groupings of four and on each desk was a large colorful name tag.

"Hello, Renee," Miss Macdonald said in greeting us.

"Hi," she replied shyly with a grin. "Can I find my desk?"

"May I," I corrected.

Miss Macdonald grinned my direction and turned back to Renee. "Yes, you may. See if you can find your name."

Letting go of our hands, our daughter ran toward the multiple groupings of desks as Miss Macdonald turned our direction. "Mr. and Mrs. Marsh, she will do wonderfully. It's obvious how much you've worked with her."

"She loves to read," I said, watching as she pointed to the top of her desk. I turned back to the teacher. "I should say for us to read to her, but she can read some too. We've been sounding out words."

The teacher nodded and tipped her head toward a cozy corner of the room. "Over there we have a bookcase full of books, levels one through three. And over there..." She pointed another direction. "...we have our work centers where the students will learn about letters and numbers. At this age their minds are wide open to new discoveries."

I tried to smile.

"You seem apprehensive," she said to me.

"I'm..."

Byron placed his arm around me. "Renee has always been home. Josey is having a little problem with the idea of her being away from us."

"I'm always open for parent helpers."

My eyes grew wide. "I'd love to do that."

"Great, let me get your contact information. I know this is

difficult, but it's part of growing up. I would love to have you help after the first two weeks."

"I can help tomorrow," I volunteered.

She smiled. "We find it's better that for the first two weeks the children and parents make a clean break during the school day. It lets the students get accustomed to the routine. After that, when the parent comes in, the children usually don't have a problem with the separation."

I nodded as I looked up to see Renee talking with another little girl.

"She seems social for being home," Miss Macdonald said.

"We've been involved in play groups and we go to the library."

She reached out to my arm. "Mrs. Marsh, you've done a great job. I can't wait to get to know Renee better."

"She is also very creative. She draws clothes for her dolls and we create patterns. I do the sewing, but she wants to." I'm not ready for her to have sharp needles.

"That's a great way to encourage her imagination." Miss Macdonald said before adding, "Now, if you'll excuse me."

Byron hugged me as we watched Renee and her new friend make discoveries around the classroom. "She will be safe," he said. "I was looking too. I saw cameras in the hallway."

Sucking in a deep breath, I exhaled. "There's also a door to the outside at the end of the hallway. Someone could—"

He shook his head.

I knew he was right. I was being overcautious. I'd considered homeschooling, but we agreed to make her childhood as normal as possible. I feigned a smile. "I'm volunteering at least once a week, more if they can use me."

"Of course, you are," he said with a grin.

By the time we and other parents were leaving, a peaceful feeling had settled, mostly instilled by Renee's innocent anticipation. It helped that we met some of the parents of a few of her new classmates, exchanging telephone numbers and agreeing to get the children together outside of school.

As we entered the hallway, I looked again at the corkboard, about to ask Renee if she could find her new friends' pictures when my stomach dropped. Tugging her hand, I instead asked her the names as we hurried away.

The tree wasn't the same as it was when we entered.

Renee's picture and name were gone.

STERLING

"He's still in Washington DC," Patrick said as the three of us gathered on two.

"If Lorna is right, this can't go on. And I'm not taking any more chances with Araneae's friends," I said, spinning one of the chairs, straddling it, and leaning forward on the back.

"What about Judge Landers?" Reid asked. "Araneae said she wants to meet with her."

I nodded. "Yes, when the judge met with me, she asked to speak to Araneae."

"I don't like it," Patrick replied. "It feels off."

Intuition. Gut.

Sometimes it was more accurate than all the computer programs Reid could run.

I ran my hand through my hair. "This is why I'm fucked," I admitted this to the only people I'd ever admit failure to. When they both looked my direction, I went on, "With Araneae, I'm off my game. I agree that Landers is a liability. Her relationship with

Rubio makes her one. But fuck, this is Araneae's mother. The woman was told her baby died. Someone actually had a fucking dead baby for her to hold. She didn't know." I stood, pushing the rolling chair away as my pacing began. There was something about moving that helped me rationalize—helped me think.

I stared at Reid and then Patrick and shook my head. "If Landers lied to me, the woman deserves a fucking Emmy. She checked herself into a psych ward. She thought her daughter died. She's lived with that for twenty-six years. Connection to Rubio or not, she wants to know her daughter."

"You're fucked because you're not looking at this like the head of the Sparrow outfit," Reid said. "You're looking at this as Araneae's man."

Her man? And here I thought she belonged to me. Maybe it was the other way, too.

My feet were still moving. "If it were Lorna?"

"I'd be fucked too," Reid answered.

I appreciated his honesty. It was why I could be totally upfront with these two. "I told Araneae I'd leave the decision to meet with Annabelle up to her. She wants to do it. It's our job to make sure the meeting is secure. We have wherever it is surrounded by Sparrows. I told Annabelle that there was no way I would approve Rubio or Pauline. Pauline had her chance."

"I think Sinful Threads is where it should happen," Patrick said. "Reid has the whole place covered in security cams. The office is small, less than a tenth of the size of Sparrow Enterprises offices. It's easier to manage."

I nodded. "I agree. Now it's up to Araneae and Annabelle to decide when that happens."

"I like it happening while McFadden is in Washington," Reid said.

"Then again, he was in Washington when the Toneys were taken. Like he's purposely ordering this shit while he's away," I said.

"Welcome back," Patrick said with a grin.

"Reid," I said, "log into Stephanie's computer. Check my schedule for tomorrow. If it's feasible, I'm going to Washington."

"He's not going to want to meet with you there. Too many questions if Sterling Sparrow walks into Senator McFadden's office."

"I don't give a fucking shit about his reputation." My feet stopped moving as I turned to Reid and Patrick. "But you're right, he does. Book me a suite at some upscale hotel, but not under my name. I don't want him to have any warning. Once we're there we'll give him the option to come to us. If he doesn't, we'll go to him and bring the damn press if we have to. I'm done with this shit. I want Araneae to have a life here in Chicago. I don't mind having her watched by you," I nodded to Patrick. "As a matter of fact, I can't see that stopping anytime soon. However, I don't want her worrying about her friends. I want her to feel like she can go to a fucking bakery."

Both men looked at me.

"Why a bakery?" Patrick asked.

"Nothing, it's just something she said once. The point is that we'll always have enemies. That's fine. They're mine. The kidnapping of Louisa was a direct attack on her. Sylvester said so himself. He said he would have taken Araneae if he could have gotten to her. That fucker is dead, but McFadden has ten ready to take his place."

"But," Reid said, "Sylvester said they wanted the evidence. There's no evidence. You said that even Annabelle agreed."

"Then why is McFadden so sure it exists?" Patrick asked.

"That's what I intend to learn. Fuck, if it does, I'd consider a deal."

"It could ruin him," Patrick said.

"Or it can save Araneae."

Reid turned toward the computer. "You have two appointments regarding some upcoming bids first thing in the morning and a meeting with the mayor in the afternoon."

"Reschedule the mayor. He'll wait," I said. "Have the plane ready for as soon as the appointments are done. Once we're in the hotel, we'll contact Hillman and set up the meeting with Rubio. That way we're set." I turned toward Patrick. "I'd like you along, but if you're there, the women are on lockdown again."

"I'll go," Reid said. "Do me good to get out."

I grinned. "And bring a crew. I want the suite watched and protected. We're not taking any chances." I turned specifically to Reid. "Are you okay with Lorna being here without you?"

"I'm at Sinful Threads," Patrick said, "and we can have a crew on one ready if she calls."

"This is a go," I said. "Tomorrow I'm face-to-face with Rubio. This shit is over."

The Thomas Jefferson Suite within the Jefferson Hotel was a good size by suite standards. With a regal entry, a kitchen, dining area with a table for ten, multiple sitting areas—the largest with a view of the Washington monument—and two bedrooms, there was plenty of room for Reid to set up surveillance as well as some of our crew to be present yet hidden.

"Hillman isn't pleased," I said to Reid, even though he'd been listening to my call and heard. "He said tomorrow because he's back in Chicago. The Senate is in special session. He claims that McFadden is needed in a committee meeting for a vote on something this afternoon, and there's no guarantee it will be resolved soon."

Reid smiled. "He didn't sound like he was any happier about the second option."

I leaned back on the sofa and undid the button of my suit jacket. It was all part of the power play. McFadden would walk in here dressed for the Senate. I wasn't going to look like I had just worked out. "No. My offer of showing up at his office in the Hart Building was not well received."

I looked at my watch. It was nearly three o'clock. With the two-hour flight and Reid coming ahead to get the technology and crew set up, we were right on schedule. The senator was due in the next half hour. Apparently, the vote wasn't as important as keeping me away from the press at the Hart Building.

Fifteen minutes later, our eyes in the lobby saw Rubio enter with another man.

"He's early," Reid said as his fingers flew on a keyboard.

He was running facial recognition on the man with Rubio. More than likely we'd talk alone. If he brought this other man into it, Reid would become visible. If McFadden entered alone, Reid would stay hidden.

Through the years, I'd met with Rubio and he'd met with me. As my mother said last week, my father even went to him after Daniel McCrie was killed. We may not like or trust one another, but there were times that our combined power was better than either of us alone. That didn't mean we wouldn't take each other out in a second—we would. That was the life we lived, the edge of legality, the fine line between power and evil.

We'd also both accomplished significant gains in our more legitimate endeavors. For that reason, it was important to keep our underworld activities in the shadows. However, if there was another attack on anyone connected to Araneae, I was ready to pull back the veil.

We also had a suit at the door and rented the room next door. I wouldn't allow more than one person to enter with McFadden or wait outside. If need be, any extras could be in the next room. Having multiple goons stationed outside the door set off alarms with hotel security.

We both stood straighter as a knock echoed from the door. Nodding to me, Reid picked up his laptop and moved to the bedroom, shutting the door.

A few seconds later, Derek, the suit at the door, opened the main entry as I stood. Pushing the door inward, Rubio entered, alone.

"Sparrow, I'm not alone." He looked around the suite. I was the only one visible.

"I thought we could discuss this matter in private."

He nodded. "He can wait outside with your man."

Nearly thirty-five years my senior, Rubio McFadden had lost height since I was a boy. It's true I was now taller, but he was definitely shorter. His once-dark hair was now whiter

than it was black, and his once-toned body had lost its definition. In short, Rubio McFadden had aged. If my father were
still alive, I like to believe he'd have aged better. If he were
alive he would be one year older than Rubio.

If my father were still alive, this meeting would include
him, not me.

My father was dead.

"Have a seat." I gestured toward the large oval dining
table.

He looked around the suite and out the large windows
before taking the seat at the head of the table. "This is highly
unusual. When your father was alive—"

"We're not here to discuss my father."

"He had more decorum than to ambush—"

I let out a laugh, interrupting him again as I sat with my
back against the wall, able to view the entire two rooms. "My
father is dead, but he was most definitely not known for his
decorum. Now, let's move on. I hardly believe I'm the one
who ambushed you, Rubio. Stay away from Araneae. I made
that clear at the club. Perhaps Hillman didn't pass along the
information."

He leaned back in the high-back chair and shook his head.
"I think you're mistaken, son. I've been here in DC."

I wasn't his son nor did I appreciate the power play, but
that wasn't my concern at the moment. "I know where you
are and where you were. I also know where Sylvester
Hicks was."

"I don't know a Hicks," he said, "and as for that woman,
Pauline is certain she's an imposter."

"Then why did you have her friend kidnapped and
demand McCrie's evidence?"

He shook his head.

I leaned forward with my hands on the glossy table, one holding the other as my elbows straightened. "I called this meeting to get the shit out in the open. You're afraid the old wives' tale is true and Araneae has McCrie's evidence. I'm here to tell you that I thought that might be true. I was wrong. She has nothing. She didn't even know her name much less have decades-old evidence."

"Then your dead daddy lied to you or never told you the truth," he said with a shit-eating grin. "I don't know what you know from those days, but they're over. I'm announcing my candidacy for president on Labor Day. I don't want any ghosts from the past coming back to life. She's a damn ghost and if you cared about her at all, you would have left her dead."

My jaw clenched as my grip of my own hands tightened. "She's off-limits. Anyone associated with her is off-limits."

"Her momma thinks it's her. It's a shame." He shook his head in mock sympathy. "It will break her heart to lose her daughter a second time, to see her dead. You should have left her that way."

"She was never dead," I said, my teeth aching from the increased pressure.

"She was to us. It was over. McCrie just couldn't let it go. He gave me six CD-ROM discs and six to your daddy, but before Daniel died, we learned he'd made copies. Son, those CDs will hurt Sparrow as much as McFadden."

"I'm not running for president," I said.

"No, but I am. And I don't even want that evidence to hurt Sparrow. As appealing as that is," he said, leaning forward, "my political career is tied to Illinois, to Chicago. It doesn't need a story like this to get out. You've closed up

Sparrow's ring." His head shook. "Too fucking fast if you ask me, but you didn't ask and you got away with it. None of the existing rings are tied to me or my outfit, not in a way that can be linked. Like I said, let the dead stay dead, or kill them if necessary."

"Why do you believe that the copies exist? I asked Judge Landers and she said she didn't believe the old wives' tale."

"No wives' tale," Rubio said. "I know what she says. I've kept that woman close, waiting for the day she slips up and I learn what McCrie did. So far, nothing."

"Again, then why?"

"Daniel told me, seconds before his last breath."

I sneered, almost chuckled.

It didn't fucking surprise me that Rubio McFadden had been the one to kill Daniel McCrie. It surprised me that he'd admit it.

"Don't tell me," he said, "that you're shocked that someone might off their own family, if it served a purpose." He looked pointedly at my gold ring—my father's gold ring.

"Takes a lot to shock me." I leaned back again, lowering my hands to the ornate arms of the chair. "Stay away from Araneae and anyone connected to her. She doesn't have the evidence. She didn't know a thing about it, but if you're certain it exists, I'll try to find it."

"I've been looking for ten years, since McCrie died. He told me that she had the key."

I shook my head. "She had no connection to him. She didn't know him."

Rubio laid his hands flat on the table. "Dying men don't lie. You should have asked more questions of Allister. Labor Day is coming in a week." He stood. "I respect you and things you've done, Sparrow. We could make this work: coexist in Chicago while I get the big white house on Pennsylvania Avenue. Somehow, that girl has the key, and I'm not letting her bring me down. I'm not letting you bring me down."

I stood too. "One fucking week. You want me to find in one week what you couldn't find in twenty-six years."

"Ten," he corrected. "I'd heard rumors, but it wasn't until McCrie was at death's door that we knew for sure that she'd lived. Your daddy came to me. We made a deal."

"I thought my father came to you to tell you he didn't hire the hit on McCrie."

"He came to me because he knew Daniel sang, and he didn't want World War III. I'm not interested in World War III. I'm interested in the presidency now. You find me that evidence, and then you can keep the girl."

I stood taller, squaring my shoulders, towering higher than McFadden. "I'm keeping her no matter what. You're backing the fuck away because if you don't, I'll turn Chicago into a war zone and your campaign will be the first thing we obliterate."

"You're the one who was hell-bent on saving the kids," he said as if it were a bad thing. "Hell, half of them came from nothing. At least with us they had a roof over their heads and food in their bellies."

"Don't fucking justify what you did." I narrowed my stare. "Their lives were hell."

"You saved them, many of them. I'll sweeten the pot. You get me that evidence. We put this behind us for good. I don't give a damn if she's really Araneae McCrie or not, my niece or not. Like I said, a family connection hasn't stopped either of us from getting rid of people in the past. Get me the evidence, and she lives and her friends stay safe, as long as they fucking stay away from the feds."

"He was in your outfit, the fed."

Rubio's cheeks rose. "Keep your friends close and your enemies closer."

"You knew?"

He didn't answer; instead he continued, "And for the sweetening part, I'll make sure any rings dealing in that precious merchandise in or around Chicago—that I can find—will also be closed down." He shook his head. "It's a win-win proposition. Maybe we can even come together, two pillars from one of the biggest cities in our country, to end child exploitation. We'll be fucking heroes, and I'll be moving into the White House."

"I can't promise a week."

He started to leave but turned back. "Time's running out, Sparrow. And don't come back here to Washington. We aren't ready for the photo ops yet. Call Hillman when you have the CDs. I'll be back in Chicago as soon as I can."

"Araneae and her friends are safe," I said again.

"Until Labor Day. Bye, now. We'll be talking again, real soon."

ARANEAE

*T*uesday morning as I entered the kitchen, my steps stilled, surprised to see Sterling still present. I watched as he stood talking to Reid with his back to me, scanning his long legs covered in his pricey suit trousers, his fit waist, and the way his long-sleeved shirt fit over his broad shoulders. There was something about seeing him dressed for work that twisted my insides, perhaps it was because I was becoming very accustomed to what he was hiding under that expensive suit.

He turned.

His dark gaze held me captive as he blatantly did the same as I'd just done, his eyes scanning from my high heels to the top of my head. Thank goodness I was wearing a padded bra under this silk blouse because under the heat of his stare, my nipples were as hard as the diamonds in my ears.

"I should stick around more in the morning," he said, walking toward me and wrapping an arm around my waist. It didn't matter that the kitchen was filled with our friends as he pulled me to him. "You're beautiful. I think I should reconsider this Sinful Threads Chicago office."

The tips of my lips moved upward as I was surrounded by more than his embrace, but also the cloud of his spicy cologne. His playful tone had me intrigued after all that he'd told me about McFadden the night before. "Why is that?"

"You look too damn good to be out there with other men. I'm thinking a permanent lockdown should be considered."

"I will stab you in your sleep." I looked beyond his broad shoulders. "Besides, I think that's why I have Patrick."

His grin grew as he turned to Patrick. "Fight them off with a stick."

Patrick smiled.

"I'm serious," Sterling went on, "use your gun if you have to."

"I'm finding," Patrick said, "the silk fashion industry is a primarily female-oriented business."

"Yes, not many gunfights," I added.

Sterling kissed my cheek and stepped away. "We can never be too careful. Women are as dangerous as men."

Lorna and I exchanged looks.

"See," Reid said, "look at the two of them scheming."

"Hey, working together got me to your level," I said with a laugh as I poured a cup of coffee. "Why are you here?" I asked Sterling.

"Other than this is where I live?"

"Yeah, other than that."

"The three of us have been working on what McFadden said. We need more. I'd like to be with you when Annabelle comes to your office. Maybe she knows more than she even realizes. We're running out of time."

Biting my lower lip, I shook my head. "I'm scared to see her, yet I feel like I need to do this alone." I looked over at Patrick. "Not like I'm alone. Patrick and Jana will be there."

"If we weren't on the time crunch, I'd agree," Sterling replied. "This can't wait."

I blew across the top of my coffee mug. "I could ask her whatever you want to know."

Sterling came closer. "You haven't spoken to her yet."

He was right. Jana had arranged the meeting for me. My hands were too shaky as I held the card she'd given to Sterling and I tried to call. I had no doubt I'd be a bundle of emotions when we spoke. Having Sterling there would be support; however, for ten years I'd been strong on my own. Being in a relationship with him didn't mean I was no longer strong. It meant I could lean on him, and sometimes it would be better if I didn't.

I shook my head. "I know, but please, I need to do this." Placing the coffee on the counter, I cupped his smooth cheeks. "This meeting wouldn't be possible without you."

He reached for my hands and kissed each palm. "I don't want to ruin this for either of you, but she was there. She told me about your birth. We need to learn what she remembers and maybe even clues about the time closer to when your father died."

I exhaled as I reclaimed my coffee. "She's coming at noon. Let me have some time with her and then you can arrive."

"How long do you think she'll be there?"

"I invited her for lunch. I figured even if we don't eat, it will help ease the tension."

He nodded as he reached for my wrist, the one not holding the mug. "You're wearing the bracelet."

I swallowed the lump forming in my throat as I retrieved my wrist and sat at the table where Lorna had fruit and a muffin waiting. "I can't explain it." I looked down at the charms. "I think that sometimes I feel a relationship with Annabelle is cheating on Josey." I shrugged. "And maybe even Lucy—Louisa's mother. Wearing this is my connection to all of them, my way of including them in this. Remember, Josey told me that she and Annabelle were friends...and Lucy added charms."

Sterling shook his head as he sat beside me. "That's not true though. Annabelle didn't give you to the Marshes. She believed you'd died."

"I'm hoping she can fill in those blanks for me."

"Sunshine, we're trying to do that, but right now we need to concentrate on finding that evidence."

A familiar uneasiness settled over me. "Why can't McFadden believe that I don't have it? I don't want it. I want to move on."

Lines of concern formed on Sterling's forehead. "He said that your father said you were the key."

"I don't know what that means."

"Maybe Annabelle does."

I looked beyond Sterling: the room had emptied. "Where is everyone?"

His lips turned upward as his dark eyes glistened. "I guess they wanted to give us a moment."

Leaning forward, I brushed my lips over his. "I love you. I'm not sorry you brought me to Chicago, to you..." I looked around the now-emptied kitchen to the view beyond the windows. "...and to this. I'm starting to love everyone here. I'm just worried that more people will get hurt because of me."

"Not on our watch."

Wringing my hands, I paced the length in front of my desk to the windows and back as the clock approached noon. Jana had picked up lunch from a local deli not far from our office. While she and Patrick would eat theirs in the conference room, I had my mother's—that was difficult to say—and mine ready on the table in my office. The memories of the meeting with Pauline continued on repeat in my head.

Sterling had said Annabelle wanted to meet with me. I kept telling myself to believe him. He wouldn't have encouraged this reunion if it would end poorly. To be honest, I wasn't sure what I'd do if this ended the way the meeting with Pauline had gone.

Through my door that was ajar, I heard the opening of the door to Jana's office. My steps stilled as my stomach twisted, adding auxiliary knots on top of knots. Closing my eyes, I listened.

"Excuse me. I have an appointment with...Araneae McCrie."

Tears filled my eyes at the sound of my real name. Annabelle pronounced it differently than I was used to hearing. She pronounced it, *uh-ron-e-eye*, like the spider.

I took a deep breath and willed my feet to move—to meet her halfway. It felt like the most difficult ten feet I'd ever walked. My limbs became tingly and my head faint. My circulation was speeding yet not doing its job of delivering oxygen to my cells. With my nerves ramping up into overdrive, I took a deep breath and reached for the doorknob.

Jana was still seated at her desk while Patrick was hidden in the conference room, the door slightly ajar. None of that mattered. My concentration was on the only other person in the room.

As my gaze met my mother's, the rest of the world disappeared.

"That would be me," I said, my voice unsteady.

ARANEAE

*A*nnabelle Landers didn't move, staring at me as if I could be a ghostly apparition, able to disappear at any moment.

This wasn't the first time I saw the woman who had given me life.

I'd seen her reflection in the mirror within the bathroom of the club. I'd looked her up online once I knew more about her. Yet none of that prepared me for this second, for the way my heart pounded in my chest, my circulation drummed in my ears, or my hand trembled on the doorknob.

The woman before me was tall and slender with a regal air. Maybe a better word was stately. Seeing her standing here in my office, holding her handbag like a shield, her shoulders back and neck straight, I envisioned her presiding over trials wearing a black robe over her lovely dress. Her blonde hair was secured in a twist behind her head, allowing her neck to appear long with a simple string of pearls.

She was me. I was her. Sterling said they had mitochondrial DNA to confirm my identity and my relationship to this woman. As we stared at one another, that scientific verification wasn't necessary.

"Oh," Annabelle gasped as her fingers of one hand came to her lips. "You're so beautiful."

Though tears were slipping down them, my cheeks moved higher while my breasts rose and fell as I fought to fill my lungs. "I-I...look like you."

I did.

If I could see into the future to when I would be Annabelle's age, I believed I would be her twin. I'd read online that she was sixty-seven years old. I'd read facts, such as she married Daniel McCrie following their graduation from University of Chicago Law School. Annabelle Landers had begun working for the state prosecutor before being elected to the Illinois Circuit Court. She had one child, a daughter who was deceased. She was later appointed to the federal court; her appointment had been spearheaded by Senator Rubio McFadden. Her husband passed away ten years ago.

It was all information, but none of it was like staring into my own eyes, ones as moist as mine.

Annabelle too was crying. "You do look like me. I always thought you would."

My head tilted. "I don't know what to do now."

Annabelle took a step closer. "May I..." She swallowed. "...may I hug you?"

It was almost too much.

I nodded as we both took another step closer.

The soft scent of vanilla filled my senses as she engulfed

my shoulders in her embrace. For a moment, we stood there, her arms around me and mine holding to her.

How do you greet the mother you never knew?

How do you greet the daughter you thought had died?

With tears and smiles seemed to be the answer to both questions.

When we finally pulled away, I gestured into my office. "We can go in here. I have lunch."

She nodded. "Thank you for agreeing to see me."

As I closed the door, I pointed to the table. "I thought we could eat."

Her smile turned sad. "Araneae, you have to know that I didn't know."

"Sterling told me."

We sat, each looking more at one another than toward the food.

Finally, she spoke, "It is hard for me to understand how you and Sterling Sparrow became...At the club, you said that the two of you are engaged?" She looked toward my left hand.

I shook my head. "It's not true. We're dating..." A smile floated across my face at the memory of our one official date. "...we have a lot happening right now. I told you that because you were staring at me. I didn't know who you were, and well, it seems that Sterling has a reputation. I thought saying he was my fiancé would protect me."

"I never thought I'd say anything like this about a Sparrow; however, when he met with me, I believed him. He cares for you and about you. While I would never have chosen a Sparrow for my daughter...." Her cheeks rose higher. "...I like saying *my* daughter... I would want you to be happy and seeing you and talking to him, I hope you are."

"I am."

We both reached for our napkins, placing them on our laps.

Annabelle tilted her head. "There are so many things I want to ask you. Did you..." She seemed to swallow her words. "...was your childhood...?" She took a deep breath. "I'm so sorry. I don't know what happened."

"My childhood was good. I was raised by loving parents."

Her head shook again. "I don't understand. Was it...? All I can think is that they put you into witness protection because of Daniel without telling me."

My eyes opened wide. "If that's the case, I was never told."

"How else could they, would they, take you from me?"

"Who is *they*?" I asked. "Who would have taken me and put me in witness protection?" My mind filled with scenes from my childhood. This scenario was not anything I'd ever considered.

"I would have assumed the FBI. I've been racking my brain since that night at the club. I've..." She looked down at the food. "...we've both been cheated out of twenty-six years."

As Annabelle set her fork back down, her hands were visibly shaking. I reached out and laid mine on top of hers. "What may I call you?" I asked.

Her light brown eyes, the same as mine, peered upward away from the salad on the table in front of her. Her attention lingered on my hand and bracelet, before returning to my question. "I know what I'd like, but I can't ask that of you."

She'd turned her hand so we were now palm to palm, hers wrapped around mine and mine wrapped around hers.

I squeezed hers. "I had a good mom." I took a deep

breath. "A great mom. I won't tarnish her memory. That doesn't mean I don't want to get to know my mother."

"I'll answer to whatever you choose to call me," Annabelle said. "As you probably know, my name is Annabelle." Her smile returned as our hands remained united. "My mother's name—your grandmother—was Amelia. When I found your name, I'd been searching for something unique, strong, and resilient that also began with the letter A."

"I didn't know about my grandmother. Is she...?"

Annabelle shook her head. "No, she passed before you. I mean, before you were born."

"I'd heard that story about why you named me Araneae from my mom."

"How? How would she know?"

I exhaled. "I don't know. She said you were friends from childhood and that my birth father had done something he thought was right, but doing it put me in danger, so you asked her to take me, to keep me safe."

"I'm sorry, Araneae. I wasn't that selfless. I wanted you. I vowed to protect you."

There was a shift in energy, but before I could process, a deep rumbling tenor filled the room.

"Then we need your help."

Though I'd felt Sterling's presence, I hadn't heard him enter, and by the look on her face, neither had my mother.

Annabelle and I turned to face Sterling.

STERLING

*I*nterrupting this reunion wasn't my goal. Saving Araneae by setting her free from the sights of McFadden was.

Araneae stood and came toward me.

"The clock is ticking," I said as she placed her delicate hand on my arm and turned to Annabelle.

"I asked Sterling to give us some time alone." Her head tilted. "I hope we can have more in the future."

Annabelle nodded. "I'd like that as well."

I walked Araneae back to her chair and assisted her in sitting before taking a seat across from Judge Landers. "I invited myself here today. You were honest with me when you came to my office. It's my turn."

"I hope for my daughter's sake that we can always be honest with one another."

"You told me," I began, "that you didn't believe the old wives' tale of your husband passing on evidence to Araneae." I looked to Araneae. "She has no idea about any of it. I've filled in as many blanks as I could. She knows what Daniel knew and who it involved."

Judge Landers lifted her hand. "I don't."

"Judge Landers, can you really say that? Can you profess to that when your daughter's life is on the line?"

She visibly paled. "Are you threatening Araneae, here in front of me?"

Araneae's hand came back to my arm. "No, he's not..." She sat taller. "...Mother." The title seemed to come uneasily from her lips, yet her saying it had Judge Lander's attention. "Sterling has been brutally honest with me. You yourself said that you named me to be strong and resilient. I am. I've been on my own since I was sixteen."

Annabelle audibly gasped. "Why?"

"We don't know," I answered. "It all coincides with Daniel's death."

"Prior to that, as I'd said," Araneae went on, "I was raised by great parents. I was raised as Renee Marsh."

Annabelle's eyes narrowed. "I was told you called yourself Kennedy Hawkins."

"When I was sixteen, my mother..." She hesitated. "...my father, the one I knew, had died in an automobile accident. My mom took me to the airport and gave me a new identity. She told me that Chicago wasn't safe, and I was never to come back."

"At sixteen? You were abandoned at sixteen?" There were new tears in her eyes.

"Not abandoned," Araneae said, "sent away, for my protection. It was what I was told."

"We believe," I said, "that Josey Marsh believed she was doing what was best for Araneae."

"That was when she told me that you had named me Araneae, and you'd given me to her for safekeeping. She said there were bad people after me, and I needed to get away from Chicago and never come back."

"Did she tell you who?" Annabelle asked.

I sat up straighter. "She warned her about the name Sparrow, my father and me."

"What? And then you searched for her?"

"It should be obvious," I said, "my intentions are to help Araneae. Yes, I found her to hurt Rubio, to get that evidence, but now..." I reached out and covered Araneae's hand. "...I will do whatever is necessary to protect her. When I walked in here, you said that had been your intention in keeping her. You told me that someone took that opportunity away from you. Today you have the opportunity again. We need to find that evidence."

"To hurt Rubio?" Annabelle asked.

"If I said yes," I asked, my tone deepening, "would you choose him over Araneae?"

Annabelle moved her gaze from me to Araneae and back. "No. I'd choose my daughter. I'd make the choice I was never allowed to make twenty-six years ago. However, if it comes to that, I may require your help, Sparrow's help."

Araneae's big light-brown eyes turned my way.

"If you need it," I said, "you have it. Right now, we need to find the evidence for him." I leaned back. "He said he had a copy and so did my father. He also said he saw it and knows it exists. Daniel told him..." I wasn't going to tell Annabelle Landers that Rubio McFadden killed her husband. "...near the end of his life that he'd made another copy. He told Rubio that Araneae is the key."

Annabelle's head shook back and forth. "Are you saying that Daniel knew our daughter was alive? And Rubio has known for ten years?"

I let out a long breath. "I can't answer about Daniel with one hundred percent assurance. My father knew. He showed me her picture..." Technically, I found her picture. "...when I was thirteen. In that picture, Araneae was seven years old. Each year I was shown an updated photo. My father told me that she was mine."

"I-I don't understand. Your father was watching her? He planned for the two of you...why?"

"All I know for sure was that he was getting at least yearly updates," I clarified. "They ended when Renee Marsh became Kennedy Hawkins. I was at the University of Michigan at the time, but I had help. We found her again. Up until I lured her back to Chicago, Araneae, without her knowledge, has been under Sparrow protection. Mine, not my father's."

Annabelle leaned back in the chair. The table was littered with most of the lunch Araneae had arranged. Outside the windows, life was occurring, the way it did. Sparrow Enterprises was making money. Sparrows were around the city doing what they did. Yet within this small office, it was time to come clean and learn what we could.

"What do you want from me?" Annabelle asked. "I never saw evidence."

"Then why would he say I was the key?" Araneae asked.

The judge's head shook. "I never understood why Daniel did anything that he did." She looked back to Araneae, her gaze going to her wrist. "He gave me the bracelet you're wearing right before you were born."

Araneae lifted her wrist. "This came from my...other mother. She gave it to me before she sent me away on the plane."

"It's the same bracelet. I couldn't believe it when I saw it at the club. I don't know how any of this happened." She tilted her head toward the bracelet. "Have you changed the picture in the locket?"

As Araneae struggled with the locket, I reached over and pried it open. "It's faded," I said. "I can't see what it is."

"It was a picture of the church where we were married."

"How did my mom get it?" Araneae asked.

"Daniel gave it to me just a day or two before you were born. We were up in Wisconsin..." She sighed. "...I blamed him for what happened to you. I wasn't supposed to leave Chicago. One morning, while I was supposed to be on bed rest, he drove me up there. The snow started falling." Her eyes closed as if she were seeing the scene from the past. "I was terrified I'd go into labor. The roads were nearly impassable. We had stopped at this little out-of-the-way motel. I didn't understand why he'd do that. He started to tell me what he'd done and why we were in danger. I refused to listen. I was a judge. I couldn't be made to testify against my husband, but if I knew..." Her sentence trailed away.

Araneae and I both nodded.

"He left me there."

"Alone in a snowstorm?" Araneae asked.

"He wasn't acting like himself. But when he came back, he was calmer. That's when he gave me the bracelet. However, back then, it only had two charms." She touched the charms. Where did you get the scissors and the diploma?"

"From someone very special. The diploma was when I graduated high school. The scissors were to commemorate the ribbon cutting of Sinful Threads."

"I'm so proud of all you've done."

Araneae glowed with Annabelle's praise.

"Back then," the judge went on, "when you were born, it only had the locket and key."

Araneae and I both looked toward one another as I reached for her wrist and lifted the charm, the one that looked like an old key. It was smaller than a standard skeleton key for a door. My mother's house still had interior doors that took skeleton keys. The one on the bracelet was less than half the size, some of the gold had chipped away, exposing the metal beneath.

Turning to me, Araneae asked, "Did he say that I'm the key or I had the key?"

"Fuck. It can't be. Where would it lead? What could it possibly open?"

We both turned to Annabelle.

"The minister who married us," she said, "gave Daniel the bracelet for our daughter. That's what Daniel told me. It had belonged to the minister's wife. He wanted it passed on and they had no children. We were married at a small church in Cambridge, Wisconsin. We were never very religious, yet I remember when Daniel returned from visiting the minister and talking to him, I thought that he had a new sense of calm. He agreed to go back to Chicago.

"Is that minister still living?" I asked.

Annabelle shook her head. "I don't know. I doubt it."

Araneae reached out to the judge. "It may be a long shot, but is there anything, a lockbox, a..." Her head shook. "...jewelry box, anything that you can think of that my father could have used to hide the CDs that Rubio thinks I have?"

"I can't think of anything. I moved after he died. The house was too big and lonely. Everything was cleaned out. A lot was donated."

"Did Rubio...? Was he around when you moved?" I asked.

She nodded. "Yes, he had people to help."

I looked to Araneae and shook my head. "Then it wasn't there. He'd know."

Her soft brown eyes swirled with ideas. She turned to Annabelle. "He went to the church and afterward he was calmer?"

"Yes, well, he said he talked to the minister. I assumed that was at the church."

"Mom, can you tell us the minister's name and the church?"

"I love hearing you call me that." She sat straighter in her seat. "The minister's name was Watkins, Kenneth Watkins. The church was..." She reached for Araneae. "...it's where you're buried."

JOSEY

Eleven years ago ~

*W*rapping my jacket around me, fending off the chill of the springtime air, I stared down at the track as members of the girls' track team gathered. The sky was blue, yet the early April sun held little warmth. At least it wasn't snowing, I thought, as I took in the greening grass. Trees were beginning to sprout blossoms and leaves.

Often Byron would arrange his schedule to attend Renee's track meets. Today wasn't one of those times. I smiled as parents I recognized waved and nodded, some carrying blankets. Through the years there had been reassurance in that many of the children who'd first met in kindergarten were still together. Though their interests varied, they'd remained friends. As Renee got older, I'd become a Girl Scout leader and active in the PTO. Byron worried that I was bringing too much attention to us, but in my mind, it was my way to stay involved and protect Renee from within.

Those girls, including Renee, who were scheduled next to run, were unzipping their sweats and pulling sweatshirts over their heads. Like many of her teammates, Renee's hair was pulled back to a high ponytail. Throwing her sweatshirt to the side of the track, she reached up and tightened her ponytail tie. I knew from experience that when she ran, her hair would swish back and forth.

My back stiffened as a vaguely familiar man took the seat near me on the bleachers. My mind tried to place him as a parent of one of Renee's classmates. I was coming up empty. Then again, the parents from all the participating schools were seated together. Maybe he was the father of one of the opponents.

My skin prickled with an uneasy feeling as he scooted closer.

I wished I could lose the sense of dread that accompanied me night and day over the last fifteen years. I longed to enjoy the life we'd created and not fear that at any moment it could be ripped out from under us.

What would it be like to not wake multiple times a night in a cold sweat with images of Allister Sparrow in my head?

After all of this time, I couldn't imagine.

It wasn't that Mr. Sparrow personally visited us through the years, but he'd sent subtle messages, enough to let us know he was watching. We'd continued to do as he instructed, sending Renee's school picture each year to the post office box. The address was the same as when she'd first been given to us, as was ours. We lived in the same house.

The man sitting beside me nodded toward the track as the girls readied themselves in the starting blocks. Renee was in the lane closest to the field, farther back than her teammates and opponents. It was an optical illusion—the way the different lanes appeared. Each lane farther from the field was just that much longer than its neighbor.

"One of those yours?" he asked.

I flinched as at the same moment he spoke, the starting gun sounded, echoing through the cool air, and the girls began to run.

"Excuse me?" I replied, my mind on Renee as she pushed herself, her bare legs below her running shorts straining and arms pumping with a baton in her grasp.

This was Chicago in the spring. It seemed like track uniforms could be warmer.

"She's grown up nice," the man said, his eyes too on the track.

I turned his way. "I'm sorry, do we know one another." I couldn't place him.

I stood and clapped as Renee came around the track and passed the baton to a teammate. Breathing heavily, she looked up to the stands and smiled. Her soft brown eyes glowed with pride. The baton hand-off was the hardest part of a relay for her, and she'd done it perfectly. Her teammate was significantly ahead of the pack.

The last runner in a relay was usually the fastest. As the first, Renee's job was to keep them in the running. No pun intended.

As I sat down, the man turned to me. "What was that cat's name?"

My stomach twisted as a cold chill ran through me. "Sir, I'm certain you're mistaken."

"Kitty," he said with a nod. "Big gray one."

The next hand-off had happened, but my eyes were no

longer on the track. I turned to the man, my blood boiling. "If you have something to say or a message to deliver, do it and leave."

"Just checking up. She's gotten real pretty, that one. There are always opportunities for her, you know, if things don't work out."

Another perfect hand-off, yet I wasn't seeing the relay as my stomach was revolting at his suggestion.

My neck straightened as my mind was besieged by memories of Neal's childhood stories. It didn't take a genius to know that his mother had talked up his abilities in math and other attributes to keep him out of what could happen to children in the Sparrow outfit. I wasn't talking about the children of people in the outfit. I meant children they acquired. Selling a prostitute's boy wasn't beneath them and she knew it.

The race ended, Renee's foursome the victors.

After standing and clapping, I sat again and turned this man's direction. With my jaw clenched I stared at this man—my gaze unblinking. As I did, I now recognized him. He was the census taker when Renee had been young. "Things are working out just fine," I said. "Leave us alone."

"Just doing my job, ma'am." He pulled a toothpick from his pocket and placed it between his teeth. "Watching her daddy too. There are lots of moving parts. Sometimes they crash."

"Byron is doing everything he was told."

"Not talking about that one."

I shook my head. "Then tell me, what is your job? Is it to intimidate me? Is it to scare me? As I said, my husband and I are doing everything we were told to do. She's loved and cared for. What someone else does isn't up to us. If your boss has a concern, voice it. Otherwise, leave us alone."

We sat in silence for a few minutes until I turned to see Renee, now wearing the team's long pants and sweatshirt, coming my way, climbing higher and higher between people as her cleats clicked upon the metal bleachers. She was already taller than me by quite a few inches and nearly as tall as Byron.

"Go away now, or I'll scream," I whispered to the man.

"Not a good idea."

Taking a drink from a water bottle, Renee sat on my other side. "Did you see the baton pass?"

I laid my hand on her knee. "Of course, I did. It was perfect. You did great. Good job. Do you know your time yet?" I was talking fast, trying to keep her attention on me.

"No, the coach said she'd get them to us later." She leaned forward, looking around me. "Hi."

The man nodded. "Nice to see you again."

"This man was just leaving," I said.

He stood. "Until next time. Stay safe."

Once he was gone, Renee leaned closer and whispered. "Who was that? He seemed kind of creepy."

"If you ever see him again, let me know."

"I don't remember seeing him before," she said.

"Still, will you promise?"

"Sure, Mom." She smiled again. "I need to get back down to the team."

I reached for her hand. "Seriously, Renee, that hand-off was great."

A glow of pink filled her cheeks, a mixture of the cool air, sunshine, and her reaction to my praise. "Thanks, Mom."

ARANEAE

*L*orna and I sat together in the penthouse kitchen waiting for the men to return from what she called the bat cave. After we all ate—together for a change —the three of them disappeared. Other than Patrick who was with me the rest of the day, I had the feeling that Sterling and Reid had been working on this since he and my mother left my office.

"I feel like there's hope," I said, sipping a glass of wine— the sweet stuff that Sterling disliked.

Lorna also had a glass of red in front of her, a thicker, more full-bodied wine than mine. She spun the glass, twisting the stem and watching the liquid slosh. "I can't imagine all the changes you've gone through."

"In the last month or my whole life?"

"Both, I guess," Lorna said with a scoff.

"The last month has been...overwhelming. I'm glad Sterling has been with me..." I smiled at her. "...and all of you. I really feel comfortable here, more than I could have imagined."

"You know, he'd been watching you for years. I wasn't really supposed to know, but after years of his digging into your life, your name came up with Reid occasionally. When Sparrow decided the time was right, I was worried."

"About?" I asked.

She inhaled and exhaled, her green eyes moving away from her glass and toward the now-dark windows with the lights of Chicago below. "We have a dynamic that I can't explain. I wasn't sure how adding another person to it, someone who Sparrow wanted and who didn't know she was wanted, would be."

"Has it always been the four of you since you and Reid married?"

"There was some tension at first. They weren't used to having a woman around and then with Mason..."

My chest tightened at the mention of the friend Sterling had told me a little about when he'd explained the darker side of Sparrow and McFadden. "I don't know much about him really. I know he was with Reid, Patrick, and Sterling in the army."

"And afterward for a while." She reached out and covered my hand. "It's why I always tell Reid I love him. Things can happen in the blink of an eye. These three..." She lifted her hand as her eyes became glassy. "...have always—as long as I've known them—been inseparable. Three is a different dynamic than four. When there were four of them, they'd often branch out in twos. It was usually your man with Mason and mine with Patrick." She shook her head. "That isn't to say..."

My pulse had kicked up. "What can I assume about Mason?"

"Nothing. That's Sparrow's story."

Getting up, she walked out the archway toward the back elevator. When she returned, she sat back down. "I know what they want me to know. One day, if Sparrow wants you to know the details, it's up to him. I shouldn't have mentioned it. His name is kind of off-limits around here. I've been thinking about your mentioning it a while ago. You even knowing it means that Sparrow trusts you more than you can know.

"For years he carried around this cloud." She blinked away the moisture from her eyes as a smile bloomed. "It's been gone since you arrived, not lessened, not intermittent. We're all happier for him than you can imagine. I know this place gets weird. I understand better than anyone how you felt the other night. I just want you to know that having you here...the first time I met you, I knew immediately that I didn't need to worry. It's like you've always been meant to be with us—with him."

I took a breath. "I can't explain it, but it feels that way to me too."

The sound of the pocket door caused both of us to turn toward the archway where Lorna had just been.

One by one, the kitchen grew fuller as all three men entered. No longer in suits, they were all casual. It was the one in the gray sweatpants and charcoal t-shirt who had my attention, the one staring at me as if he hadn't just recently eaten and I was his dinner.

"What did you learn and decide?" I asked, ignoring the way my body twisted and nipples hardened under his gaze.

Stop it, Araneae. You're in a room full of people.

That shouldn't happen, yet it did.

"We might be on to something," Sterling said.

Reid was holding the key, no longer attached to my bracelet. In his large hand, it appeared even smaller. "This is brass, covered in an imitation gold. That's why it appeared to be flaking."

"Do you think it can open something?" Lorna asked.

"I do. I've been researching keys and lockboxes all afternoon and evening. There are many that have a similar key. Most are antique or made to look antique. Based on the size, I think the lockbox is small, about the size of a letter box."

"So my mother helped?" I asked.

"We hope," Sterling said, sitting down at the table with us. Reaching for my wine glass, he took a sip and immediately his lips and nose scrunched. "Ugh. How do you drink that?"

I took it back. "I like the sweet stuff."

"That size of box," Patrick said, "one they couldn't open, if it was at the church could easily have been moved or discarded. The only way to know is to look. Tomorrow, the church is going to be searched."

"Really?" I asked excitedly. "I want to go."

Sterling reached for my knee under the table. Similar to the night of the lockdown, I was wearing yoga pants, a t-shirt, and soft socks. He squeezed it gently with his large hand. "We'll talk about it upstairs."

My lips came together, physically stopping me from arguing, yet the words were right there. I understood he didn't want to do it in front of others, but by God, we would be discussing this.

Less than an hour later, up in our room with my hand on my hip, I declared, "I'm going with you."

"You're the one who never wants to leave Sinful Threads," Sterling said, "always concerned about taking time away."

I stripped my shirt off, pulling it over my head and stepped out of my yoga pants. Sterling's t-shirt was on the floor of our closet joining the pile of discarded clothes.

My eyes went to him, the way his sweatpants hung low, the trail of dark hair going down into the V created by his trim waist and hip bones. Making a concerted effort, I moved my gaze higher until it met his. "Don't throw my own words back at me. This is about me. Besides, it's a church in a small picturesque town in Wisconsin. It's not like when you were headed down to Boulder in the middle of a kidnapping. We can leave and drive first thing tomorrow morning and be back before afternoon. We can both work after if we don't find anything. I'll let Jana know."

Sterling shook his head. "Nothing to Jana yet. And we aren't driving. It's only two and a half hours, but we're concerned..." He seemed to weigh his words.

"About what?" I asked, wearing only my bra and panties as I walked to the bathroom to ready for bed.

"What your mother said could have been a plant," he said following me, "to throw us off. Or it could be a setup. There are too many possibilities." He came up behind me, his dark eyes peering over my head at our reflection as he wrapped his arms around me. His jaw was tight and brow furrowed, his expression adding more warning to his words.

I spun in his embrace, my eyes coming to his bare chest. Placing my hands over his broad shoulders, I looked upward. "This is not a lockdown situation."

"Sunshine—"

"No," I interrupted. "Absolutely not. If that's what you're thinking, get it out of your mind right now."

His chest inflated as he inhaled. "You have to trust—"

I laid a finger over his lips. "I do trust you. I trust you, Reid, and Patrick, just like you told me to do when we were at the cabin. It took me a while, but I understood what was happening when you went to Boulder. I didn't like it. That situation was dangerous. This is where my parents were married. I want to see it."

He kissed my lingering finger. "What about the other thing your mother said?"

That it's also where I was buried.

"I've been thinking about that too. I want to see it." When he didn't respond, I went on, "I want to see it with you. It'll probably be emotional, but remember, you promised to be with me when I learned good and bad. I'm not really buried there, but a child is. That makes me sad."

"The three of us talked about lockdown," he admitted.

My head shook.

"I want to trust your mother."

"Me too."

He ran his hand through his hair as he took another step. "If she's sending us on a wild goose chase, it could be to make you vulnerable."

"You said that McFadden agreed I was off-limits until Labor Day. We still have five days." I followed him back into the bedroom. "Won't I be safest with you?"

He spun toward me, the tall windows behind him. In the dark reflection of the glass, I saw the way the muscles in his back tightened. Facing me, his gaze darkened, raking over my body, both exposed and unexposed parts, and warming my skin. Lower, an erection was coming to life.

A smile came to my lips. "Aren't I?"

"Not right now," he said matter-of-factly.

My cheeks rose higher. "You don't scare me, Mr. Sparrow."

He came closer, running a finger over my cheek. "I never want you to be scared. I want you to always know you're safe." He reached for my waist and pulled me closer until his growing erection probed my stomach. "The only one to touch you is me."

I craned my neck, looking up at him. "You're the only one I want touching me. However, if you don't agree that I'm going with you tomorrow, I'm going to give you a dose of your own medicine."

"Oh yeah? What would that be?"

"What's good for girls is good for boys."

"Sunshine, I'm not a boy."

"No, you're very much a man. I'm also not a girl; nevertheless, if you're not good..." I left the sentence open-ended.

He reached behind me, unsnapping my bra.

"Sterling."

"You should know by now, I'm always good."

I took a step back. "Promise me that I'm going to Cambridge, Wisconsin."

All at once, I yelped as he lifted me, placing me on the edge of our bed.

"That's not a promise," I said, trying to ignore what his lips were doing, how they were kissing and nipping the side of my neck from behind my ear to my collarbone. "Sterling."

He took a step back, his dark eyes closing before opening

again. "Be ready by six. We want to get to the church before people are there."

My head tilted as I smiled beneath veiled lids. "Now, where were we?"

His answer wasn't verbal, though it did involve his mouth —all of it. His lips, tongue, and teeth.

ARANEAE

*S*terling's plane touched down in Madison, Wisconsin, at a private airport. When Sterling said to be ready by six in the morning, he meant wheels up at six. I didn't mind. I'd hardly slept with my thoughts on what we may find. If we didn't find the evidence that Sterling had alluded to in our talks, we were back to no answers. If we did, I didn't want to see it. I wanted the rose-colored glasses he described.

It was hard enough to know that beyond the stories things like child exploitation occurred, that men and women placed dollar signs above the lives of children, that there were really people out there who paid to fulfill sick fantasies. Knowing it was enough to turn my stomach. I couldn't see it.

The flight from Chicago to Madison was less than an hour, yet the tension in the plane was palpable, radiating off Patrick and Sterling in thick waves reverberating through the air. After the initial greeting, Keaton stayed away from the three of us, aware of our moods. There was a lot riding on this theory and we all knew it.

Sterling had reassured me numerous times that no matter if there was evidence for us to find or if we didn't, I was safe. He promised double security details on my friends. I didn't want to believe that the evidence existed or that my uncle or Sterling's father had been involved, yet at the same time, I wanted it over. I wanted to not be afraid for my friends. I wanted a life like we had in Canada or on Lake Michigan. I wanted to not need to look over my shoulder or fear being without Sterling or Patrick. I wanted to maybe one day walk down Michigan Avenue or Lake Shore Drive alone and enjoy the scenery.

Patrick said there would be a car waiting for the three of us at the airport in Madison. Reid was back in Chicago doing what he did from the confines of their lair and watching over Lorna and the rest of Sparrow.

I recalled what Sterling had said, that this could be a ruse to focus our attention elsewhere, leaving parts of Sparrow vulnerable. Or this could be a setup. I didn't want to believe either of those options because it meant Annabelle purposely led us this way for Rubio.

Along with my fantasies of walking the main streets of Chicago, I envisioned a relationship with my birth mother, one where we met for lunch at a cafe or enjoyed one another's company as we browsed stores along Lake Shore Drive.

We all sucked in a breath as the door to the plane opened. Beyond, the sky was filled with the purples and pinks that follow a sunrise. It was early Wednesday morning and it seemed as though Madison was quiet, waiting for the hustle and bustle of the workday to begin.

Sterling placed his hand in the small of my back, with Patrick a step ahead. "Come on, sunshine. I'm not letting you out of my sight."

I nodded, sandwiched between the two mountains of men as we scurried across the tarmac, through the small airport to the waiting car.

Each wearing blue jeans and a simple t-shirt, Sterling and I were both casual. It was Patrick who continued his role as bodyguard in a dark suit as he sat shotgun with the driver he'd hired, and Sterling and I sat in the back seat. The car was a simple, inconspicuous black sedan. The drive from Madison to Cambridge lasted about thirty minutes as Sterling searched his phone for more information on the church where my parents were married.

"It's the oldest Scandinavian Methodist Church in the world, built in 1851," he said. "The building is protected under the National Registry of Historic Places."

If my father, Daniel McCrie, hid the evidence here, it was a smart move. He was probably confident that the building would remain standing, and as a bonus, there would have been no record, such as with a safety deposit box or storage container."

I let out a deep breath. "How do we get in and where do we search?"

"Getting inside won't be a problem. There's no security system," Patrick said. "And very old locks."

"How do you know that?" I asked and then added, "Never mind. I should learn not to doubt you."

He went on, "The original structure—the chapel—has a basement and a steeple with a bell tower. More recently, there's been an addition to the building which also has a base-

ment. From the plans I've accessed, the newer section's basement is subdivided into a kitchen and classrooms. The first
floor of that newer section has meeting rooms, more classrooms, and offices. The original building is where church
services are still held."

"Are you thinking the basement of the original building?"
Sterling asked.

"That or the steeple," Patrick replied. "My guess is that
the original basement is not fit for use as part of the building.
It makes sense that it would be a good storage area."

My pulse kicked up as we passed a *Welcome to Cambridge*
sign.

By the minute, the sky was lightening. Suddenly I worried
that we would be seen.

"We'll go around back. There's an access door that goes
directly to the basement level. Take the car," Patrick told the
driver, "and wait elsewhere where you won't be seen. Come
back when one of us calls or texts."

"Yes, sir," the driver said, pulling around into the rear
parking lot.

The church itself was small by today's standards, yet the
stone walls and tall steeple, combined with the stained-glass
windows, held a romantic charm. I reached for Sterling's hand
as a small fenced-in area to the side of the church came
into view.

He followed my gaze. "You can stay in the car. You don't
need to get out."

I swallowed the tears bubbling in my throat, forming a
lump ready to erupt, and shook my head. "I want to stay with
you. Let's go into the church first."

Sterling nodded, tugging me closer and planting a kiss on my forehead. "You're so strong. I am amazed."

"You wouldn't say that if you could read my thoughts. I'm a mess."

He kissed my forehead again and forced a smile. "Then you're my favorite kind of mess."

The car stopped in the parking lot near a short sidewalk leading to concrete steps that were bordered by a wrought-iron fence. The three of us got out of the car, looking all directions for any witnesses to our breaking and entering. Momentarily, my gaze lingered on the fenced area in the distance with a variety of different-sized headstones.

The stairway where we'd been dropped off descended below the ground to an old wooden door with a dirty window. The grass on either side of the sidewalk was coated in morning dew as the late summer air began to warm with the rising of the sun. A few leaves had lost their hold of trees, blowing in small cyclones upon the pavement; however, as we descended into the cavern of the stairs, the breeze ceased to find us.

With Patrick ahead of us, my hand shook in Sterling's grasp.

This sort of activity may not be unusual for these two, but it was my first time to break and enter, and I was as nervous about being caught as I was about finding the evidence.

As if he'd had a key, Patrick did something to the lock and turned the old tarnished brass knob. After a bit of stickiness, probably caused by old paint combined with a rarely used door, a push of his shoulder moved the door inward. Musti-ness filled my senses as we stepped into the concrete rectangle seeming to span the entire length and width of the chapel above.

I lifted my free hand to my nose as our shoes upon the cement caused swirls of dust to come to life. The illumination from the window and Patrick's phone brought dimness where there had only been black. Scanning the room, the addition of light revealed a lost world inhabited mostly by dust, cobwebs, and spider webs, their intricate designs hanging from rafters and attaching to support beams.

"I don't think they come down here much," Sterling said as we continued to turn, taking in the entire basement.

"There are so many boxes," I said. "How will we find it if it's here?"

Patrick handed each of us a pair of blue latex gloves from his suit coat pocket—because everyone carries those. We covered our hands and spread out, searching and opening boxes. Some were so old that touching them caused the cardboard to disintegrate in our grasp. Choir robes from forever ago and hymnals that at one time were the standard were among our discoveries. Other findings included files full of records long forgotten—most with writing that was no longer legible—that filled multitudes of boxes left to mildew on rusting metal shelves.

"I'm going up to the steeple," Patrick finally said.

"I want to see the chapel?" I said to Sterling, asking as much as stating.

He shook his head. "I was so sure this was it. I'm sorry. I thought..." His words trailed away as disappointment infiltrated his tone.

"Please, before people get here. I want to see where my parents were married."

Taking one last look around at the decayed past of this church, he nodded and held my hand, our latex gloves still in place as he first ascended the wooden steps. His weight caused the wood to creak as the rubber soles of my tennis shoes squeaked in the silence. Step by step, we progressed upward in the narrow staircase.

More than once the stairs turned until we finally came to a landing. Above the landing, there were more stairs. I peered upward into the darkness, knowing that was where Patrick had gone. At the landing, Sterling reached for the old decorative doorknob and pulled the wooden door toward us.

The door opened to the vestibule of the chapel.

Together, we stepped out into the fresher air.

The old wood floor was well worn yet beautifully maintained. Above the doors to the outside was a striking stained-glass window, the morning sun sending colors from the design to the white plaster walls within.

One more set of double doors and we were inside the chapel.

I sucked in a breath as Sterling squeezed my hand.

"It's lovely," I said, my gaze searching everywhere from the rows of wooden pews to the tall windows along the side and the huge stained-glass window above the altar. The minister's pulpit was to one side and a place for a choir was secluded off with more beautiful wood trim. To the other side was a large grand piano.

I turned to Sterling with tears in my eyes. "Thank you."

He shook his head. "It seems this trip has been a waste of time."

"No, don't you see? If it weren't for you, I wouldn't be here, seeing this. I know my father did bad things. I know their marriage wasn't perfect, but they created me. They loved one another when they were here. And I would have lived my entire life without knowing this, without seeing this. It's all possible because of you."

Letting go of my hand, he wrapped his arm around my back and pulled me to his side. "One day, I'd like to be the one saying I do."

His declaration washed away a bit of my sadness. "Mr. Sparrow, if that's a proposal, you'll need to do better. Remember the asking part?"

His finger ran over my cheek, the scent of the gloves prevailing, yet the sentiment still there. "That's right. What were those words again?"

I lifted myself to my toes and kissed his cheek. "When you remember, let me know." I tilted my head toward the side of the church. "Before the driver comes I'd like to go see..."

"Are you sure?" he asked.

"I am."

STERLING

"Okay, sunshine, but first, let's go back in there..." I tilted my head toward the stairway. "...and wait for Patrick. Hopefully he found something."

Araneae looked down at her watch. "It's a little after eight thirty. What time do the people start working?"

"The offices open at nine. I'd like to be long gone by then."

We slipped back through the door the direction we'd come, my hand wrapped securely around hers as footsteps from above came closer. I didn't need to ask. I could tell by the expression on Patrick's face that his excursion had been as fruitful as ours in the basement. He simply shook his head as he descended the wooden steps in front of us. With Araneae secured between us, I took up the rear.

Stilling our steps, we peered one last time around the basement, taking in remnants left over the centuries, those of memories, logs, and mementos. These were items—or what was left of them—that at one time someone thought to save. Or maybe they were things that no one cared to discard. Regardless, we hadn't given ourselves enough time to thoroughly search every nook and crevice.

We needed to get out of this church now. And yet, by the magnitude of debris, I doubted that a week would be long enough to search.

We didn't have a week.

Our time was running out.

We tried and came up empty—yet I wasn't willing to accept defeat.

Once outside, Patrick secured the door and texted the driver as I stuffed Araneae's and my blue latex gloves into one of the pockets of my jeans and again secured her hand. Together we walked toward the small graveyard.

Again, her small hand trembled in my grasp. That was her only outward sign of apprehension. With her neck straight and shoulders back, she stepped determinedly toward the enclosed graveyard. Letting go of my hand, she reached for the latch.

"Araneae," I said, stopping her. "I never meant for me finding you to bring you here."

She looked up with her soft chocolate eyes, full of a magnitude of emotions. "I'm glad it did."

So fucking strong.

Awe simply didn't come close to describing the admiration I had for this beautiful, resilient woman beside me. I'd been wrong when I'd said she was fragile. That description didn't afford her the credit she deserved for all she'd endured in the past twenty-six years or for what I'd subjected her to in the last month.

In my eyes, her strength surpassed mine or even Patrick's or Reid's.

Yes, each of the three of us could look death in the face and walk away unscathed. That took a backbone of steel and a dead, nonfunctioning heart.

Araneae faced untold challenges and met them with love and emotion, baring herself in a way that scared the shit out of me. She faced the loss of parents and then the possibility of a family, only to have Pauline throw it in her face, and yet she didn't stop.

She opened herself to Annabelle.

She was willing to risk it all for Louisa.

She had taken a man, one with not all pure motives, and allowed him to see that there's more to life than success, money, and revenge.

I tugged Araneae's hand as she began to enter. "I love you so much."

Her small hand reached up to my cheek. "Sterling, I love you too. Thank you again for keeping your promise, being with me for the good and bad, and for bringing me here. I'm sorry we didn't find what we wanted," she went on, "but I feel like I've found so much more than a few compact discs. With each day since you bulldozed your way into my life, I'm finding more of me."

I kissed the top of her head, her silky blonde hair beneath my lips filling my senses with her shampoo and hairspray.

Taking a deep breath, we stepped carefully between the gravestones. As I scanned the writing, I saw there were some graves dating back to the 1800s. Few were into the second half of the 1900s, and then we came to one that was only a few inches high in the front, a bit taller in the back. A small rectangular-shaped stone. Carved upon the surface was a tiny angel, one with a baby's body and face.

Araneae McCrie
From birth to heaven
Our Angel, may she know she was and will always be loved, until we meet again.

Letting go of my hand, Araneae fell to her knees as she ran her fingers over the engraved stone. Without looking up, she spoke, her voice cracking yet filled with the determination uniquely hers. "It's surreal to see my own name."

I moved down to my haunches, wrapping an arm around her as the sedan entered the parking lot. "We should go."

She peered toward me. "Do you think we could find out who this is and give her a proper burial?"

I shook my head as I stood. "No, the coffin is empty."

"What?" she asked, still kneeling on the ground.

I offered her my hand and helped her stand. "From what I understand, there was a body. Rubio and my father had it exhumed."

Her expression changed, morphing to one of shock as she stood and brushed off her knees. "Why? Why would they do that?"

I shook my head. "My father never told me. My mother mentioned it last week and McFadden confirmed it. Mother said it was to do DNA testing, and Allister told her that he'd been lied to. He said the baby was you."

"No, you said..."

I reached for her shoulders. "I said *you*..." I emphasized the word. "...are Araneae McCrie and of that I'm confident. The mitochondrial DNA verified it. Sitting at a table with you and Annabelle, not only your coloring but your manner-isms confirmed it. You are Araneae McCrie. My father lied. It was what he did."

"It makes me sad to think an infant died and was never properly honored."

My mind went not to one infant, but tens—no, hundreds—of children who were never properly honored: those who lived through the hell of the Sparrow and McFadden outfits.

I reached for Araneae's hand. As we carefully stepped around the headstones and graves, making our way to the iron gate, another car pulled into the parking lot.

Leaning against the sedan waiting for us, Patrick looked up, his hand moving under his jacket as he watched the car that was joining our gathering.

Shit.

"We need to go," I whispered.

Araneae nodded as we shut the gate and hurried to the sedan.

The recent addition to the parking lot was an older model Buick, not black like our sedan, but a shade of red closer to maroon. As we hurried toward the sedan, the driver's door opened and a woman approximately in her fifties stepped out.

"May I help you?" she asked.

Our feet stopped as for a moment we remained silent.

"I'm Jackie Fellows," she said. "I'm the senior minister here. Are you looking for someone?"

"No," I replied. "We'll be on our way."

She took a step toward us, looking closer at Araneae than at me. "Miss, are you all right? Would you like to talk to someone?"

"I'm fine, thank you," Araneae replied.

"You look sad."

Araneae's gaze went from Patrick to me and back to the minister. "I came to see a grave, and now, it was...more emotional than I expected."

The woman took another step closer. "I don't have meetings until later." She finally looked up at me and forced a smile. "Please, come in the church and we can talk."

ARANEAE

The woman began walking toward the church. I peered upward at Sterling's expression, knowing that going inside the church and speaking to this woman wasn't what he wanted.

"Maybe she can help," I whispered.

"I don't like this." His deep tone left little room for rebuttal.

I let go of his hand. "Then stay with Patrick. I'll go in alone."

"Hell no," he growled, retrieving my hand as we walked past Patrick and the black sedan, following Jackie Fellows, not into the basement where we'd been, but into an entry taking us into the newer addition, a sprawling, more modern wing. The outside lawn was deep green, and above the path, recently fallen leaves blew in the light breeze. The peaceful surroundings were contrary to the quandary within my mind.

After Pastor Fellows unlocked double glass doors, she

asked us to follow her through a wide entry and down a hallway. The walls were lined with bulletin boards filled with
announcements of all kinds and brightly colored paper
borders, reminding me of my elementary school.

The office where she stopped had a nameplate near the
door: *Pastor Jackie Fellows*. The next line said: *Senior Minister*.

I took a deep breath as we entered her small office as she
turned on lights and opened the blinds. The view through the
window was out to the street in front of the church, not the
parking lot or cemetery.

"May I get the two of you something to drink? Coffee
or water?"

"No, we're in a hurry," Sterling replied.

"No, *thank you*," I corrected, reaching for Sterling's arm.
"As I said, this has been more emotional for me than I
planned."

"Please, have a seat..." She motioned to two chairs across
from a standard desk. "My secretary will be here shortly, but
we can keep this private if you prefer. First..." She leaned
forward in her chair as Sterling and I sat. "...as I said, I'm
Jackie. And you are?"

"I-I'm..." I began first. "...Kennedy Hawkins."

"Mrs. Hawkins?"

"Miss," I replied, "and my—"

"Kennedy and I are dating," Sterling replied. "I'm her
boyfriend."

I held back a smile, still unsure about that title. As he
mentioned last night, Sterling Sparrow was hardly a boy. It
was also clear that he wasn't offering his name.

"Kennedy," Jackie's tone was soothing, despite the scary-guy act coming from the man beside me. "Would you like to speak alone?"

"No," I answered quickly. "He's been helping me uncover some family secrets. You see I was adopted, and now I'm trying to make sense of an unknown family history."

My mostly truthful answer seemed to relax the pastor a bit.

"Well, as you probably know," she began, "this is a very old church. Our chapel dates back to 1851. What is it about our church and our graveyard that you believe is connected to your family history?"

"From stories I've been able to piece together," I answered, "at one time, my father was close with a minister here. I believe his name was Kenneth Watkins."

Jackie nodded. "He was the senior minister here for quite a stint. While many ministers like to move about, I understand why he was here for so long. I'll admit presiding over this church is a gem."

"Is he...may I contact him?" I asked.

"No, I'm sorry. He's deceased. I'm the..." She seemed to be thinking. "...third senior pastor since Minister Watkins."

I let out a long breath at another dead end.

"Kennedy, what were you hoping to find?"

I shrugged, gazing from the pastor to Sterling and back. His dark gaze was fixed on me and his jaw clenched. It was no secret he was uncomfortable and wanted to leave. "I really don't know," I answered honestly. "There's an old wives' tale—"

Sterling sat taller, every cell in his body emitting his disapproval of what I was saying.

I swallowed. "Supposedly, my father was close to Minister

Watkins, and my father left something with the minister for safekeeping. I don't even know what it was, but I know I'm supposed to find it."

"That's quite a story. A hidden treasure?"

A smile came to my face. "I know it sounds farfetched. It's fine." I started to stand. "Thank you for your time. We can—"

"Kennedy..."

I stopped.

"Can you give me any more information about this hidden treasure?"

I looked to Sterling and opened my palm his direction. "I have this key."

Begrudgingly, Sterling reached into the pocket of his jeans and removed the small key, placing it in my palm.

Jackie Fellows exhaled and leaned back in her chair. "This is highly unusual."

"I know. I'm sorry to waste—"

"Can you tell me whose grave you were visiting?"

I didn't want to tell her mine. Instead, my mind searched for names that I'd read on the headstones. The truth was that I hadn't paid that close of attention to any but mine. And then I remembered a name that I'd read.

"Valentine Shadows," I replied. "I know it's a long shot, but I read that name in a family bible."

"The Shadows were a well-established family in Cambridge before their children moved away wanting the big city. If you need more assistance with information on them, I'd be happy to assist you."

I stood as did Sterling. "Thank you again."

"Kennedy," Pastor Fellows said, "one more thing. I'm not sure if this will help you or not. However, being connected to the Shadows...well, I've always been curious. The senior minister before me told me about something. He also didn't know what it was. However, for years we've held on to it."

My eyes widened as I looked again between Jackie and Sterling. "What?"

She stood and went to a large bookshelf behind her desk, one filling the expanse of the wall nearly to the ceiling. The spines of many of the books appeared old while there were also newer editions. Walking the length of the shelf and back, she murmured to herself. She reached upward, standing on her tiptoes to retrieve something from a higher, less-accessible shelf.

"May I help you?" Sterling offered.

"Thank you. It's the one..." She pointed. "...with the worn leather spine."

Sterling reached above her, tipping the book back. As he did, his neck straightened.

He lowered the book. Turning it in his large hands, he revealed a lock where the pages should be. "This isn't a book."

Minister Fellows took it from his hand and turned to me. "It's something that has been passed on between senior ministers for years. There was some discussion of breaking the lock, but it seemed that the mystery superseded the need to learn its contents. Kenneth Watkins was a pillar, a man highly regarded in this community. I hope that for his memory, if your key fits, you will respect his loyalty to your father. I...well, no one wants to believe Pastor Watkins would be hiding anything that would bring shame on his name or this church."

She handed me the lockbox.

My pulse accelerated as I held the box that appeared from

a distance to be a leather-bound book. In my grasp, it was considerably lighter than a book its size should be. I swallowed back the emotion as some contents within rattled. "Thank you."

"Do you want to see if your key works?" she asked.

My hands were once again shaking. "I-I think...if you don't mind. I would like to do that in private."

She nodded and stepped around the desk. "I'll give you two a moment. If it fits, it's yours. If it doesn't, please leave it on my desk and maybe another day the mystery will be solved."

Once the door shut, I laid the box on the minister's desk and turned to Sterling. His gaze was dark, yet his expression had changed from one of concern and irritation that I was speaking to the minister to one of anticipation.

"Fuck," he growled under his breath. "This could be it."

I fumbled with the key, finally handing it his way. "Please do it. You're with me. That's all I want. I can't open it. I can't see if there are pictures."

"McFadden said CDs."

I extended my hand with the key. "Please, Sterling."

Maybe the man beside me wasn't the villain but Prince Charming, and instead of a shoe that needed to fit, it was a key.

His chest expanded and contracted. With his gaze set on me, I nodded again.

Taking the key from my hand, he inserted it into the keyhole and turned...

JOSEY

Ten years ago ~

*B*yron shut the door of our bedroom, closing us away from the world—our safe place that was no longer safe.

Renee and a friend were down the hall in her bedroom doing homework and listening to music. Normally, I might tell them to turn the music down, but at present, the loud tunes were a barrier keeping Byron's and my conversation private.

While the January wind blew snow through the air outside of our home, ice ran through my veins. I walked to the window and closed the curtains, no longer confident of our safety or security.

It was no longer veiled threats, but outright warnings.

Our voices were hushed yet urgent.

"It's come. I know it. We have to move now," I said.

His eyes shut. "I can try to talk to him."

"You're dead." Neal was dead. "You've been telling me that for years. What makes you think Allister Sparrow will talk to you now?"

Byron reached for my shoulders. "We won't let them have her—won't let him."

My eyes closed at the reality of my biggest fear—greatest nightmare—coming true. "The call said..." I swallowed back the bile bubbling in my gut. "...her birth father lied. He was found dead. Story is that he hanged himself. The man on the phone said her time is up and to await instructions." Tears over spilled my gray eyes as I tried unsuccessfully to rein in the fear and frustration. "We've done everything he asked. We've complied and now he knows where we are, where you work, where she goes to school. He knows everything. We complied and by doing so, played into his hand."

"He doesn't know everything," Byron said.

"What do you mean?"

"I told you from the beginning that I've been planning and saving. We could...disappear."

"All three of us?"

He nodded.

I let out a breath and sank to the edge of the bed. "Will it be safe for her?"

"I made a connection. He's not through the outfit. He's not through any outfit. He's from Boeing. He makes extra money with government contracts and well, he knows things, how to make things look legit. He can help."

I shook my head. "I'm so tired of lying. I want to go away..." I looked up. "...maybe Washington state or Montana, somewhere remote, somewhere without crime."

"Baby, that place doesn't exist."

"We have to get out of Chicago," I pleaded.

"If you think all three of us can get into a car, plane, or train and disappear into the sunset, I'm afraid you're wrong."

I looked up at my husband, really seeing what the last sixteen years had done to him, how they'd aged him. The lines in his face were deeper. His back slouched, rounding what was once proud, the physical result of carrying the burden of our deceptions.

"But you said the three—"

"This man," Byron interrupted, "I've told him some of our needs, not all. He thinks the best chance for Renee is to separate from us. Sparrow will be looking for three of us, not one."

My breath caught in my chest. "No. I can't do that. I can't. She's sixteen years old. What will we do, leave her? I couldn't..." I stood. "...I won't." I recalled the veiled threats from the recurring visits by that man—the census taker and track meet spectator. "Byron, you know what will happen to her if they find her. You know." I laid my hand on the front of his shirt. "In here. In your heart, you know. I would die before I allowed her into that life. If Sparrow is upset with her birth father, he's not above taking it out on her."

Byron's jaw set as his stare disappeared for a moment behind closed eyes. When his eyes opened, he made a declaration I never expected.

"I have to die in her place."

I gasped, taking a step back. "What? No. I don't want to lose either of you."

He shook his head. "Listen, Josey. There's a plan. We can't all travel together. According to my resource, he suggested making a clean break. I will *die*—disappear first."

"Are you leaving us?"

"Hell no. I'll go ahead and get something set up for us. My contact can help. If Sparrow believes it, maybe it will satisfy him, stop him from looking."

I paced, turning every few steps like a caged animal. "And then what?"

Byron went to the closet and pushed over the sliding door. Inside were years and years of life's accumulations: clothes that no longer fit, shoes no longer in style, as well as boxes of pictures chronicling our happy family. From under a stack of shoe boxes, he retrieved a manila envelope, one I couldn't recall seeing before.

He handed it my direction.

"What is this?" I asked, not sure I wanted to know.

"It contains fake identifications for all three of us."

Untucking the lip of the envelope, I dumped the contents from within onto the cover of our bed. Birth certificates, passports, and four IDs became visible. I reached for one with Renee's picture and then another. "Why does she have two?"

"Because she's sixteen. Some airlines will allow her to fly alone, but not all. He said it was a safety net."

I read the name: Kennedy Hawkins. The reality hit me like a punch to my gut, a momentary loss of air as dread flowed through my body. "I-I can't..." I picked up the one with my picture. "Why are our names different?"

Byron reached for my hands and directed me to sit on the bed. "It's her best and possibly only chance. Sparrow's influence is far-reaching. We saw that years ago when I tried to get employment in other states. If he wants to find us, he will. We have few options. Separating, letting Renee go, will make her less of a target. He'll be looking for all three of us. He knows how much we care for her. He'd never suspect that we'd separate."

"I-I..." Words were hard to form. "But I do love her. You love her." I searched his eyes. "Tell me you do. Tell me this hasn't all been an act."

"Josey, I fucking love her more than if she were our own. We've always known she wasn't. We've always known this could happen."

"So we..." Standing, I turned circles. "...what? Put her on a plane and never see her again? How does she live? How does she survive? What if they find her?"

"I told you that I've been saving money. I've accumulated enough to keep her in a good private school through high school, and if she chooses a state school or gets scholarships, it will cover most of her tuition and board through her undergraduate years. We always wanted her to go to college. I'm not saying it's ideal. I'm saying that this is the best way to hide her from Sparrow. I've researched private schools. I found one that if they can be convinced that through the death of her parents, arrangements were set for her emancipation, they'll allow her to stay there."

I let out a long sigh. "What about us?"

He sighed. "Giving all of that money to her won't leave us with much, but I think I have a solution."

My head was pounding. He wanted to send Renee away. He wanted to give her all we've saved, yet he thought he had a solution. "What?"

"That's what I need to go ahead and check out. There's a community in Maine." He forced a smile. "You said you wanted remote. This place is completely off the grid. No telephones. No internet. No cell phones. Nothing. They help people who need help and everyone works together to keep the community self-sufficient. It will be a place where we can disappear."

My eyes grew wide, staring at my husband as if he were someone I'd never met. "You want to go to a what? A commune? A cult? And send Renee to a private boarding school where we won't be able to reach or contact her?"

"Josey, I want all three of us to live to see tomorrow. I don't want Renee living in a commune. I want her to have a life, for her to have a chance at a life. I want to wake up next to you for the next thirty years and not share a shallow grave. That's what I want."

ARANEAE

$\mathcal{A}$fter thanking Minister Fellows, Sterling and I left the church with the lockbox in tow. The world seemed a new place as we passed other workers arriving and the late summer air continued to burn off the morning dew.

Patrick met us at the sedan, his questioning stare penetrating through the darkness of his now-donned sunglasses. We rode in virtual silence until we reached the airport and boarded the plane. Once aboard with the door closed, the three of us were a chorus of voices asking as well as telling.

"There are no pictures," Sterling said, so far being the only one to look inside and see the contents. "There are CDs, but more than McFadden said. He'd told me there would be six. I didn't take the time to count, but I'd estimate that there are at least a dozen. There were also a few floppy disks and multiple envelopes with documents. I didn't take the time to look at any of it closely."

I shook my head, leaning against the back of a tall chair

sitting at the round table at the front of the plane with Patrick and Sterling. "So we take it all to McFadden and life goes on?"

"No," both men said in unison.

"What? I want this over."

"So do we," Sterling responded, "but we're not handing over information that we don't know what it entails."

"You're going to copy it, aren't you?" I asked pointedly, looking at both men. "You're not going to let this die."

"We're going to take it to Reid and learn the contents," Patrick said in his calming tone.

"And then *you're* going to decide what is shared," I added, "the three of you.

"No, Araneae," Sterling replied. "The one making that decision would be you."

"What?"

"It's yours. You may not want to know what it contains, but I've been thinking about something you said. You asked me if I found you for the purpose of finding the evidence so I would be in control of its dissemination."

I nodded, remembering the conversation.

"I did," he said matter-of-factly.

My chest grew tight at his confession.

"And I was wrong," he went on. "That said, finding you, Araneae, wasn't wrong. The choice is yours completely with what happens to whatever's in this box. First, let Reid find out what it contains."

I sucked in a breath, looking into Sterling's dark eyes and back to Patrick's as my mind swirled with the ramifications. "Tell me," I declared, "if there's evidence about Sparrow, about your father's involvement, what will that mean for you, for all of you? That FBI agent, Wesley Hunter, he wants evidence against you. He wants me to testify. I don't want to know what's on there. I don't want to do that."

"In a way," Sterling said, "that's what your mother said about not wanting to know what your father did or what he had."

"She said that even if she knew, she couldn't be compelled to testify against him because he was her husband." My heartbeat accelerated as I stared at Sterling. "Do you remember those words?"

The plane was now high in the sky as Sterling unbuckled his seat belt and came my way. His expression was suddenly dark, darker than my question should have instilled. With a tug, my seat belt came undone. I hesitated as he encouraged me to stand.

Yet as I did, he reached for my wrist and without a word led me through the main cabin and back to the bedroom.

Once the door was shut, I found myself pinned against the wall, his solid body on mine and his dark, penetrating gaze taking my breath away.

"Sterling..."

His lips came to mine, demanding, possessive, bruising.

His hard chest pressed against mine, flattening my breasts as his arms created a cage near my face. When we finally pulled apart, I looked up expectantly, wanting to hear the words.

"You are mine," he declared, yet his expression was not one of adoration. "You fucking have been for nineteen years. For most of that time you didn't know, you didn't understand. I knew you were mine. Now I know so much more." He leaned back, looking down over my t-shirt and jeans. "I know every fucking curve you have hidden under those clothes. I know the way your body responds to not only my actions but also my words and even expressions. I fucking love how wet you get, how hard your perfect nipples become, and the way you say my name all breathy as you're falling apart."

My breasts moved against his chest, fighting for air to fill my lungs.

"I fucking know the words you mentioned. I know them because a beautiful, magnificent, intelligent, loving, and amazing woman taught them to me." His finger caressed my cheek. "She taught me more than that. In a short time, she taught me that I was capable of more than power and violence. She showed me that I can love. That's the woman I want to share my name, my life, my bed forever."

He took a step back.

"Sterling?"

His head shook. "I won't use those words, not yet. I never want you to think that I'd propose to you to stay out of prison or to keep my family name out of the news. Araneae, you deserve so much fucking more than that."

"But...it's a solution."

"No, sunshine. It's forever and I want to spend it with you once we know what forever means."

He came closer and brushed a chaste kiss over my lips. "And if you ever take my control away like that again in front of Patrick or anyone, your ass is mine."

I took a step closer and placing my hands on his shoulders, lifted my tennis-shoe-covered feet up to my tiptoes. "Yes, Mr. Sparrow."

He reached down as his fingers splayed over my backside. "It's already mine. One more thing."

"What?"

"Lockdown. All of us, until this is settled. Even Sinful Threads."

"What?"

"Chicago office. Jana gets the rest of the week off. You can handle business from the penthouse."

I considered arguing and telling him that my business was off-limits to his rules, but then again, McFadden's deadline was looming. Today was Wednesday. Labor Day was Monday —in five days.

I could follow Sterling's rules for five more days if when they were done, we could move on. "When this is over," I said, repeating something we'd discussed before, "you promised me more control."

He leaned forward until our foreheads touched. "When it's over."

I smiled. "Then I can wait."

STERLING

"I want to know what Reid knows, when he knows it," Araneae said after handing me the lockbox as we settled into the back seat of one of my reinforced SUVs.

After the near miss the other day by the drive-by SUV and what we may have possibly discovered, there were no precautions I wouldn't take. With Patrick in the shotgun position and Garrett driving, we were on our way to the apartment where Reid was waiting—practically biting at the bit to get his hands on the contents of the lockbox.

I reached for Araneae's hand. "Do you want to know?"

Araneae's bottom lip disappeared for a moment as I watched her thoughts swirl through her soft brown eyes. "I do and I don't."

My head shook as Garrett navigated the Chicago streets, our vehicle stilled sporadically by stoplights and traffic while Patrick continually kept an eagle eye on our surroundings. It was early afternoon in the Windy City, and as usual, downtown traffic was at its normal gridlock. Taking a breath, I peered up at the buildings, some of their top floors lost in the low bank of clouds that had recently settled over the city.

Since our return, the sky had filled with heavy gray clouds, the signaling of a cold front coming our way. On the calendar, summer still had a few more weeks, yet many considered the Labor Day holiday the unofficial end. Pools throughout the city closed. Schools throughout the country reopened, reducing the number of families visiting over their children's summer breaks.

I found it ironic that the same deadline had been given to us. The clock was ticking with a lot riding on the contents of this box. All of that, combined with the gloomy skies, had us all on edge. The tension within the car was growing thicker by the moment.

Taking a look to my side, Araneae was staring out her window. Her gaze clouded as if she weren't seeing the skyscrapers and overcast conditions. If I could guess, her mind was still back in Cambridge—the church where her parents had married and the graveyard where she was supposedly buried.

It was no secret that I wanted us to leave the church and wasn't pleased about her decision to talk to the new minister. With each step toward the church and while in that office, my thoughts were on how to best inform Araneae that I disapproved—admittedly, most of my explanations included reddening her sexy round ass. And then...

I almost couldn't believe my ears when Pastor Fellows mentioned something handed down since Watkins or possibly before.

Now, watching Araneae with that faraway gaze, I wanted to reassure her that we'd find our way through this, that she was safe, and maybe even that one day we'd prove to the world that she was the real Araneae McCrie.

Of course, I noticed how she'd introduced herself as Kennedy Hawkins.

I reached over and secured her hand. "You do and you don't want to know," I said, repeating what she had just told me.

Her head bobbed as if her emotions were beginning to overpower our discovery.

"I've told you what I think this contains," I said honestly. I squeezed her hand. "I've been honest with you. I knew it would be too much information all at once, so it's taken time. Still, you know more than I wish you did. Not because my family was involved, but because I would do anything if you could live your entire life and never know that this ugliness exists."

Patrick spoke, redirecting our attention. "Sparrow. Araneae."

Both of our gazes moved to the front seat.

"I spoke with Jana," Patrick said, "before we disembarked the plane. She just sent me a new text message. The Chicago Sinful Threads office is locked and secure. She's on her way home and available to do whatever she can do for you from there."

"Is she safe?" Araneae asked.

I nodded Patrick's direction, silently telling him to send a team of Sparrows to her neighborhood and watch over her. At this point, I wasn't sure of anything.

"We'll send extra eyes to watch over her," Patrick replied.

"And her son and her husband," Araneae added.

With one finger of my free hand, I turned Araneae's beautiful face back toward me, running the pad of my finger over her cheek. I leaned closer, inhaling the sweet scent of her lotions and perfumes. "This...this..." I began, "is what I didn't want. I don't want you worrying about your safety and that of your friends."

"I'm not worried about mine."

I loved her confidence.

"Sometimes, I wish I could keep you in Ontario or on a yacht, keep you away from the darkness."

"See," she replied with a smile, "I think you see the world differently than I see it."

I hoped I did.

"You see it in one way," she went on, "but really, Sterling, it's multidimensional. There is bad. There is evil. More than likely, in that box we'll find evidence of that. You've lived with this knowledge most of your life. You've given me a glimpse of it because I need to realize that it exists..." Her lips turned upward. "...for my safety."

"You're finally catching on."

"However," she continued, "what you seem to not see is that the world you describe is a subset of a bigger, much more beautiful place. When I look at you, I don't see only darkness. I see a man who is doing his best to teach me about the world I was born into while at the same time shielding me from its ugliness. And I love you for that. So...going back to the box..." Her shoulders straightened. "...I want to know what it contains. I want a promise from you that the three of you will tell me everything—not necessarily in detail—but don't shield me for my safety, my naiveté, or anything else. If you can make me that promise, I don't need to be there when it's discovered."

It amazed me that she could see me the way she did, that she could see me as more than a man who made decisions that affected others' lives, who used his money and influence to seek more, and who would kill for her.

"I want to shield you."

"I know," she replied.

"I promise you'll learn everything."

"And you'll be with me when I do?"

"Yes."

The car turned, passing the risen gate before descending into the tunnels of our garage. As it did, I let out a long breath, thankful to be within our safety structure. "We're all here," I said.

Patrick turned back my way. "Not Lorna."

It was a punch to my gut. "What? Where is she? We're on lockdown."

"She went shopping this morning before it was declared. Reid called and told her. She said she'd be home but hasn't returned. He's been trying to reach her for the last ninety minutes."

"Send Sparrows," I said. "What about the tracker on her phone?"

"Sparrows have already been sent. The tracker indicates that she's at the South Loop Market."

"Did she have a driver?" I asked, my mind racked with scenarios.

"No, she took one of the cars from the garage."

"Track that too."

"Reid's on it."

As Garrett pulled up to the elevator within the garage, Patrick, Araneae, and I got out of the car. I leaned toward Garrett's window. "Go to one, and we'll let you know what's next."

"Wait," Patrick said, staring at his phone.

"What is it?" I asked.

"They found the car she drove. All four tires have been slashed. When they found it, a tow truck was already there."

"Fuck," I growled.

Patrick continued to swipe his screen. "Lorna just pinged the backup tracker." He looked up at me. "The market isn't far from here. I'm sure that Reid wants to go out looking for her, but I think it would be better if Garrett and I go."

Araneae's eyes were glassy as her now-trembling hand held tightly to my arm.

"Fuck," I said with a tilt of my head, "if it were her..."

"It's not," Patrick reassured. "Lorna understands. She hasn't called Reid back for a reason. Instead, she's used the tracker in her purse to ping back. We'll find her. She's avoiding someone or someones. Sparrow, we'll get her. Go to Reid. Tell him we won't be back without her."

I inhaled, wanting to be the one to go with Patrick while also knowing that my presence would only complicate matters more. With a quick nod, I said, "Go. Bring her back and if you find who's after her..." I didn't need to finish the sentence.

Patrick nodded as he opened the door and got back in the car with Garrett.

Laying my hand over Araneae's, I did my best to comfort her, to erase a bit of the worry from her expression. "Distraction. That's what this is. McFadden tried to find this information for ten years. He put us under a deadline. Now he's trying to distract us so he can carry out his threat."

"What did you mean about the tracker in her purse?" she asked.

I inhaled, touching the sensor next to the elevator as the screen lit up.

"Do I have a tracker with me besides the one on my phone?" she asked.

I couldn't lie to her. "They're sewn into all your purses and handbags as well as your satchel."

"Lorna knew about it and was able to use it to call for help?"

I nodded as the doors to the elevator opened. We both stepped inside.

"Sterling, once she's safe, I want to know all of this. I get that you don't want to worry me, but what if I needed to contact you or Reid and couldn't use my phone? If you've given me a means, I should know it."

I was determined that wouldn't happen. Araneae McCrie was not going out and about by herself. She wouldn't need to ping Patrick or me. One of us would be present. Instead of saying all of that, I asked, "You're not upset the additional trackers exist?"

The elevator was moving upward to P.

"I suppose I should be upset. Fuck, I don't know what I should think anymore. I know that keeping us all safe is your priority. I guess that I want to be safe too. I want everyone safe. If that means learning your and Reid's spy shit, then I want to know how to use it."

The elevator doors opened on P to our quiet apartment.

According to the security app on my phone, the elevator hadn't been used to this floor since Lorna left, sometime after we had this morning. If I didn't have that confirmation, I wouldn't be able to kiss Araneae and step back into the elevator.

"Wait," she said. "You're leaving me here on lockdown by myself?"

"I need to take this to Reid." I lifted the box I'd been holding.

"Sterling?"

I held the doors open with my free hand. "Sunshine, I never said that any of this was easy, but you're strong. You can do it. Call Jana. Don't tell her anything about the evidence. Talk to her about whatever you would at the office. You're welcome to use our office here in the apartment." I'd never called it *ours* before, but I liked the way it sounded. I liked sharing everything I had with Araneae. "Your laptop is still upstairs. I'll be back when I'm able. If you need me, call, and as soon as I learn anything about Lorna, you will too."

Her breasts moved higher as her lips formed a straight line. Finally, she nodded. "Go, make this all end."

A sad smile floated across my face. "This with McFadden will end, but the life, it goes on forever." The doors started to close when Araneae's hand came between them, causing them to bounce open again. "What?"

"I wanted to tell you that I love you and to please stay safe." She stepped back and smiled as the doors once again closed before I could tell her the same.

Damn she was amazing.

Pulling my phone from my pocket as the elevator descended to two, I typed out a quick text message:

. . .

"YOU AMAZE ME. I LOVE YOU TOO."

ARANEAE

*S*terling's text message made me smile as I made my way through the empty apartment. Once in our room, I was momentarily mesmerized by the sight outside the tall windows. Over the last month, I'd seen bright blue skies, sprinklings of clouds, and astounding sunsets ablaze in shades of reds, purples, and oranges. This sight was different, in an eerie sort of way. I stepped closer to the glass.

Beyond the panes there was nothing.

Nothing was a poor choice of word.

I moved closer, placing my palms upon the cool glass. Leaning forward, I peered out and then down. The view beyond the window was filled with a swirl of white and gray, a suspended mist—not falling like rain or rising like steam. Except for the churning, the moisture was stagnant, surrounding our building in a new cloak of invisibility.

Taking a step back, I stood taller. Refusing to allow my thoughts to turn negative, I chose to view the cloud cover as the thought that had just floated across my mind. Perhaps instead of gloom, it was part of Sterling's infrared protection.

That was how I would see it.

As the afternoon progressed, I tried to do as Sterling suggested and keep my mind on Sinful Threads. There was another issue with not only the warehouse here in Chicago but one in Atlanta too. The analytical side of me wanted to sit down and run the numbers, yet my mind was again on one of my friends, one who could be in danger because of me. Instead of going to Sterling's office or staying in our bedroom, I set my laptop up on the kitchen breakfast bar and made myself a sandwich.

At nearly four thirty, my phone finally rang with the name I'd been wanting. *STERLING* was on the screen.

"Hello?" I answered.

"Patrick has Lorna; they're on their way home."

I let out a long breath as I leaned back against the barstool. "Is she all right?"

He chuckled. "She's good, considering. She managed to corral the two people she thought were following her. They had no idea who they were dealing with. As they followed her into where she knew they'd be cornered, she sent messages via her purse to Patrick. Now, she's on her way home and let's just say that the two suspects are being taken in for questioning."

"The police?" I asked, immediately knowing that wasn't the case.

"Sure, sunshine. Something like that."

"I don't care as long as Lorna is safe."

Was that true?

Had I gotten so accustomed to this life, the darker side of Sparrow, that I could accept it?

Pushing my question away, I asked, "Has Reid had a chance to even think about the box?"

"Some. Now he'll be able to devote more time to it."

"Thank you, Sterling, for letting me know about Lorna."

"I promised."

My smile grew bigger. "Yes, you did."

Disconnecting our call, I took a new look around the kitchen. The clouds and haze were beginning to lose their density. Though the view was mostly white, it seemed brighter. Perhaps the illumination had not really changed; the brightness was brought on by the knowledge that Lorna was safe.

The reason wasn't as important as the fact that I felt lighter.

The world was brighter.

Since I doubted that calling for food delivery was an option, with my new sense of safety, I decided it was my chance to cook for everyone. After what had happened to Lorna, it should be her turn to take a long bath and relax. Before I began my search of the pantry, freezers, and refrigerator, I sent a message to Jana, Winnie, and Louisa saying I was logging out for the night and would be back in the morning.

With soft music playing, I poured myself a glass of wine and began my search for ingredients. As the sweet liquid covered my taste buds, I had a realization.

I was once again under lockdown in this gilded cage, and yet at the moment, I didn't care.

What had happened to me over the last few weeks, the last month?

I wasn't certain I knew.

If before I'd met Sterling Sparrow, someone would have

told me that I'd be listening to music, drinking wine, washing potatoes, chopping and sautéing vegetables, and preparing salmon for five while contentedly locked in a penthouse apartment in Chicago, I would have told them that they were certifiably crazy.

Yet here I was.

Maybe I was the one who was officially crazy.

As I placed red potatoes in the oven, the slide of the pocket door from down the hall caught my attention. Wiping my hands on my jeans—I'd forgone the cute apron—I hurried toward the elevator. When I reached the hallway, Sterling was stepping from the elevator.

"Where's Lorna?" I asked, disappointment palpable in my voice.

He reached for my shoulders. "She's down at her place."

My expression fell. "I-I thought I'd see her."

He pulled me closer. "She did great today. That doesn't mean she wasn't shaken up. Reid's with her."

I nodded, looking up to his gaze. "I made dinner for everyone. May I...or Patrick take some to them?"

Leaning down, he kissed my forehead. "That was nice. Yes, I'll let them know it's coming."

As his hands fell to my waist, I looked up. "What's wrong? What aren't you telling me?"

"About Lorna, nothing much. She's shaken up. She held it together well, but once she was with Patrick and safe, she broke down. That's not like her. She's been through enough that she isn't easily rattled. I would ask Reid to concentrate on the CDs and floppy disks, but right now..." His words trailed away.

"No, you're right. He should be with Lorna. Did he find anything earlier?"

"They're encrypted."

"Will that stop him?"

"No, it won't stop him. It's slowed him down, as well as has the situation with Lorna."

I sighed, falling against Sterling's chest as his strong arms surrounded me, bringing me the comfort of his spicy scent along with the thundering of his heart under my ear.

I looked up at his clenched jaw. "Today is Wednesday and it's almost over. That gives us five days."

"Reid will crack them before then."

I liked Sterling's confidence. "I still need to put the salmon in the oven. Are you staying with me or going back downstairs?"

"Patrick and I are good at what Reid does, but there's a chance that if we mess with the CDs, we could screw up the data." His large hands caressed my back as he spoke. "I have a phone call I need to make, but if you'll give me a minute in my office—*our* office..." He corrected. "...alone, I'd rather stay up here with you."

My tired smile grew. "I'd like that." I reached up and kissed his cheek. "I'll pour you a glass of wine—not my sweet stuff—and you can meet me in the kitchen."

"Sunshine, after today, I think I want something stronger. I have it in the office." After another kiss to my forehead, he went on, "I'll be out as soon as I can."

For a moment, I stood and watched as Sterling walked toward his office. He was still wearing the clothes from our trip to Cambridge, his long legs covered in worn denim. On his toned torso and strong arms was the fitted t-shirt he'd worn all day. His steps were determined, his shoulders broad and straight. No matter what was happening, he was still Sterling Sparrow, the ruler of Chicago. With that title came the weight of the concerns of not only this city, but of our friends, and yet there was still something powerful and regal in his presence. At the same time, I sensed a chink in his armor, something I would never have seen had I not been granted the privilege of knowing the man behind the mask.

That instinct made me want to go to him and comfort him in a way only we could comfort one another. I started to follow him down the hall when the office door closed behind him.

You're being silly, I told myself.

He was just worried about Lorna.

Agreeing with my own reasoning, I changed direction and made my way to the kitchen, content to complete our meal.

STERLING

*T*he call was complete. Carlos from the cartel in Denver wanted to speak directly to me. He'd sent a scouting crew to South Chicago as well as some of the best areas within the city proper for heroin sales. His scouts claimed that there was another racket in the city, one I didn't disclose. My mind was a total blur, yet I sent the info to a couple of capos and promised to get back to Carlos with more information, assuring him our deal was secure and soon he'd have a valuable heroin network here in Chicago.

I stared around my home office, seeing none of it, thinking instead about the lockbox. I'd been mostly honest with Araneae—completely honest with all I'd said. The data on the CDs was encrypted and Reid was having difficulty with the old formats. If they'd been created more recently, he would have had their information right away. It seemed like it should be the opposite—newer should be tougher—but it wasn't. The obsolete programs, the one McCrie had used, were no longer compatible with today's technology.

Hell, Reid's technology wasn't today's. It was tomorrow's.

Getting the information from them was like trying to read Egyptian hieroglyphs with an iPad. That may be a bad example as there was probably an app for that. The point was that Reid was having difficulty making the old data work with the new technology.

We hadn't tried the floppy disks yet to see what they contained. That was an entire lower level of technology.

The information I hadn't talked to Araneae about—the omitted contents of the lockbox—were the documents in the envelopes. They contained account and transfer numbers/information for overseas accounts set up with shell companies, as well as stock certificates in McCrie's name with his beneficiaries named as first his child or children. In the case of no children, the assets of the stocks were to be bequeathed to his wife, Annabelle Landers.

Technology was Reid's specialty.

Finances were my and Patrick's repertoire.

While he'd been gone rescuing Lorna, I was the one discovering the details on Daniel McCrie's investments.

At various times before Araneae was born, Daniel McCrie invested over $250,000 in Apple stock and $300,000 in Walmart—a strange yet successful combination. The stock matured—split, grew, fucking multiplied exponentially— remaining untouched for over twenty-five years. If Araneae was able to prove that she was the daughter of Daniel McCrie, in the stock investment alone, his due diligence and financial expertise will yield her over five billion in wealth.

That amount doesn't include the money he also hid in the

offshore accounts. Those investments could be more difficult to access; nevertheless, in those accounts there too was certain to be a fortune.

I found myself torn between being happy for her and the reality that once she knew of her wealth, she would no longer need me to stay safe. Though she would forever be mine, Araneae could hire her own fucking security team. She could build her own secure fortress. She could hire investors to turn her newfound wealth into trillions.

She could choose to leave me and go on with her life.

It didn't matter what she decided; Araneae would always be under the protection of Sparrows. I'd made that declaration and I would honor it—a man's word is either his most valuable tool or his most respected weapon. Even if she chose to go her own way, I'd keep my word.

The idea of losing her ripped at my soul, preparing me for a loss I wasn't confident I could survive.

Since the moment of my discovery, my mind had been reeling with what that money could do for her as well as for her and Louisa's investment in Sinful Threads. Their profits now were decent, but nothing like that kind of wealth could provide in expansion and exposure.

The reality of my find gnawed at my gut, reminding me of my mother's warning. Genevieve Sparrow told me not to find Araneae, to leave the dead as they'd been. She warned me that doing so would bring harm to more than my goal—Rubio McFadden. It would obliterate *our* world.

With her warning running through my consciousness, I went to the highboy, opened a cupboard door, and found a crystal decanter of whiskey—Charbay Release III. Pouring two fingers in the tumbler, I listened as my mother's warning rang like a clanging bell in my head.

She'd been fucking right.

Fucking king of Chicago.

I could take a man's life and not blink an eye. I could take a company's money or evict them from their property. I could stop small two-bit drug dealers and open my streets to a Denver cartel. Politicians came to me for support. I greased their hands and they greased mine. My realm had given me all I needed, but I'd wanted more.

I'd wanted revenge.

For years, I'd anticipated that Araneae would lead me to the evidence. I'd prepared myself for what that discovery would bring, how to release it—leak it to the press—and then I'd watch McFadden fall from his fucking pedestal.

I'd lusted after the woman who'd been mine for nearly two decades.

I'd planned on claiming her, taking her, and making her mine. My plan was fucking perfect. The only annihilation would be the destruction that I controlled—McFadden.

And then my plan changed.

Lifting the crystal tumbler, I took a stiff drink, downing both fingers of whiskey.

Pouring myself another, I continued my train of thought.

Araneae was to be my acquisition, possession, the queen born to this world to fit upon my arm. She was to be at my disposal for my desires and to sit on a shelf when I was busy.

That fucking arrangement was blown to oblivion the moment I stared into her chocolate eyes, the night I had her body pinned against the wall of the office in that dingy distribution center. The fuse had been lit, the explosion imminent, yet I was too enthralled to notice.

Some fucking king of Chicago.

Araneae McCrie wasn't my possession or my acquisition.

Yes, I'd claimed her.

That didn't matter.

In every fucking way, Araneae McCrie had me, all of me—including a heart I didn't know I possessed. I'd even promised to follow through on *her* plans with the evidence—letting her decide. I'd said that. I stood by my word. I wouldn't take it back.

The reality was that if the evidence was there and she chose to, Araneae could watch both McFadden and Sparrow fall. She could do that and walk away wealthier than she ever imagined.

I'd done that—through my persistence I'd given her that ability.

With the bait dangled for years in front of me, I'd entered my father's trap, been snared, and now was about to fall, sinking to the depths of my own doing. Allister's plan to kill me in the war didn't work. His plan to destroy me with the Sparrow underground didn't succeed.

His dying words were to tell me that he wasn't done—there was a plan in motion.

Six years ago~

"You can't kill me," Allister Sparrow said, his back straight and shoulders squared. "I'm your father."

"This ring you've created has to go. I warned you to close it down or I would." My words were strong and my jaw clenched although my blood was circulating at untold speed, threatening my nerve as the anticipation within me grew.

"You have no idea what you're talking about. It's bigger than you. You can't stop it."

I was finally here. I'd arrived at the day that I'd imagined since I was a teenager.

The Chicago wind blew around us, highlighting our precarious positions.

"You're still a boy," he sneered. "You think my men will follow you? You're lying to yourself. Sparrow is made up of my men—ones I handpicked. They'll revolt if anything happens to me." His dark gaze narrowed. "Now, back away, boy, and stop playing men's games."

He'd made the mistake of meeting me at a construction site for a building going up under the supervision of Sparrow Enterprises. A recent deluge of rain and a thundering downpour had left the fresh concrete shiny and the skeleton frame of the birthing skyscraper slippery.

The message, relayed in person, not via technology, had asked him to meet three floors up. There was a concern with the rivets, alarm over the use of inferior supplies, someone skimming from Sparrow. He couldn't resist a chance to tell me that I was overreacting, that I didn't know what I was talking about. I counted on his superior attitude, knowing it would be his downfall.

Allister was older and he'd say wiser, but with youth, I had strength on my side. There was more than that, I possessed a hatred for the man whose DNA I held, a hatred that had been suppressed for too long. As I stared into his dead eyes, I recalled the photos on his computer and the abuse he'd inflicted. I heard his laughter at the plights of those who couldn't defend themselves. I remembered my mother's tears. Twenty-six years of memories flooded my mind.

As a child, I'd suffered under his hand and his words.

I was never a victim.

I was patient.

As years passed, I was confident that my revenge would come and when it did, it would be sweet.

The time had arrived. Allister Sparrow had recently announced the possibility of running for mayor of Chicago. With my mother's connections and her status as an alderman on the City Council and my father's business success, word on the street was that he'd be a shoo-in.

Allister Sparrow didn't want the office to help the city. He wanted the office because McFadden was in politics and he couldn't stand the idea of Rubio having the upper hand in anything. When McFadden had only been an Illinois senator, Allister didn't care. Now that Rubio McFadden was a US senator, my father wanted a piece of the pie. As mayor, he could grow the Sparrow outfit and conceal the illegal dealings.

Allister turned away from me—fucking turned his back on me—and began to walk toward the construction lift we'd ridden up to this height.

"Dad." My one word caused him to turn back my way.

I wanted him to witness his own demise, to observe its arrival.

I wouldn't shoot a man in the back.

Allister Sparrow wouldn't be killed from behind.

My father's chin jutted forward as he smugly waited for my next word, his long wool coat blowing in the wind. Instead of being intimidated by his stance, I moved forward. Defensively, he took a step back, his feet slipping as he wobbled on the steel beam nearly fifty feet above the ground. High enough to break a skull upon impact, yet not high enough on this closed site to catch anyone's attention.

With the blanket of nightfall and my man's assistance in rerouting the security lighting, we two Sparrows were birds invisible to the rest of Chicago.

In my imagination, I'd been the one to squeeze the life out of my father, to bring him to his knees, and to hear him finally acknowledge that I was capable of not only running Sparrow but doing it better. If time prevailed, I imagined him apologizing for the things he'd done, to my mother—his abuse, as well as his mistresses. To the children in the rings...

Some fantasies were never meant to happen.

As a gust of wind whipped up around us, his long coat became a sail. Allister's hard-soled shoe slipped backward a split second before both of his feet came off the beam. With a grunt, he reached out. His long fingers grabbed ahold of the wet beam, suspending his body high in the air.

"Sterling, help me."

It was the scene from Lion King and I was Scar.

I knelt down and stared into his dark, dead eyes.

My father was too old and weak to lift himself. Relief flooded his expression as I reached for his hand. Unlike the fictional lion brother, I didn't pry Allister's fingers from the horizontal beam. Instead, I took what was mine, utilizing a pair of sharp pliers I'd brought for the occasion.

The old bone in his fourth finger of his right hand broke easily under my grasp with not much pressure from the pliers, its crack barely audible over the rush of blood through my ears.

His scream echoed through the night sky before he growled his final words. "I'm not done, Sterling. I'll win from the grave. Mark my words."

"From hell, Dad. From hell."

As my father fell to the shiny concrete below, I removed the golden family crest ring from his bloody digit before wrapping what remained of his finger in plastic and placing it in my pocket until I could dispose of it properly.

A few hours later, two members of the Chicago police department met me in my office at Sparrow Enterprises to deliver the sad news. I didn't normally work in the office that late; however, as I explained, I'd been waiting for my father. He'd asked to meet with me. Reid had the text message from my father as well as my image on Sparrow's security footage throughout the entire evening.

Twisting the golden ring on my right hand, I mustered all of the sympathy I could at the news of my father's tragic accident and early demise.

Present-

I finished the second two fingers of whiskey and poured a third.

"Fucking did it, didn't you, Dad?" I looked down, not up. "You're probably laughing at me now, you son of a bitch."

There was a light knock on the door as Araneae pushed it

open, her chocolate eyes opened wide. "Sterling, are you all right?"

My chest moved up and down with breaths as I tried to right the spinning room. "Long day, sunshine."

As if a dream, she came to me, placing her petite hands on my chest. "I know we're under lockdown, but we need to go immediately."

The alcohol was making me fuzzy. I didn't drink like this on a normal basis. I also hadn't eaten. That wasn't a great combination. "No," I declared definitively. "We're staying put. That's what lockdown means."

"No, I called Patrick. He's getting the plane ready."

Patrick. Fuck that.

He took orders from me, not from her.

Placing the tumbler on the highboy, I reached for Araneae's shoulders. "Why can't you do as I say just once?"

"Sterling, Louisa is in labor."

ARANEAE

Sterling's gaze fluttered over me as if he were trying to comprehend my words.

"What?" he asked, the scent of whiskey thick on his breath.

"Louisa's in labor."

He took a step back and ran his hand through his hair. "That food you said you made?"

"It's in the kitchen."

He looked around the office. "Shit, I'm sorry, Araneae. I thought we were here for the night."

"Sterling, tell me what's wrong." I saw the empty tumbler with the scant remnants of amber liquid. From the sight of his dark eyes, I could guess it wasn't his first glass.

His lips came to the top of my head. "Like I said, long day." He inhaled. "And it sounds like it's getting longer. Did you say you called Patrick?"

I nodded. "Let's eat first. A few minutes won't make a big

difference. Besides, Marianne needs to get back to the airport, and they need to refuel the plane." When he looked at me like I was too full of information, I laughed. "Patrick told me that. I wouldn't have known."

After a few deep breaths, he opened the cabinet door, revealing the small refrigerator and pulled out a water bottle. Removing the cap, he downed all of the contents, setting the empty bottle on the top of the highboy beside the empty tumbler. "Okay. First, your amazing cooking, and then we're headed to Boulder."

I took his arm. "The hospital is in Denver."

"Is everything all right? There aren't any effects from last Saturday, are there?"

I was taken aback by his tone of genuine concern, as if the whiskey had removed a layer of his natural shield, the one that hid his true emotions in most circumstances.

"As far as I know she's fine. Her contractions are still about five minutes apart. Some are strong while others aren't. She called me and as soon as we hung up, Winnie called."

We'd made it to the kitchen, where Sterling went to the refrigerator and removed another bottle of water before sitting at the breakfast bar. As I sat the plates down in front of him, I asked one more time, "Is something wrong? Is there something you haven't told me?"

His jaw clenched as he stared my way as if contemplating his response. After waiting for his answer that didn't come, I turned and started walking back to get the food from the stove. As I did, he reached for my hand and pulled me back his direction landing me between his thighs.

"Today, in Cambridge..." His cheeks rose as a new brighter light came to his gaze.

"Yes?"

He reached for my hands. "You're so fucking amazing."

"Well, if that leads you to drinking—"

"No," he interrupted. "I didn't want to talk to that minister."

It was my smile's turn to bloom. "That was rather obvious, Sterling."

His head shook. "You don't get it."

"What don't I get?"

"Me."

I intertwined our fingers. "I thought you said that I do. I get you forever. Have you changed your mind?"

"Hell no. It's that anyone else would have known I didn't want to go into that church and would have told her no."

My shoulder moved up and down. "I'm working on that "Yes, Mr. Sparrow" response."

"Don't, sunshine. I mean it's sexy as hell and makes me instantly hard, but I admire your tenacity. We wouldn't have found whatever is inside that lockbox without you."

"You wouldn't have needed to find it without me. It seems I've brought all the baggage the old wives' tale warned you about, what your mother—"

Sterling's finger came to my lips. "I don't believe that." He inhaled and exhaled. "No matter what, I won't regret finding you, Araneae. You're the fucking best thing I've ever had in my life."

Moving his finger from my lips, I brushed mine against his, our kiss soft. "I'm glad you found me. Now, let's eat and get on the plane."

Once we were both eating, he said, "I should take a shower."

"I'll make you a deal."

"Oh yeah...?" His tone was returning not only to normal, but with his more calculating, sexy tenor.

"Yeah."

"What deal would that be?"

"Eat and we'll get Patrick or Garrett to drive us to the plane. Then once we're on the plane and on our way to Denver, I'll shower with you."

Sterling's cheeks rose. "When I was a kid, my nannies would try to get me to eat. Never once was there a deal like that."

"Well, good," I said with a chuckle.

Shaking his head, he continued to eat.

Although only a little over an hour had passed since the time I walked into Sterling's office and the time Garrett drove the SUV, pulling up at the private airport—where we'd already been this morning and afternoon—the evening sky was beginning to darken. The clouds had cleared, leaving a chill in the early September air.

As the SUV came to a stop, I noticed other cars. Before asking, I looked to Sterling and Patrick. By the keen sense of their gazes, it was clear that whatever had been bothering Sterling earlier was forgotten, at least temporarily, and they had new fires at hand.

"Four Sparrows," Patrick said.

"I don't like them riding on the plane with us," Sterling said, "but it makes sense. Having them with us, we'll never be without protection."

Before I could speak, under the lights of the airport's parking lot, the doors of the other cars opened and four rather large men stepped out, each looking a tad scarier than the one before.

"Do these men work for you?" I asked, hoping the answer was yes.

"Have them gather over there," Sterling said, motioning toward the rear of the plane, the part painted like a sparrow's tail. "I'll get Araneae up and inside to the back cabin. Then have all of them sit in front at the table with you, the partitions closed. Just because they're protecting her, it doesn't mean they need to be near her."

Patrick nodded knowingly. "Give me two minutes."

"Why don't you want—?" I started to ask.

"These men wouldn't be on this flight if we didn't trust them," Sterling said. "They'll protect you with their lives. That doesn't mean I want them close to you."

I nodded, knowing I was out of my league with what was happening, totally trusting Sterling and Patrick's decisions. "Okay."

The group of men met with Patrick in a small circle as Sterling and I walked up the stairs to the cabin of the plane. Keaton and the new attendant named Millie met us at the door. We'd seen them both this morning.

"Mr. Sparrow," Keaton said, nodding to Sterling. He turned to me and smiled. "Ms. McCrie."

"Hello." I looked to both of them. "I'm so sorry to change your plans again."

"Not a problem," Keaton said.

I knew it was. I also knew from Jana that no one would complain to Sterling even if they thought it was an inconvenience. It made me wonder if all these people had pasts that somehow intertwined with Sterling and his crusade to right his father's wrongs.

"Patrick and the other associates will be and are to stay in the front of the plane," Sterling instructed. "Help them if they need anything, but they're not to cross the partitions."

"Yes, sir," Keaton answered.

Millie's eyes were a bit wider. I wasn't certain she was as accustomed to all of this as Jana had been. While that thought settled in my mind, I hoped that her inexperience was a good thing. A few steps behind, Millie followed us through an archway to the main cabin, stopping to close the partitions on either side.

As Sterling and I sat in the belted seats, she came closer. "Is there anything I can get you, Mr. Sparrow, Ms. McCrie?"

"We have baggage that should be taken to the bedroom. Confirm that it's there before takeoff. Once we're in flight, we're not to be disturbed."

"Yes, sir," she said with a nod before disappearing toward the back of the plane.

I leaned closer. "So does that mean...about that shower?"

Sterling's dark eyes burned with a smoldering light I'd missed earlier in the evening. "You made me a deal."

"I did."

"No one backs out of a deal with Sterling Sparrow."

My lips curled upward. "While that hadn't been my plan, now I'm suddenly intrigued about what the resulting conse-quences might entail."

With a grin, Sterling shook his head. "Have you heard from Louisa?"

I looked down at my phone. "Not recently. The most up

to date was a text from Winnie saying that she's with Louisa's family in the waiting room and there's no news."

Sterling's hand covered mine on the armrest. "She's going to be fine and so is the baby."

"Kennedy."

"Is that for sure?" he asked.

"Well, it was before she was kidnapped because of me."

"What do you think about that?" His dark stare bore into me. "The name, not the kidnapping."

I sighed. "I like that my name will carry on without me."

He reached for my chin and sighed. "Once this is done, I'm certain we can petition for your identity. With your mother's assistance and the DNA results, it may take a while, but it should be doable."

"Can't Reid just push some buttons?"

"He could, but if he did that, it might be more difficult to prove you really are Araneae and not just someone who changed her name."

I turned his way. "Why would it matter? I don't care what anyone else thinks. You believe I'm me. My mother does. I do. No one else matters."

Sterling inhaled and exhaled.

"What?"

"Sunshine, let's take one day at a time."

He was right.

"There may come a day when you want the world to recognize you as Araneae McCrie. I will support whatever you decide."

I turned my hand until our palms were touching and fingers intertwined. "You keep saying that."

He nodded.

"It's not that I doubt my ability to make a decision. This isn't about which dress to produce or if we should branch out into bed linens—"

"That's a great idea," he interrupted with more enthusiasm than I expected.

I smirked. "I haven't talked to Louisa about it yet, but I thought of it a few weeks ago. I mean, people spend a third of their lives in bed."

The tips of his lips quirked upward. "I'd like to increase that percentage."

"Anyway, as I was saying, these decisions...about what to do with the evidence, depending on what's there and my name...I feel like they have further-reaching implications."

"They could."

"Then I'm asking for your advice."

His finger touched my nose. "Your decision. I said that. I'm not going back on that no matter what we find. I gave you my word. A man's word is either—"

"Either his most valuable tool or his most respected weapon," I said, interrupting and repeating what he'd said numerous times. "I'm asking for your input. That won't be breaking your word. It will be keeping it."

"How do you figure?"

"Excuse me."

We both looked up at Millie.

"Yes," Sterling said.

"Your bags are in the bedroom. Once we're in flight, I'll bring some cheese and fruit and water bottles into the bedroom, and then you won't need to be disturbed."

"Thank you, Millie," I said before Sterling could correct

her for what he would consider overstepping. After all, he told her that we needed nothing. "I would love some snacks."

Her smile beamed. "Marianne said we're ready to take off and all the gentlemen are seated."

Sterling nodded. Once she was gone, he turned back to me. "Explain what you just said."

"I would love some snacks?"

He shook his head as his gaze darkened. "Araneae."

"You promised me, Sterling Sparrow, that I wouldn't face any of this alone. You've been there with Pauline, with my mother, talking to McFadden." I took a deep breath. "You were there in Cambridge when I saw my grave. I need you...no, I *want* you to be with me, guiding me, helping me, and that's what you've done. You may have bulldozed into my life, but you've supported me through this crazy maze. Please don't stop now."

Our lips met as the speed of the plane increased, the wheels lifting off the ground as we flew higher into the darkening sky.

JOSEY

Ten years ago ~

"Today," Byron said as he prepared to leave for work.

My chest ached, my head ached, and my heart ached.

I looked around our bedroom, the one we'd shared for the last sixteen years. Beyond was a hallway that led to other bedrooms, one being Renee's. The living room was quaint and the kitchen cozy. Out in the backyard where we'd had the deck, we'd added a screened porch. It was absolutely lovely in the warmer months. We'd spend time together sitting and eating out there.

It wasn't warmer now.

The early-morning January winds were blowing a dusting of recent snow in swirls and cyclones under the streetlights as spider webs of frost decorated the corners of our windows.

"Kiss Renee," I managed to say as tears bubbled in my throat. "It will be the last time."

"Josey, I've never left this house without telling both of my girls how much I loved them."

His words broke me as I fell into his chest. He wrapped his arms around me, holding me tight. "You can do this. We have to do this, for her."

His friend, the one who made the IDs, had helped, making a connection with someone in the state police. Later tonight he would make a home visit, one for Renee to witness, and inform us of our loss. This evening we'd be informed that Byron Marsh had died in an automobile accident on I-90 on his way home from work. An impaired driver had swerved lanes to reach an exit he'd almost missed. The driver hit Byron, sending him into a concrete lane divider. Byron died upon impact. The policeman will recommend we don't view the body, especially Renee.

The plan was for me to keep Renee out of school and away from the news and social media. She wouldn't know that there were no reports of Byron's death or that the accident hadn't occurred. For her safety, I needed to be convincing. And then once the airline tickets were accessed, I was to take her to the airport with her new identity.

Byron had secured her spot at St. Mary of the Forest with a generous donation, information on her parents' death, and certification of her emancipation, so she was set through graduation with them. She would be in Boulder, Colorado, in a new world from Chicago.

At the same time, there was a second scenario playing out, the reason that time was of the essence. Sparrow sent a new scout, someone who could ultimately be the one to take us out. I didn't know his name, but Byron did. I should say Neal did. The scout had been with the Sparrow outfit for most of his life, along with his friend Joey—the boy Neal befriended, the man whose debt cost Neal and Becky their lives once.

That man from Sparrow gave Neal—aka Byron—a week to disappear, be wiped clean from the world and the grid. There were many bad things about the world where Neal was raised. There was also honor in darkness. This man remembered what Neal had done for Joey. He'd watched as Neal was pulled down time after time yet never gave up on the man he called his brother.

We had no doubt that once we were gone, this man—Neal wouldn't tell me his name—would take credit for our demise. We didn't care as long as we were all safe.

Neal received the ultimatum saying that Sparrow wanted us all gone, but he wanted Byron gone first. While there would be no news of the accident, Allister would see Renee's and my grief and know that his man had removed one of his targets.

Byron promised that Renee and I would also disappear within a week after him. We knew that if we didn't comply, we would vanish and it wouldn't be the way we wanted.

That night as I prepared dinner, a knock came to our front door. My hands shook as I laid the large spoon by the stove and went to the door.

I listened, not truly hearing what the man in uniform was saying. After suppressing my tears all day, I fell to the floor with a wail, a cry for the life we were all losing.

Renee came running from behind me. "Mom, what's the matter?"

Her big brown eyes looked from me to the officer as she laid an arm over my shoulders. "Mom? Mom?"

My heart shattered as I sat up on my knees and pulled my

five-foot, six-inch daughter into my embrace, tugging her also to her knees. "It's your daddy."

"What?" She looked up at the officer. "No, tell me he's all right. Maybe you have the wrong person."

She was fiercer than me, determined to right the wrong this man was claiming, to correct his lie and uncover our secrets.

"Renee," I whispered, standing and wrapping her in my arms. I turned to the officer. "May we...can we see him?"

"I don't recommend that, ma'am. We can identify him through possessions. He's...well, I don't recommend seeing him."

Renee and I waited as the officer retrieved a plastic bag containing Byron's wallet, his ID, and his watch. I held the bag in my shaking hands as I nodded with tears coming down my face. "They're his."

"Ma'am, we'll have a report for your insurance company in twenty-four hours if you can come down to the station...." His words faded away as my head buzzed with emotions.

At some point, he was gone.

I was sitting on the couch, my daughter's head in my lap as we cried.

Her, for the only father she ever knew.

Me, for a life I'd never again have.

Sometime within the next hours or days, I saw beyond my bubble of despair.

I could go to the grave hating Allister Sparrow, and I most certainly would. Nevertheless, the last sixteen years were more than I'd ever dreamt of having. For over a decade and a half I'd lived more than some people ever experience: a husband and daughter. A home and a life.

I had to walk away, but I could do that, knowing that Renee would be saved; she would be free to continue and find her own slice of life. After all, she was named after a spider, Araneae. The daughter I shared with that woman in the hospital, Judge Landers, had grown into a beautiful, strong, resilient, vivacious young woman. The judge had named her and we'd raised her.

We had to believe that together that would carry her through.

ARANEAE

Touching down in Denver, my thoughts were on Louisa. The mysteries surrounding my life as well as the possible contents of the lockbox were momentarily forgotten. All that mattered was getting to the medical center and seeing my best friend.

Sterling reassuringly reached for my hand resting on my jean-clad legs. After our shower, we'd both changed into casual clothes, me in a t-shirt with jeans and a jean jacket and Sterling in dark blue jeans and a white button-down shirt. With his sleeves rolled up and shirt unbuttoned, he was back to his model status, not the CEO of a worldwide real estate company.

"It's the middle of the night," he said. "Aren't you exhausted?"

I shrugged. "I'm too excited. I can't believe it's finally time for Kennedy to be born."

"Any news?" he asked, tilting his head toward my phone.

"No. I just sent a text to Winnie, to let her know we're here. From what I've heard, labor can last for hours." I tried to read the thoughts swirling through Sterling's dark stare. "Are you worried about last week?"

"No, like I said, we've been watching them. I'm concerned for everyone's health, but the doctor we had at Winnie's checked Louisa out before we sent her to the medical center. And then they released her. It should all be fine." He took a deep breath. "Winnie has stayed true to our story. Jason and Louisa aren't fully certain of everything that happened but know they're being protected. I'm more concerned that they think my motives are more altruistic than they are."

The tips of my lips moved upward as I cupped his recently shaved cheek with the palm of my free hand and let my fingers skim over the smooth skin. "You're my knight in shining armor."

"No, sunshine. My armor is black as coal."

"That's not true, Sterling."

We both lurched forward as the plane came to a stop. Out the window the sky was dark, yet the lights of the private airport illuminated the tarmac and hangars.

"Would you tell me something if I asked?"

Small creases formed around his eyes. "I won't lie to you, Araneae. However, there are also things I won't discuss."

I nodded as we undid our seat belts, stood, and I began to walk forward.

"Wait," he said, stopping my onward progress, "until the Sparrows are off the plane."

I'd almost forgotten about the men in the room in front of us.

Wrapping his arm around my waist, Sterling pulled me

close, surrounding me in his clean, spicy scent. His voice was a low whisper. "Whatever you want to ask, do it now, before there are others to hear."

Looking up at the granite features forming—the expression he wore when around others was taking over—I smiled at the way I was beginning to understand the very complicated man before me.

"Jana's story..." I said. "I was just wondering how many of the others, the people hopelessly devoted to you, those who bend to your schedule, and show up at the penthouse without question. How many of them have similar stories?"

"Like I said about Jana, those aren't my stories to tell."

"But there are others?"

He didn't answer.

I pressed my hand against his chest over the buttons of his shirt. "You can do your best to convince me that you're not a knight, but you are. You're not perfect." I grinned. "Sometimes you're a real asshole."

"So I've been told."

"That doesn't negate the fact that you're also good. I hope one day you'll see that."

Before Sterling could respond, the partition opened and Patrick nodded toward the door to the outside. "We're all set. The car is waiting," Patrick said.

As Sterling reached for my hand, the one on his chest, I said, "Thank you for not fighting me about this trip. I know you'd rather have us all in Chicago behind the infrared technology."

Letting go of my hand, he placed his in the small of my back. Straightening his broad shoulders, he led me toward the door and steps. Nodding at Keaton, Millie, and Marianne, his dark eyes scanned the tarmac. A few steps ahead of us, Patrick was doing the same, searching beyond the lights of the airstrip for what could be hidden in the darkness.

Our steps quickened as we made our way to the car.

Once we were inside the back seat with one of the large men from earlier driving and Patrick as copilot, Sterling sighed and whispered in his deep tenor, "I would much rather be home."

That one statement would be all that was uttered while in the presence of this new man. Since I hadn't been introduced, it meant that Sterling wanted me to stay quiet. I hadn't cared for all of his rules in the beginning, yet with time, they'd settled in.

What seemed ridiculous a month ago was now common practice.

Fear of his punishment no longer lurked in the recesses of my consciousness. I'd come to realize that I liked some of them too much for them to be considered deterrents. It was more than consequences that influenced my willingness to concede to his rules. It was trust and respect for Sterling's mission.

I was his.

I now accepted that without question.

In doing so, it made him mine, and I liked that thought too.

Sterling protected what was his. He'd brought me into a world that played by different rules. He'd also shown me the man behind the mask. Currently, his features were hard and unrelenting. This was the face the world saw.

In the last month, I received the gift of seeing whom the world didn't. I knew the man who was loving and compassionate, the man who carried the weight of Chicago on his shoulders and yet could emit so much passion it radiated like lasers from his dark eyes.

Sighing, I leaned back. As the car moved through the night, I let my mind do what it had been doing for most of the plane ride: think about Louisa. Ten years replayed in my head, meeting her at St. Mary of the Forest, attending the same college, becoming what I'd suspect it would be like to be sisters.

The winter I arrived in Colorado, the second semester had already begun. Completely alone, I wasn't sure who I could trust. Prior to my arrival, the school had been told the story of my parents' death in an automobile accident, Phillip and Debbie Hawkins. There was a counselor there as well as the headmistress of the school, both of whom took me under their wings, reassuring me that I would be safe and looked after.

I recalled not knowing how any of it would work.

Everything was foreign and unknown.

I tried to do as Josey had said and be strong, but at sixteen and alone, I wasn't sure how to do it. I knew there were others who at sixteen were far worse off than being placed in an elite boarding school. Josey had warned me that if I were found, my future would be unsure.

Life in a private school in the mountains of Colorado was starkly different than my life in Mount Pleasant, Illinois. Gone was the community, the homes of my friends and their families, even their pets. The cat I'd had since I was young passed away at the ripe old age of thirteen. He'd been a great cat; however, I was certain had he been alive, I wouldn't have been able to bring him to Colorado.

The commute to and from class was now a walk instead of a drive. My home that I'd shared with Josey and Byron was also gone, simply a memory of what life had been. With the exception of the one picture and the charm bracelet, that life was as if it had never existed. Even my name was different.

Every now and then, I'd recall the way my mother helped me with my homework, patient and diligent, and the way she'd taught me to sew. It was my father who helped me with my math. While Josey nurtured my creativity in all things, Byron instilled my love of numbers. Those memories would bring a smile to my face and a tear to my eye.

The first few days at St. Mary's were some of the loneliest of my entire life.

Each student—it was an all-girls school—had her own dorm room. My home went from a three-bedroom ranch in suburbia to a single room containing a desk, bed, closet, and dresser. I'd arrived with no possessions except the clothes on my back. The room I'd been assigned had the basic needs, sheets, pillows, and blankets on the bed, and towels and wash-cloths for the communal bathroom.

The second day, instead of attending classes, Mrs. Shep-herd, the counselor I'd met the day before, took me into Denver to shop for my needed supplies. Somehow, according to Josey, Byron had set up a trust fund in my new name that allowed me spending money. I wasn't confident in what I had to spend, only that Mrs. Shepherd assured me that I was able to purchase what I needed.

Perhaps that was part of my reasoning for refusing Ster-ling's order, the one that came in the empty box, the one to move to Chicago with nothing. I'd done that before, made a move without bringing tangible memories. Yes, the clothes and cosmetics he'd supplied were luxurious. Nevertheless, I couldn't and wouldn't lose everything again.

It was the third day at St. Mary's as I sat eating breakfast in the cafeteria that I met Louisa. She and two other girls our age sat down with me at my otherwise-empty table and introduced themselves. I was taken aback, so shocked and lonely that at first, I forgot how to respond beyond polite answers. As time passed, we found more and more things we had in common. By spring break that year, Louisa invited me to go on vacation with her family. I'd already met her parents and sister during the times they'd come to campus and take Louisa out to eat or times she'd go home for a night.

The years in my mind blur as I think about how the Nelsons took me in and gave me what I'd lost—at least a bit of it—of a family. If it hadn't been for the Nelsons, I couldn't imagine how I would have turned out. Entering an all-girls school at sixteen years of age, knowing no one, and having no one was undoubtedly the scariest moment of my life.

A grin came to my face as I turned toward Sterling.

Sterling Sparrow was intimidating and domineering, yet he wasn't scary, not to me.

I had to wonder how all the pieces of my multiple lives prepared me for where I was today, for being Araneae McCrie.

ARANEAE

*E*ntering a hospital in the middle of the night, or should I say morning, was nothing like entering it during the day. The large rotating glass door spun until Sterling, Patrick, and I were inside. Silence met us as the shiny floors surrounding the middle waiting area reflected the dimmed lighting. Within the center of two-story-tall pillars were large plants and groupings of chairs. Up to the second-floor railing, the hallways were barren. The gift shop was closed, and the white grand piano was without a player. Even the guest services desk, which was most likely manned by volunteers, was empty.

It wasn't like we needed a volunteer's guidance. We had the knower of most things leading us. We had Patrick. I didn't even think to question as to whether or not he knew where he was going. Another thing I'd learned over the last month was not to doubt his knowledge. Sterling and I followed him toward the bank of elevators. With each step, Sterling continued his constant surveillance of our surroundings.

We rode upward in silence, my mind on Louisa, while the two men with me were monitoring our safety. The elevator doors opened to our desired floor without a stop on any other.

Apparently, the lack of visitors at this time was to our advantage.

Following behind Patrick, it was Lindsey, Louisa's sister, whom I saw first. Beside her was a large handsome man I didn't recognize; however, as soon as we entered, his eyes widened at the sight of Sterling.

Probably my imagination.

"Kenni!" Lindsey squealed as she jumped up and ran my way, wrapping her arms around my neck.

"Lindsey..." I stepped back and took her in from her long, dark hair and blue eyes to her athletic body. She was a carbon copy of a younger Louisa. "How's Lou doing?" I looked around the room, waving to Calvin, Louisa's father, and Winnie. There were also members of Jason's family present. I'd met them a time or two, but I couldn't recall their names.

Hell, when it came to names, hearing the one they were calling me now sounded foreign. I was used to being Ms. Hawkins at work, but this was different.

"She's doing great." Lindsey's nose scrunched. "I think. This is all new but I know she's ready."

I laughed. Louisa had been telling me she was ready for the last month.

"When did you get in from Boston?" I asked.

"A few hours ago." She pointed to the good-looking man. "This is Marcel."

Marcel nodded, his gaze moving between me, Patrick, and Sterling.

"We've been dating for a few weeks," Lindsey said.

"Hello, Marcel. Nice to meet you. I'm...Kennedy Hawkins." I tried not to hesitate. After I finished introducing Sterling and Patrick to our intimate group, Winnie came forward.

"Kennedy..." She turned to Sterling. "Mr. Sparrow."

I wasn't sure of all the details of what had transpired here last weekend in Boulder, what kind of understanding Winnie and Sterling had come to. Whatever it was, the tension seemed to ripple through the air with a palpable bit of unease.

"Ms. Douglas," Patrick said, redirecting her attention. As he did, Lucy, Louisa's mother, entered our area, coming toward us through double doors.

"Kennedy," she said with a smile. "I'm so glad you made it. Would you like to come back and see Louisa?"

Tears filled my eyes as one of the many mothers I'd known embraced me. When we pulled back, I asked, "May I? Is it okay?"

She smiled and nodded at Sterling and Patrick.

As she did, I began another set of introductions. "Lucy Nelson, this is my boyfriend..." Yes, there needed to be a better term. "...Sterling Sparrow and our friend Patrick Kelly." I hadn't been told not to introduce them or use their real names; however, there was something out of place with having them here—my new life in my old life.

Then again, Marcel, the man beside Lindsey, gave off the same air.

You're being paranoid, I told myself.

"Nice to meet you," Lucy said with a nod. "The hospital

only allows two people back in the LDR room at a time, besides Jason. I think we're getting close to meeting Kennedy Lucille." She smiled my way. "I know Louisa wants to see you."

Sterling squeezed my hand drawing my attention back to him. A small part of me hesitated to turn his direction, to see his expression. I knew that no matter his opinion, I was going through those double doors to see Louisa. My experience at the church in Cambridge taught me that while Sterling wouldn't make a scene here, he'd be certain to bring it up later.

Why bring me here if I wasn't allowed out of his sight?

With a deep breath I refocused on the man at my side. When I turned, I saw and heard the opposite of what I expected.

"Tell her hello from me, sunshine."

A smile bloomed over my face.

Sterling and Patrick had probably thought this scenario through and expected as much. Hell, knowing them, there were Sparrows dressed as medical staff beyond the doors. I decided to not let that thought fester.

"Thank you," I mouthed Sterling's direction before I turned and followed Lucy through the double doors.

Once alone, Lucy turned my way. "Kenni, I have to ask. Are you safe?"

Since I met her, Lucy had been similar to Josey in many ways—one was the way she was always a straight shooter. That was a quality that had endeared her to me. At this moment, her straightforwardness was less endearing and more alarming.

As her question filled my ears, my steps stilled as the

mysteries of my life washed over me. Warning bells rang in my head. "Why would you ask that?"

She reached for my hand. "Honey, we love you. We always have. But I can't help but worry." She tilted her head toward the waiting room. "That man."

"Sterling," I said defensively, almost adding that he was in real estate, "...we're dating. He helped me get here so fast."

Lucy let out a long breath as if she were weighing her words. "Kenni, the day after you arrived at St. Mary of the Forest..." She swallowed.

The hairs on the back of my neck stood to attention as the alarm bells grew louder, their ring now a shrill squeal. "Tell me."

"Mrs. Gore..." The headmistress of St. Mary of the Forest. "...called and asked me to come to her office. She told me about you and your unique situation. She was moved by all you'd endured and wanted to help. However, the board of trustees had strict rules about the interaction of faculty and students. So she asked if Calvin and I would assist with looking after you and welcoming you to St. Mary of the Forest and to Colorado."

"What?" My mind was having difficulty keeping up. "You're telling me that none of it was real? Y-you...Lou...?"

Lucy squeezed my hand, the one still in her grasp. "Honey, Mrs. Gore gave me a letter. In it, it said that you might be in danger. A name was mentioned. Not an entire name but a last name."

"That was ten years ago." My head was shaking. "Why would you want me around if you thought I could bring danger?"

"That was never a question. We have two daughters and

when I looked at you, I saw them. You needed someone and our hearts were open. Kennedy, we grew to love you. I asked Louisa to introduce herself. I never told her about the warning."

"You didn't think to tell me?"

"I wanted to believe it wasn't true. I didn't want to scare you. And the name, it wasn't connected to a first name. I didn't know for sure..."

My head shook.

"I don't know if you remember," Lucy went on, "but one time we were all skiing and the lifts stopped. Once we made it back to the condo, it had been broken into. We knew there was a risk in agreeing, but you were worth it."

"I do remember that." I blinked as tears prickled the back of my eyes. "But you lied to me. The whole thing, making me feel like I was part of the family, it all was a lie."

"No. We never lied to you. I asked Louisa to introduce herself; the rest was real. You two were meant to be friends. As I said, Louisa never knew Mrs. Gore asked us to help. She doesn't know now."

I worked to swallow the lump in my throat. "Then why are you choosing this time to tell me this?"

"Because I'm concerned about you with him."

My emotions were all over the place as I stared into Lucy's eyes.

It took a moment as we stood in the quiet hallway a few yards from the sparsely manned nurses' station. Finally, standing taller, I found my voice. "I can say with one hundred percent certainty that Sterling Sparrow has been the most honest person in my life. He's been open with me." *In ways you apparently haven't.* I didn't say the last part, although my breaking heart told me that it was true.

"Winnie mentioned the other man is always with you," Lucy said.

"Sterling is overprotective."

"You know you can tell me if there's more. I'll do my best to help you. That's always been my goal."

I took a deep breath, fighting the feeling that I'd just lost another parent. Maybe she's being honest. Perhaps Lucy had been looking out for me, but with her confession, I heard more. I'd come too far in the last month to let emotions bog me down. In her confession, I also heard the opportunity for obtaining more information on my past. "Did you know anything about my parents?"

"Debbie and Phillip Hawkins?"

I didn't answer.

Finally, Lucy nodded. "In that letter, one that accompanied the information about your trust fund...No one else read it. It was sealed, only to be opened by the person or persons who would commit to watching over you."

"Was it from my parents?"

Her eyes closed. "I was never supposed to tell you. From what I understood, everything they prepared for you was because they loved you and they wanted you to be safe."

My mind filled once again with thoughts of Josey and Byron. He was gone. I was there when the police officer informed us. However, I'd never known what happened to Josey. "Lucy, if my mom is still alive, any information you have may help me find her."

"The letter wasn't from a woman. The signature was from Neal Curry."

ARANEAE

*N*eal Curry?

My eyes narrowed as I took a step back, away from Lucy's touch. "I-I've never heard that name before in my life."

At least Josey had mentioned Araneae.

"Maybe he was the Hawkinses' representative," she suggested. "I don't know."

"The Hawkinses weren't real," I said, tired of living with lies.

"I always suspected."

"The last time I saw my mom, she told me to become Kennedy Hawkins for my safety. I did. Sterling has given me more. He's shown me who I really am."

"And that is...?" she asked.

I shook my head, not ready to disclose that information. "It will all come out soon enough. I want to see Louisa."

Her head tilted. "The last time you saw your mother? Was that before their automobile accident?"

She was talking about the fictitious automobile accident the Hawkinses suffered.

Instead of answering, I said, "You said that birth was close. Take me to Louisa or I'll ask the nurses."

Again Lucy reached out to me. This time I took a step back and straightened my neck.

Her blue eyes flushed with sadness. "Kennedy, I told you this today because I'm concerned about Mr. Sparrow. I wanted to call you as soon as Louisa told me that you were dating him. I started to call, and then I was afraid your phone might be tapped. I didn't tell you this information to hurt you but to protect you." Her head shook. "I'm not sure what he's told you, but please think of yourself and of your friends. Powerful people usually get that clout by leaving skeletons in their wake. I'm not saying literal dead people. I'm saying secrets and lies that one day could come back to haunt him. I don't want you or Louisa to be hurt."

Her speech hit me wrong. Suddenly, everyone was concerned for my well-being.

Where have these people been?

What was real and what were lies?

Those same questions continued to swirl through my mind as I asked again to see Louisa.

"Calvin, Louisa, Jason, and I...we all want what is best for you."

"I love Sterling. He loves me."

"We love you."

And you've lied to me for ten years. I didn't say that either.

"Lucy, may we go to Louisa?"

She nodded. Together we passed the nurses' station on our way to an LDR room. Lucy pushed the door inward. I didn't notice the living room-like furnishings, the large TV, or even the window to the dark night sky. Instead, my gaze went to the person who for the last ten years I'd considered my best friend.

Unfortunately, in the last five minutes, a cloud of uncertainty had descended, making me question everything. And then as if the sun broke through the clouds, my gaze and Louisa's met.

"Kenni," Louisa called out, her genuine expression filled with happiness and sincerity.

Concentrating on the here and now, I quickly went forward, wrapping Louisa in a hug. For no reason—or maybe for a million reasons—as we embraced and I closed my eyes, a flood of tears trickled down my cheeks.

Louisa and I hadn't seen one another since my last day in Boulder at Sinful Threads, before Sterling kidnapped me to Canada. In our ten years of friendship, it was our longest separation. And yet in this instant, we were reunited. As we hugged, I wanted to believe what Lucy said. I wanted to believe that the only nudge Lucy had given Louisa was for her to introduce herself to me.

I wanted to believe our friendship was real.

When I pulled back our eyes met and I said, "I've missed you so much."

Before she could respond, Louisa's blue eyes closed and her expression changed. With a groan, her lips came together.

Jason came forward, smiling at me as he reached for Louisa's hand. "Breathe, beautiful. Breathe."

As I stepped back and away from the bed, Lucy came next

to me and wrapped her arm around my waist. "I told you we are close to delivery."

I fought my instinct to flinch away from her touch as I watched my best friend work her way through a contraction.

After a minute or more, Louisa's grip of Jason's hand loosened, and she turned my way. "Jeez, these are getting stronger." A smile came to her lips. "I'm so glad you made it. I hoped you would."

I couldn't help but smile. My best friend was strong and positive even in the midst of giving birth. "Of course," I said. "I told you that you couldn't keep me away." I looked to Jason. "Are you both all right?"

He nodded. "Tell him thank you."

Jason's gratitude and Sterling's earlier words twisted my insides. It hurt to know that while Jason was thanking Sterling, I was the person responsible for their traumatic events. "I will."

"What are you talking about?" Lucy asked.

Before we could answer, Louisa's face scrunched again, and she reached out for Jason's hand. As she rode out another contraction, the door to her room opened and two people, both dressed in scrubs, came inside.

"Ladies and gentleman, I think it's time." One of the women looked to me, the new face in the room. "I'm Dr. Gorman. We've been watching the monitors."

I stepped back as the other person—I assumed a nurse—donned latex gloves and went to the foot of the bed. Her hands went under the sheet, making me feel a bit uncomfortable, like I was intruding. Before I could speak, the nurse did.

"Yes, ten centimeters. We're fully dilated." She looked up at Louisa and to Dr. Gorman. "Are we ready to push?"

I thought the nurse's use of the personal pronoun *we* was misleading. Though I'd never given birth, I was confident only Louisa would be doing the work.

Louisa's blue eyes went from the nurse to Jason.

The glance exchanged between the two of them was one of the tenderest expressions of wordless devotion I'd ever witnessed. Simply being an observer filled my heart with joy.

Louisa nodded as Jason smoothed back her long brown hair away from her flushed face. "You've got this."

Louisa turned Lucy's and my way. "I love you both—"

I lifted my hands. "I'll be right outside in the waiting room. I'll let them all know that it's showtime."

Pink filled Louisa's pallid cheeks. "Private show, but we'll let you know as soon as Kennedy Lucille makes her debut."

With the mention of the baby's name, Lucy reached for my hand.

Instead of flinching, I gave hers a squeeze. Next, I made my way back to the waiting room. As soon as I passed beyond the double doors, in the connecting hallway I was met with my own wordless expression. Unlike Jason's to Louisa, Sterling's was darker, less adoring, and more like one of questioning.

"You were gone a while," he said, his voice low, his tenor rumbling.

"I'm sure my trackers were being followed. I wasn't far."

"It's to keep you—"

I placed a finger over his strong lips. "It's baby time." My smile grew. "Thank you again. I couldn't have made it here in time for the birth if I'd flown commercially."

His lips quirked. "Especially with a detour to Wichita."

"Yeah, I'd like to avoid those."

His arm snaked around my lower back as we walked together to the waiting room.

I spoke to everyone. "They kicked me out." All eyes turned to me. "It's time."

The entire room buzzed with excitement.

Looking back up at Sterling, I asked, "May we step out of here for a moment? I need to tell Reid something."

Sterling's jaw clenched as his shoulders straightened. "Patrick?"

"Sure. He'll find out anyway." As I'd mentioned many times, the three men shared a brain.

Once the three of us were in a nearly empty hallway— nearly, because I noticed one of the men from the plane casually reading a magazine, sitting in a nearby grouping of chairs —I turned to Patrick and Sterling. "When Lucy first took me back, she asked me if I was safe."

Sterling's brow furrowed. "Why would she—?"

"I swear," I interrupted, "I've never before heard what she just told me. She said that when I moved here at sixteen, the headmistress of the school asked her if she and Calvin would keep an eye on me." The words shouldn't evoke emotion, but they did.

"You're saying that Lucy Nelson has had information that she's only now revealing?" Patrick asked.

I sighed. "Yes. The reason she's doing it now is that she was given a letter saying that I might be in danger and to watch for the name Sparrow."

The cords in Sterling's neck protruded as the strain on his jaw increased.

"She said something else," I added. "She said the letter she

received telling of my possible danger was signed by a man
—Neal Curry."

Both Patrick and Sterling exchanged looks.

"Does that name mean anything to you?" I asked.

Patrick shook his head while Sterling's eyes darkened. "I-I
don't know," he finally said.

"Can you pass this on to Reid?" I asked.

Patrick's phone was in his hand. "Sending it to him now.
He may be asleep, but he'll get the message as soon as
he wakes."

Sighing, I leaned into Sterling. "I keep forgetting that it's
the middle of the night."

The man with the magazine was looking our way. He
nodded to Sterling who nodded in return.

"Is this level of protection overkill?" I asked.

He hugged me closer to his chest. "Nothing is overkill
when it comes to keeping you safe."

STERLING

I wasn't comfortable with the situation. If I hadn't promised Araneae connection to her best friend from the beginning, we wouldn't be here. We'd be safely tucked away with Lorna and Reid, high in the sky in Chicago. The medical center was too open, too exposed, and yet I didn't see any options to avoid where we were. Instead, we did the best with what we had. Between Patrick and I, we'd taken all the precautions we could, men watching the entrances and exits and men stationed near the entrance to the women's wing and the labor and delivery department—the one Araneae had just seen. Even the nursery was being watched. That was being monitored by Shelly, Patrick's operative here. A woman in the nursery was less suspicious than a man. Marcel, the man Lindsey introduced as her boyfriend, was also a Sparrow.

Watching over someone and fraternizing were two different things.

That would be dealt with, just not here and now.

It was obvious by his expression that he didn't plan on seeing me in Boulder.

The task at hand was too much for our four associates and the ones we had here on the ground. That meant that once again we'd called on Carlos's men for help. As Araneae went back into the waiting room to her old world, my gaze went to the window in the hallway.

The sky was beginning to lighten, yet even with the breaking of dawn, the outside protection from the cartel was nowhere to be seen. That didn't mean they'd let us down. It meant that they were the shadows of this domain. That's what they did, how they operated, what they preferred. My men weren't from here, weren't recognizable. That was why the Sparrows were inside and the cartel was outside.

Before Patrick and I made our way back into the waiting room, I turned my direction to him. "What do you think about what Araneae said about Neal Curry?"

His head shook. "I think it's a fucking clue, maybe the missing piece Reid needs to track down the Marshes."

I ran my hand through my hair. "Again, the warning about the Sparrows."

Though his lips flattened, Patrick didn't answer.

If my father had helped hide her, why were the warnings always about Sparrow?

"My father knew she was alive—he'd shown me her pictures—until McCrie was killed. That's when Josey Marsh rushed Araneae to the airport and Kennedy ended up here." I was thinking aloud, unsatisfied to be in the waiting room around too many people. "If Lucille Nelson is telling the truth..." There was no motivation for her to lie. She could have simply never told Araneae. "...then the letter accompanied Araneae to the boarding school. It was the same time as McCrie died and Araneae was moved away." I ran my hand through my hair. "I don't think my father killed nor ordered McCrie killed. The other day, McFadden practically admitted to ordering the kill of McCrie. Something we may never know is *why*."

Patrick nodded. "What happened ten years ago? What rocked the boat? What caused McFadden to turn on McCrie and Allister to turn on Araneae?"

"It was the same time as when they exhumed the remains in the grave in Cambridge," I said. "The same time my mother said my father thought he'd been lied to, that Araneae was really in the grave, not the teenager he'd been watching."

"No offense, Sparrow, but I don't trust your mother, her memory or honesty."

"It's fucking hard to learn secrets that have been buried for a decade or more," I admitted with exasperation in my tone. "I agree with you, but my mother seemed adamant. What I don't trust—or should I say *who* I don't trust—was her source. My father could have easily lied."

"It seems," Patrick said, "the only living player in the three-way scenario with Allister, Daniel, and Rubio...is Rubio."

"Who the hell is or was Neal Curry?"

"Someone who knew Araneae was alive after she was rushed out of Chicago. Someone who knew exactly where she'd show up."

"The obvious answer would be the Marshes," I said. "After all, Araneae said her mother rushed her to the airport and gave her the new identity. We need to be sure the letter addressed Araneae as Kennedy."

Patrick nodded as he looked down at his phone.

"Reid probably isn't awake," I said. "When he is, I want to know what he can learn about Neal Curry as soon as he learns it."

Our man back in Chicago had a full plate. What with our normal activities in and around the city, learning the contents of the lockbox, and tracking down Neal Curry, it was a lot for even Reid. Patrick and I needed to get back to Chicago to do our part.

Patrick looked up from the screen of his phone. "Reid's awake. He just texted me and said he's on the Curry thing." Patrick continued to read. "It sounds like he's also been up most of the night. When Lorna fell asleep, he went to two."

"Did he say how she's doing?"

Patrick's eyes moved from the screen to my gaze. With a slight shake of his head, his lips curled upward.

"Fine," I replied to his smirk. "Araneae is making me soft."

"It's not soft, Sparrow. It's compassion. Doesn't always work in this world, but it's not a bad thing to have, especially not for the right people."

I grunted.

It was new for me, and it wasn't.

The people who resided in our apartment were there for one reason. I fucking gave a shit about them. They were to me like the people in the waiting room were to Araneae. They were the weakness of Araneae's that I'd purposely exploited. She gave a shit about those people. That's why we had Sparrows here on the ground until this thing with McFadden and Araneae was settled.

I just wasn't certain what settled would mean. According to my mother, it meant obliteration.

"Lorna's still asleep," Patrick replied, pulling me from my thoughts and relaying the information on his screen. "Reid also said he's making progress breaking the encryption. With the age of the data storage, he believes the bit key will be comparatively shorter than if it had been encrypted today. His biggest problem was breaking into the out-of-date storage devices without damaging the data."

It could be compared to video games. I never had time for that shit. The war I played was real. However, we have capos with excellent hacking skills, surfers of the dark web, who began their education as gamers. Reid had to figure out how to essentially play a twenty-six-year-old video game on a new, incompatible console.

"He broke through the issues with reading the CDs," Patrick said, "and has multiple computers running, devoted to finding the encryption scheme."

In my head I imagined the screens upon the wall on floor two, the data spinning and running with all the possibilities until the right one was found. With the computer power we had in our operation, literally thousands of possible schemes could be attempted per second.

The door from the waiting room opened.

Araneae's cheeks were wet and eyes red.

"What is it?" I asked, rushing toward her.

"She's here."

My pulse increased as I reached for Araneae's shoulders. "And...is she—?"

Araneae reached for her phone and swiped the screen, bringing a picture to life.

ARANEAE

"*L*ook," I said as I held up my phone. "Isn't she beautiful?"

Sterling shook his head as he pulled me close. "Fuck, Araneae."

"What?" I craned my neck upward.

"The tears. In our world, they usually mean something bad."

With my arms around his waist and his around mine, the world felt right. "This is what I was talking about, Sterling. You always jump to the most negative conclusion. Kennedy Lucille is here. She's beautiful and according to Lucy she has a very loud cry. She also has ten fingers, ten toes, weighs seven pounds and twelve ounces, and is twenty-one inches long."

"Sunshine, those most negative conclusions keep us on top of all possible scenarios." Sterling turned to Patrick. "Message Darius for the car and Marianne for the plane. We're headed home."

What?

"No, not yet," I said.

Sterling didn't need to answer, not verbally. The answer was crystal clear in his dark eyes and set chiseled jaw.

"Please, I want to hold her, just for a moment. Then we can go. I know there are a million fires in Chicago. I want to know what's in that box, on those CDs and floppy disks, and in the documents. I do. But...give me a half hour."

Sterling's gaze went to Patrick. And while he didn't say a word, Patrick nodded.

"The plane will be ready in an hour," Patrick said. "Marianne needs to file the flight plan back to Chicago."

I sighed. "Thank you."

As I started to step away, I stopped. "After we go...will...will there still be people watching them?"

Sterling nodded. "Yes, they're all safe and they'll stay that way."

He'd said that before the horrible incident with Louisa. Nevertheless, he'd also told me that since that episode, the number of eyes on them—the number of Sparrows—had increased. "Thank you."

Through the window, the sky was lightening. It was morning and we'd all been up for the entire night. Hell, we'd started the day by flying to Cambridge. I'd knelt at the empty grave of a small baby, and now I was going to hold another with a full life before her.

Going back into the waiting room, I sat beside Winnie. "I can't wait to hold her."

She feigned a smile in my direction. Maybe it wasn't forced. Perhaps it was the lack of sleep. "I-I was nervous to see you again, to see him."

"Him? Do you mean Sterling?"

She nodded. "May I tell you something?" Her voice was a low whisper.

I scanned the room around us, thankful that Sterling and Patrick were still in the hallway. With those who were around us, it truly didn't matter our volume. Everyone else in the room was talking, looking at the same picture we'd all received, and discussing Kennedy's information. It was then that I noticed Calvin, Louisa's father, and Jason's parents were missing from the room.

Of course, the grandparents would be back with their precious new granddaughter. My mind fluttered to an unknown place, an image of me holding a dark-haired baby with Annabelle and Genevieve present. Maybe it was my lack of sleep encouraging my imagination. However, if this were an unreal dream and I could make alterations, I also wanted to add Josey to that room.

It didn't matter.

The image was purely fiction.

First, Sterling and I weren't that serious—or were we? And then I couldn't in a million years imagine Genevieve Sparrow welcoming me or a child of mine, even if it were also Sterling's, into the Sparrow family.

"Kennedy?"

"Um," I said, dismissing my imagination. "What did you want to tell me?"

"He contacted me again."

"Who?"

"Agent Hunter."

I let out a long sigh as my pulse kicked up—again thankful Sterling and Patrick were not in the room. "Seriously, Winnie, there is so much going on. You can't talk to him. I'm not asking you to lie. Just don't talk to him."

Tears welled up in her eyes. "I thought I was helping you. I know now that was wrong, but that doesn't mean the whole thing with Louisa didn't scare me."

I reached out and laid my hand upon her jean-covered knee. "I'm sure. I was scared and I wasn't here. But don't you see that it was Sparrows who saved her? He does good things."

"Real estate," Winnie said, "you mentioned that."

"I wish I could tell you more. I do. I can't. For the rest of this week, I want you to close everything down with Sinful Threads—all operations across the country." Sterling had told me and Jana to work from home. Extending the order nation-wide was my idea; after all, Sinful Threads was my company. Perhaps I was learning to live in this new world. "I promise this is for a good reason. Tell all the managers that everyone will be paid for their normal time. Tell them that it's a long weekend bonus in celebration of Mr. and Mrs. Toney's new daughter."

Winnie's eyes grew wider with each word. She looked at her watch. "Immediately, for the next two days. You want production stopped when we're already behind on the dress orders? We have crews planned to work Monday, too. They're expecting the overtime."

"Two days, Winnie. That's all. No one works on Labor Day. We'll be in full swing on Tuesday."

"What's happening? Can't you tell me something?"

"I can tell you that you're safe, and if you meet again with Agent Hunter, we'll know."

"Am I being watched?"

"Not in a bad way. After this weekend, we're hoping it's all done. Life will go back to normal."

"Kenni, what's normal for you anymore?"

My cheeks rose. "I can't tell you that either, but I can say that I like it. I'm comfortable and safe." I looked into her gaze. "I'm loved. I really am. And I love him too."

"I can see that. I can. But you should know that I didn't reach out to Wesley. He cornered me while I was at the market. We didn't talk long. I can't control where he finds me."

I looked her directly in the eye and spoke low. "Winnie, you know what happened to Louisa and Jason. This is serious stuff. Involving the FBI will not help. It will make it worse. Let Sterling handle this. He's on it. Stay home or with Louisa until after the holiday."

Her lips disappeared between her teeth as she looked down and then back up. "Wesley told me to make a deal and save myself. He said there's something about illegal activities and Sinful Threads. Could someone in Sinful Threads be working for Mr. Sparrow?"

My head shook from side to side. "No, not in a nefarious way."

"I told him I didn't know anything." She sighed. "I liked Wesley. I really did. Now I don't know who to trust."

I knew that feeling. I'd had it. "I trust Sterling and Patrick implicitly. I'll tell them what Agent Hunter said. We'll get to the bottom of that." Or should I say we'll add it to our growing list of to-dos.

The double doors opened and all four smiling grandparents came through. Lucy spoke, "They have paper gowns back there and before you touch her, you need to sanitize your hands, but if you girls want to go back, they'll let all three of you."

Girls?

I guess that was what came from one generation to the next. The younger, no matter how old, were always younger.

My gaze went between Winnie and Lindsey. "Let's go."

A few minutes later, covered in a blue paper gown, I sat in a large glider as Jason came toward me with Kennedy in his careful grasp. "Aunt Kennedy, we're very happy to introduce you to Kennedy Lucille Toney." He placed the beautiful baby wrapped in a light blanket in my waiting arms.

Her little face scrunched as her eyes opened and closed.

"It's bright out here, sweetie," I said.

Unwrapping the blanket, I peered down at her perfect little body covered only in a tiny diaper. As I opened her grasp of one fist, she wrapped her long slender fingers around my one finger. With tears in my eyes, I looked over to Louisa.

She was smiling my way with Jason at her side.

"She's beautiful," I said, my voice filled with emotion. She was also wearing a tiny stocking cap. "May I take off her hat to see her hair?"

"Yes," Louisa said. "It's light, like Jason's." Her eyes glistened with unshed tears. "Like yours, Kenni."

It was. Her hair was a fine, soft yellow coating, barely visible, and as soft as silk to the touch.

"Hello, Kennedy," I whispered. "Your aunt Aran—Kennedy is going to spoil you rotten."

I didn't want to give her up, to pass her on to Winnie or Lindsey, yet I knew Sterling was waiting. Finally, I looked around. "I can't be selfish. Who is next?"

Once Kennedy was safe and secure in Lindsey's arms, I went to Louisa. "I love you...both...all of you. I have to get back to Chicago, but I promise I'll be back."

Louisa reached for my hand. "Jimmy Hoffa?"

I smiled and shook my head. "Nope, no idea where he's buried." Considering he went missing in the 1970s, I was certain that he wasn't one of Sterling's skeletons.

His father's or my uncle's?

Now those were genuine possibilities.

"Stay safe," Jason said.

"I will. You too."

Jason nodded. "We have help and..." He looked to Kennedy in Lindsey's arms. "...we'll take it."

"All I can tell you is that you're important to me. That makes you important to him."

After giving a round of hugs, I made my way out of the room. The nurses' desk was much busier than it had been, men and women in scrubs coming and going, watching monitors and typing information.

There was a normalcy about the medical center, now that it was morning that was reassuring. In the waiting room, I said my goodbyes to Lucy and Calvin, wondering how these people would fit into my new world.

What was normal?

I wasn't sure I knew anymore.

And then as I opened the door to the outer hallway and a devilishly handsome man turned his dark stare my way, I knew.

Sterling Sparrow was my new normal.

"Sunshine," he said, "we need to get back. Reid has cracked the first CD."

"Broken it?" I asked, aghast.

"No, he's got the data. Only eleven more to go."

JOSEY/REBECCA

Present

"*D*o you ever think about her?" I asked Neal one morning as I woke after a vivid dream starring our daughter. In my imagination she was still sixteen, beautiful with so much life ahead.

He reached for my hand. "I do. I think about searching for her, but I'm sometimes afraid of what we'll find."

"We've been disconnected from everything for so long." I looked around our two-room cabin. The door to the bedroom was open to the larger room, a space shared by a living area and a small kitchen. The wooden floors were clean as were the windows and our simple furnishings. We had a fireplace for heat and windows that opened for cooling. The community where we've lived for the last ten years could be considered a cult, but to us it was simply our home.

The people within had welcomed us, no questions asked. They'd taken us in and given us our own space. The people here came from all walks of life. Rarely did we discuss the world outside of our bubble, yet when we did, most of us were content with our decision to become one with the land.

We learned their ways.

The most important rules were kindness and participation. No acts of violence were tolerated. It meant immediate expulsion. And we all worked together to keep food on the tables, logs in the fireplaces, and clothes on our backs.

The community in northern Maine was completely self-sufficient with few exceptions. Every quarter, a group of the men went to the nearby town. They sold our crops or our creations and purchased supplies.

Under the covering of a religious organization, our community was exempt from certain laws. That allowed the residents to live off the grid, so to speak. We had no taxes, no bills, and no credit cards. No anything that connected us to the world we'd left.

When we'd moved here, we took back our real names.

It was a risk. It was the name Allister Sparrow knew if he ever believed we were still alive.

Neal's friend had supplied us with other identifications.

Our fear was that his friend knew the names he'd given us. He also knew the name he'd given Renee. By returning to Neal and Becky Curry, we cut all of our ties to Renee. That was how I still referred to her.

Renee.

She should be set as Kennedy Hawkins by now, but to me, she'd always be our Renee. The daughter we'd watched grow up. The one we'd had the privilege to love.

STERLING

*R*eid, Patrick, and I were all on two as Thursday afternoon grew into Thursday evening. While the lack of sleep over the last thirty-six hours had our nerves on edge, having Araneae and Lorna, as well as the three of us, safely secured within our current lockdown gave me a small amount of comfort. That along with the constant eyes on Araneae's friends in Denver and Boulder and it almost seemed as if we might find the light at the end of this tunnel.

Seven CDs were opened.

Five to go.

And four floppy disks.

Daniel McCrie had hit pay dirt, at least for when he did this. Technology was nothing like it is today. He copied screenshots of online auction sites with photographs of boys and girls that had been up for sale and rent. I'd heard when I was young, by eavesdropping when I shouldn't, that most kids lasted a few months to maybe a year in what my father's men called the stables. Once their usefulness was done, they were sold, oftentimes out of the country. It was an elaborate operation.

When I closed the doors on Sparrow's ring, I had complaints from all over the world. What Rubio had said about me doing it too abruptly was almost right. My father's disgruntled middlemen, the ones who skimmed their profits in the exportation, began to revolt. It could have been noticed if I hadn't taken care of it when I did. After a few associates wound up in acid baths within barrels near the shipyards, word spread fast.

Upon two CDs there were even snippets of a live feed. Unfortunately, the capacity of storage on a CD was significantly lower than what we had today with flash drives. The total capacity of the average home computer around the time of Araneae's birth was less than a single flash drive today. The snippets were only a few seconds long, yet they showed enough.

I'd heard of the live feed, but had never seen it.

Patrons were able to make their requests and pay to view in real time whatever they requested. The snippets included text bubbles of customers making suggestions and bids. As moneymakers go, it was a brilliant setup. Instead of satisfying one customer with one kid, thousands could tune in and watch. As a moral—even in my immoral world—human being, it turned my stomach.

With all I'd seen, it took a lot of sick shit to make me queasy.

This did it.

This crossed the line.

"Do you think you can track the patrons?" I asked as we

replayed the snippet. "Look right there." Reid paused the snippet and I pointed at the bubble near the bid.

Reid shook his head. "Eventually, maybe. This was twenty-six years ago. Those accounts are undoubtedly gone. The IP address could get me to the region, city, or town, but I'd venture it will tell me that the user was in the greater Chicago area."

"Not narrowing it down much," I said, disheartened.

Even in my nearly thirty-three-year-old mind, as the pictures came up on the screen, I found myself transported back to my father's office, complete with the dark surroundings, the reeking stench of cigarette and cigar smoke, and the revolting laughter of his men.

I fucking hated that sensation. Everything about this made my skin crawl.

With each discovery, I reminded myself that I wasn't that petrified young teenager. I was a man, the ruler of Chicago's underground, and the one who took down my father and others who made the decision not to follow me. I was also the man who'd put a stop to the Sparrow side of this horrendous ring, helped the victims I could—the ones I could find and who wanted saving.

The pictures themselves wouldn't lead to the downfall of McFadden or Sparrow. The victims couldn't even be identified conclusively. The children were numbered not named. And then we saw it, a URL link within the live-feed snippet.

"Look at that," Reid said, enlarging a still shot of the live feed. In the lower-right-hand corner was the link to place bids. That link should have led to either one of the outfits.

No longer active, it was at least the beginning of his current search.

Silently, I hoped it went to McFadden and not Sparrow.

That wasn't to save Sparrow Enterprises or my memory of my father—Sparrow Enterprises was diverse and solvent and my memory of Allister Sparrow was already tarnished. My hope was for one reason: I didn't want to have to explain the concept to Araneae and admit it was my father's ring.

"McFadden," I said, "told me that McCrie gave him six CDs and my father six. Do you think that in this box we have a copy of each one?"

"If that's the case," Patrick replied, "then six of these incriminate each outfit." He looked to me. "I'm sure at the time he knew which was which."

I leaned back in my chair as Reid's fingers continued to fly. On another screen, the computer was working out the encryption scheme of the next CD. Each one had a different one. He'd definitely taken his time to do this as thoroughly as possible.

"Rubio didn't say," I said, "but if I were to theorize, I'd speculate that McCrie took each man his own dirty laundry, to prove he had it. He thought it would bring him something in payment."

"It fucking killed him," Reid said.

Who knew Reid was listening?

"Not immediately. It bought him time," I said, standing and pacing a small trek. "Why did McCrie give Araneae up at birth?"

"Do we know he did?" Patrick asked. "We know for almost certain from the good judge that she believed Araneae was dead. She gave birth and they handed her a dead baby."

My head shook as one of the computers emitted a chime. We all looked that direction. The screen that had been rolling with thousands and hundreds of thousands of schemes was now still, a string of numbers and letters on the screen.

"Number eight," Reid said confidently.

"I keep going back," I began, "to my father saying that Daniel McCrie owed him. I can't imagine my father helping McCrie out of the kindness of his heart." He didn't fucking have a heart.

"Maybe it was quid pro quo?" Patrick offered.

"McCrie gave my father the CDs that implicated Sparrow. He gave Rubio the CDs that implicated McFadden. He hid copies. Eventually, McFadden killed him."

"You have a sixteen-year jump in there—a hole," Patrick said.

"Fuck, I'm aware."

Reid turned away from the screens, spinning his chair, his dark eyes zeroing in on me. "Before speaking with Judge Landers, we thought what?"

"That she gave Araneae up to protect her."

"Daniel McCrie was her father," Reid said. "He saw the shit on these CDs. He worked for McFadden and also for your father. He knew what both men were capable of doing."

"So you're saying," I said, "McCrie gave her up to protect her. He hid her existence from even his wife, for her safety?"

Reid shrugged. "It makes sense. I can't imagine lying to Lorna, but if it were to save my kid's life, to save her from ending up as one of these pictures, I just might do it."

"And she'd kick your ass if she ever learned," Patrick added.

"McCrie isn't around for Judge Landers to kick his ass."

"Right now, I think she's just amazed her daughter is alive." My head began to nod. "You know, you might be right about her dad. We figured her mother would try to save her, why not her father?" I stopped my pacing and turned to my two confidants. "Why did he go to my father? Why not McFadden, his brother-in-law?"

"Maybe that's the reason. Maybe he thought Allister could hide her from his own family. We are mostly certain that Rubio called the hit on McCrie. If he'd order his brother-in-law dead, what would stop him from putting his niece in a sex-and-exploitation ring?"

"Why would my father help him? What was in it for him?" Allister Sparrow wasn't the type of man to hand out favors, not one this big.

Reid spun the chair and lifted the four CDs still in their plastic cases up in the air. "This. Maybe McCrie told Allister that he had copies. He offered them to him after Araneae was no longer a child, no longer prime for this ring."

"And then," I said, the pieces clicking into place, "when my father heard rumors about the whole thing being a ruse, about Araneae really being the dead baby, he was livid. McCrie panicked and went to McFadden to do what...? Offer him the same deal? McFadden didn't believe that she was ever alive."

"Because that was what her mother said and your father announced," Patrick said. "Your father told your mother he'd been lied to. McFadden got wind. He was sick of McCrie's shit and offed him. Problem officially solved."

"In the meantime," Reid said, "somehow the Marshes—whoever in the fuck they were—got wind of McCrie's demise. If they were reporting to Allister, they were aware of at least the Sparrow outfit. They assumed, like many others, that

McCrie's death was a Sparrow hit. They freaked out and went on the run..."

I stopped walking again. "It would make sense that they were afraid of Allister. Why they warned both Araneae and Mrs. Nelson about the name Sparrow. Fuck, they might not have even known that McFadden was part of the equation."

"And now," Reid went on, "McFadden thought all his troubles were over. The baby in the casket was Araneae. He killed McCrie. He'd kept Annabelle close. No loose ends until you showed up with the rumored-to-be-deceased Araneae McCrie on your arm a month and a half before he planned to announce his candidacy for president. You fucking imploded his world."

Nodding, I sat back down. "Damn. If we're right, we've been close to figuring this out for years, but now, with the evidence we've got it." I looked to both Reid and Patrick. "Can we trace the money from the 737 pilot's wife's shell company to McFadden to prove he paid to have the plane crash-landed or at least raise suspicion that he was involved? What about the fire in Araneae's apartment?"

"I've been on that," Patrick said. "Shelly got the fire inspector's report. They've ruled it arson with two pending cases of manslaughter."

"Why manslaughter? Why not murder?"

"There's no evidence the fire was set to cover up the killing or to cause their deaths; instead, the evidence supports that the couple died as a result of the fire, not before it. The medical examiner's report has to do with smoke inhalation. They weren't dead before. If they had been, they wouldn't have inhaled the smoke."

I nodded. "But no suspects?"

"None," Patrick replied. "We were looking into the blond insurance agent, but now we know that was Agent Wesley Hunter."

"Aka Mark, aka Walsh," I said. "Fuck, he has as many names as Araneae."

"What are we going to do with this information and what about the stocks?" Patrick asked.

He too had looked through the documents. We varied a little on the net worth, but either way, if Araneae could prove her identity, she will be a very wealthy woman.

"I'm not sure about the evidence," I admitted. "I told Araneae that I'd leave that decision to her. I haven't decided what to lead with...the evidence or her wealth."

"You could start with I have some bad news and some good news," Reid said with a chuckle as he turned back to the computer screens. "Fuck."

"Is that the bad news?" Patrick asked.

"No," Reid replied with a shake of his head. "I'd say it's good. I just found the closed account where bids were sent for the live auction. It bounced off a shit-ton of virtual servers, went through some archaic firewalls, and ended up right back here."

"Here? Tell me," I said, "that it's not Sparrow."

"It's not Sparrow."

ARANEAE

I woke as Sterling climbed into bed. The room around us was mostly dark with only the sliver of the moon shining through the large windows. Yet in the dimness, I could make out his handsome features, his furrowed brow as he slid between the soft sheets. Curling my body, I rolled closer. "Good night."

"Sunshine, I didn't mean to wake you."

I sat up, leaning on my elbow. "I've been tossing and turning. You'd think after being awake all of last night, I'd be exhausted. I think that's it. I'm too tired to sleep. My mind is all over the place. Will you tell me what you've found?"

With a deep sigh reverberating through our bedroom, Sterling reached his arm around me, pulled me closer, and wrapped me in his embrace as his spicy scent filled my senses. "You did it. What they all feared you'd do, you did it."

My body grew heavy with the weight of the evidence. "Is it...McFadden or Sparrow?"

"Both."

I spun to face him. "I don't want to turn in Sparrow. I don't. It's not just because I love you. It's because it wasn't *you*. You didn't run whatever is on those CDs. Your father did it. You've stopped it. You've done more than that; you've helped victims." When he didn't answer, I went on, "You said it was my choice. I don't want people to know."

"Do you want to know details?"

"No. I'd rather not."

"There was one thing even I didn't know about." He shook his head. "It was sick."

"Who did it?"

"McFadden's outfit. Reid was able to trace an old URL. Even when shit is wiped clean, it survives in cyberspace. You just need to know how to find it."

"Could it still be happening?"

"We don't know," Sterling said. "Today's dark web isn't easy to navigate. Finding the sites isn't as tough as following where they go. I could say, yes, there are things out there like we found. Is McFadden currently involved? We can't say. However, we can prove that over twenty-five years ago he was."

"Children?" I asked, the word thick on my tongue.

Sterling nodded. "Assuming the evidence was recent when your father hid it, I'd say if any of the victims are still alive, today they would be anywhere from my age to maybe forty." He rolled toward me, until my head was on my pillow and he was over me. "I think it should all be made public."

"Why? You and your business shouldn't suffer for what your father did."

"Because before I had you with me, I wanted to shove this

in McFadden's face. I wanted to hand him a gun and watch him take his own life, unable to come back from this fall. I wanted Sparrow to take over McFadden's men. I wanted to reign over every dark corner of this city."

"Then do that," I said honestly. "I just have one stipulation."

"What is that?"

"That I'm beside you."

"What if you change your mind?"

My hands went to Sterling's now-bare shoulders and splayed over his chest, feeling the indentions of his torso. "Why would I change my mind?"

"Maybe because you won't need me or maybe the best answer is that I've already tarnished your light. Because of me you're condoning the hiding of evidence and being an accessory to homicide."

With my eyes adjusting to the silvery shimmer from the moon, I stared up at Sterling's eyes. "There's more. I can see it in your eyes. Tell me what you haven't said."

"Details on the evidence?"

"Has Reid cracked all the CDs?"

"Yes. He needs some special technology for the floppy disks. They haven't aged well. They can't hold much information, so we have no idea what they'll contain."

"My father hid all of this?" I asked.

"Yes."

My hand went to his cheek. "Then he brought me into this darkness, not you. You found me. You saved me."

"Sunshine, I don't know how else to say this, but your father did more than that."

My eyes opened wide. "Do I want to know?"

"He also hid information on offshore accounts and some stocks he purchased, complete with the paperwork bequeathing the accumulated funds to his child or children. In the case of no children, they were to go to Annabelle."

I was having difficulty understanding why Sterling thought this was so important. "So there's some money. How much are we talking?"

"Billions."

I gasped.

What?

"What did you just say?"

"In the stocks alone, Patrick and I figure between four to six billion."

"What? I-I don't know what to do with that kind of money."

"You hire people. That's what you do; people to help you manage it. You can hire your own bodyguards. You can build your own safe house."

I blinked my eyes as if seeing clearer would help me understand. "I don't want any of those things. I want what I have." I swallowed. "Unless now that you got what you wanted, you don't want me."

His lips met with mine. "Never think that. I want you more than life itself. I don't care if you claim the money or not. I've told you, when it comes to money, I do all right. I want you safe. I also want you here because you want to be, not because you need to be for your safety or because I kidnapped you."

My lips curled upward. "I told you that you kidnapped me."

"Only to Ontario."

"I don't have to think about it. If what you say is true, I'll talk to Annabelle. I suppose if she wants to keep it, she can refuse to help me verify my identity. No matter what, Sterling Sparrow, you're not getting rid of me, and I'm not getting rid of you. It took me some time, but you convinced me." I lifted my lips to his. "I belong to you and you belong to me."

"What about the evidence?" he asked.

"Let's sleep on it. My uncle's deadline is before Monday. We still have a few days."

"You're amazing."

"Hey," I said, remembering my conversation with Winnie. "I know we have a thousand things happening and deadlines, but what does illegal activity mean to you?"

Sterling lay back against his pillow. "It could mean many things. Why?"

"Something to do with Sinful Threads."

"We'll talk to Reid about it."

"I'm sure it can wait," I volunteered. "I want this McFadden thing taken care of first." The room grew quiet until I asked another question, "Sterling?"

"Hmm."

"Can you give me other options for McFadden? If you take the evidence to him and he takes the bait and kills himself, how will that help the children if the ring is still going? I mean, won't someone else just take over?"

"Exposing the ring, his outfit, brings light to the under-world. It could end up exposing more."

"Or helping? Right?" I sat up. "You're no longer involved in this. Agent Hunter wanted my information or wanted me to testify against you. What if we gave him or someone else the information and pointed him at Rubio instead of you?"

"Like you said," Sterling replied, "we have a few days. Let's think about all the possibilities. No going rogue. This is too big and too dangerous."

I leaned over his chest, bringing our noses together. "Yes, Mr. Sparrow."

"Oh, sunshine, you know what that does to me."

"Yes, Mr. Sparrow..." I lowered my hand under the covers, over his tight abs, and lower. Wrapping my fingers around his erection, I moved my hand up and down. "...I believe I found more evidence."

"You think?"

No, I was certain.

All at once, our world flipped. I was on my back with Sterling's toned torso covering me. With his nose touching mine, I stared up into his dark stare as a giggle escaped my lips.

His head shook. "Only you could have that beautiful smile..." His finger traced my lips. "...and a laugh after that conversation."

Sterling lifted himself higher, taking me in, inch by inch, from the top of my head to where his body covered mine. His gaze sent heat to my skin while leaving goose bumps in its wake.

"Only you could be thinking about sex," I said.

His head shook once more. "It has nothing to do with the conversation and everything to do with the evidence you were just stroking." He reached for the straps of my satin nightgown. "I believe you started this, but, sunshine, I plan on finishing it."

My body was at his disposal. That meant there was only one thing I could say. "Yes, Mr. Sparrow."

STERLING

*S*itting in a conference room on floor one—the working area of the Sparrow outfit—I listened as two of our Sparrow capos reported on the heroin distribution Carlos's men had discovered on their scouting mission.

"You're saying it's centered in the warehouse district?" I asked.

"Yes, sir. It's small but profitable. A group of rogue wannabes utilizing the tools they already have," the first man said. "The trucks of other businesses. They don't steal them. They are employed by the trucking company."

This was my city. No one created an operation without taking it through Sparrow. If I approved, I received the standard cut. If I disapproved, the operation went elsewhere or we eliminated it. The fact that this had been happening under our noses meant there would be heads rolling somewhere. Or bodies in acid.

The possibilities were numerous.

"They're transporting the heroin via drivers that service multiple small warehouses," the first man continued. "It's not one business but many. The drivers are contracted, not employed by the individual companies."

I was getting the picture. "These drivers are transporting heroin within their standard shipments."

"Yes," the second man said. "Some of the businesses have reported discrepancies in their merchandise numbers. Say for instance that a company is moving merchandise, let's say medical supplies. When that merchandise leaves the warehouse for the distribution center, the quantity is verified often by weight. It's standard. The only one to touch the merchandise between stops is the driver or the loading/unloading crew. Somewhere along the way, the driver stops. He or she replaces a small portion of the merchandise with the drugs. The shipment is then delivered. Someone on the inside of the distribution center separates out the heroin from the medical supplies and holds it until it's picked up for distribution."

"Then the merchandise quantity on both ends doesn't match," I said.

"Right. The weight could be verified if the pallets are weighed. That's why they have to remove some of the merchandise. If they only added the heroin, the weight would be off, or boxes and pallets would be noticeably different."

"How fucking long has this been going on in my city?"

Both men shook their heads. "Boss, the truth seems to be that it has been happening for at least a few months. We've traced it to some rogue Disciples."

The Disciples were one of the street gangs known to be in Chicago. Officially there are fifty-nine gangs in Chicago with nearly one hundred thousand members. They were here because we allowed it. They paid their share and in exchange, I or McFadden allowed them the use of our streets. While McFadden and Sparrow both benefited, we also made the rules.

"Rogue? I want a meeting set up with various gang leaders. It sounds like they have some punks ready to try a takedown. We're stopping this before they end up clashing on the street."

"These truck drivers were mostly hired in the last six months, working for the contract trucking companies," man two said. "Not just one trucking contractor. They're spreading the joy to keep it under the radar."

"I want names of the trucking companies and names of the companies they run merchandise to and from."

The first man pulled his phone from his pocket. "I have the trucking companies. They're the ones who are doing the transporting and paying off the lower management at the warehouses and distribution centers to take the blame for the discrepancies." He pulled up a list of only a few trucking contractors.

"That's not very many," I said, looking at his screen. "Send me the list."

"No, not many," man number one said. "But they work for multiple various companies. The plan is good. Say one company is caught with numbers not meshing; they don't see the bigger picture."

After a ding on the computer before me, I pulled up the trucking companies that he'd listed. He was right. They contracted out to hundreds of smaller companies. "Do you think all the drivers are involved?"

Both men shook their heads. "No. This is still small.

We've narrowed it down to around fifteen drivers," man number one said.

"Fifteen drivers who have over twenty stops—twenty different warehouses or distribution centers that they service," the second man said.

"Get me the list of the companies where they deliver or pick up."

"We have a partial one," the first man said, looking again at his phone.

My computer dinged as his list came through.

As I scrolled the list of diverse companies, one jumped off the screen at me.

Sinful Threads.

Fuck.

"And you said the management at these warehouses are aware of what's happening?"

Both men nodded again; number two spoke. "Yes. They're aware because they have to make excuses for the number discrepancies. Allowing their company to be used also gets them a cut. I'd venture to guess some are making more on this than they receive in their paychecks."

"Sometimes they even need to adjust security footage," man number one said.

We'd been too concerned over Araneae's safety and the evidence she was supposed to possess that we'd allowed the problems that brought her to Chicago to go unchecked. I'd paid Franco Francesca to alter the quantities of merchandise for Sinful Threads for the reason of luring her here. We had no idea that the continued issues, number discrepancies, and blips on the security footage were part of a bigger picture.

"We're closing this down. I want word on the street that

no one starts their own operation on my streets and gets away with it. I also want the leaders to know the Denver cartel has my approval. We'll get the maps squared away. Give everyone their space and hopefully keep the casualties to a minimum."

No, I wasn't saving the city from drugs. I wasn't a crusader for good. I was regulating the drugs and the markets. I was profiting off of people's addictions. I would shed blood to keep the lines of sales and distribution clear. I'd also order the shedding of blood to make my point. I would shut down the operation within the trucking contractors. For most of the businesses, I didn't give a fuck.

There was one company that I did.

I had no doubt that Franco Francesca's hands were dirty, that he was involved.

The trick was making him pay without it hurting Sinful Threads.

We needed to find out how deep it was in Sinful Threads.

Now.

ARANEAE

*M*onday afternoon, I sat with my hand in Sterling's alongside Patrick, Reid, and Lorna as we gathered around a ridiculously large television, waiting for Senator McFadden's presidential announcement. We weren't in our apartment. Sterling still had his rules about who could be invited into that space. Instead, we were in a large living-room-type room on the floor that Sterling, Reid, and Patrick referred to as two. We'd been escorted with optimum secrecy, only being shown the room where we were. It was something out of a spy movie, but since we were able to be joined by others, the small accommodation was worth it.

I also decided that I'd hold onto the blindfold I'd worn to get here, for future use. When I mentioned that to the possessive man at my side, I was met with a sexy gleam to his dark eyes.

Yes, that did the twisty-turny thing to my insides.

I smiled at our guests. This truly was a day we all made possible.

The information regarding McFadden's presidential announcement had been leaked to the press on purpose by his camp, wanting full exposure. As a senator from Illinois, more specifically from Chicago, his declaration was to come with Millennium Park as the backdrop. Part of me wanted to be there in person, to watch the scene unfold, but not surprisingly, Sterling didn't approve.

Something about safety.

He said that so often, it was difficult to recall each particular time.

He was right.

Here in our glass tower we were safe from the fallout.

Those of us in the room were the only ones who knew what was coming. We'd all helped.

Two days before~

With Patrick guarding Jana's outer office, Sterling and I waited impatiently within my office at Sinful Threads. The Saturday sky beyond the windows was crystal blue as South Wacker Street and the canal below at street level was filled with people on this last official weekend of summer.

Sterling reached for my hand. "Last chance, sunshine. Are you confident this is what you want to do?"

Pulling my lip from between my teeth, I nodded. "It is.

When I called her, she said she wanted to see me again. I think it's time to be completely open with her."

Sterling's expression told me he wasn't confident in my plan. It wasn't just his expression but the tension radiating from him, emitting in waves like the infrared barrier that I imagined hid our safe world ninety-seven stories in the air.

"Involving her is a risk."

"It is," I admitted. "I guess after losing Josey and hearing Lucy's confession, I want to know where exactly Annabelle and I stand. You are right about me. I do trust people. I've trusted you and look where it's brought me. I can't allow myself to cut Annabelle out of my life simply because I've lost other mothers. I want to lay it all out on the line and then either we go it together as mother and daughter or I move on with..." I lifted my hand to Sterling's chest, feeling the rhythm of his heart beneath his well-fitting t-shirt. "...our family."

His eyes widened. "Our family?"

"Don't jump to conclusions," I said with a laugh. "I mean you, Patrick, Reid, and Lorna. We're a family and I'm good with it."

"With all the baby talk with Louisa," Sterling said, "you had me concerned."

"Well, Kennedy is adorable, but those contractions didn't look fun. And Mr. Know-It-All, you're the one who knew I had the birth control insert before our first time. Nothing has changed."

"That's where you're wrong." He cupped my cheek. "Everything has changed since I brought you into this world and my life."

Our lips came together as the room around us disappeared. No longer were the windows filled with sunshine on my radar. All that mattered was that the most powerful, handsomest man I had ever known was supporting me, loving me, and making me feel complete.

He'd told me about the heroin ring using small businesses. While the term *small* in association with *Sinful Threads* made me bristle, I understood that in comparison to a conglomerate like Sparrow Enterprises it was small. I also understood why Agent Hunter had believed that Sinful Threads was being used in an illegal operation. Apparently, it was. It wasn't Sterling's doing. It wasn't even Franco's doing, though it was clear he was a willing participant. Unfortunately, so was Vanessa, the second-shift manager at the distribution center.

With operations at a current standstill, we had more pressing concerns. However, neither of those individuals would be reporting back to Sinful Threads. All of the employees would be vetted and either released or retained. With Patrick's help, I would clean up the Chicago workings of Sinful Threads.

My smile grew as our kiss ended and I stared up into Sterling's darkened gaze. "I can see you're worried."

"I don't want you to get hurt."

"You keep telling me that I'm safe."

"It's your heart. I think if Annabelle disagrees with your plan, it will hurt you here." His hand fell over my breasts.

"Are you sure you don't just want to touch my breasts?"

His scowl morphed before my eyes, bringing out his sexy smile. "I most definitely like touching your breasts. I'll take any excuse."

I shook my head. "My heart has been hurt before. Just

promise me it won't be hurt by you and I think I'll be all right."

"That is a promise I will keep forever."

We both turned at the sound of Patrick greeting my mother. I took a deep breath.

"Do you want to talk to her alone?" Sterling asked.

"No, I want you beside me."

He simply nodded, his features stalled somewhere between granite and the smile he'd just given me.

I opened the door to the front office. "Hello. Thank you for coming."

"You called, Araneae. I hope you'll do that more often."

"I'd like that," I said, gesturing toward my office.

"Maybe in less formal settings," she said.

"Judge Landers," Sterling said in greeting as he offered his hand.

As they shook, my mother smiled. "This truly is a whole new world for me, Mr. Sparrow."

"For all of us," he said. "Please, you're Araneae's mother. Call me Sterling, if you'd like."

"Sterling, please call me Annabelle."

Sterling nodded and gestured toward the small conference table. "Annabelle, Araneae, I believe we have a few things to discuss."

I took a deep breath and turned to Annabelle. "Mother..." I liked using the title. "...I'd like to share with you how we got to where we are today. I knew nothing about you, my birth father, or the world you inhabited."

Annabelle nodded. "I should tell you that I didn't know much about this world when I was younger. I was willingly naïve even while living within it." She sat in the chair to my right as Sterling sat in the one to my left, leaving me at the head of the table. "For years, I tried not to be a part."

"This is all new to me too," I said, "but it's important that I share with you what I've learned. Apparently, there have been rumors about me since my birth."

"Araneae, I never believed them. I've told Rubio, your uncle, for years that they were all false, only stories of lore, such as fables told between old men."

I shook my head. "They're all true."

Annabelle sat back as her light brown eyes opened wide and her lips formed a straight line. "W-what do you mean? Did you find something?"

I looked to Sterling and back to my mother. "Yes. With Sterling's help, we've uncovered everything that has led us to here."

Her gaze narrowed toward Sterling.

"Mother," I said, bringing her eyes back to me, "I realize there has been bad blood between the Sparrows, McCries, and McFaddens."

"One could say that."

"I'm going to be straightforward with you. I promise everything I say has been verified. Will you believe me?"

She inhaled and exhaled. "I want to."

"I will probably tell you things you don't want to believe, yet through all of this, I've asked one thing of Sterling." I turned back to him. "I asked him to be honest with me." I turned back to Annabelle. "My entire life has been covered in secrets and lies. He has kept that promise. Despite the fact that some of what he told me was hard to hear, through it all, he's been beside me."

She exhaled. "I do know some things. Let's see how what you have been told compares to what I remember."

"It isn't all stories of lore, Mother. The other day after talking to you, we found the evidence my father hid."

Her head shook. "No, that's not possible. It doesn't exist."

I reached out until our hands touched. "Mom, until a month ago, you didn't think I existed."

She twisted her hand until we were palm to palm and held mine. "I never wanted to believe the evidence was real. I wanted to think that Daniel would have been honest with Rubio and Allister."

"He was," Sterling added. "He gave each man a copy of the evidence against their own organization. He proved he had it."

"But you just said—"

I interrupted, "We found the copies he hid."

"Evidence against Sparrow *and* McFadden," Sterling added.

"And you're sure of what it contains?" she asked.

"Yes," Sterling answered. "I have a man who excels at uncovering hidden data. If it has anything to do with technology, he can crack it."

Annabelle nodded. "You wanted me to know this why?"

"Because, Mother, I need your help. I'd like your advice."

Tears came to her eyes as her cheeks rose. "This is...I can't find words."

"Judge—Annabelle," Sterling said, correcting his greeting, "as I'm certain you're aware, this fabled evidence has the potential for mass casualties. While my father, not I, was guilty of the crimes uncovered, it will still reflect upon Sparrow and Sparrow Enterprises. As for Rubio, he was in charge twenty-six years ago. This is a direct connection. A direct hit with a Tomahawk missile—deadly accurate."

"What are you asking me? Do you want me to approve this obliteration of his world, my world, while leaving yours intact?"

ARANEAE

"No," I said, "Sterling wants all the information against both men disseminated."

Her light brown eyes went to Sterling. "Why would you want that?"

"It's a very long story, Judge Landers. When I took over in this world, I continued many of my father's practices. One I immediately shut down included the use, trafficking, and exploitation of children." His head shook. "I was shown that world by my father when I was still quite young. I also had a very good friend who believed he lost his sister to one of the Chicago rings. I do bad things. I won't lie to you or Araneae. However, when it comes to children, I draw the line."

"You're certain that this is the evidence Daniel hid?"

I nodded.

Her complexion paled. "And you're saying Rubio is still involved?"

"That's more difficult to prove," Sterling answered. "He

was involved. We have proof. The reason I want all the evidence brought forward is for the victims and their families. Maybe it will help one or more reunite or bring closure."

Again, there were tears in my mother's eyes. "Daniel had told me a little bit about it. I wouldn't listen. I didn't want to know." She turned to me. "How did you find it? You told me that you were raised by good people and at sixteen you were on your own. How then do you have this evidence?"

I lifted my wrist, the one with the old charm bracelet. "The key is now gone," I said. "After talking to you, we started putting the clues together. You said my father was calmer after going to the church in Cambridge where you were married. You said he came back with the bracelet. The evidence was hidden at the church where you and my father married. The key that was previously on this bracelet opened a lockbox he'd given to the minister to keep."

She covered her lips with the tips of her fingers. "The picture in the locket."

"Yes," I said, "it was the clue to the location."

"Daniel asked me years later where the bracelet had gone. I told him I'd given it to the nurse at the hospital to be buried with you."

I shrugged. "I don't know how Josey got it. I remember that she wore it all the time. When she took me to the airport ten years ago, she gave it to me. I kept it because it was hers." I lifted my eyes from the gold charms back to Annabelle. "And now I know it was yours too. It's very special to me.

"Through the years, since Sterling ended Sparrow's involvement in the business of child trafficking, he has worked to help victims of it. I know this because I've met some of them."

Annabelle looked between Sterling and me. "Why do you feel so strongly about this?"

"I was thirteen," Sterling began, "the first time I saw photos of the victims. I wasn't that far off from the ages of some of those on my father's computer. I knew in my gut that if some of the men who worked for my father had their way, it could be me on the screen. The only thing that saved me was my last name. To be honest, we have reason to believe that this ring was why Araneae was hidden from you. We can't confirm it, but we have made the assumption that Daniel hid her from Rubio for her own protection."

"From Rubio?"

"Like I said the other day, when I was thirteen," Sterling went on, "my father showed me Araneae's picture. He said Daniel owed him and if I proved myself, one day I could have her. Since that day, I knew she was meant for me. Each year until she was sixteen, he received new pictures and showed them to me."

Annabelle's head shook. "I still can't believe that your father knew she was alive." Her lips pursed before her eyes opened wide and she went on, "Oh my, the way you pronounce her name. Did you hear it from Allister?"

"I did," he answered.

"You say it differently," I said to my mother.

"I do. Before you were born, I proposed the name to Daniel. He agreed if he could alter the pronunciation. I consented, but in my head, I always pronounced it like the spider. I thought it made you strong." Her lips curled upward. "And you are." She straightened her posture. "Rubio and Pauline are my family." She looked at me. "Your family. Rubio has been supportive of me since Daniel died."

"He didn't die," Sterling said matter-of-factly. "He was killed by Rubio, maybe not by his hands."

Though she didn't verbally respond to Sterling's proclamation, Annabelle's complexion paled even further, her breathing grew shallow, and her now-glassy gaze stayed fixed on him.

"My father had Araneae's coffin exhumed," Sterling continued, "and reported that it was her inside. My father was irate. I don't know if he was lied to or he simply lied for his own reasons." He turned to me. "As I told you, I have the DNA proof. This is your daughter. Anyway, we believe that Daniel reminded Rubio about the hidden evidence. Rubio thought Araneae had been confirmed dead and knew you thought the same. The only other person to hinder his political ambitions, the only one with access to the hidden evidence was Daniel."

"There's something else," I said, standing and walking to my desk. After gathering the two envelopes from the lockbox, I returned to the table. "My father also left these in the lockbox."

For a moment, Annabelle simply stared at the envelopes, her head slowly shaking. "That's my husband's handwriting." She looked up. "This is all so difficult to face." She took a deep breath and looked down again at the envelopes. "What do they contain?"

"Information on offshore accounts," Sterling said without hesitation. "We haven't yet been able to verify their existence or the amounts they contain."

"He told me there was money." Her head shook. "I didn't listen."

I pushed one of the envelopes closer to her. "This one

contains stock shares. Before I was born he made investments in two budding companies."

"He was very good at what he did. He was so smart at finances. If only..." Her words trailed away.

"Annabelle, he was excellent," Sterling said. "He invested in Walmart and Apple. His investments are now worth between four to six billion dollars."

Her eyes widened as the recently regained color drained from her cheeks.

Sterling went on, "The shares were legally bequeathed to his child or children, or in the case of no children, to you."

My mother stared at me. "We have to prove that you're you."

It was my turn to cry. "You don't want it?"

"I don't need it. I'm fine. I have everything I'd want, except you. Now that I have you, there is no amount of money that could make me risk that."

I let out a long breath. "Mother, Rubio McFadden literally threatened me. He tried to kill me before I got back to Chicago. He also arranged the kidnapping of my best friend to get my attention and demanded we find the evidence. I suppose he decided that since I am alive, the hidden evidence must also be real. He gave us until Monday to produce it."

Again, she looked between Sterling and me. "The judge in me wants proof. Can you prove this?"

"We'd rather keep the kidnapping out of the news and away from the authorities. We took care of it. Her friend is safe," Sterling said. "The attempted murder was the crash-landing of a commercial jetliner that was supposed to hold Araneae. There is a money trail to the pilot, to his wife. The pilot died days later in a freak accident. That is all verifiable."

"That money trail leads to Rubio?"

"Not directly but yes," Sterling answered.

"I don't want to believe this. I know what people think about me and him. It's not..." She shook her head. "...friends —family. That's what we've been to each other through the years as well as colleagues. At least, I thought we were. We enjoy one another's company, but not in the way people think." Her head shook again. "However, who you describe isn't the man I know. And yet in the pit of my stomach, I do believe what you're saying."

Oh, was she saying that they weren't romantically involved?

I hoped that was it.

"Over the years," she went on, "I've been approached by federal law enforcement agents; really, ever since before you were born when Daniel supposedly had that evidence. That's what they've wanted. I can give you the name of the agent from the Chicago field office."

"Did Rubio know you talked to them?" Sterling asked.

"No. I didn't have anything to share with them. I thought he'd take it wrong." She turned her attention to both of us. "Most recently, I've been in contact with Agent Wesley Hunter." She turned to me. "Araneae, you found the evidence. I can't advise you on what to do with it." She looked up at Sterling. "All I know is that I have my daughter. I don't want to lose her."

ARANEAE

Sunday~

With Winnie's assistance, we contacted Agent Wesley Hunter, or I did. Before our meeting, I made the choice to hand him six CDs. While Sterling was set on exposing both sides, I couldn't do it. I wouldn't give the FBI reason to further investigate Sterling.

I met Agent Hunter at a busy cafe early Sunday morning on Division Street in a bustling part of Chicago. The place was lively with patrons. The outdoor seating was filled as coffee drinkers and diners enjoyed the remnants of summer.

Surprisingly, the location of our meeting was chosen by Sterling. He wanted it made public so I could be better watched. I knew Patrick was a booth away. I also knew Reid was seated on the other side of the restaurant. What I didn't know was how many of the other patrons were Sparrows.

Technically, we were near our deadline with McFadden and anything could happen.

As I was sipping a cup of coffee, the man I'd first met as Mark approached my table.

"Ms. McCrie."

"Agent Hunter."

He took the seat opposite me in the booth. "As you can imagine, I was surprised to get your call."

"I'm here out of civic duty."

His head tilted.

"You see, I didn't have what you wanted when you ambushed me. However, things have changed."

"What has changed?" he asked as he leaned forward. "Are you ready to testify against Mr. Sparrow?"

Instead of answering, I went on, "I have been rumored to be the holder of evidence hidden by my birth father. As you probably know, I didn't even know my true identity until recently. The idea that as an infant I was given evidence was ludicrous."

"Yet you're saying things have changed?"

I reached into my purse and pulled out the six CDs Reid entrusted to me. He knew which were against Sparrow and which were against McFadden. It didn't take much convincing on my part for Reid to see my reasoning.

It saddened me that the Sparrow victims and their families would not have the closure they deserved. However, that didn't supersede my desire to protect the man who protected me. I wasn't brought into Sterling Sparrow's life to shatter his glass tower. I was brought to reign beside him.

Lifting my wrist, I showed Agent Hunter my bracelet. "This was given to a nurse to have buried with me. When my birth mother handed it over, she believed I was dead. She had no way of knowing the bracelet would be given to my adoptive mother and then on to me. In this locket is a faded picture of the church where my parents were married."

He lifted his hand. "The church in Cambridge has been thoroughly searched."

"The lockbox was on a shelf in the minister's office. From the spine, it looked like a book."

I had his attention. "These were in the box." I pushed the six CDs his direction.

Agent Hunter looked down at the half-dozen CDs. "Is this all that was in the box?"

"No," I answered honestly. "There were four floppy disks."

"Did you bring them?"

"Yes, but not really." I reached into my purse and pulled out the mutilated floppy disks, now held within a plastic bag. There was no way to get information off of them. We will never know what they contained, but neither will the FBI. "They disintegrated upon insertion into a reader."

"I'm surprised you're willing to turn in your boyfriend," Agent Hunter said.

"I'm not. Mr. Sparrow is unconnected to this evidence apart from his assistance in helping me find it."

Agent Hunter looked from the CDs to me. "Then what is this?"

"It's hard evidence against the man who ran the outfit you infiltrated. I know you must have more, but this..." I pointed at the CDs. "...is irrefutable."

Indecision washed over his face.

I leaned forward. "Tomorrow he is announcing his candidacy for president. I have copies of the CDs. I expect the FBI to do its job and end not only his political run but also the ring if it's still in existence. If it isn't, these CDs should stop him from gaining further power. If the FBI doesn't do its job, I'll send copies to every news outlet in the country. Either the FBI can get the headline or be the headline for suppressing evidence on a political figure."

"Are you suggesting I've suppressed evidence?"

"I'm suggesting that you were within the McFadden outfit as a man named Walsh for two years, and the outfit is still going strong. I'm not certain why you want Sterling, a real estate mogul, but I'm giving you Senator Rubio McFadden on a silver platter. I suggest you make the right move."

He shook his head. "Sterling Sparrow is dangerous. You're playing into his hands. You'll never be safe as long as you're with him."

I reached for my purse and glanced to the side, my gaze meeting Patrick's. "Good day, Agent Hunter. I'll give you twenty-four hours. After that, FBI cover-up will be the trending hashtag."

As I stepped out of the booth, Patrick stood and walked directly behind me.

ARANEAE

Monday-

The special broadcast began. McFadden had all the fanfare associated with a broad political statement. He had the red, white, and blue swags lining the constructed stage. There was a huge American flag behind the podium as well as an Illinois flag hanging by a pole to the side. As the cameras panned the park, the glistening water of Lake Michigan could be seen. The crowd was gathering.

Sterling squeezed my hand as he too glanced around the room.

"Thank you for including me," Annabelle said. She forced a smile. "It's my first time being blindfolded."

I wanted to tell her it was mine too, but I had hopes for

more. However, I didn't think we'd gotten that far in our relationship.

"Purely precautionary," Patrick answered.

Winnie sighed. "I can't believe you included me in this."

I reached out to her on my other side. "You're in this now. You know what you do and we're trusting you. Your assistance in getting Agent Hunter to meet with me made this happen."

"Are we ever going to fill Louisa in?"

"She knows enough," Sterling said.

"Did you tell Wesley about the drugs at the warehouse and distribution center?" Winnie asked.

I turned toward my mother. "Not belonging to anyone here," I clarified.

She shook her head. "I'm done wearing blinders."

"No, really," I replied. "It's a small operation using unknowing businesses."

Annabelle lifted her hand. "I can't know about it in case it crosses my bench."

I looked at Sterling, most confident that the newly discovered ring would be dealt with without the assistance of law enforcement. I turned to Winnie. "I didn't. More pressing matters..." I tilted my head toward the television.

A reporter was speaking, orating the attributes of Senator McFadden and discussing the unusual move to declare before midterm elections.

Sterling had sent word to Hillman that he would meet with Rubio tomorrow morning. It was enough to extend our deadline.

"He's going up on the stage," Reid said.

We all waited as Rubio McFadden took the podium with Pauline at his side.

As time passed and McFadden continued to speak, I grew more agitated. Looking at Sterling, I silently asked what was going to happen. With a slight shake of his head, he wordlessly told me he wasn't sure.

"Oh!" Lorna exclaimed.

"That's not Wesley," Winnie said.

It wasn't Agent Hunter who had stepped onto the stage. It was a man in a suit with four men in FBI swat gear behind him. McFadden seemed confused, as if perhaps this was part of their planned performance.

"Special agent from the Chicago field office," Patrick said.

The reporters were scurrying and giving play-by-play on their microphones as the crowd grew loud and the man in the suit put Senator McFadden in handcuffs. As the cameras panned, Pauline came into view. Her expression was horrified as the color drained from her cheeks.

I looked to Winnie. "I'm glad she's not wearing Sinful Threads."

"Public humiliation," Sterling said, leaning back on the sofa where we sat.

"How long until they release the information on his indictment?" I asked.

"It will depend," my mother answered. "I'm sure his attorneys will be working to keep everything suppressed."

The newsfeeds were abuzz with speculation for days until the charges were finally announced.

. . .

SENATOR   RUBIO   MCFADDEN   OF   ILLINOIS
CURRENTLY HELD WITHOUT BOND HAS BEEN OFFI-
CIALLY CHARGED IN CONNECTION TO AN ILLEGAL
HUMAN   TRAFFICKING   RING.   HE   VEHEMENTLY
DENIES ANY SUCH CONNECTION.

When I looked up from my phone, Sterling was standing on the edge of the back patio of the cabin. He wasn't looking at me, but out to the shimmering waves on Paul Bunyan's lake. His broad shoulders were straight and his long legs were covered in blue jeans. On his feet were his hiking boots. From his profile he seemed lost in thought.

Tucking my phone and hands into the pockets of my jacket, I warded off the chill as the cool autumn breeze rustled the changing leaves and pine branches surrounding the cabin. As I stood, the crisp gusts blew my long hair around my face. I went to him and placed my hand on his shoulder; as I did, he turned.

"What are you thinking?" I asked.

The tips of his lips moved upward. "I'm thinking that I don't deserve what you've done."

I didn't think he was referring to what *we'd* done this morning as we awoke at this stunning cabin. How we'd made love while the sun rose over the treetops, showering our bedroom in red and gold hues. Or how we'd taken each other higher than the clouds and then lounged in one another's arms in the afterglow of our union as the sky beyond the windows brightened to a crystal-clear blue.

"I love you, Sterling."

Snaking his arm around my waist, he pulled me closer into

his warmth and security. "Why didn't you turn over all the CDs?"

"Because you're not guilty. Rubio is. Your father was."

"I'm guilty of many other crimes. If you only knew what I've done, what I'll keep doing—"

I covered his mouth with mine, silencing his words. Soon his hands moved from my waist to my cheeks, holding our kiss in place, bruising my lips as his tongue sought entrance and our kiss deepened. My moans joined the autumn sounds, floating through the air.

Damn, I was ready to go back inside, back up to our room.

When we pulled apart, Sterling's dark gaze searched mine. "I've done some awful things, but the best fucking thing I did was collect you. You're mine. I don't want to ever let you go."

"Then don't."

My pulse quickened as without warning, Sterling fell to one knee before me and reached for my hand.

"Oh my. What?"

His dark gaze shimmered. At first, he simply turned my hand to palm up. As if reading my future, he traced the lines of my palm print. "I promised you that when this was over..."

Excitement coursed through me. "My palm print? The elevator?"

He looked up. "Yes, for emergencies. I still want Patrick or me..."

Yada, yada, safety...

I didn't care about his stipulations. Just having my palm print work, allowing me access to the garage, to the outside, was what I'd wanted. Using it may never be on my agenda. Knowing I could was priceless.

Sterling's gaze continued to deepen as his baritone tenor

drowned out the breeze, and leaves swirled in cyclones around us. "Sunshine, I've known you were mine for nearly two decades. I never knew how you'd change me. I was afraid that after I took you, I'd dim your light. That still worries me. What I didn't expect was that my cold black heart could ever know love.

"It continually amazes me that you see good in me, that you can see past what you know is present and see what I never realized was there. You make me want to be a better man."

With a quirk of his grin, Sterling reached into the pocket of his jeans. As he brought the object closer, the center diamond glistened.

Tears prickled my eyes as my breathing ceased.

"I know you want to make Araneae McCrie your legal name."

I did.

"However, I have another option for you."

My lips curled as tears filled my eyes. "An option, that's a choice."

"Yes, another choice for you." He swallowed, his dark gaze fixed on mine. "Araneae McCrie, will you consider a different last name? Will you marry me and become Araneae Sparrow?"

Will.

I couldn't answer, not verbally. The lump in my throat was too big. Instead, I nodded and nodded and nodded again as tears fell from my eyes.

After slipping the incredibly gorgeous ring over my finger, Sterling stood and again cupped my cheeks. "I love you."

"You've changed my life in so many ways," I said. "You showed me who I really am and who I can be. Because of you,

I have my mother back. I have new great friends and my old friends are safe. You uncovered the secrets and lies, and through it all, you kept your word—your promises. I'll be proud to be your wife." I brushed my lips against his. "I mean we were always meant to be together. Isn't that what you said?"

"And I'm always right," he said with a smirk.

"My answer is yes."

As he took my hand, we walked toward the edge of the hill, looking down at the lake. "This is yours, Araneae," he said. "Chicago is yours. Whatever you desire is yours."

I leaned into him, taking the strength of his arm now around me. As we stood, I tried to also give back—share my light—as our bodies melted against one another. Finally, I looked up with a grin. "You promised me a ride to the lake. Let's get the ATV and this time it's my turn to drive."

"Oh hell no. Keeping you safe is my lifelong mission."

As he reached again for my hand, I stared down at the diamond engagement ring. "Sterling, it's beautiful."

"Not as beautiful as the woman wearing it, my fiancée."

Fiancé.

I had one of those now too and this time it was real.

STERLING

Epilogue

Three months later~

Patrick looked my way. "The roads are not good and getting worse. The helicopter pilot says if the winds keep up, he can't fly."

Fuck.

I paced the office of my cabin watching the snow accumulating outside the windows as inside, the staff and others prepared for Araneae's and my wedding. The living room with the two-story windows had been transformed into a chapel. Sparkling lights and evergreen combined with the view out the windows made it a winter wonderland. No expense was spared.

It wasn't that money had ever been an issue, but after the

court's recent ruling that Araneae McCrie was now alive and the cashing in of the stocks her father had purchased, finances were less of a concern. Of course, Araneae had strong opinions about the use of her newfound wealth.

I wouldn't have expected any less.

She had plans for improvements and expansions regarding Sinful Threads. Louisa loved the idea of branching out into bed linens. Even with my limited knowledge of their merchandise, as a businessman I saw the opportunity. Araneae had been right that most people spend a third of their lives in bed. Why not let them sleep on Sinful Threads sheets?

Then again, it was my goal that when it came to the two of us, we'd increase that percentage. However, the bed wasn't the most important element of the equation. It was the connection between my soon-to-be wife and me. I'd gladly make love to her in bed or fuck her against the wall or even on the kitchen counter. Thankfully, while I was up for all the possibilities, so was my fiancée.

Araneae's other plan for her increased assets involved creating a foundation for victims of child and adult trafficking and exploitation. With Annabelle's assistance with the legalities, they were working on the best way to help. Araneae's desires were all-encompassing. She wanted counseling, medical treatment, and education. Dr. Dixon was one hundred percent on board and ready to take on the medical aspect. She herself hadn't been a victim, but her sister was. While her sister wasn't saved, I may have had something to do with financing Renita's education, giving her a means to help others where her sister wasn't. I financed it, but she was the one who turned hard work into a medical career.

It's my observation that sometimes victim was a term that could be expanded beyond the individual who experienced the atrocity and include their support system as well.

It would take a while to get Araneae's plans up and running. With her determination and Annabelle's help, I had no doubt that the Sparrow Institute would one day be a reality.

As time passed, it was painfully obvious that Araneae's light had fucked with my dark more than the other way around.

I looked over at Patrick, dressed in a custom tuxedo. Reid was with us, looking good too in his tuxedo. I had been hidden away from Araneae all day while she was upstairs with her mother, Lorna, Louisa, and Winnie along with a staff of hairdressers and makeup people. In my opinion, the staff wasn't necessary. Araneae was stunning first thing in the morning with no makeup, sex-mussed hair, and the patches of red on her skin where my beard growth left a trail reminding us both where I'd been. She didn't need professionals to enhance her beauty in any way.

My mother, Louisa's parents, and her sister and Marcel, as well as Jason and baby Kennedy were also here. It was fucking Grand Central Station. Every damn bedroom in this cabin was occupied, including the spare bedrooms above the garages. That was, except one.

What do you get the woman you love for her wedding when she had the world at her fingertips?

Araneae Sparrow was about to become the queen of Chicago, and there was nothing she couldn't have.

I came up with an idea.

The name Lucy Nelson provided was the opening to both

old and new information. With some detective work from Reid and his men, we'd found the one thing—or should I say the two people—Araneae wanted in her life.

That discovery also revealed more of the secrets and reasons on how Renee Marsh had become Kennedy Hawkins. Keeping the Marshes, or Currys, a secret from my fiancée was one of the most difficult things I'd done since I brought Araneae into my life. I'd promised her honesty and I'd provided it. I also told her there were things I couldn't disclose.

Currently, the Marshes fit in that category.

It was a needle in a proverbial haystack, but as luck would have it, a few years ago Neal Curry had been photographed. It was for an educational paper published on the subject of secluded communities—a master's thesis written during the recent nationwide obsession with cults. The paper was published in a little-read refereed journal. Neal happened to be among a group of men from a small community in Maine who visited a town every three months to buy and sell goods. The paper made a point that the candid photographs were taken without the subjects' knowledge or permission and the names of the community members were provided secondhand by townspeople. Since the members refused interviews, the author could not stand behind the accuracy yet chose to publish the photos as evidence of the community's existence.

Being the only lead we'd had in over ten years, Reid, Patrick, and I had to check it out.

To say that both of the Currys were shocked upon our arrival to their Maine community would be an understatement. We later learned that Neal, aka Byron, had been part of the Sparrow outfit since childhood. Allister had set him and his wife up to raise Araneae. When they learned of McCrie's death, they were also informed my father was coming after them.

I don't know if what they were told or believed was true, but if it had been, these two people saved my fiancée's life. I owed them an eternal debt, not vengeance as Allister may have planned.

The woman Araneae remembers as Josey now goes by her legal name, Rebecca. Once I convinced her to talk to me—not an easy process—I showed her a recent picture of Araneae from the many on my phone.

My fiancée was so fucking beautiful, I'd take her picture constantly if I wasn't busy showing her how important she was to me. That's on my agenda for the next fifty or so years.

Reid looked up from the computer on the table before him. Working from a laptop was a definite downgrade from our lair in Chicago. "This sounds crazy, Sparrow, but I found a man near the airport where the Currys are currently stuck. He drives a snowplow. He guarantees he can get them here. It will just take a little longer."

I looked at my watch. The wedding was supposed to start in ninety minutes. "Tell them yes. We'll wait. I don't know what I'll tell Araneae, but we'll wait."

"He said there'd be a fee," Reid said.

My eyes opened wider. "I don't give a fuck. Just get them here."

Reid typed out his response. "In good weather the drive is around an hour and fifteen minutes."

"Just have them keep us posted. I'll get Annabelle to help with the delay." I'd told her about my impending surprise, not wanting the presence of the people who raised her daughter to upset her. As with most things, she was supportive.

Araneae's mother was taking our engagement and wedding better than Genevieve. However, even my mother was coming around. It helped when I told her that it was Araneae who contained the casualties of our world to Rubio and his top men. I also think Annabelle helped to convince my mother that the joining of our two families truly was as I'd said—the perfect union.

Two families in Chicago's elite.

The royal wedding was about to occur.

With Araneae still upstairs, Annabelle greeted the Currys as soon as they arrived.

"Hello," Rebecca said meekly, seemingly overwhelmed by the travel and perhaps our home. Her gaze darted around until it landed on Annabelle.

As I started to speak, to welcome them, Annabelle gasped. "I remember you...from the hospital."

Rebecca reached out to Annabelle's arm. "Please know that we loved her."

There were tears in Annabelle's eyes. "I believe you. It was out of both of our control. She loved you too and speaks highly of you."

I'm not fucking emotional, but watching the two women embrace one another was the final chipping away of the rock-hard coating that had covered my heart.

I didn't shed a tear.

Hell no.

Are there winter allergies?
I think there could be.

With all the guests seated, I made my way to the front of the room by the windows with Patrick and Reid at my side. On one side of the aisle was my mother. On the other side were the Currys and Annabelle. I couldn't help but notice how Rebecca and Annabelle were putting their heads together, whispering, and even holding one another's hands. It must have been surreal to each of them, to know that together they had been and now would be part of Araneae's life.

When the music started, the procession began. Winnie, Lorna, and then Louisa descended the stairs, all smiling as they came closer. It was as the music changed that my vision tunneled. Coming down the stairs in a long white gown, her scooped neckline and long veil trimmed in soft white faux fur, was the woman who was made for me. Her golden hair was up, showcasing her slender neck. Hanging from her ears were the diamond earrings I'd given to her the night she boarded the plane to be mine.

As our gazes met, I wondered if she'd see her gift—the Marshes—because from where I stood, it seemed as if she too had tunnel vision. We only had eyes for one another.

The most gorgeous light-chocolate stare looked up at me as the officiant said his words. I couldn't tell you exactly what they were. I only knew what they meant. Their meaning did more than cement my father's nearly twenty-year-old proclamation that Araneae was mine. His words gave both Araneae and I more than either of us had ever had on our own.

Love.

Security.

His words obliterated the secrets and lies of the past.

And assured us promises for a future.

Beyond my beautiful bride was proof that the union he was performing also gave us family.

When the final words were spoken and I kissed my bride, she whispered, "I have a gift for you." The gleam in her eyes was contagious.

What could she possibly give me that I couldn't buy?

"Sunshine, the only gift I want is you."

Her cheeks rose. "We'll see."

As Louisa handed her back her bouquet, Araneae turned toward our guests and an audible gasp escaped her lips. This time as she alternated her stare from the Currys to me, the earlier gleam was gone, replaced by an onslaught of tears.

I reached for her cheeks, wiping away the moisture. "Don't cry. They didn't want to miss their daughter's wedding."

Lifting the front of the skirt of her dress, Araneae hurried toward the Currys, wrapping her arms around both of them. "How?" she asked, looking at Mr. Curry. "Daddy, you...died."

Annabelle reached out to her daughter's shoulder. "So did you."

Later, as emotions settled and the joyous occasion prevailed, while Araneae and I sat at the center of the table, and foods and wines were being consumed, my wife leaned my way. "With the gift you gave me, I almost forgot to give you yours."

"I told you, all I need is you."

She reached down to the pearl-covered handbag near her feet and lifted it. Unsnapping the clasp, she reached inside.

When she looked back up, the earlier shimmer was back in her soft brown gaze.

"What is it?" I asked. She had my curiosity piqued.

Keeping her hand below the table's edge, she opened her fingers, exposing the small remote control in her grasp—the one to the custom-made vibrator.

My smile grew. "That only works if you're wearing..." My eyebrows danced.

"Then it will work," she said as pink filled her cheeks.

Taking the remote and placing it in the pocket of my tuxedo, I knew beyond a shadow of a doubt, Araneae Sparrow was made for me.

Sterling and Araneae's story is complete.

If you'd like to learn more about what the future holds for those they love, you don't want to miss TWISTED, book 1 of TANGLED WEB. Preorder today by tapping on the title.

Turn the page for a sneak peek.

TANGLED WEB: BOOK 1

The underworld of Chicago is far from forgiving. It's a world where knowledge means power, power money, and money everything.

My name is Mason Pierce. I paid the ultimate price to have it all. I gave my life.

That doesn't mean I ceased to exist, only to live.

Going where the job takes me and living in the shadows, with deadly accuracy I utilize the skills inherent to me, not knowing from where they came, not recalling what I'd lost.

And then it came back.
Not *it*.
Her.
Laurel Carlson.

I shouldn't want her, desire her, or need her, yet with each meeting I know she is exactly what I have to have. Laurel has the ability to do what I thought was impossible, to bring me back to life.

My gut tells me that it's a deadly mistake to open my world to her, to show her my twisted existence. However, my body won't take no for an answer.

I've made dangerous mistakes before.
This time, will the price be too high?

From New York Times bestselling author Aleatha Romig comes a brand-new dark romance set in the same dangerous underworld as *SECRETS*. You do not need to read the *Web of Sin* trilogy to get caught in this new and intriguing saga, *Tangled Web*.

TWISTED is book one of the *TANGLED WEB* trilogy.

Have you been Aleatha'd?

Are you ready for the dangerous and mysterious world of Web of Sin to continue in Tangled Web, a new trilogy, coming May of 2019?

Preorder TWISTED, book 1, today.

WHAT TO DO NOW

LEND IT: Did you enjoy Promises? Do you have a friend who'd enjoy Promises? Lies may be lent one time. Sharing is caring!

RECOMMEND IT: Do you have multiple friends who'd enjoy my dark romance saga? Tell them about it! Call, text, post, tweet...your recommendation is the nicest gift you can give to an author!

REVIEW IT: Tell the world. Please go to the retailer where you purchased this book, as well as Goodreads, and write a review. Please share your thoughts about Promises on:

*Amazon, *PROMISES* Customer Reviews

*Barnes & Noble, *PROMISES,* Customer Reviews

*iBooks, *PROMISES* Customer Reviews

*Goodreads.com/Aleatha Romig

BOOKS BY NEW YORK TIMES BESTSELLING AUTHOR ALEATHA ROMIG

TANGLED WEB:

TWISTED
Coming May 21, 2019

OBSESSED
Coming June 25, 2019

BOUND
Coming July 30, 2019

WEB OF SIN:

SECRETS
Coming Oct. 30, 2018

LIES
Coming Dec. 4, 2018

PROMISES
Coming Jan. 8, 2019

THE INFIDELITY SERIES:

BETRAYAL

Book #1

Released October 2015

CUNNING

Book #2

Released January 2016

DECEPTION

Book #3

Released May 2016

ENTRAPMENT

Book #4

Released September 2016

FIDELITY

Book #5

Released January 2017

RESPECT

A stand-alone Infidelity novel

Released January 2018

THE CONSEQUENCES SERIES:

CONSEQUENCES

(Book #1)

Released August 2011

TRUTH

(Book #2)

Released October 2012

CONVICTED

(Book #3)

Released October 2013

REVEALED

(Book #4)

Previously titled: Behind His Eyes Convicted: The Missing Years

Re-released June 2014

BEYOND THE CONSEQUENCES

(Book #5)

Released January 2015

RIPPLES

Released Oct 2017

CONSEQUENCES COMPANION READS:

BEHIND HIS EYES-CONSEQUENCES

Released January 2014

BEHIND HIS EYES-TRUTH

Released March 2014

THE LIGHT DUET:

Published through Thomas and Mercer Amazon exclusive

INTO THE LIGHT

Released 2016

AWAY FROM THE DARK

Released 2016

TALES FROM THE DARK SIDE SERIES:

INSIDIOUS

(All books in this series are stand-alone erotic thrillers)

Released October 2014

DUPLICITY

(Completely unrelated to book #1)

Release TBA

ALEATHA'S LIGHTER ONES:

PLUS ONE

Stand-alone fun, sexy romance

Released May 2017

A SECRET ONE

Fun, sexy novella

Released April 2018

ANOTHER ONE

Stand-alone fun, sexy romance

Releasing May 2018

ONE NIGHT

Stand-alone, sexy contemporary romance

September 2017

THE VAULT:

UNEXPECTED

Released August 27, 2018

UNCONVENTIONAL

Released individually

January 1, 2018

ABOUT THE AUTHOR

Aleatha Romig is a New York Times, Wall Street Journal, and USA Today bestselling author who lives in Indiana, USA. She has raised three children with her high school sweetheart and husband of over thirty years. Before she became a full-time author, she worked days as a dental hygienist and spent her nights writing. Now, when she's not imagining mind-blowing twists and turns, she likes to spend her time with her family and friends. Her other pastimes include reading and creating heroes/anti-heroes who haunt your dreams!

Aleatha impresses with her versatility in writing. She released her first novel, CONSEQUENCES, in August of 2011. CONSEQUENCES, a dark romance, became a bestselling series with five novels and two companions released from 2011 through 2015. The compelling and epic story of Anthony and Claire Rawlings has graced more than half a million e-readers. Her first stand-alone smart, sexy thriller INSIDIOUS was next. Then Aleatha released the five-novel INFIDELITY series, a romantic suspense saga, that took the reading world by storm, the final book landing on three of the top bestseller lists. She ventured into traditional publishing with Thomas and Mercer. Her books INTO THE LIGHT and AWAY FROM THE DARK were published through this mystery/thriller publisher in 2016. In the spring of 2017, Aleatha again ventured into a different genre with her first fun and sexy stand-alone romantic comedy with the USA Today bestseller PLUS ONE. She continued with ONE NIGHT and ANOTHER ONE. If you like fun, sexy, novellas that make your heart pound, try her UNCONVENTIONAL and UNEXPECTED. In 2018 Aleatha returned to her dark romance roots with WEB OF SIN.

Aleatha is a "Published Author's Network" member of the Romance Writers of America and PEN America. She is represented by Kevan Lyon of Marsal Lyon Literary Agency.

facebook.com/Aleatharomig

twitter.com/aleatharomig

instagram.com/aleatharomig

ACKNOWLEDGMENTS

I would like to thank everyone who encouraged me to return to my dark-romance roots and those who supported me while I was enjoying the lighter side.

Sterling and Araneae's story wouldn't have been possible without the constant support of my husband and partner in life, Mr. Jeff. His patience as well as that of my family and friends while I spent days, weeks, and months immersed in the Web of Sin was remarkable.

Thank you to Danielle Sanchez, my friend and PR support. Your encouragement and excitement helped me get this trilogy underway.

I also want to give a special thank-you to my beta readers for their commitment and dedication as I bombarded them with chapters, often five a day. Thank you, Kirsten, Sherry, Angie, Val, Ilona, and Jeff. Your comments and concerns made this trilogy into the story it is today.

Thank you also to Renita McKinney for providing sensitivity editing, helping to create an accurate world of diversity within Web of Sin. I also appreciated how much you loved Sterling, and oh, the cardiologist!

My undying gratitude to Lisa Aurello for your amazing editing skills and most importantly your patience with a crazy author. You're the best.

Finally, thank you to YOU—readers, bloggers, and fellow authors—for reading, supporting, and sharing. It takes a community and I'm so blessed to be within yours.

Made in the USA
Columbia, SC
28 July 2019